DIRECT ACTION

# DIRECT ACTION

## JD SVENSON

[Lacuna]
2019

Published in 2019 by Lacuna in Armidale, New South Wales, Australia
www.lacunapublishing.com

Lacuna is an imprint of Golden Orb Creative
PO Box 428, Armidale, NSW 2350, Australia
www.goldenorbcreative.com

All enquiries to the publisher: general@lacunapublishing.com

Cover design, text design by Golden Orb Creative: www.goldenorbcreative.com
Typeset in 11pt Minion Pro
Cover image by AS Photo Studio, used under licence from Shutterstock.com
(photo ID: 765429313).

A National Library of Australia Cataloguing-in-Publication entry has been created for this title:

ISBN 9781922198389 (pbk)
ISBN 9781922198396 (ebook)

*To Max and Hugo.*

# 1

---

*Proxima.*

    *Rigel.*

        *Barnard.*

            *Wolf.*

Under the arc light, stargirl held the thin flannie around herself, reciting, stamping her feet against the cold within.

*Luyten's. Sirius. Methuselah. Lah.* She liked that one, with its sound a creamy whipcrack on her tongue. Methuselah, that most ancient of stars: the mother; she from which they all came. At the *big bang*. When everyone was stardust – her; them, the coppers she could see across the road, in their hotdog-van copshop, fan-cooled behind their desks. The people at the cavernous PCYC hall today – queuing for watered down juice, in the cheap plastic cups she held out to them but hated because they would end up in the sea or tossed for future generations to find. *A few breeding pairs wandering the arctic circle.* There was a bin nearby and she leaned on it, vomiting in. No-one knew. No-one understood. There had been no other way.

Times like now she would name the constellations too. *Cassiopeia. Triangulum. Andromeda:* her namesake, with its syllables that bounced back from her teeth like from a skin drum. She'd breathe their sacred names and look up at the sky, starting from the beginning when she forgot the order, from closest to furthest, from this, her tiny blue ellipsis orbiting the sun. The order was important. It calmed her, like the metal of the bin, cool under her fingers. There was no cool any more, she thought, as the depthless sadness bolted in. Above, the sky was dry as a cornhusk, the dirt beneath her feet dessicated, empty of all but the memory of rain.

The water at Liddell had been warm, when she'd stepped into it. The smell – so thick it had clogged her nose – hypoxic peat and seaweed. And carp. Bloody carp, clear beneath the surface – one metallic streak and then another, in the dark water. *This is what we humans do*, she remembered thinking. *Make muck out of paradise.* Her mind had chased them then – *little fishy, I don't belong here either. Come with me? Be my talisman, make me safe?* Hah. *Safe.* Since when had she ever wanted safe? Or had it, for that matter. She felt safer right now, watching the Muswellbrook constables with all their relaxed camaraderie and paperwork, moving about, ink-dark firearms slouched at their waists.

She stood, wiped her mouth, and breathed the stars' names again. Looking up at them made her remember. Yes. She could rest, now; they had done it. Nothing more was required of her. She was Gaia. She crossed the floodlit road and walked in.

# 2

On Level 60 of the ninety-floor shard of glass that held Sydney's magic circle law firms at a seemly distance from the populace below, Cressida Mitsok leant with one hand against the glossy wall of the corridor and tried to stop shaking. *For God's sake*, she moaned inwardly. *It's just a fucking partnership meeting. Remember the stadium*, she thought, watching the white specks of yachts tango the afternoon easterly below. *Remember desal. That gorgeous rack of steel on Botany Headland condensing drinking water out of salt because of you. And what about Pacific Highway, Coffs to Yamba? You won a bloody award for that.* The sliver of pride that swelled elbowed out terror momentarily. *Six years as a Senior Associate and eleven with the firm, you've **earnt** this. They **know** you.* In the muted lighting she opened her handbag and looked inside again. *Just a nibble*, she reasoned. Just one shot of that creamy sweetness, that divine release against her teeth. *C'mon. One.*

*No.*

*Save it for the Porsche*, she told herself. *Besides. You'll get chocolate on your teeth.*

Here was the door. In the veneer reflection Cressida reviewed her appearance. On the glossy wood her skin shone like steam on silver, her collarbones as fine as a dancer's against the lemon silk of her top. That five kilos she'd put on during WestConnex had stayed at bay under Inge's iron watch and, of course, the weekly triathlons; the skirt now skimmed pleasingly rather than bulged across her hips. And while the rest of her outfit was sharp as a tack, the hair was left intentionally messy, essential to the golden triad for female solicitors: attractive but approachable; capable, yet feminine; and young – most importantly, young – but not *too* young. Still diverting ... *fertile* ... but not flaky. After years of careful attention, of scouring magazines and clocking the outfits the other female solicitors wore, of finding out where they shopped and where they had their hair done, she knew that at last she looked like the real thing. *Partner material, bitches*, she thought in the direction of those on the other side of the door. She closed her eyes, nailed a smile to her face, and knocked.

On the other side of the door, two feet away in French cuffs and a fresh Majorca tan, the Sydney Managing Partner of Hannes Swartling regarded her from the nearest end of a vast boardroom table. Behind him all eighty-five partners of the firm looked on: forty from the Sydney office, fifteen from Melbourne, and at least thirty shadowy figures around the table on video links from the Asian and European representatives. The anointing of a new member to their ranks was a hallowed event, and their expressions were both haughty and expectant. She smiled at them, trying to remain calm, and also to keep her gaze from the small stack of documents that lay among the clutter of plates on the table. The Managing Partner offered her a chair and she took it. 'Cressida, welcome,' he said. 'Thank you for joining us. Coffee?'

'Black thanks, Michael,' she said, smoothing her hair. A liveried butler noted her order on a pad and glided out.

And there were the boxes. As much as she tried to affect nonchalance, they pulled her gaze like tiny black holes. Small, black and velvet-lined, one sat in front of each of the Partners, like miniature portals to the other side. The side of Partnership: of three-course gratis lunches, 10am starts and 4pm knock-offs. Of calling the shots instead of taking them in the tit. Of *profit sharing*. And no more *bloody billable hour targets*. All of which, as every Senior Associate had engraved on their heart, spelled unimaginable freedom, respite, and bliss.

Despite the promise of all that, however, there were only three applicants this year: herself; a scary-brilliant patent lawyer called Dr Margaret Minters; and some young upstart from tax who fancied his chances of ascension before thirty like they all did. But the boxes were what she was focused on – if only sheer force of intention could compel their contents one way and not the other, like she seemed to be able to do for everything else in her life. The boxes each contained two marbles: one yellow, one blue. When the time came, the silver canister in front of Michael would be handed around and each partner would deposit a yellow or a blue; in conscious adaptation of the archaic ritual, a single blue was sufficient to kill her application.

'Well,' said Michael, surveying the faces. 'I think we'd all agree. Ms Mitsok has put in a very impressive application.' There came a general murmuring of agreement, and Cressida flushed. *Relax*, she thought. *Your arms are water.* 'For my part,' he said, turning to her, 'I am certain you would be a wonderful addition to the Partnership.'

'Thank you,' said Cressida, proffering a carefully modulated smile.

'But this is an opportunity for questions. To iron out any remaining issues. If there are any, of course …' He regarded the room. 'Partners?'

Cressida watched and waited as little butterflies flip-flopped in her stomach. Richard Branagan, her direct supervising partner in Building & Construction, gave her an encouraging smile from halfway down the table and she smiled back. *In an hour I'm meeting Felipe at the Westin*, she thought. *And the delightful Tiffany D. In the 'modern master bedroom well-appointed for quiet yet energising escapes'. Chocolate. Porsche. Yacht.*

For a moment there was silence, and for a second, then another, there came a flush of hope – would they go straight to the vote? The Managing Partner would pick up that canister, she'd be asked to wait again outside, and they'd go straight to popping in their little marbles. She swallowed, smiling.

But then a voice began from down the table.

'You do realise …'

Cressida searched quickly for its owner. Ah yes. Foster. Sixtyish, grey tie, Insurance. He'd never liked her. She braced herself but regarded him coolly.

'… that you'll be the youngest female appointment to Partnership in this firm's sixty-six year history?'

She feigned surprise. 'No,' she said, smiling. 'Well. I apologise that it took me so long.'

A chuckle ran the length of the table and Cressida relaxed, just an inch.

'But doesn't that mean, Miss Mitsok,' another voice piped up. *Fuck.* '… that you're likely to have other priorities soon? Family, for example?'

Her heart dropped to her stomach. Wenn Davis, Perth Environment and Planning; no women in his practice. Her mind raced. Could he really, actually ask that? But that was the thing, she knew. He bloody could. He could ask *anything*, especially when confidentiality undertakings bound everything HR that ever happened at the firm. And yet – the appearance of gender tolerance was also essential, so duly there was a rustle of concern at his words. Knowing the territory, Davis pressed on.

'Come, gentlemen,' he chided them. 'We all know this meeting is entirely in camera. There has to be an honest discussion – the firm's future relies on it.'

Cressida held up her hand, palm out, all reason and measure.

'It's fine,' she said. 'If you're wondering whether I'm going to disappear in a few years – abandoning the firm's most important clients to the demands of … *motherhood*, for example' – she spoke the word with distaste – 'the answer is no. I'll be quite content as a childless Alpha Female with several million in blue chip, thanks.' And thank God Felipe wasn't clucky. 'Have you heard how expensive those child creatures are? I'd rather keep the money myself.'

The table laughed, more warmly this time. Cressida chalked up another point in her favour. Her coffee arrived and she sipped it, scalding herself but not flinching. The butler retreated to a corner and waited.

'Well,' the Managing Partner said as the room settled, 'if there are no other questions?' He reached for the black compendium in front of him, and Cressida's stomach did somersaults.

'Hang on a minute, Michael.' The assembled heads turned, and a tiny frown creased Cressida's brow. So there *was* a woman in the room after all. And one Cressida didn't recognise. That was odd. Almost every single staffer of Hannes Swartling she knew either by introduction and careful grooming during the time she had been with the firm, or from memorising their bios on the firm website. But she didn't remember this face. For something to do she picked up her coffee cup and sipped it, but it was empty and she put it down again.

'I see from your application that you're a building and construction lawyer,' the woman said. 'But some time ago you spent' – she inspected the document in front of her – 'two years at ASIC. Prosecuting white-collar crime, of all things. Just *on* that … Do you anticipate your relationship with your father will affect your role in the Partnership?'

Cressida blinked. One. It only took one.

'I'm sorry, and you are …?'

'Ah, Cressida,' Michael said, turning to her, 'this is Debra Bollos. Up from Melbourne. New Head of Finance down there. But you've been most recently in our Hong Kong office, is that right, Debra?'

'Five years,' the woman said, with an eye-roll that seemed meant to speak volumes. About what, exactly, Cressida wasn't sure. Her own Southeast Asian work had been the highlight of her career – plenty of work, distant supervision, and a lean enough team to be able to get on with it. Plus Asian men were much more polite to women, she'd found. The Muslim countries had been the best – unlike most Australian male lawyers she'd worked with, they didn't drink alcohol like drains.

A man in a green tie next to her leant forward. 'Actually yes,' he said, while Cressida racked her brain for his name. Andrew somebody; Tax, Melbourne.

'Ah. Andrew, hello,' said Cressida.

'Hi,' he said. 'Yes, I was going to ask about that.' He glanced at Debra. 'He's coming up for parole soon, isn't he?'

Cressida stared. Four years it had been since her father had been arrested, seven since he'd been found out, and here they were, questioning her about it as if it was yesterday. She swallowed and spoke.

'Debra, Andrew,' she began. 'My father's past in this firm has nothing to do with mine.' She turned to the Managing Partner, letting a sliver of irritation grate. 'Surely my application is sufficient on its face without needing to refer to irrelevant matters.' She regarded the rest of the table again. Her people. Something these two irrelevant anomalies were not. 'Those that know me know this aspect of my private life is of no concern,' she added, smiling.

'But you must appreciate, Cressida,' Debra persisted, 'not many Senior Associates applying for partnership have involvement in a major fraud on their copybook.'

Cressida flicked her gaze back and narrowed her eyes.

'I beg your pardon?'

'I mean,' Debra continued, with a smile both patronising and incredulous, 'wasn't there some suggestion that you were involved in *working* on the dust case? *With* him, on the very same fraudulent material that led to his arrest?'

Cressida stared.

'If I were you I'd check my facts before saying something like that,' she said, 'or you might find yourself served with defamation proceedings.'

Debra's mouth dropped open and a murmur issued from around the table, but Cressida held her gaze.

'I mean it,' she said. 'No charges were ever laid.'

But her voice was lost in the rise of outraged ridicule that followed her words. They didn't understand. She was sick of people making wild allegations about her without the facts. And why here, of all places, among her *colleagues*, did she have to defend herself?

Then another voice rose amid the din. As heads turned and the noise subsided, Cress instantly knew who it was. She would recognise that honey drawl anywhere. Brian Prendergast, charismatic Head Partner in Mergers & Acquisitions. Cressida had met him only rarely, but every time she had, he'd looked and sounded like his insides were lined with bitcoin. He was the sort of person who got people to do what he wanted without their even realising, and Cressida knew it would be no different now. He held his hands up, pausing for the ruckus to subside. She held her breath and waited.

'Debra,' he began, his voice replete with the relaxed and reasoned authority of someone who knew people would listen. 'You probably haven't come across our Cressida a great deal.'

*Our Cressida.* She savoured the thrill. How lucky that she had resisted mouthing off.

'No I haven't,' said Debra. 'But if she goes around threatening senior partners with defamation in a partnership meeting, she's not someone I—'

'If I could just finish,' Brian interrupted, aiming that platinum smile, and the glances that echoed at Debra from around the table were enough to silence her. 'It's correct that we *were* fortunate to have Cressida spend some time at the Australian Securities and Investment Commission,' he said. 'And I say fortunate, because those of us here would remember the good use she put that prosecutorial training to on her return. You would all remember John Gray's acquittal on the eight hundred million dollar insider trading charge – or more particularly, the legal fees he paid us, which were nearly more.' There was nodding and a chuckle round the table. 'And the best of us wouldn't have lasted half the time Cressida did in our Szechuan office,' he said, voice rising with both humour and emphasis. 'Two years, wasn't it?' he said, turning to her. 'Not including the six months you spent learning Mandarin beforehand, am I right?'

Cressida flushed in embarrassment, at the same time weak with relief at the diversion. 'Something like that.'

'But all jokes aside,' Brian continued, his voice dropping to a tone of gravitas, 'not only the language preparation, but Cressida's natural' – he looked at her with obvious admiration – '*star quality* is the only way to put it, and her fine legal mind came in *very* handy closing a nearly impossible deal while she was at our China office. Some of you would remember the construction of the Dagangshan Dam.' He paused briefly, then added, 'In fact, if it weren't for Cressida, I doubt we would still *have* a Western China office. We were very proud of her.' He turned to look at her again. 'That business with Mr Mitsok is well in the past now, for both Cressida and us as a firm,' he continued. 'In my view we would be committing almost as great a crime, if I could be so bold, if we were to hold his acts against his daughter now. She has my vote for the Partnership, that's certain.'

Cressida took a deep breath and tried not to levitate off the chair. At last. It wouldn't do to look too eager, she thought, concentrating on keeping a straight face. As if on cue, the door opened and a succession of waiters came in with pale pink, glistening glasses of alternating schnapps and champagne on trays. Cressida stared straight ahead, focusing on a painting on the wall at the far end of the room. *Steady*, she told herself. *Steady*.

'That's all very well,' said Andrew. 'But I'm not convinced.'

There was a murmuring round the table. Cressida sucked in her breath and stared at him.

'If I could elaborate,' Cressida said, an amount of serenity having been restored to her by Brian's words. 'Of *course* I helped him,' she said. 'I was twenty-five, and he was my *father*. But if you are suggesting that I had even the tiniest inkling that the other affidavits were …'

But then she stopped. There was no point. He was either for her or against her, and anything she said herself wasn't going to change that. Her strength was in the rest of them. They'd stand by her. Of course they would.

'Michael,' she said, turning to the Managing Partner. 'Surely this is not the appropriate forum for this. If my father's conviction is so damning of my partnership application, perhaps someone could indicate why I was asked to put one in?'

Andrew stroked his tie and regarded her. 'No offence was meant, Cressida. But if it's not discussed here, then where? To have that blot on your record only two years into practice …'

She clamped her jaw shut and tried not to scream at him. *He was my father. I trusted him. How was I to know that he was up to his neck in it? It's alright for you*, she thought, *you tax lawyer. You arrogant, self-satisfied princelet of Melbourne aristocracy, with your inheritance of class and knowledge from five generations of law royalty; any blots on your record would have been promptly swept under the carpet by the boys' club, unlike my father who came here as a scato immigrant and had to prevail over every adversity with spit and toilet paper.* It probably wouldn't help her application if she got up and strangled him, though. Fortunately for both of them, at that moment Brian intervened.

'Come now, Andrew,' Brian said, 'Cressida cannot be asked to account for matters that were never established in a court of law. She is a fine ... Oh.'

With a flicker the fluorescents lights above went out, the video links went dark, and the assembled partners became suit-shaped shadows. A murmur of surprise went up and in the dim green glow of the exit signs the Managing Partner moved to the door. He opened it to scan the corridor.

'Would you believe it,' he said, returning. 'The whole floor's out. We'll um ... Sorry, Cressida. We'll have to reconvene.'

There was a collective groan, and then the Partners started getting up. Jackets were shouldered amid talk of retirement to the nearest bar for a beverage. Cressida looked on incredulously.

'What?' said Cressida. 'But ...'

It will take weeks to do that, she wanted to shout! Eleven years it had taken to get to this meeting. Eleven years of virtual imprisonment in the four walls of her office, day in, day out, whether in Sydney or Vientiane or Sweden or bloody Szechuan Province, through weekends and public holidays and even, two years running, Christmas Day. Of a Senior Associate's courting and kowtowing, eating food and drinking wine she didn't want, just to be drunk enough to laugh at the jokes of corporate clients she couldn't stand, in everything from girlie bars in Singapore to interminable yacht cruises in Sydney Harbour she couldn't escape (which was almost worse). And here they were, acting like the cancellation of her promotion to Partner was nothing. How could they be so *indifferent*? Then the room was empty, Debra and Andrew trailing out.

'Better luck next time, Cressida,' said Debra. Andrew smirked and drained a schnapps from the sideboard, regarding her, then followed.

Cressida grabbed a glass of the champagne and downed it in three gulps. The bottle's ornate gold label shone in the half-light – Châteauneuf-du-Pape; it retailed for six hundred dollars a bottle, she knew. *Well at least I've cost you all an hour or two's billing*, she thought, collaring a glass of the schnapps. *Or just an hour's if you're doing motor accidents.* Sucking down half, she pushed herself away from the table and looked out the window, trying to dispel her rage. *Hang on.* Beyond the harbour's sheet of moonlit water the entire North Shore was black, the only lights those lining the base of the Harbour Bridge or the headlights of cars crawling across it. How quiet it was, she thought. And when had she ever in her life sat in a room by herself in the dark? In the silence she could feel the surge of her heart in her chest. For once in her life there was nowhere to go, nowhere to be; it was almost restful. Then a door slammed outside in the silent corridor and she jumped. With a shiver she swallowed the schnapps, collected her gym bag from behind the shadowed reception desk, and followed the Partners into the fire escape.

## 3

The hip. It was always the hip Robert loved the most. That sweeping curve, giving itself to the lean of his inked brush like a lover; the torso, almost perfection; the nipped waist reaching down, with its muscular invitation to grasping and grip; those too – but the hips – how he loved the sweet release of them – he would poise with his brush on the paper, waiting, waiting – and then—

'What the?'

The ceiling light had gone out.

Colin's Estuary brogue came from across the darkness. 'That's a turn-up.'

Robert cringed and reached for the light switch.

'Wait a sec.'

But when he flicked it, nothing happened. With an exasperated sigh he found the door handle. In the corridor, shadowed figures were emerging from their offices. He stepped back into the room, quickly, before anyone saw him. Dammit. A second later there was a knock at the door and a muffled voice called in.

'Mr Premier?'

'Fuck me,' said Colin, as something fell over with a crash.

'Just a minute,' Robert called, trying not to sound panicked. 'Colin darling, can you get your clothes on?'

'I'm trying, I'm *trying* ...'

The door opened and a flashlight bounced in, catching the white flash of his lover's thigh in its glow. A stream of words and justifications flooded to Robert's throat but stuck there, while Colin continued to swear in Cockney. A security guard in a dark suit stepped in and cleared his throat. It wasn't one Robert recognised. That wasn't unusual though: they always seemed to be new.

'Evening, Premier. There seems to be a bit of a power issue. Help you out of the building, can I?'

'Um, yes please.' Robert turned, awkwardly. 'This is my—' Oh God, why could he never find the *words*. 'My, er ...'

'Your drawing model, sir. Yes. Hi, Colin.'

'Evening.' Colin grimaced and waved as the officer turned the torch back on him, continuing to pull his jeans on over one bare muscular leg.

The officer sighed.

'Would you like this?' The guard handed him the torch. 'I'll wait outside.'

Robert's cheeks burned. *Oh God, the drawings*, he suddenly remembered. He reached out for the easel and it collapsed, the A0 size sketchpad crumbling to the ground in a flurry. He gathered it up but couldn't find the inkwell or the brush. *Great. That'll be a nice black stain on the carpet to explain later.*

'Come *on*, Colin,' Robert muttered through gritted teeth. 'Darling, I'm sorry,' he said, as Colin struggled into the other pants leg, 'appearances – I'll wait for you in the corridor.'

Robert shoved the drawing pad behind a filing cabinet and threw his shoulders back, donning the glamour of his office like armour, and thrust open the door. Outside, three security detail stood unreadable in the dimness.

'Evening, sir.'

Down the corridor another guard in hi-vis was cheerfully directing people towards the green exit sign.

'Just make your way to the exits, Members,' he was saying, 'fire exit that way ...'

Robert stepped closer to one of the guards and spoke to him, inches from his ear.

'We've been working together for some time now – night classes, you know,' he said. 'It helps to have a hobby I've found, don't you think? A man needs a hobby.'

'Sign him in, did you, Mr Premier?'

Robert swallowed.

'All visitors have to be signed in, don't they. Very important security policy,' the guard said, face deadpan as he glanced at the other two. The silence lengthened.

'Oh for fuck's sake.' Robert pulled out his wallet and handed the officer a hundred-dollar note. The other two stood motionless. '*Colin*,' he bellowed back into the room. The guard smiled and took a step in, just as Colin emerged.

'Right then, are we?' the guard said, 'This way. Mr Charleton, if you'll follow security that way—'

'What's going on?' Robert demanded, trying to get his gravitas back. 'Power out in the whole building?'

The security guard looked sideways at Colin, considering.

'Seems so.'

'Where's bloody Carl? Oi Carl,' Robert yelled back down the corridor as the guards started herding Colin out, looking for the Minister for Energy. 'Nice job. I thought we hired you to stop this happening.' He smirked and craned past the security guards to look. 'Where is he?'

'Same place you're going, Mr Premier. Cabinet members this way,' he said, indicating the other direction down the hallway.

'Where are we going? What about – Mr Charleton?'

'Mr Charleton will be fine.'

'But – why aren't we going that way? No. He has to come too. *Colin*,' he called out, craning to see him. Colin turned around. The guards stopped.

'I'm not going anywhere unless Mr Charleton comes with me.'

The first security guard sighed and turned to another of the guards.

'He checks out, right, Stewart?'

'Yes sir.'

'Alright. Damo,' he nodded at him.

The third security guard stepped towards Colin.

'If you'll come this way, sir.'

For a split second visible relief washed over Colin's face and then he smiled in that cheerful way of his.

'Right then,' he said, and followed.

# 4

The fire escape down Cressida's building had become one long concrete column crowded with people, all shouting to be heard over each other and the exhaust fans that screamed above. In the green pools of light thrown by the exit signs, Cressida fell in between a man piggybacking a sequinned woman screeching with laughter and brandishing a cocktail glass, and another complaining about not getting the tray of drinks he had ordered from the bar on the top floor. In her three-inch heels she had to lower her foot to each step carefully before attempting the next, gripping the railing and trying to put out of her mind the people stacked behind her, while sweat streamed down her neck and made her head itch. *You try doing this in Prada pumps, plus three glasses of alcohol*, she told them, weighing up whether to take the shoes off. For the most part the crowd seemed drink-warmed and tolerant though, all solicitude and laughter in the departure from routine; the next time the line stalled she bent down and yanked her shoes off, apologising to the oyster patent-leather as she stuffed them in her bag.

The respite in her arches and back was immediate. Fuck. That was better. She looked up, assessing whether to wait for a gap in the crowd or try to assert her way back in. Then on the next landing she spotted the receptionist from Building & Construction and Winnie from Tax, and relief at the sight of familiar faces rushed in. Next to them was a frail woman with fine grey hair who also looked familiar. She stopped beside Cressida, her top lip beaded with sweat, and passed a bony wrist across her forehead. Ah, Cressida remembered, Brian Prendergast's receptionist. The woman mouthed something at her.

'Sorry – what was that?' Cressida yelled, leaning forward. 'It's Esma, isn't it?'

'Yes,' the woman said, breathing heavily but attempting a smile. 'Thank you.' She held her face close to Cressida's ear. 'I don't suppose you'd walk in front of me, would you, just so I can grab you as I fall past?'

'Of course,' Cressida laughed. As conga twins the two of them inched forward, Esma's thin fingers spiking Cress's shoulders and Cress holding onto the railing for support. When they reached the bouncing torchlights of security on the ground floor, both fell against the wall to catch their breath. There was a hand towel in Cress's gym bag somewhere, and with relief she found it and dabbed carefully at her sweat-glossed face, wondering at the same time why she was bothering – her mascara would already be resembling an ageing English rocker's. But she could hardly meet Felipe looking like a drowned rat.

'How will you get home?' Cressida asked Esma, fishing around in her bag for a hand mirror before she realised it would be too dark to see anything by – she'd have to fix herself up at the Westin; hopefully there'd be enough time before Felipe got there.

'Driving, I thought,' she said, looking with some alarm out the plate-glass window onto the street. 'How about you?'

'I'm at the Westin tonight actually,' Cress replied. 'Minibreak.'

'Oh gosh. I remember those,' Esma laughed, mopping her face with a handkerchief. 'Well – go on then, don't let me hold you up!'

Cressida laughed, digging her shoes out of her bag and putting them on.

'Thanks. Alright then. See you.'

They waved and Cressida rejoined the crowd heading towards the double doors onto the street, astonished by the number of people still coming down the stairs. It was amazing to think that she worked a few metres from these people every day, and aside from the Tax crew had never met any of them. Outside the revolving doors the heat of the day still soaked the air; thank God the Westin was only a two-minute walk. How good it would be to get underneath one of those hot, ludicrously plentiful showers in their suite. Except – oh shit. The suite. *Tiffany Delux*. She had booked her as a special treat for Felipe: three hours, full service. Oh God. The rate was five hundred dollars an hour, and bang, whoops, she didn't have the promise of a coming partnership salary to pay for it now. What was she going to do – call her and cancel? God, it had taken enough courage – plus two glasses of white – to book her in the first place. *And* they probably had a massive cancellation fee. She stood on the kerb, wondering what to do. There was nothing for it. She'd have to phone and hope to get out of it with just an hour or something. But what on earth was the name of the place again? The web search page was blank though – *Safari cannot open the page* ... And when she dialled there was nothing but a loud beeping noise, and a screen that said *Emergency calls only*. Plus a missed call from Richard. *Scato*.

A man arrived in front of her, holding out a five-dollar note. His tie was loose and the front of his shirt was soaked with sweat.

'Sorry, 'scuse me. Do you have any change?' he said. 'I'm trying to ring my wife.'

'Oh,' said Cressida, dropping the phone and going red. *Relax, he can't tell you're dialling a brothel*, she thought. 'What, is your building blacked out too?' she said, busying herself picking up the phone and fumbling for her wallet.

'Are you kidding?' The man frowned, nodding down the hill. 'The whole city's out. Why do you think there's fifty people at the bus stop?'

'Oh,' Cressida said, looking. That's right. The whole North Shore too. The bus queue stretched down the block, mingling with the line at the taxi rank next to it. A fire truck was inching through the traffic. *Shit*. What was the point of going to the Westin then? But that would mean Felipe would be waiting on the street. She quickly dug some change from her wallet and handed it to him, waving away the note. 'Is your mobile not working either?'

At the bus stop people groaned at the sight of one full bus then another trundling past. On a third, two people hung off the back, and the groan turned to a cheer. He shook his head. 'Can't get through.'

'Radio said they were prioritising Emergency calls. Access Overload Control,' a man in the queue said, knowledgeably. In a strobe of flashing blue lights the fire truck lumbered up the kerb and four men swung down.

'Do you know – are the phone towers out?' the man at the bus stop called out to them. 'What's going on, anyway? I thought this new mob were supposed to be better at running the show.' He looked around at the others in the queue for agreement.

'Yeah, not sure at the moment, mate,' the firefighter said, reaching for what looked like an enormous crowbar from the back of the truck. 'Most have battery backup so they'll work for a bit. Your phone's probably working, just jammed with everyone trying to make calls. I'd keep trying.' He turned and jogged towards the Hannes Swartling building after the other two, and as they watched they entered by a side door.

Cressida stepped to the edge of the road, craning round it to check the traffic.

'Terrorist attack is what I heard,' the man at the bus stop was saying.

'What? I doubt it. More likely a power surge. I know one thing, I wouldn't want to be them in all that clobber. In this heat?' said another man.

'Sorry, gotta go,' said Cress, ducking behind a car and dodging others to the other side. Weaving through the crowd she hurried along the footpath, looking for Felipe's characteristic figure. He would tower over everyone in his usual non-surgical-days uniform of Momotaro denim and a tight Calvin Klein Slim Fit black t-shirt (bought in a three pack), the pecs and shoulders of daily ocean swims notable underneath. But when she got to the Westin, the doors to the hotel were closed and the foyer was dark, with no sign of Felipe. She perched on an aluminium bench seat and speed-dialled his number, not remembering until the high-pitched beep that the phone wasn't working. Where was he? She untied her ponytail, shaking it out to loosen some of the sweat, and looked up at the exact second the space above was sheared by lightning. Momentarily the masses in the square below were visible, and it was like finding herself in a giant nightclub; in the returning dark, people's faces were unreadable, black bobbing heads converging. Yells and crashes sounded from the murky dark down closer to the harbour. She was thirsty, and a headache was beginning to flower behind her left temple. Suddenly she felt small, and surrounded, fear coiling in her stomach. Whether Felipe turned up or not, how on earth was she going to get home? Then her phone rang.

'Pip,' she said, collapsing into the bench seat at the sound of a friendly voice. Pip Buchanan, her office-mate for the first two years of her time at Hannes Swartling.

'Cressida, I heard. How awful!'

'I know. It's total bedlam here. Fifty people at the bus stop and no-one's going anywhere.'

'I'm talking about the partnership vote, silly.'

'What? Oh. Yes. I know. *Malakas*,' she said, using her father's favourite expletive. 'How did you hear?'

'Um.' There was a pause and a rustle on the handset, then Pip continued, 'Brian Prendergast told me actually. Where are you?'

'Outside the Westin. What about you?'

'In a water taxi. We were at Aria – the bloody lights went out right in the middle of the spanner crab. Anyway, they couldn't take cards without any power, could they, so we didn't have to pay. Is it still going where you are?'

'Yep,' Cressida said, watching a gaggle of people surge around a taxi, yelling and banging on the roof. 'Cripes, now a fight's breaking out over a cab.'

'Oh God, really? They'll get it back on soon,' Pip said. 'I bloody hope so, anyway. I'll get rapidly homicidal in this weather without air conditioning. How are you getting home?'

'At least you're down by the harbour. I'm bang in the thick of it in a wool skirt and stockings. Um, not sure yet,' she said. 'Walking, probably.'

'Poor you. I'd come and get you if I could. By the way it's pouring here. Hope the rain stays away from where you are.'

'Jesus, really? That'd put the icing on it. I …' Just at that moment a fat drop landed on Cressida's knee, and more pinged on the seat next to her, then out of nowhere a sheet of water roared across the square from the sky behind the Hannes Swartling building. Three weeks of forty degrees and it was raining *now*? Cressida scrambled for the tiny umbrella in her handbag.

'Hang on,' she yelled. 'I'd better go. Are you okay getting home?'

'Yeah I'm fine. You too I hope. Good luck finding Felipe!' her friend yelled back, and Cressida hung up. Feeling like a gazelle on ice, she ran across the paving to the overhang of the nearest building, where thirty other people huddled looking out at the rain. Down at the bus stop, the queuing workers stood with heads bent sideways like horses in a field. One woman had her face to the sky letting the drops pelt her cheeks. Cressida half longed to do the same, feel the rain wash the sweat from her face and where it stuck to her clothing, but that would ruin her blowdry so she didn't. Looking around she decided there was only one thing for it. She'd have to walk, and hope Felipe could look after himself. Quickly she closed the umbrella and fished her running shoes out of her gym bag, standing awkwardly to slip off her heels and jam first one foot then the other into the runners. She stashed her heels in her handbag and put the umbrella up again, pressing the speed dial to Felipe again with the other hand. Hopefully the mobile phone fairy was still on the job. He picked up on the first ring.

'Felipe? Oh thank God,' she said, feeling another wash of relief. 'I've been looking everywhere for you.'

'Darling, where are you?' he said. 'Are you alright? You sound distressed.'

'There's a bloody blackout here. And it's pouring.'

'Cressida, what are you yelling for?' he said, irritated. 'What's all that racket in the background?'

'It's the rain. Sorry. Look I've been trying to call you. It took ages even to get out of the building, let alone on a bus. Where are you?'

'What do you mean? I'm at the hospital of course ...'

'Oh,' said Cressida, stopping. Someone behind her ran into her and swore, and she apologised, cupping the hand with the umbrella in it round the phone. 'But ... but I thought you were meeting me at the hotel?'

'Yes, look I *know*, darling, I'm so sorry – to tell you the truth I clean forgot! They're down an orthopod registrar here and it's bedlam; I haven't had a minute to think.'

'Oh. Yes, of course,' said Cressida, concealing the disappointment in her voice. It was alright. He'd remember about the partnership vote later, when the chaos had died down.

'And I did say to you, Cressida, that I wasn't sure about this the night before such an important triathlon meet.'

Oh God, the triathlon. Felipe was obsessed with them, in part because he was certain it helped with seniority on the Australian Orthopaedic Association Board, of which he was a member. Cressida wasn't convinced, but she wasn't about to argue.

'Yes, yes of course absolutely ... Hey, um, we just had the partnership vote, Felipe ... remember?'

'I'm sorry, Cressida, I can hardly hear you – can we talk about this later? I'll get a taxi and ... oh, there's one. Excuse me.' Then there was the sound of a scuffle and a door slamming. 'Oh for goodness sake. Now I've seen *everything*.'

'What?'

'Oh nothing. Just a bloody wardsman jumped the queue for the only taxi there's been for half an hour. Can you flag one and come here?'

She looked around. On the street below, four taxis were bumper to bumper under the grey sheets of rain, but their signs were dark.

'Ah ...' she said. 'Look, how about I get home as soon as I can and drive over. Only, well, it's total gridlock here. How's the street outside the hospital?'

'I wouldn't know, Cressida, I'm in the car park underneath.' The irritation in his voice went up a notch. 'Where the taxi rank is. Oh—' There were muffled words on the end of the phone again. 'It's alright, all is well, Peter can give me a lift. See you. No need to drop over. I'll see you in the morning.'

'Oh. But ...' she began, and the phone went dead. She looked down at it and swallowed. It was okay, it was a long way from the hospital to here. What did she expect him to do – come all the way down and pick her up? The two bars of chocolate in her bag were glinting at her again, and before she knew it she had ripped the wrapping off the Jelly Popping Candy Beanies and devoured half of it, falling into its consuming decadence as the rain coursed over her umbrella. Hadn't *that* whole chocolate/Porsche plan turned out well, she thought, watching water stream into the drain in the gutter beside her. She looked down at her shoes. They were soaked, and the bottom half of her skirt was drenched from the angle of the downpour. Then a pool of light flooded the street ahead and she looked up to see a helicopter bank above the buildings, its searchlight backlighting the shards of rain. At least it warded off the dark. She squeezed the water out of her skirt and began to walk.

On Elizabeth Street the restaurants and nightclubs were like toys run out of batteries, the bar owners standing and looking forlornly out into the street, while next to them disgorged patrons leant against walls finishing clear-glass beers. Police were everywhere, doling out witches hats along the edge of the roadway to keep the crowd on the footpath. It took her forty minutes to make it along Oxford Street to Bondi Junction, but at the bus terminus she squeezed onto a bus full of wet office workers and exhausted-looking European backpackers, and stood for the journey up the hill to North Bondi. On the kerb at the corner of Military Road the bus let her out and she stood to watch it go, a box of golden-lit noise, red tail-lights and steam winding its way up the hill. The street was slick with rain and as the bus receded, like a tide the silence settled in, broken only by a deep, bouncy ping that echoed from the golf course on the other side of the road – frogs? Distantly she could hear the roar of the sea from the foot of the cliffs, and then a night bird called, far off. She felt caught like a fly in amber in the strangeness of it, between the heavy sky and the wet ground, listening as nature extended its fingers into the gaps left by the stillness. And there was that alone feeling she'd had in the boardroom, again, after everyone had left. As if the frogs and the birds were the only other things living. Quickly she shook off the feeling and started for home.

At her apartment building all she wanted was to get inside, heeling off her wet shoes and shucking her skirt in the hallway. As she fell against the wall she flicked the light out of habit, too tired to find the torch on her phone in the dark. By feel she identified a juice left over from that morning in the fridge, the sediment that had floated to the top meeting her tongue. *Blecch.* Spinach, kale and beetroot would never have flirted in the kitchen at a party. The expensive cold-press juicer made a dark shape on the counter. Hopefully the five kilos of veggies in the crisper would keep. She fell on her bed and coaxed open a window, noticing again the silence thick on the hot night air. But then, some flats away, there was laughter, and she felt herself relax. Someone was having a blackout party. The human race did still exist. She fell onto the pillow, fast asleep.

# 5

---

Eighteen months as Premier, four years in senior ministry, and nearly twenty years as a member of parliament, and the whole time this place had been in the bowels of the building and Robert had had no idea. He always felt like he was the last to know things, but from the protestations and questioning of the other Cabinet members ahead of them, it seemed like for once he wasn't the only one. He had peeled off his jacket twenty minutes ago, and stopped to loosen his tie on the last landing – buggered if he was going to take it off; there were still standards to maintain – and by the fourth floor down, his shirt was soaked. They had already descended eight levels of stairs, and Parliament House only had seven storeys. The security guards would only say that all would be explained when they got to something called 'cog', as they called it. It wasn't really very satisfactory. He was the Premier of New South Wales for goodness sake, supposed to be security briefed at the highest levels, but it seemed like even this was something he wasn't fully informed about. He would take it up with the relevant people after this was over.

Meanwhile, how on earth was he going to explain Colin? A few steps ahead of him, his lover's low jeans and canvas shoulder bag with its raggedy Greenpeace iron-on on the flap clearly marked him as non-staff, his dayglo-yellow No Sweat ethical hitops cringingly flashy; the Minister for Energy and his own irritating deputy, fresh as a daisy in her navy suit despite the heat, were only metres in front. For three years they had managed to keep their relationship secret, no small feat given Colin's passion for getting physical outside the bedroom. Robert reached out and gave his hand an unobtrusive squeeze – reassuring to himself or Colin, he wasn't sure, but it made him feel better. They would just explain it somehow. The most important thing was that Colin was safe.

Robert's legs were shaking by the time they finally arrived. At the foot of the stairs four security guards waited next to a metal detector and the standard conveyor belt x-ray machine arrangement. What, more security? But anyone here had done all that to get into Parliament House to begin with. Maybe these people weren't all from Parliament House though. Looking at them he would have no idea. There were more than two thousand workers in the building, and he only really knew members of his own Cabinet and, maybe, one or two of their longer serving staffers. Could never be too careful, he supposed. A security detail in a dark suit stepped forward.

'Honourable Members …'

People raised their hands and called for quiet and he began again.

'Honourable Members, you are about to enter Unit COG – Continuation of Government. Once you have cleared security please file in in an orderly fashion and help yourselves to refreshments. A security briefing is due at twenty hundred hours. We hope to have as much information for you as possible then.'

Robert's stomach lurched. Continuation of *government*? What the hell was going on?

'Damo,' someone called out. 'Come on, it's just a blackout for fuck's sake – is all this really necessary?'

'I'm sorry, madam,' Damo replied, 'it is.'

Colin turned to look at Robert. His face was calm but there was concern in his eyes. Robert swallowed, dredging up presidential as well as he could.

'Go on.'

Belts and shoes and jackets were shucked, phones and laptops deposited in trays and passed through the x-ray, MPs patted down and caressed with the explosives tester wand. Robert sighed and pushed his hand through his hair. This was really going to ruin his weekend, he thought, irrationally. He had been intending to surprise Colin with lunch at Wild Duck. It had been so long since they'd been there, and the weather was flawless.

Damo was standing in front of him. He was indicating a corridor off to the right Robert hadn't noticed before.

'This way, Mr Premier.'

'Sorry?'

'Necessary to segregate you, Mr Premier. Extra precaution.'

'Oh,' Robert said, grinning tightly. He craned to see past Damo to the crowd behind. 'Colin.'

'I'm sorry, sir,' said the security guard, shaking his head as Colin stopped and turned. 'Highest levels only.'

'Oh.' The Premier's stomach fizzed. 'Oh – alright – Colin – I'll see you – later …' he said, waving optimistically.

Colin gave that reassuring grin. 'Copy that,' he said, and was gone.

Damo nodded and Robert stepped ahead of him. They came to another door. Robert turned to him.

'What about the scanner?'

'No need,' the officer said, holding up a swipe card until the door hissed open. For some reason Robert's heart was going like crazy, and sweat had sprung out on his palms. Something was seriously wrong, and he was *Premier*. He would be expected to know what to do. *Quick, think of something.* Inside was a large space that looked like a dated hotel room, all '70s laminate and vinyl, except that along one side was a bank of televisions, three telephones, and two laptops. It must have dated from when the back extension to Parliament was built. Two large men in suits, and another in an Australian Federal Police uniform stood by the buffet drinking out of plastic cups, white spiral cords at their ears. When he entered they stopped their conversation and turned around.

'Ah, Mr Premier,' one said, stepping towards him. 'Have a seat.' The TVs on the wall flashed on, and he saw … what were the Federal Minister for Home Affairs and the … wasn't that the Federal Resources Minister? What were they doing on videolink?

'Mr Premier.' The officer sat down across from him and pushed a white card with blue writing and a raised gold insignia across the gap. 'Joe Fitzgibbon, Senior Constable, AFP.' Then he passed him a document. TOP SECRET, said the title, MAJOR INCIDENT: POWER SUPPLY. Oh gosh. So. Not a blackout then. There was a carafe of water on the table and a stack of plastic cups; Robert reached for one and filled it.

'Goodness,' he said, scanning the document. 'Senior Constable – I'm sorry but this needs the presence of my Cabinet to discuss this. The Deputy Premier and the Energy Minister – they were in the crowd a moment ago. Could they be collected please?'

'The Honourable Federal Members requested only you at this time, Mr Premier.'

Robert swallowed. There was going to be a tonne of fresh hell to pay for this, and no more Saturday pub lunches for a while. He took a deep breath.

'Right,' he said. 'Better get them live then.'

# 6

In the morning Cressida woke to someone banging on her door. It wouldn't be Felipe because he had a key. Cressida yanked the windows shut against the hot air outside and squinted at the clock radio. Off. Oh for God's sake, she thought, pulling on her cream silk dressing gown. Hadn't someone sorted out the power *yet*? She padded across the floorboards to the front door and squinted through the peephole. Helena stood there, her curly brown-haired head dwarfed by enormous wraparound sunglasses.

'Oh thank God,' said her stepmother when Cressida opened the door, running into the flat and slamming the heavy timber behind her so hard the potplant next to it fell off the shelf. She did a lap of the loungeroom checking the windows were locked and fell on Cressida in a cloud of L'eau d'Issey. 'The world's ending, Cressida – you have to come home.' She cupped her hands around Cressida's face, her eyes wide. 'Haven't you heard? Terrorists. We're under attack. Joan next door said she'd heard it was the electrical union. Quick, pack some clothing. What is your *skirt* doing in the hallway? Is someone else here?' She peered out the window as if to look for terrorists running down the street, then hurried into Cressida's bedroom and started hauling clothes out of drawers. 'The police have said—'

'Helena,' Cressida cut her off. Rubbing her eyes, she began in her best low, firm voice, 'What are you talking about?'

'Oh for God's sake, Cressida, haven't you heard? On the radio. Terrorists have sabotaged three power stations. *Three*. That's why there's no power. We have to get out of here.'

'What? Jesus,' Cressida said, not sure whether to run in circles like Helena or go back to bed and pretend it wasn't happening. Neither would be particularly helpful, she decided. Instead she carefully sat on her bed and picked up her phone, which of course was now flat, only a fancy slab of glass and plastic in her hand. She put it down and calmly flipped open her laptop. At least *it* was still charged. The Sydney Porsche dealership's page was still open from yesterday, and she flicked from it to the *Herald* website. Then she remembered the modem would be dead. She stood up and found Helena's handbag.

'Your phone is still charged?' she said, rootling.

'What are you doing?' asked Helena, digging through the bottom of Cressida's wardrobe. She found a duffel bag and started throwing things into it. Cressida opened the settings function on Helena's phone and switched on the wireless hotspot, groaning inwardly at the little blue circle while her laptop looked for the signal.

'I'm just checking to make sure you have in fact gone mad ...'

Ah. Five bars. *Excellent.* She clicked refresh on the page. Convulsively it loaded.

'Ah,' said Cressida. 'Holy fuck.'

*Terror Australis*, the *Sydney Morning Herald* website blurted, in large white letters over a picture of flames and a close up of a firefighter in a gas mask. *Overnight three major NSW power stations, servicing sixty percent of the Sydney metropolitan area, were destroyed by fire,* she read. *Police suspect terrorism ...*

'Oh my God,' she began. 'This says ...'

Then she realised she was about to say exactly the same thing Helena had. Maybe not the bit about the world ending, but at least the terrorist/power station part.

'What do you think I've been *telling* you?' Helena said, zipping the duffel. 'Is that everything?' She stood up, thinking. 'I'll go and pack some cans from your kitchen. We've got plenty at home, but you never know how long this is going to last ...'

Cressida looked out the window, wondering why everything looked so normal. Her first thought was that at least the triathlon was off. Then she thought maybe it was odd to be thinking that at a time like this. There was something else. Then she remembered. *Felipe.* In seconds she was in motion, dropping her silk robe to the floor and pulling on shorts and a t-shirt, grabbing some sportswear from her bottom drawers, some undies and her hairdryer, her trenchcoat off its hanger. Oh God. The hairdryer. There was no power. She looked in the mirror. Despite all attempts to prevent it, her blowdry had been ruined by the rain, her normally buttery locks a puffy snakeskin mess. There was a wide headband on the dresser and she grabbed that, slipping it over her head and hair and tucking in the ends at the back so it looked like a turban. It would have to do.

'Jesus, Cressida, don't you eat canned food?' she heard Helena exclaim from the kitchen. 'All I can find here are dried mushrooms and diet drink powder. And about fifty kilos of carrots and celery in your fridge. What's that?' she asked, peering around the door jamb to the laundry where Cressida was wrestling a backpack off a high shelf.

'My emergency pack,' said Cressida, grunting. The heavy bag fell into her arms and she dragged it out to the kitchen like a corpse, leaning it up against a cupboard. She filled a glass from the sink.

'No, don't. You have to boil it. You have an emergency pack?' said Helena, her voice holding a mixture of disbelief and approval.

Cressida unclasped the pack and pulled out a transistor radio from the top.

'Sure. Don't you? I think there are some purification tablets in here somewhere. What frequency's the ABC?' They both looked at each other as she tried the *on* button on the radio, sharing relief when the device burred into life. 'Why do we have to boil it?'

'133.5. No idea. Since when have you had an emergency pack?'

'I don't know,' she said, piling the vegetables from the fridge into a cloth bag as Helena watched. 'I never thought I'd have to use it. I just liked packing it. Ah.' She twiddled the dial on the radio and found the station, then turned the volume up. It was halfway through a bulletin warning them to stay away from train stations and shopping centres. They exchanged a look and Cressida swore and threw the tap water in the sink, then both of them ran into the hallway.

'Can you take that?' She pointed into her room at her laptop. 'Wait a minute. *Alessa*. She was ...'

'Alessa's fine,' Helena said, touching Cressida's arm. 'She's at home. Her plane got in yesterday afternoon. Not happy about the lack of hot water, of course, and her bags never turned up on the concourse. But other than that she's fine.'

Alessa. Her sister, in town slumming it with the provincials. It was the obligatory fortnight in March and, as usual, or at least once the missing suitcases arrived, she would be fresh from a Singapore fashion mall in a new capsule outfit from some edgy new designer. Last time it was lots of leather and dangly earrings. Cressida looked down at her own ensemble. She'd have to change. Quickly she went to her room and shucked her shorts, slipping on instead the cream linen Leona Edmiston shift.

'What are you doing?' Helena said from the doorway.

'A terrorist attack is no reason to look sloppy,' she said, adding a pale silk scarf and her weekend pearls, yellow rather than eggshell. Quickly she applied tinted SPF and bronzer, three-second eyeliner and a dash of gloss, picked up the duffel and started herding Helena towards the door.

'What about Dad?'

'I know,' Helena said and stopped, turning to her, eyes filling with tears. 'I've tried ringing them all morning, but I can't get through. I did once on the mobile and it went straight to voicemail.' Her eyes were dark. 'I guess they have contingencies for this sort of thing.' Then she brightened. 'Well. At least we know we don't have to worry about Jerome. No need for power stations on ships.'

'Yeah,' Cressida snorted. Her brother had been on the *Sea Shepherd* for weeks. They'd have wall to wall solar, surely. Or was that hull to hull? 'I guess not.'

When they opened the door the heat hit them like wind from a furnace, sweat stickying Cressida's eyelids almost immediately. Helena held her handbag over her head against the sun's blaze, took the duffel and ran towards the car. When she had popped the boot of the vast green Jag she ran back to take Cressida's laptop.

'Actually, Helena,' Cressida said, lugging the backpack and the cloth bag of veggies into the boot of her Fiat, 'we have to go via Felipe's. I just want to check he's okay. Hey – you're looking a little peaky.' She stopped and asked, 'Are you alright?'

'What? Oh. Yes.' There was a pause and Helena lifted her sunglasses to wipe her eyes. 'It's just so awful,' she said, looking up at Cressida. 'I mean – what about the babies?'

'The babies?'

'You know. The ones in hospital. And the old people, on respirators ...'

'Oh Helena, yes,' said Cressida, squeezing her into a hug. Children were usually first on her stepmother's mind when anything happened. 'Yes. I guess we don't know what the damage is yet though.' She tried to sound reassuring. 'I remember Felipe once saying something about hospitals having backup generators. Anyway,' she said, thumbing a stray tear from Helena's cheek, 'let's pick up some ice on the way to your place, then we can have a cold drink.' How long did servo ice fridges stay cold without power? 'Then we'll try and find a proper news bulletin.'

'I've got some,' Helena murmured, still distracted. Then her stepmother was looking up at her, small and scared.

'Can I come with you?'

'In my car? Of course.'

'Oh but what about the Jag?' she said, looking at the boot and then down the road. 'Will it be safe here? There's looters ...'

Cressida looked uncertainly up and down the street. It was deserted, but the vast green vehicle *was* an eye-catching car.

'You drive home and I'll follow,' she said, 'then I'll go and get Felipe by myself. It won't take long.'

'Are you mad?' Helena said, grabbing Cressida's hand, 'I'm not letting you out of my sight. Besides, Leo would kill me if anything happened to you.'

Cressida doubted her father would have much of an opinion one way or the other, but knew it would hurt Helena's feelings to say so, so she didn't.

'Okay,' she said. 'How about you drive it to your place, then we both go in my car?'

'Oh you're so sensible, Cressida,' Helena said, falling against her in a damp-eyed hug.

'Come on.' Cressida pushed her gently into the driver's seat of the Jag. 'Wait here while I go get mine.'

The Porsche still pending, Cressida's current car was a two-door Fiat she had bought after seeing it at a popup at Bondi Junction Westfield. Tiny, white and bubble-shaped, the creamy red upholstery and little red badge on the boot had beguiled her pen onto the papers before the salesperson had even had to wave the brochure. The air conditioning had gone on the blink after the last service though and only worked with the fan at full blast now, but Cressida had come to enjoy sitting in its arctic gale. She tossed the bag in the back, plugged her phone into the cigarette lighter, and turned the radio on. There was a bottle of water in the footwell and she reached for it, unscrewing the top and gulping half. Warm, but good. So-o-o good. *Well I'm sure the Porsche dealership will understand if I don't turn up for my appointment*, she thought, wiping her lips. Then another thought arose and she nearly spat out the mouthful. *Oh God. The prostitute. The hotel room.* She'd forgotten to ring them. Surely this counted as Act of God or something for the purposes of any cancellation fee. As she tailed Helena down the curve of Military Road, the burn of disappointment at last night's deferral of the vote took up residence again in her stomach. Thank God that, other than Pip and briefly Felipe, she hadn't told anyone about her application.

Driving down Campbell Parade was like passing through the main street of a ghost town. The usual passage of early morning joggers was absent, the beach deserted. An enormous armoured personnel carrier dominated the square outside the chicken shop, its occupants in full army fatigues directing traffic at the intersection under lights that flashed amber. Nearby, police in white overalls picked their way across broken glass outside the convenience store. It was startling to see the soldiers, as if war had arrived overnight.

Her stomach was rumbling. How was she going to keep the juice diet up now, without power for the machine? Fruit, she thought. Surely there'll be a fruit shop open. But all three vendors along Bondi Road were shuttered. At Bondi Junction the traffic slowed to a crawl as more gloved traffic police directed cars around intersections. The same service was on every frequency on the radio, as if there had been some kind of government appropriation because of the terrorist attack, and the bulletin about avoiding high-density areas was on repeat. Then came a news bulletin that the power was expected to be out for at least a week, and her heart sank. That meant no partnership vote for at least a week. *Damn.* With these things, momentum was so important. More delay meant more time since her most recent achievements, making them dim in their minds. Then as she slowed for the turnoff to Carrington Street it occurred to her that the power stations might even be owned by a Hannes Swartling client. If they were, she realised, it would be all hands on deck – and none of the Partners would be the least bit interested in her little application.

The road to Bondi Junction Westfield was blocked by enormous orange bollards, and further down, a phalanx of black-clothed officers lined the street down to the shopping centre. They wore hard hats and balaclavas, their bodies a bristle of artillery and communication devices. Ahead of her she watched Helena pick her way carefully through the traffic, her small head dwarfed by the matronly stretch of the back of the car. It had been her father's car, before, and Cressida hated that Helena still drove it. On every road trip it broke down, and seemed to need its own rest stop and milkshake in the shade every two hours. But Helena said driving it made her feel closer to Leo. The car was in fact a lot like him, Cressida thought: big and showy, but, well, hopeless when it came to the most important things. Being there, for example. She had seen photos of herself in it as a child, a small serious face against its white bench seat under the crook of her mother's arm, her mother a smiling blonde face behind the moulded steering wheel. They'd gone everywhere in it in those days. The good days, before the investigators arrived. To the beach, the drive-in, the seaside cafes her father had loved to frequent on his rare days off from the firm. In his little straw fedora he'd lope up from a swim in the ocean, his tasselled towel slung over one shoulder, and sit and talk to the old fellows in Greek while the four of them ate fish and chips spread on the table from the shop next door. Her stepmother would do the crossword in the paper. She, Jerome, Alessa and Helena. And before that, of course, her mother. Screw the crossword, Peggy would sit right on Leo's lap as he drank his short black, laughing and making kind fun of her husband in the heavy, rich language Cressida couldn't understand, that embarrassed as well as intrigued her.

Ahead of her, the Jag stalled at an intersection, making cars behind her honk and drive around them both. As Cressida swung into the driveway and parked under the smooth-barked apple tree, she decided she had to tell her stepmother once and for all that the Jag had to go. Those days were gone now, and so should everything that went with them. She watched Helena push the heavy car door shut with difficulty and walk round to the passenger side of the Fiat, dabbing her face with her scarf.

'Ai,' said Helena, angling herself into Cressida's passsenger seat. 'Did they have to kill our airconditioners on the hottest day of the year? An iced tea. That's what I need. If only I could get an *iced tea*.'

'You should get rid of that car you know, Helena. It's a liability.'

'What? Oh. Yes. I know, I stalled it back there,' she said, taking off her sunglasses and wiping sweat from her eyelids with her leopard-print scarf.

'It's an expensive piece of junk. I mean, what's the yearly petrol consumption on that thing? Enough to take you to Europe twice a year, I imagine.'

'Oh Cressida,' her stepmother said, giving her a sympathetic smile as she put her sunglasses back on. 'You know why I keep it. Imagine how your father would feel, finally getting out of gaol to find we had sold it. It's only in a few months, you know.'

'Yeah,' she said. That was a whole other thing she didn't want to think about.

Helena sighed. 'You know Cressida, he really ...'

The front door to the house opened and her sister Alessa stepped out, wearing a pair of Helena's swimmers and a towel.

'Oh thank God. What took you so long?' she said, flapping a pale manicured hand. 'What on earth is that on your head? Come on, come on – you're letting all the heat in.'

Cressida's hand went self-consciously to her scalp. Oh, the *headband*. Quickly she pulled it off and shook out her hair, immediately regretting it when she looked in the rearview mirror. Fluffy was an understatement.

'We're about to go and pick up Felipe,' Helena was explaining. Then she turned, stricken by a sudden thought. 'Cressida, hang on – you haven't had *breakfast*.'

Cressida laughed. Mother to her core.

'It's fine,' she said, putting the Fiat in reverse. 'I'll have something when I get back. Are you sure you don't want to wait here? It's so *hot*.'

'Felipe can wait,' Alessa called, declaratively. 'The toilet's flooded.'

'Oh God,' Helena groaned, putting her face in her hands.

'Jesus,' Cressida said, and turned off the car.

'Plus I need Cressida's laptop,' her sister added.

Cressida sighed and hauled her bag from the back seat of the car, collected the vegetables and the backpack while Helena took the duffel, and mounted the steps to greet her sister.

'Alessa,' she said, leaning in to kiss the cheek held out to her. 'Nice to see you.'

'And you.'

With its high ceilings and tall windows cloaked in heavy curtains, the three-storey Federation was always an oasis of cool in hot weather. Helena had just had most of its six-bedroom expanse repainted in Santorini colours, all Mediterranean blue and blinding white, but in the lounge off the entranceway, everything was still her mother's: the pale walls and muted grey carpet, the metal and porcelain fittings and accessories, the Gauguin print over the couch. It made Cressida feel serene just being near the things Peggy had chosen. Even Alessa wasn't going to make her feel tense today, she decided. That was the game they always played with each other anyway – who could be the more offhand, the more detached, the more smoothly critical of the other, while affecting a demeanour of total innocence. To date it was a game that Alessa always seemed to win.

Looking in at the marble ground-floor bathroom though, Cressida felt anything but serene. Thankfully there was no actual physical contents in the toilet bowl, but the water was up to the rim. Did plumbing fail during a blackout?

'I'll deal with that when I get back,' she said. 'Helena, it's really better if I go get Felipe on my own. Alessa, how was your flight?'

'It was a flight,' said Alessa with flat humour, subsiding into the white reproduction Eames chair next to the kitchen. The lushly upholstered fifties icon with its moulded plywood framework and matching Ottoman, on which her sister's mauve painted toenails currently reclined, had been her father's favourite, and Cressida was surprised to feel a fizz of resentment to see her sister sitting in it. It didn't help that the chair's curved white headrest was reminiscent of the fancy Partner chair Cressida had seen in Alessa's office when she'd videocalled her at work in Singapore.

'They even had a decent wine list,' Alessa was saying, scrolling distractedly through her phone. 'Of course you never know with Qantas. I always fly Emirates, but they've cut their direct to Sydney. Not a big enough market in Australia apparently.'

'How tiresome for you,' Cressida said, finding two glasses in the cupboard. 'You know I'd turn that off if you want it charged when you need it. Helena, sit down and I'll make you a drink. Oh. Does anyone realise there's a pond around the refrigerator?'

'Oh!' said Helena. 'I cleared it out last night! Must be from the freezer defrosting. Damn …'

'It's alright, I've got it.'

Cressida found two towels in the pool ensuite and threw them on the floor to soak up the water. 'Helena, have you got any fruit? Oh.' Beside the kettle was a thick, textured envelope, an ampersand brand name scored on one corner in pale, embossed lettering. 'The samples arrived.'

'Yes!' Helena said, smiling. 'I thought I'd leave that for you to open.'

Cressida glanced at Alessa, weighing it up. To open them now and risk her sister's reaction, or hold on until later when she could open them in private? She swallowed. 'You got the esky out,' she continued, picking up a bottle of soda and opening it with a fizz. 'What a good idea.' She poured two glasses and added ice.

'I know, can you believe it? I got the last bag of ice at the service station this morning,' Helena said, getting up. 'It was bedlam. People were queuing for petrol halfway down the block. Quick, open it.' She grinned, with clear excitement. 'I want to see them.'

'See what?' said Alessa, still looking at her phone.

'Cressida's …' Helena began, but Cressida silenced her with a look.

'Just some paperwork,' said Cressida, delivering the drinks. Alessa eyed her for a moment, but returned to the screen in her hand. Back at the kettle, with careful nonchalance Cressia sliced open the envelope and tipped it up. The contents fell out successively into her hand: invitation, wishing well insert, RSVP, place card, bridal registry card. All white with wide pink stripes, layered with embossed black print and a silver love-heart motif. The sample invitation was triple folded and sealed with a double layer of real wax. So crisp and flawless. Expensive. Behind her Helena had come to stand at her shoulder. On seeing them she let out a sigh.

'Oh,' she breathed. 'They're *lovely*.'

They were. Brimming with the promise of all things sought for. Perfection. Love. Wealth. Children. Despite what she'd said to the Partners, and even Felipe. Cressida glanced behind at Helena and saw that her eyes were damp.

'This would never happen in Singapore,' Alessa was saying. 'There are blackouts all the time and people just cope. Cressida, your laptop?' she said, getting up. 'I have to send an email before 10am.'

'It's in my bag,' Cressida said. 'Don't you have a spare battery?'

Too late though. Alessa was at her shoulder.

'Yes, I have a spare battery. Yes, it's also flat. Oh God, Cressida, *pink*. That's so two years ago.' She returned to her seat. 'It's all Tahitian seafoam at the moment, didn't your wedding stylist tell you? God I'm parched. I can't cope with this dry air.' She held her face up to spritz on something from a small silver canister, then fanned her face with the boarding pass.

'I'm surprised to hear you know anything about it,' Cressida said, quietly. 'I don't see you getting married any time soon.'

Alessa looked at her, deadpan, and Cressida held her gaze.

'Cress …' said Helena.

'And what the hell is Tahitian seafoam, anyway?'

'You know, blue. Bluey green,' Alessa said, eyes still locked on Cress's. 'Tiffany colour.' She sighed, then looked down at the phone again. 'You do have a wedding stylist, don't you?'

A stylist? thought Cressida. It's eighteen months out from the wedding and I don't even have a *dress*. Her stepmother kept making jokes about her getting cold feet. It wasn't that; there just hadn't been time to look at designs, much less get one made. It was a crucial decision. At least the honeymoon was sorted. She'd finally managed to persuade Felipe to do something a bit interesting – he'd wanted a month in Europe looking at architecture, followed by skiing in Switzerland, but she'd convinced him to build in two weeks in Fiji. There was an orphanage Helena helped sponsor there and she was going to volunteer. She was really looking forward to that part, at least.

'Alessa, hush,' Helena said, giving Cressida's shoulder a squeeze. 'They're lovely. Cressida, you wanted fruit? There's some on the sideboard. Don't you think it's just awful?' she said to Alessa, perching on the Lexington two-seater opposite. 'What were these people thinking? Oh thank you, what's this?' She took the canister from Alessa. 'Elderflower water. What, do I just spray it on like this?' She squirted it cautiously, then laughed as some landed in her eye. 'Cressida, here, have some of this, it's wonderful!'

'No thanks,' Cressida said, wrestling the laptop out of its bag. 'Here you go,' she said, dumping it on Alessa's lap. She inspected the bowl of fruit on the table. Of what was there, apples were the lowest GI. She took one and bit into it, closing her eyes and savouring the crunch. Fibre really had something going for it, she thought, wishing she didn't let Alessa get her so riled.

'Where's the "on" button?' Alessa said, peering at the keyboard.

'Oh sorry,' said Cressida, flicking it. 'I thought you'd know.'

'Mine has biometrics.'

'Oh you two, it's too hot,' Helena said, flapping her hand in front of her face and holding the drink to her cheek.

Cressida flipped open her backpack, pulled out the transistor radio from the top and turned it on. Still music. *I guess they can only say the same thing so many times*, she thought.

'Alessa, what are you doing sending an email anyway?' Helena continued. 'You're meant to be on holiday.'

'Yeah tell that to the Americans,' Alessa said, rolling her eyes and finding the wireless hotspot function on her phone. 'We're doing the carve-out of Weibo in an IPO and I've got to get this to the board of directors before they meet at ten.'

'The what of what? Hey I don't think the internet's working, you know.'

Alessa rolled her eyes. 'What's known as a corporate float to you. Of course, I left all this with Antonio,' she said, airily. Presumably that was some minor underling at her firm, Cressida thought; she'd heard her mention him before. A 'minor underling' Senior Associate, same pay rate as her. 'But you never know with those boys,' Alessa continued. 'I like to keep an eye on them. Cat's away and rats playing and all that. And it's, you know, a multi-billion-dollar deal, so it has to be done exactly right.' She sighed, smiling blandly.

'I thought that was what they were paying you for,' Cressida said. 'To get it right.'

Alessa looked at her. 'I'm sorry? They are, and that's why I just said I'm keeping an eye on them. What, aren't I allowed to have a couple of weeks off once a year?'

'No, I'm not saying that,' Cressida said with a sigh. 'I just mean, it just seems a bit unfair to leave a junior doing all the work and not giving them any recognition for it.'

'That's ridiculous,' Alessa said flatly. 'That's the way the system works. You work like a demon for fifteen years – or in my case, eight,' she said, 'make pots of money for the firm and see hardly any of it, and then you get rewarded. That's what Dad did, that's what I'm doing, and so, by the way, is Antonio. Just on that,' – she paused to sip her drink – 'how *are* your partnership aspirations going? Getting a bit long in the tooth for an SA, aren't you? Having a bit of trouble making the grade?'

Cressida bristled, inwardly counting to ten.

'Yeah well,' she began, 'it's easier for people at outer Alpha Centauri, like you. Where there're no other contenders.'

Alessa opened her mouth to respond, but Helena cut in.

'I don't know how you do it,' her stepmother said, smiling and shaking her head at them both with frank admiration. 'Both of you. All I have to manage every day is a handful of sweet little children, and *that's* enough to send me spare. Oh,' she sighed, looking out to the backyard, 'we were meant to be going to the pool on Monday. I'll have to put a sign up. They've been looking forward to it for weeks. Do you think they'll have the power back on by then? How will they cope in this heat, without the air conditioning?'

'Same way we are, I guess,' Cressida said, dropping her gaze from Alessa, who returned hers to the computer screen. 'With a lot of ice cubes.'

# 7

As they drove to Felipe's in Elizabeth Bay, Darley Road was bumper to bumper, and at Syd Einfield Drive towards the Junction, cars turning right were being searched. Flashlights were shone into gloveboxes and under seats by black-clothed police while the car's occupants waited on the roadside, mattresses and doonas ejected so boot linings could be palpated. 'That's a bit of overkill, isn't it?' said Cress. 'I mean – what are they expecting to find?'

'She loves you enormously, you know. And you shouldn't tease her about still being single.'

'Yeah,' she sighed. 'Like she didn't, all those years before I met Felipe. And then tortures me about not having made Partner yet. At least I've got a *life*. Where do all these people think they're going to go, anyway?' she said, watching the line of cars in front of them inch forward. 'The black-out's everywhere.'

'But it's different for her, you know – in Singapore. And she works so much,' said Helena. 'You know they've set up Moore Park Stadium as an emergency centre. Twenty-five generators for the hot water and fridges.'

The lights changed and Cressida thought of the vegetables she'd left at Helena's. She couldn't use her juicer anyway; may as well donate them.

'Really? Maybe they'd like my carrots and celery. What about a few of those cans of food we brought from my place, could we spare them?'

'Absolutely,' nodded Helena. 'I was thinking the same thing. We can go this afternoon. Hey is that service station open? How are you for petrol? Oh.' Bright orange witches hats blocked the entrance. 'It's closed.'

Cressida glanced at the gauge. Two thirds full. She'd have to keep a lookout for an open one; it would get low soon enough. And try and drive as little as possible until things were back to normal.

In Felipe's cul de sac up from the harbour, the road was lined with fire trucks and police cars mounted on the kerb.

'Hang on,' said Helena, 'is that police tape?'

Cressida slowed and followed Helena's gaze. A blue and white strip was looped across the street ahead of them. She stopped. Next to them was a tiny space across an empty driveway. Cressida jammed the car into reverse.

'Cressida, wait – there's no way you'll fit ...'

Cressida grimaced as the back of the Fiat bounced against the car behind her. With the motor still running she picked up her charging phone from the footwell and dialled. Felipe picked up on the first ring. He was shouting at someone.

'Look, for God's sake ... It's quite a simple matter of ... Sorry, one minute. Cressida,' he answered, sounding relieved. 'At *last*. Are you on your way? The police have bloody decided to take over my building.'

'I'm about fifty feet from your apartment,' she said, ducking under the tape. 'Where are you?' Then she saw him, standing by the entrance to the Rex. He was waving his hands at two police officers, and he didn't look happy.

'All I want to do is go up for *five minutes*. Look, *less*,' he was exclaim-ing. 'Up three flights, into my flat, down again before you even notice. Actually, why don't we even *do* it that way – you turn around and ... Oh Cressida, thank God,' he said, squeezing her to him. 'What happened to your hair? Look, I'm trying to persuade these *clever, sensible* people to let me go up for a *teensy-weensy minute* and retrieve my medical bag from my flat. The one I need for those *life-saving operations* on Monday,' he added, putting an arm around her as he gave the police officers a tight grin. The medical bag. Felipe would only ever use his own personal collection of instruments when he carried out operations. He had an autoclave in his kitchen to sterilise them every night, and normally the hinged black bag went everywhere with him. He'd even negotiated a special clause in his hospitals' insurance policies to allow him to use them. His voice dropped to measured consultant-persuasive: 'I'm sure as fellow members of the emergency services …'

'I thought you said you were an ortho,' one of the officers said. 'That's hardly emergency.'

'That may be,' said Felipe, sighing in exasperation, 'but they can still be life-saving. Look, that's not the point – it's not like there's even any danger up there – Mrs Ahmadi lives on the first floor, for goodness sake. If it's explosives you're worried about, what am I going to do, shake the building with my footsteps going past up the fire escape?'

The officer gave Felipe's broadset form a pointed once-over.

'Anything's possible.'

Felipe rolled his eyes, and Cressida could see by his intake of breath that a blast was coming.

'Hi,' she cut in, holding out her hand to the first officer and smiling broadly. 'Cressida Mitsok. Nice to meet you. And you are …?'

'Constable Glie,' said the second officer, glancing past her down the street, impatient.

'Hello,' Cressida said. 'Look, officers, it's too hot for this, isn't it? Thank you so much for being here. What a total drama. I don't envy you two trying to do crowd control right now; it's like everyone's got heatstroke.' She looked up at the apartment block above them. 'Was anything found?'

'Forensics are up there now. The best thing you could do for both of us is get back behind the tape. I can't do anything about your boyfriend's bag right now. We should be able to clear the area in a few hours. If it's safe, he can get it then.'

'Sure, officer. That sounds very sensible,' she said, taking Felipe's elbow. 'Thanks again.'

Felipe sighed and eyed Constable Glie. 'But *please* – it's life-saving equipment.'

'And I don't want to be using it on you if you go up there and get yourself blown up. Back behind the line.'

Cressida steered Felipe away from the building towards the car.

'Unbelievable,' Felipe said, once they were out of earshot, running a hand through his grey-washed hair. 'Two corrections for digiti minimi *and* a metatarsal tomorrow, and the possibility of no instruments. "A few hours". It could take *days*.' He looked down at Cressida with a sigh and took her hand, kissing the back of it with vehemence. 'But how are *you*, my gorgeous creature?' he asked, and leant in to kiss her hair. 'Have you lost your brush?'

'Happy to see you,' she said, pressing herself into his armpit. 'No blow-drier. This way.' She pointed down the street. 'Maybe you can come back for the bag tonight?'

'With police on every corner? In this mood they'll be arresting people just for popping out for a litre of milk. I think not,' he said. Cressida looked at him quizzically. 'All along Cowper Wharf Road they were, this morning when I went out for my run,' he explained, shaking his head. 'Police. At least I think they were. Could have been army for all we know. Impossible to tell. Lots of black and self-important attitudes, anyway. The place's barmy. Terrorism suspected, but have they arrested anyone yet? No. How can they tell it's terrorism? Helena,' he greeted her, peering past her into the back seat of the Fiat with a look of chagrin.

'Felipe,' Helena exclaimed, and swung her door open. 'Hang on, you come in the front.'

'Thank God,' he muttered. 'Cressida, you know I've *said* this isn't the most practical car for a man of my size ...'

'Are you alright?' asked Helena, squinting up at him with one hand shielding against the glare. 'Was there a bomb?' She levered the seat forward and climbed into the back as Felipe folded himself into the front.

'Oh God no.' He waved his hand dismissively, straightening. 'Complete overreaction. The lady downstairs is Persian, always getting packages from Iran.' He sighed. 'Spices or some such. Cressida darling,' he said, peering in through the passenger window as Cressida started the car, 'there's no way you'll be able to turn around with all these emergency vehicles in the way ... Anyway, one was misdelivered to another resident by TNT yesterday afternoon, left in the corridor and then this morning the recipient said it was ticking. *Ticking*.' He accentuated the word with the click of the seatbelt as Cressida spun the wheel one way and then back trying to ease the car out of the space. 'This isn't *Get Smart*. She threw it back into the corridor and called the police. And look at this,' he said, indicating another police car that was crawling past. 'How many millions are we spending on this completely hysterical overreaction? What was it, three power stations? It was probably climate whiners, for God's sake. Terrorism? Poppycock.'

Cressida glanced in the rearview mirror and saw Helena's face still looking stricken.

'But what was it?' she asked, leaning forward. 'The thing in the package.'

'Oh, I don't know.' He sighed and squinted up the street at the apartment block. 'Are you alright, Cressida? You seem to be taking rather a long time to …'

'Sorry,' said Cressida, peering over the bonnet. 'With any luck this one'll be it … Ah, yes,' she said, breathing a sigh of relief as they made it out into the traffic again.

'They've sent forensics up to find out,' he continued. 'Not that we'll ever hear, of course. If the police have any pride they'll be far too embarrassed to tell us. Sumac, probably. Anyway. How's things back *chez* Helena?' He attempted to turn to look at her but there wasn't the room so he turned back. 'Sweltering, I suppose? What's that?'

Cressida followed his gaze. There was a large white object at his feet.

'Block ice,' said Helena. 'There was a fellow on the footpath back there with a refrigerated trailer. There was a bit of a queue – but I got some while I was waiting. Twenty dollars a block, mind you.'

'Gosh,' said Felipe. 'Enterprising.'

'Felipe – how was the hospital? All those people on respirators, it must have been awful – what did you do?'

He shook his head. 'Utter bedlam. Thankfully I wasn't mid-operation, but I heard in Emergency they were hand-bagging people. Unbelievable. I mean, we have generators, but they kept cutting out …' said Felipe, winding down the window. 'Cressida, I might just turn that off – I feel like I'm parachuting,' he said, turning the air-conditioner dial. 'I think they've realised they need to upgrade the lot after this episode.'

There was a noise from the footwell and with surprise Cressida realised it was her phone, ringing.

'Oh Felipe, answer that, will you?' she said, navigating some cars double parked on Kent Street.

'What? Oh,' said Felipe, peering with difficulty between his knees. 'I would if I could find the damn thing …'

Eyes still on the road Cressida caught the charger chord and fished the handset out of the footwell, handing it to him.

'Oh, thank you.' He spoke gruffly into it. 'Hello? Cressida Mitsok's phone. Oh. Yes, I'll hand it right over,' he said, and held it out to her. 'It's some fellow called Michael.'

They stopped, waiting for the traffic to move around an enormous personnel carrier mounted on the curb.

'Can you put it on speaker? It's just a tad hard to hold the phone right now …'

'Hang on,' he said into the phone again, fiddling about with the screen for a moment and then continuing loudly, enunciating every word, 'are you there? I've put you on speaker.'

'Er, yes? Hello?'

It sounded like the Managing Partner from work.

'Michael? It's Cressida.'

'Oh good. Hope you're nearby, Cressida. The CEO of SinoGen's here from China. Private chopper from Melbourne, current mood foul. I'm not sure whether you knew, but they own the plants that were destroyed. All three. Eraring, Bayswater *and* Liddell.'

'Shit,' said Cressida. That answered that question. 'All hands on deck, then.'

'Meeting at my place. Twelve noon. We need you on planning law. Have you got a pen?'

'Felipe – can you …'

'Hmm? Oh, yes.' He extracted a fountain pen from his breast pocket with a flourish. 'Fire away.'

'Seventy View Street, Woollahra. See you there.'

# 8

---

Following the sector's recent privatisation, the newly-minted owners of the destroyed power stations were Chinese, and currently sat at Michael Roland's glass-topped patio table looking decidedly anxious. Two pedestal fans and a portable air conditioner hummed beside them, and a spread of yum cha delicacies was mouldering untouched on the table. Around it sat a roll call of Sydney Partners relevant to energy law in the firm; with surprise Cressida noticed Pip was there, the only other Senior Associate. She sat on a seat between Brian and the air-conditioning unit, wearing her serious face. Cressida raised her hand in greeting, but her friend was engrossed in the conversation. She watched through the sliding doors from the kitchen for a moment, trying to assess the vibe. Butterflies flip-flopped in her stomach – the prospect of talking directly to a client when you weren't a Partner, especially in front of those who were, was pretty intimidating. Still, she reassured herself, Michael seemed to think her China experience would mean something, so maybe that was her authority. Just don't say anything stupid, she told herself. Her practice group's supervising Partner, Richard, saw her through the glass and rose.

'How's it going?' he said, entering the sliding door and joining her looking out at the meeting. He held a bottle of craft beer, its sides slick with condensation.

'Chaos,' she said. 'You? Hey – how did you score that?'

He grinned. 'Aha!' He turned and opened the fridge behind them, revealing row on row of dew-sheened beverages. 'Take your pick. Apparently Michael's had an in-home Tesla for ages. Said AGL gave it to him as a bonus on their float in '06.'

'Michael's got a *powerwall*?' said Cressida, standing to enjoy the gust of cold air from the fridge for a moment. 'How fortunate.' She selected a bottle of mineral water and cracked its top with relish. 'What about the spread? Looks like they got it catered by the local takeaway.'

'Michael's deep freeze.'

'Hah!' Cressida laughed. 'Oh to be a Managing Partner. So – how's it going out there?'

'Enough kittens to open a pet shop.' Richard shrugged. 'Mainly because they're sure their other plants are next.'

'Seems reasonable. At least until someone's in custody. Or, rather a lot of people, probably.'

Richard sipped his drink.

'Yeah well. The client's convinced it's environmental.'

'It fits,' Cressida shrugged. 'I mean, why would you bother otherwise? If it was just general bloodshed and disorder you wanted, wouldn't you do something straightforward, like, I don't know, a train station or something?'

'Yeah maybe,' he said. 'Although apparently ISIL have claimed responsibility.'

'ISIL,' said Cressida. Her voice was flat.

'I heard it on the radio this morning. Four people turned themselves in to Wyong copshop. They're calling them the Climate Four. Didn't say they were ISIL, but who knows?'

'Yeah, great,' she said, rolling her eyes. 'I just figured with how nuts the greenies have been going on that big coal mine in Queensland, it made sense that it was environmental. Not that the greenies weren't nuts already. Look at my brother.'

Richard laughed and rolled his eyes.

'God.' He shook his head with a laugh. 'Is he *still* on that boat?'

'It's whale hunt season. He's out there,' she shrugged, feeling the same sense of annoyance she always felt when the topic of Jerome came up. There came an outburst in Mandarin from the terrace and they looked up; the man sitting next to the speaker echoed the other just as rapidly in English.

'Hey I got your missed call, by the way,' said Cressida, turning. 'Was it urgent? I was going to call you back, but then there was this blackout thingie, and I didn't get a chance.'

Richard laughed. 'Well, God,' he said, passing his hand over his face.

'Now that you mention it, that might have hit the skids as well. How does the biggest transport project the state's ever seen sound? I'm serious,' he added, at Cressida's *come on* look. 'Bigger spend than the M one, two and four put together.' He put his beer down. 'InterConnex. They're doing the extension into Victoria at last, and adding Queensland to it for good measure. Two fifteen billion dollars in value, big enough to make Coffs to Yamba look like a wallaby track. You as lead legal counsel on it, by the way. WestConnex loved you so much they told all their friends about you. Jesus girl, you look like I just said you'd won the lottery,' he said, grinning. 'Launch in eight weeks, PM's invited, black tie, the usual. They want to officially issue the call for detailed proposals there – which means a draft T and C ready for review by the client in four.'

Cressida frowned. 'And they're not worried about, you know, *this*?'

Richard picked up his beer again. 'They're assuming the power will get sorted out in time.' He shrugged. 'And that it's important to – or should I say, be *seen* to – get on with business as usual as much as possible, blah blah blah. Anyway – Brian's set up an office in his basement, said you can work there. It's either that or fly down to Melbourne with Tax, I'm afraid.' He laughed, as they shared a look of mock horror. 'At least until the power's back on.'

'But … I'm not a Partner yet,' Cressida said, her mind yet devouring the possibilities. It wouldn't matter that she was only an SA though, she knew. Pulling off a project like this would make her a serious acquisition – maybe even directly at Partner level – for any law firm in the country.

'Oh yes, that,' Richard said. 'The vote.' He paused, and looked at her with sympathy. 'Look I *did* manage to have a quick chat to Michael, and he thinks we can get the Partners together again in—'

The sliding door opened and the Managing Partner stuck his head in. 'Ah, Cressida,' he said. 'Can you two join us in here? Cressida – I was hoping you could run Mr Zhou through the planning issues for a potential rebuild. Best case scenario of course …'

'Of course,' said Cressida, finishing her drink. But she grabbed Richard's elbow as he pushed himself away from the bench.

'So,' she whispered. 'When?'

'When what?'

'The partnership vote.'

'Oh,' Richard said. 'Cressida, you understand, it's tricky right now … That's really Brian's decision. Okay, okay … I'll ask him – we can try for, maybe, three weeks?'

She smiled.

'Fabulous,' she said, and stepped out into the patio. 'Mr Zhou. Hi everyone,' she acknowledged, shaking the CEO's hand. A chair was brought and she sat down on it, giving the client her most winning smile.

'Cressida,' Michael began. 'It was our Szechuan office in China you were in, is that right?'

She nodded. 'Chengdu. Beautiful.' The CEO laughed and said something to his translator. It sounded to Cressida like 'that monkey prostitute's asshole'. Oh yes. She had missed the richness of Chinese vernacular.

'Cressida,' Michael continued, 'how can we fast track the red tape on your environment side of things for SinoGen? What's the situation now that Part 6A has commenced? Would you mind running Terry through it?'

'Certainly,' she said, turning to the CEO. A fresh drink appeared at her shoulder and she took it, sipping delicately then placing it carefully on the glass. The man adjacent looked at her, ready to translate. 'It's okay,' she said to him in Mandarin. 'I speak Mandarin.'

At that, Mr Zhou's eyes flew open and the two men shared a disbelieving glance, then the CEO fell back in his chair with a bark of laughter.

'Oh thank God,' said Mr Zhou in Mandarin. 'Call me Terry.' He sighed and shook his head, then slapped both thighs and laughed. 'You would have heard me call Chengdu a whore's asshole then. And you are not so stupid an egg as the rest of these chrysanthemum faces.' The translator reddened and Cressida tried not to laugh. It meant having a face like an anus. 'Anus vagina, someone said it takes two years to get approval?' he said. 'That's fucking mad.'

'Sorry,' she said with a sympathetic smile. 'There's a lot of regulation in this country.'

'But I don't have that kind of *time*,' he said, rolling his eyes in exasperation. 'Fucking shareholders, you know, breathing down my neck.' He glanced over at Michael and mimed a cut-throat motion with one finger.

'Sorry,' said Cressida to Michael. 'Do you want me to translate?'

'What? No, no,' Michael said. 'You just do your thing and let us know the upshot.'

She turned back to Mr Zhou. 'Best guess for a switch-on date, assuming you get funding? Um ... five years?'

His eyes flew open.

'It takes at least two years before they'll even pass the paperwork,' she said. 'You'll have to wait for the Director General's environmental criteria, do the environmental assessments, put the thing out for public comment, wait for submissions, respond to them, probably do more environmental assessments, wait for the approval panel to be convened, and then it could take another six months to a year before you get a decision.'

'Fuck a cat,' said Terry. 'That's it. I'm going to Texas. They know how to get things done over there. Five years? What am I supposed to tell the fucking bank? The board will have my balls.' He wiped a hand across his face and pulled at his shirt collar where a ring of sweat had formed. 'Why is it so fucking hot here? I thought Australia was meant to be paradise. This is worse than Chengdu.' He looked at her. 'You look alright though. You single?'

Cress snorted. 'Um, no. Sorry, yes, it's usually cooler in March. Anyway, look, you can ask for consideration to be expedited,' she said, sitting back and sipping her drink. 'But even then, that's about how long it will take. Till the first clod can be turned, anyway.'

'An*us*,' said Terry. He looked around. 'Does anyone have any pilsener? I hate your country's horsepiss beer.' He threw the contents of his glass on the lawn behind him. 'Has that pretentious wanker got any Asahi in his fridge?' He pointed his chin at Michael.

'Um … Mr Zhou wants to know if you have any Asahi.'

'Oh. Um, no. Crown?'

'I think anything other than beer at this point.'

'Richard,' Michael said, still smiling at the CEO. Richard hauled himself up and went into the kitchen, returning with a can of Canadian Club and handing it to Mr Zhou, who tasted it, burst into a grin and sank half, waving the empty can in thanks when he was done. He turned back to Cressida.

'Much better. Arrgh. What choice do I have?' he shrugged. 'Your coal is the cheapest. Cunt-struck fuck. Five *years*?'

'Yep.' Cressida sighed. 'Though the good news is,' she said, 'the government here have snuffed the National Energy Guarantee, so no Paris targets. And despite what the rest of the world is doing they're still committed to coal, so' – she shrugged – 'you're good.'

Terry shook his head.

'National Energy Guarantee,' he said, and rolled his eyes. 'I will never understand you Australians. Why would you want to make fucking solar panels when you can just dig up cash. Anyway.' He crushed the can and held it up in cheers. 'Thanks.'

When the client and Partners had gone, Cressida subsided into a patio chair beside Pip and watched her demolish the remaining duck pancakes. Her workmate's curves were resplendent that day in a turquoise velveteen dress atop black platform sandals. Where Cressida was rail thin, Pip was more Monica Lewinsky, but she really *worked* it, Cressida thought. She was the only Senior Associate Cressida knew who could get away with fishnet stockings and five-inch heels as workwear. With her dark hair and blue-grey eyes that were like coins falling through water, Cressida knew she never lacked for right-swipes on Tinder.

'Pip,' Cressida said. She leaned across to kiss her colleague's cheek, catching a whiff of her heavy perfume as she touched the moist skin, and inspected the table. 'It's been ages.' Nothing on it she could eat, she thought. Wall to wall fat and carbs. Although there was a plate of melon on the end. She'd read somewhere it took more energy to digest melon than it contained, so she settled on that, delicately arresting a slice from the bone china.

'You really nailed it there, Cressida,' Pip said, munching and mopping up sweet sauce with a pancake. 'I wish I had your brain.'

'Hah!' laughed Cressida, holding the slice of melon between two fingers and sucking off the juice. 'How do you know that? I was speaking Chinese.'

'Yeah, *and* that. The whole thing. You're the real thing,' Pip said.

'Yeah well,' she said, wiping her fingers on a napkin, 'at one point he was calling everyone anus faces, so be glad you missed it. Anyway' – she took in Pip's outfit with an appreciative glance again – 'I wish I had *your* dress sense. Dressing down, I see.'

'Oh this old thing,' Pip laughed. 'Collette Dinnigan on sale, three years ago. I love this muted palette thing you're doing today, though,' she said. 'Silk on a weekend. *You* can talk about dress sense.'

'Alessa's in town.' Cressida sighed, knowing that to Pip, at least, that would explain it. The mention of her name brought back the burn of her sister's words. All through their childhood Alessa had been the cool one, the popular one, the one who always *knew* what the uber-on-trend colour and style was for hair, shoes, year twelve formal dresses, all the things that had mattered to her as a too-skinny fifteen-year-old – and now, it seemed, wedding invitations. Tahitian foam. Sounded like something they'd use to fluoride your teeth at the dentist.

'Ah. How's she coping with no power?' said Pip. 'Not well, I imagine.'

'Oh darling, this sort of thing happens *all the time* in Singapore, don't you know?' said Cress, reaching for another slice of melon. 'I'm not sure what all the fuss is about. Meanwhile she's complaining about absolutely *everything*. "The toilet's blocked. My laptop doesn't work. Isn't there anything other than canned food? I want a shower."' It was good to vent about it with Pip. At least Pip knew her sister well enough to understand, *and* she was on her side. 'I agree with the last one though. I *hate* not being able to have a hot shower,' she said, mopping her face with a serviette. 'Even a lukewarm one to wash off the bloody humidity. Can you believe this? What kind of idiots blow up a power station?' She blew out air so it fluffed her fringe and rolled her eyes at Pip.

'Very *intense* ones,' Pip said, rolling her eyes in return. 'Nobody I've ever met, anyway. I suppose it had to happen some time though. I mean, why should the UK and the US get all the fun? I feel like we've arrived now, you know, as a country – we've had our very own terrorist attack.' She threw a grape into her mouth.

'It's hardly *fun*, Pip,' chided Cressida, frowning. 'I mean, there are a bunch of people out there who are finding this really difficult. There's even, like, you know, emergency shelters. Helena said there's one at Moore Park Stadium.'

'Oh I know that, silly. But the main thing is, it's not us, is it? Goodness, doesn't this look like an entrail,' she said, picking up the last rice paper roll from a plate. 'I'm just taking the Oscar Wilde approach to life; that it's far too important a thing to be taken seriously. Hey – on the note of things serious – how's the wedding planning going?'

'Oh God I don't know,' Cressida said, falling back against the wicker chair. 'I can't believe it's only eighteen months away. There seems to be so much to *do*.'

'Is Alessa helping? That's her job, you know. As your only sister.'

'Hmph. Yeah right. No. Not really. Other than to tell me my invitations look dated. "So two years ago" she said.'

'You're *kidding*. Charming. Best off without her then. Well like I said, tell me if there's anything I can do. Bummer about the partnership vote, by the way. They're crazy to treat you like that.'

'Yeah, crazy. Some woman from Melbourne brought up Dad though, so what chance did I have?' She looked out at the pool. 'Fucked if I know how she even *knew* about him. On the other hand, of course, there was that three-week run in *The Australian*, I guess,' she snorted. 'Anyway I ended up threatening her with defamation, so it was pretty much doomed from the start. So let's not go on too much about my *brains*,' she laughed.

Pip's mouth dropped open. She covered a laugh with her hand. 'You threatened Debra Bollos with *defamation*?'

'Is that her name.' It seemed odd that Pip knew it. But knowledge was power at Hannes Swartling, so maybe it wasn't that surprising. Maybe they'd worked on a deal together or something. 'Anyway. Overall I'm putting the whole thing down to misadventure. Trying not to take it personally. I'm sure they'll reschedule it when they can.'

'Hmm,' said Pip, looking thoughtful. 'Yeah. I guess so. Though something similar happened in Singapore last week, I'm told' – she stretched forward for a dumpling – 'and they *did* reschedule it – for forty-eight hours later.' She bit into the soggy morsel. 'Because of course we know from your sister that blackouts happen there *all the time*.'

Cressida paused with her glass halfway to the table.

'What, you mean there was a partnership vote put off because of a blackout there as well?'

'As it happens, yes. Esma told me. They re-did it two days later. The guy got in, too. But I'm sure they'll get round to it. Why wouldn't they? Unless that whole thing with your dad *does* turn out to be a problem …'

'Oh for God's sake,' Cressida said, getting up and starting to stack the platters. She always tried to resist clearing up crockery at work functions – a dangerous habit for anyone female and remotely ambitious – but it helped hide her agitation. And besides, it was only Pip. 'Yes, probably. And if that's it I'll … Well. I don't know. Sue them for discrimination. Doesn't the ICCPR say something about discrimination for that? I don't know. Human rights law always bored me to tears.'

'Oh Cressida.' Pip laughed and poured herself a half glass of champagne from the bottle warming on the table. 'I don't think that will help. I'm sure the vote will be fine. Give it time.'

'Yeah, because eleven years isn't long enough,' Cressida sighed, pushing open the sliding door with her shoulder. 'Do you want a lift somewhere? Your place is on my way home.'

'No that's okay. I've got an engagement. Not a real one like yours, of course,' she said with a laugh, 'but one I'm hoping will be just as much fun.' She smiled and drained her drink.

'This mystery man again,' said Cressida. 'I don't know why you're being so secretive. I won't tell anyone.'

'Don't ask, don't tell, that's my policy.' Pip smirked and kissed Cressida on the cheek. 'Besides, I seem more mysterious that way. See you at Brian's.'

'Oh yeah, Brian's,' said Cress, dumping the crockery on the marble island in the kitchen. 'Richard mentioned it. What's happening at Brian's, exactly?'

Pip got up and aimed a toe into one of her wedges. 'That's where M and A are hanging out until the power's back. He's got battery-backed solar power and a *great* little Balinese cabana going on in his ground floor,' she said, bending into her handbag and flipping open a compact to inspect her teeth for yum cha. 'You should join us.' Pip almost made working for Hannes Swartling sound like fun.

'He's got batteries too? Gosh, I'm feeling *very* late adopting. Sounds good. Oh by the way. I almost forgot. New project. Couple of tollways north and south. Bigger than all three Ms combined. You interested?'

Pip's eyes snagged on her. 'Do you mean *InterConnex*? I thought that was Richard's baby.'

'For some mystifying reason' – Cress grinned – 'he's made me project manager.'

'*You?*' Pip exhaled, looking impressed. 'Wow. Plum gig.'

'Come on. You always wanted to do more infrastructure stuff.'

'I'd love to!' she said, leaning in to hug Cress. 'Thanks for asking me.'

'No problem,' said Cress, feeling a flush of pleasure at her friend's gratitude. 'There's a truckload to do. Draft Terms and Conditions on the first stage by mid next month, ready for the Call for Detailed Proposals at the launch in eight weeks. Nothing two brilliant chicks and half the Building and Construction group can't accomplish together and at lightning speed,' she said. 'I'd like to get out to the sites for a few days once the power's back, visit all of it, how does that sound? Let's check in together at Brian's first thing Monday.'

'Excellent, Cressida. Thanks. See you.'

☼

Back at Helena's Alessa was reclining, nymph-like, by the pool under the shade of the striped umbrella. Her nose was in a fat paperback and she wore one of Helena's white kaftans and a sarong tied elaborately as a bandanna around her head. Felipe was next to her, glasses perched on his nose, naked to the waist and flipping through a stapled wad of paper.

'Darling,' he said, getting up. 'Join us?' He sat down and circled her with his arms. 'The water's perfect.'

'I will. I just got the most amazing news though,' she exclaimed, sitting carefully on the end of the banana lounge between his feet. 'Richard's put me on a massive new road project! As *lead counsel*,' she said. 'It's going to be a tonne of work.' She rolled her eyes and rested her chin in her hands, then looked at Alessa. 'Is my laptop still charged? I need to start getting together the precedents ...'

'Flat as a tack I'm afraid,' Alessa said, still in her book.

'Oh,' said Cressida. 'Great.'

'It's a *Satur*day, darling,' Felipe said, leaning forward to massage her shoulders. 'Forget about work. Relax, come for a swim. I did forty-seven laps before lunch, didn't I, Alessa? Have to keep our condition up,' he said, squeezing Cressida's bicep between two meaty fingers.

Cressida lifted her arm out of his grasp and peered into the water. 'Are you sure it's alright? Without the filter? Anyway my bathers are at the flat. Hang on a minute, isn't that ...' She picked up the document next to Felipe on the coffee table. 'I thought so – *Orthopaedia Today*. What are you talking about? *You're* working.'

'That's different,' he said, taking the article back.

'I wonder if ... what about *your* laptop, Felipe? I can just log on remotely with my phone ...' Except it was nearly out of battery. Maybe she could do it sitting in the car with the car charger in – but then, petrol wasn't unlimited either ...

'My laptop's at home as well, I'm afraid.' Felipe shrugged. 'I can get it for you later though, when I go back for my bag. Assuming they're letting us in the *building* now of course.' He sighed. 'Look,' he said, regarding her over the top of his glasses, 'Why don't you do a quick workout and then we can go out for dinner at that new French place in Crow's Nest?'

'That would be great,' said Cressida. 'Except there's a blackout.'

'Oh. Damn. Keep forgetting. Alessa – don't suppose you have any other ideas?'

'I've been pondering it all afternoon,' Alessa said, putting down her book and looking pained. 'I reckon we're going to find that everything's closed. Appalling. Right when I arrive wanting modern Australian three hat.'

'Michael's house has solar power. I was just there. We had yum cha,' Cressida said, and was rewarded by Alessa's mouth drop. She looked into the house through the open bi-fold doors. 'Where's Helena?'

'She went out, she wouldn't tell me where,' said Alessa. 'She had a conspiratorial glint in her eye though.'

'Oh no,' said Cressida.

'I know.'

'Yes well I'm hoping it doesn't involve any large furry animals this time,' Alessa said. 'I did get an email from Jerome before your laptop went flat, incidentally.'

'Oh really? That's a first. He's alive then. What did it say?'

'You wouldn't believe it,' Alessa said. 'He said we should be going out in protest in support of the terrorists.' She cocked her head to one side, remembering. 'That "at last someone is taking direct action on this crime against future generations AKA climate change, and you should both be burning your practising certificates in front of the Supreme Court in protest at their arrests". Quote unquote.'

'Does anyone even do that anymore?' asked Cressida, leaning back on Felipe's chest. 'Richard said there'd been four arrests. Are these the same ones? The Eraring Four or something?'

Alessa shrugged. 'Don't know. We can ask though. Next time you email. He's probably got better access to news than we do.'

'So impulsive,' Cressida said. 'If he's so passionate about them why isn't *he* back here protesting?' Her brother. She loved him to pieces, but sometimes he was so … well, so twenty-seven.

There must be some way she could get onto a charged laptop though, she thought, regarding the world over Felipe's forearms. She looked at the pool. It did look inviting. Her shift was sticking to her in the heat.

'Alright,' she said. 'Alessa, where are those bathers?'

'Helena's room, third drawer down,' she said, and glanced up at her sister. 'Try not to mess anything up in there. Helena likes to keep it neat.'

Cressida gritted her teeth. 'Of course.' When her sister said something like that it made her feel like going in and doing exactly what she'd said not to, while also dropping a couple of her earrings in the nearest tray of cat litter for good measure. She wouldn't, of course. But it felt good to think it.

There was the heavy slam of a car door and Helena appeared at the back gate wearing a trilby with her leopard-skin scarf tied over it and down under her chin. She was carrying a long black case that looked like a violin, along with a plastic bag of shopping. She murmured hello and kept going. Cressida followed and found her standing on the other side of her bed, looking flustered.

'What's that?' Cressida said, standing in the doorway.

Helena looked down at the plastic bag on the bed.

'That? Nothing. Just a few bits and pieces. Alessa and Felipe said they were going for a jog. I thought all of you would be out.'

'In this heat?' she said, noticing something long and thin in the plastic bag. 'Wait, is that … since when did you play baseball, Helena?'

'It's not for that,' Helena said, grabbing the bat. 'It's just, well, you know … Cressida, there are looters out there. Police everywhere. The alarm system's not working. We need to be *safe*.'

'Oh Helena,' Cressida said, walking round to her side of the bed and taking it from her. 'You're completely safe. We're all here, for goodness sake. What else have you got in there?' She opened the plastic bag. Inside were two small black and white canisters, some D-bolts, something that looked like a torch, and a kilo of chops.

'But what if they have guns?' Helena said. 'Marjorie down the road told me that number 52 got broken into. They cleaned the place out. No-one was home, thank goodness. But it … it worries me.'

Cressida pulled out the torch.

'Where did you get all this stuff?' she asked, digging through the bag. 'Helena, that's what the door locks are for.'

'Wellington Surplus on Carrington Street. They took cash. Don't touch that,' Helena said. 'It's a flashlight with 2.5 million volt stun gun. They smashed their sliding door, Cressida. With a tyre iron they found in the back shed. I have a right to take precautions.'

Cressida squatted down beside the bed. The long black case was under it.

'And what is this?'

'Nothing. Oh, don't look. It's better if you don't. Please,' Helena said, putting her face in her hands. Cressida pulled out the case and opened it. Inside was a rifle.

'Helena. How did you get this? You have to take it back.'

'No,' Helena said. 'I used Leo's … Leo's clay target licence. It's the only one they would give me. I wanted a handgun, but you need a different permit for that.'

'A *handgun*. Helena, are you out of your mind? The few people that get killed in home invasions are *the ones that have the guns*. Everyone knows that. And if the other guy has one, you have three times the chance. Or something.'

'Really?'

'Why did they let you have this? You didn't …'

Helena grimaced and nodded. 'Well he did make me power of attorney.'

'You're telling me they let you buy a gun as someone's attorney,' Cressida said. 'That is the nuttiest thing I've ever heard. Helena. I mean it. You need to take it back.'

'Cressida? Did you find the bathers?' came Alessa's voice from the hallway. At the look on Helena's face Cressida shut the case quickly and slid it back under the bed. 'Just about to,' she called out, standing up. 'Take it back, Helena. Or else I will,' she said quietly. More loudly, she said, 'What a good idea, Helena. We'll fire up the barbie. Give me those chops and I'll put them in the esky.'

# 9

Head still pressed against the headrest, Robert opened one eye at a squint and found the clock on the dashboard between the adjacent hulking shoulders of the pilots. Twelve more minutes, going by what they'd said earlier when he'd managed to be heard asking across the scream of the engine. Surely he could hold out for that long. He had given up trying to speak to his ever-present security detail in the next seat, concentrating instead on his breathing and trying not to let loose the fist of panic that was welling in his throat. He had always hated flying, and helicopters were a whole extra layer of nightmare. Whenever he and Colin had holidayed anywhere, the trip had only been accomplished with twice as many Serepax as the label directed and sustained administration of the drinks trolley. And he wasn't above holding Colin's hand on takeoff either, or at least hooking a foot quietly round his ankle if the nearby seats were full. But it was Sunday, and he hadn't seen Colin since the corridor outside COG two days ago, and this contraption was a long way from Emirates business class. He'd tried focusing on the horizon, thinking perhaps looking off into the distance would help. It didn't; the horizon's relentless bucking just made him feel sicker. Away from them stretched vast tiered mounds of grey and yellow earth, the trucks moving across them only just visible, kicking up dust soundlessly as if he was watching a silent movie. He'd never been to the state Resources Minister's electorate, and he could see why. It was fucking miles from anywhere, and mainly dirt.

Finally they lowered to the earth and with desperate fingers Robert unbuckled himself, his palms slippery with sweat. Inside the aircraft hangar the air conditioner hit him like a blow. Ah. *Power*. He nearly collapsed on the cool concrete there and then, wanting to be enveloped in its icy body hug. But you couldn't do that when you were Premier. You could barely do *anything*. His phone rang. He checked the screen. Carl, the state Energy Minister. He pressed.

'Bob. You nearly here? Julie's rung three times already.'

Robert turned to Damo.

'How long?'

'Eighteen minutes, sir.'

'We'll be there in twenty. Well,' Robert corrected, glancing at Damo, 'eighteen.'

'There'll be a coldie waiting for you.'

The mood was sombre when he arrived in the vast farmhouse dining room. The state Resource Minister's personal property had become a de facto safe house of sorts, with easy access by air an hour from Sydney in an area still with power, and plenty of room in some pimped up shearers quarters for the various Cabinet members. Security had of course tried to convince them all to stay in that sweaty bunker below Parliament House, but as he walked in he was annoyed to see that the Deputy Premier, Michaela Flanagan, was present, together with two junior members of his Cabinet whose names eluded him. They were all gathered around the microphone implant in the middle of a vast timber dining table. As he approached, Carl simultaneously dialled a number on the pad next to it and handed him a long-neck. Robert took the drink and nodded to those assembled, sitting down. The phone picked up.

'Julie,' Carl said, leaning towards the speaker. 'You there, mate?'

'I am,' came the Minister for Home Affairs' rounded vowels. 'As is Mr Royce,' she added. 'So we're just waiting for Josh.'

'Yes, the treasurer will be here in a minute,' said the Federal Minister for Resources. 'How's it going over there?' He chuckled. 'Brings a whole new meaning to keeping the lights on.'

Robert's phone pinged and he looked down at it. Colin. *Where are you?? I need to talk to you!* Followed by the requisite pink hearts and rainbows. Robert swallowed and held it at a discreet angle to type his reply. *Darling, in a meeting. Call you as soon as I can.*

'Barton, I'm glad you see this as a matter of amusement,' said the Federal Minister for Home Affairs in clipped tones. 'What I want to know is, Premier, how are you going with arrests?'

Robert looked up, reddening even though he knew no-one could have possibly seen. Arrests. Yes.

'Yes quite. Carl,' he said, gruffly, 'why isn't the Police Minister here? Any updates on that?'

'Ah, he's at the Sydney control centre I believe, Premier,' said Carl, blanching. 'I'll just see if I can …' He pulled out his mobile and searched for the number. Michaela chipped in, leaning towards the phone.

'Good afternoon, Ministers. Michaela Flanagan. Deputy Premier. I'm so glad you raised that,' she purred. 'I understand the Federal Police are intending to charge the perpetrators – when they're found – with terrorism. It seems that it would be the AFP that is coordinating arrests then, wouldn't it? More a Federal matter?'

There was a pause.

'My instructions are that the MoU with the AFP relies on full cooperation from NSW Police,' the Federal Minister for Resources replied. 'Those being the authority present on the ground.'

'Yes of course, Minister,' Robert said, glaring at Michaela. She was always just that little bit too bold. One of the security detail approached the table as a light started to flash on the phone.

'Police Minister now on line two,' he said, nodding at the console.

'Oh, oh goodness,' Carl said, putting his phone down. 'If we just click on that he'll join the call …?'

'Should do, sir.'

Michaela held a hand up. 'We'll get to the Police Minister in a moment,' she continued smoothly. Robert stared at her. You didn't keep the Police Minister waiting at a time like this. Unless you were Michaela Flanagan, evidently. 'But first, if we could just ask one thing before we do – the matter of the power plants themselves,' she said, glancing at Robert. 'Perhaps Carl as Energy Minister could fill us in. How long until we can get power restored?'

Restored? Why hadn't he thought of that. Of course that was the most important thing. Yes. How about how to get the power back?

'Thank you, Michaela, certainly,' began Carl. 'Look, you know, I won't lie. This is not ideal. I'd say we've lost at least 7K megawatt hours of electricity capacity. I mean there's a bunch of renewables and a few pussy gas-fired plants about the place, but these babies – the three that got hit, that's Eraring, Liddell and Bayswater – that's a fuck of a lot of power, if you know what I'm saying. Love to hear about the chances of getting it from the other states by the way,' he said, leaning into the microphone while holding Michaela in a look. 'Because right now that's all we've got. Even a national rationing scheme might be necessary.' They nodded at each other and he leant back. 'If I could be so bold.'

'And we can assume,' Michaela said, taking her turn to lean forward, 'that the Commonwealth will trigger the company's rights under the *Terrorism Insurance Act*, am I right? Make the necessary declarations and so on? Any news on that at your end?'

'Ms Flanagan,' said the Minister for Home Affairs, pleasantly, 'I don't follow.'

'Oh. I'm sorry,' Michaela said. 'The *Terrorism Insurance Act*. Clapped-out old thing you guys passed a few years ago, seems it might come into its own now. Provides that the Commonwealth will foot the bill for any costs from terrorism incidents excluded by an insurance contract. Under the usual terrorism ouster, I mean.'

'Oh *that*,' said the Minister, in a tone that sounded to Robert like she hadn't understood a word. 'Yes I'm sure we can come to an arrangement. We need those arrests first though, don't we. And as we have said, all the resources of the Commonwealth are available in that regard.'

'Thank you, Minister,' Michaela said. It was like watching a rat bare its teeth. 'That *is* good to know. And let us know if you need anything from us to make that declaration.' She sipped on the glass of white wine at her elbow.

'Of …?'

'Of a declared terrorist incident under your Act,' said Michaela, rolling her eyes at Carl. 'To trigger the reinsurance. Look – I'm sure Treasury can fill you in. Josh. He's coming on soon isn't he? He's the responsible Minister.'

'I know who my own Treasurer is, Ms Flanagan. Thank you.'

'Yes of course. It's just that if it's less than ten billion dollars damage to infrastructure, your Act provides that the Federal Government steps in and covers the cost the insurer won't. Because of the usual terrorism exemptions in the insurance contracts, of course.'

'Presumably we have a discretion as well,' said Julie, dryly. 'As to whether we want to.'

'Well, of course you do, Minister, but I can't imagine why—'

'Ah – thank you for that careful summary, Michaela,' said Barton. 'As Federal Minister for Resources I'm with you one hundred per cent. One *hundred* per cent. And I'm sure Josh as Treasurer will be too, and Energy. Singing from one song sheet there, no question. We need to get those plants up and running again as soon as possible.'

'You've got our agreement there,' said Michaela. 'Haven't they, Robert?' She was looking at him. 'Robert?'

'What? Oh,' he said, putting his phone back face down on the table. 'Sorry. Yes.' Then he glanced at Michaela and spoke pointedly into the microphone. 'Especially at the prices the other states are charging for their electricity right now.' Two could play this game. 'See what you can do about that.'

'You give me some arrests,' said the Minister for Home Affairs, 'and I'll give you whatever you want. Can we have your Police Minister on the call now, please?'

'Sure – oh,' said Michaela. The light had stopped flashing. 'He's gone.'

'Sorry, chaps,' the Federal Minister for Resources chimed in. 'Just had a text from Josh. He's a bit tied up at the moment, he says. Can we reschedule? Say this afternoon?'

Robert kept his face carefully expressionless, hoping frantically that it meant at least this excruciating conversation would be over, and also that now he could call Colin, which he would do as soon as everyone rang off.

'Just going to make a phone call,' he said when they did, smiling at Carl cheerfully. 'Won't be a sec.'

He stepped out into the hallway but there was a security detail snoozing at one end. Damn.

'Um, sorry, Carl, need my bags for a minute,' he said, as the State Minister for Energy took up deep conversation with Michaela on the white leather couch. 'Can you tell me which one's mine?'

'Oh, sure, Bob – you're last one down the hall. Think Damo already put your bags in there, mate.' He grinned and turned back to Michaela.

'Ah, great, thanks.'

The wood-panelled hallway seemed to go on forever but at last he found the room, and his two matching leather suitcases were in it. The room was tiny and had an awful lavender and white lace bedspread, but it was private. He shut the door and pressed Colin's speed dial on his phone, praying for reception. Colin answered on the second ring. At the sound of his lover's chipper Cockney, Robert's body suffused with warmth.

'Ahh, darlin',' said Colin. 'Bout fookin' time I talked to you. How are you?'

'Oh,' Robert said, dabbing at his eyes, which had stupidly dampened. 'All the better for speaking to you. Is everything okay?'

'Oh yeah, you know – they're all fookin' loonie round here and won't let us go anywhere, but I've got me paints so I'm – I'm alright. You?'

'Oh you know,' said Robert, passing a hand across his face, 'out in the middle of nowhere without you, but other than that fine. The Feds have themselves all in a tizzy and demanding arrests, of course, but that's to be expected. I suppose they think I can just plant evidence or something. Or have someone else do it. Mind you I would have thought that was their department on a Commonwealth crime. Anyway. What's up?'

'It's fantastic though, isn't it! You must be so excited now that this has happened.'

'Sorry, what?'

'Well – I mean, come on, you were telling me about how the fossil fuel mob is such a pain in the arse, always wanting something from you. Now's your chance!'

'Um …'

'Well three of their power plants have been blown up, right? So …'

'So?'

'Renewable energy!'

'Sorry – what?'

'Oh my *darlin'* – finally, you guys can actually lead the world! The technology's ready, you know it is! You guys have the most amazing solar access on the planet! You could start now – wall to wall solar plants. Oh Robert – I'm going to be so proud of you!'

Robert closed his eyes and exhaled. He loved Colin dearly, but his lover really did know how to get caught up in things.

'Colin …'

'Yes? What?' he said, with an expectant pause.

'It's not … it's not like that. It can't be.'

'What? Why not?' Now there was an edge to his voice. Robert leant back against the wall, not knowing whether to laugh or cry. Their views on politics – or the way the world *is*, as Colin preferred to describe it – were wildly divergent and they had come to unspoken agreement years ago to discuss it as little as possible.

'Because …' He didn't even know where to start. He remembered the image of the four of them sitting out there on the phone to the Federal Ministers, Michaela in her crisp blue suit, and nearly laughed. Solar power. They'd laugh in his face.

'Because what?'

'Because it's never going to happen, that's why!'

There was a silence, and it was almost as if Colin was there in the room with him, glaring at him.

'Not without leadership from people in power, no.'

In power, Robert thought. *In power.*

'If you'll excuse the pun, Colin,' he said, keeping his voice gentle, 'there's nothing "in power" about me. And any mention of renewables right now is going to blow up any chance I have of any, just as much as those loonies did. I'm sorry. I can't.' For a moment all he could hear was the sound of his own breathing against the receiver, and the sound of muffled voices outside in the kitchen. 'Colin? Are you still there?'

'Yeah,' he said.

'I'm really sorry. Look, can we talk about something else now? How's the food there?'

'The food?'

'Yeah. Are they ordering in pizza for you? Any alcohol?'

'Oh. No. No, they're not. Wow, Robert, I'm sorry. Look, I have to go. They're … well actually, it's just that, you know, I was so excited about talking to you about this and now … well now I just feel like shite. Sorry. Not your fault. We'll talk later, okay?'

Robert sighed.

'Okay, darling. Look, I'm sorry, okay? Being Premier is really fuckin' hard sometimes.'

'Yeah sure, I understand,' said Colin. He wouldn't, though. None of them did. 'I guess that's why they got you to do it.'

# 10

On Monday morning Brian Prendergast's ground floor looked to Cressida more like a hipster open-plan cafe than the back entrance to a Woollahra town house. Gigantic hardwood doors opened onto a blue-tiled plunge pool, itself ringed by wooden benches that backed onto a commercial kitchen and bar where, it was rumoured, cocktails had once been mixed for Emilio Dolce. In her opinion the head Partner of Mergers and Acquisitions was more Maldives than Byron Bay, but a hippie streak in corporate design was big at the moment and God knew he could afford to get an interior designer in every two years to tell him that. The most glamorous thing Cressida had actually been there for before were client cocktail parties where male reps made a fool of themselves in the pool and female solicitors tried to avoid getting thrown in with them; it was somewhat of a relief to be there in the daytime.

When it became clear that the blackout would not be sorted by the following week, the place had become a satellite office of Hannes Swartling M&A. When Cressida arrived at 7am, via her flat for something to wear, bacon and eggs brought by Tesla steamed in a row of bain maries on the breakfast bar, next to three types of cereal, a large bowl of yoghurt, and the glossy moons of several poached fruits. Outside the pool was one long, inviting slice of blue water reflecting back the sky. Misting pedestal fans circulated cool air across the room and black thickets of phone and laptop cords feasted like leeches on power boards against the wall. But aside from a waiter setting out cutlery, the place was empty.

From behind a sliding door at the back of the room came the sound of splashing water. Adjacent was a stack of bathsheets on a chair, next to a pile of bound documents. Oh, *a shower.* And a *blowdry! Yes please.* She snagged one of the towels and selected a licorice tea bag from the rosewood box on the counter while she waited, thinking back to the emergency centre they had visited the previous day; the hordes of overexcited children, feet bopping on the waxed gymnasium floors as they ran circuits of the basketball court, through the rows of camp beds and piled belongings, their dishevelled parents queuing for hot water and nappies. If only the perpetrators had given some *warning*, she thought, filling the cup and setting it down on a platform between two benches. But then, that probably wasn't the point, was it.

There was one spot left on one of the overborne power boards and she plugged her laptop into it, flooded with a renewed sense of ease when it winked into life. Stage one of reconnection to the world, she thought, sipping her tea. Her plan was first to do some background reading on InterConnex, then start getting the legal team together and make contact with the project managers in each state to get in the loop on the stakeholder meetings. There were concept plans and options to review, geotech reports and environmental assessments to read, approval application documents to prepare, all towards the finalisation of the T & C document in time for the launch in May. If it was anything like the other State motorways, she thought, watching the light dance on the pool, the tendering alone would be a nightmare. One day, she reflected with an odd detachment as the printer doled out the finance documents Richard had emailed her, she and Felipe would be able to afford a place like this. He was already on four hundred k, and once she was a Partner, her income would be almost the same. It was a vertiginous feeling, to have everything she had worked for be so close. It was hers, *hers.* As long as nothing went wrong.

The water stopped and the door to the ensuite opened. Richard emerged with a towel around his waist. As he reached into the gym bag on the carpet he noticed Cressida.

'Oh Cress, hi,' he said. 'Nice to see you. Brought you some light reading.' He pointed at the foot-high pile of bound documents on a chair. 'Road documents,' he said with a grin. 'Have you seen Michael yet? He *really* wanted to see you.'

'Um, no?' she said, glancing at the pile. 'Is he around?'

'Upstairs,' said Richard, giving a can of aerosol deodorant a vigorous shake. 'I'd take a coffee. He looked serious.'

'Right ...' Cressida said. A meeting, upstairs, instead of down here where the business happened? Odd. 'Thanks.' It must be something to do with the partnership vote, she decided as she climbed the stairs with her tea. Telling her about when it was rescheduled for. Nothing worse than that, no doubt. Hopefully whatever it was would be quick – she was itching to get back to the road project.

Arriving into the foyer at the top of the stairwell felt like crossing into an inner sanctum. Gold-framed mirrors and hardwood tables were pressed against the walls, and a Persian rug lined the parquet floor that stretched to the front door. To her right was a loungeroom scattered with square leather couches and a glass-topped coffee table. The temperature was at least ten degrees lower than downstairs, and Cressida felt herself relax just from the feel of the air-con on her damp skin. On the far side of the loungeroom, Michael was standing by a large plate-glass window staring down at the pool.

'Ah, Cressida,' he said, crossing the floor. He clasped her hand. 'Good to see you.' He indicated a couch. 'Take a seat. Had breakfast?'

'Um, no, actually,' she said. Unless you counted the apple she'd had in the car. Dinner the night before had been raw vegetables and tinned tuna. She was ravenous, but the thought of chowing down on a bowl of muesli and yoghurt in front of the Managing Partner was not appealing. 'It can wait,' she said.

He turned around and said, 'Sandra said what, ten minutes, Brian?'

Cressida looked up to see Brian Prendergast standing in the kitchen at the cappucino machine. What was he doing here? *Oh but it's his house, silly*, she remembered. He's just making his morning coffee. Brian nodded. Cressida frowned and tried to read Michael's face. The Managing Partner and a Senior Partner she didn't know well, calling a private meeting with her? And with a person she didn't know? The only time she'd heard of that was on Level 65 when people were given the shove. They'd call someone independent in to make sure it was all 'impartial' – and witnessed should there be a dispute over who said what later. Her heart dropped into her stomach. Was *that* why the partnership vote hadn't been rescheduled yet? They were planning to *sack* her?

But as she stood up and reached over to shake Brian's hand across the bench, the thing she noticed immediately was how distracted he was. It was like someone had flicked the dimmer switch on his usual energy. His smile as he held out a plate of croissants and danishes to her was only half its usual intensity.

'Who's Sandra?' asked Cressida, taking a pastry and trying to sound offhand.

Michael lowered himself onto the couch opposite and ran a hand across his face. 'It's complicated, Cressida. I'll explain when she gets here,' he said. 'How's things?'

Brian sat at an angle in a chair on the other side of her and nursed his coffee.

'Fine, thanks,' she said, warily. 'Except for my partnership application of course. When *is* the vote rescheduled for by the way?' she said, taking a dainty mouthful of her tea as she looked at Michael over the rim. Instead of answering, Michael gave a pained looked at Brian, who gave a show of grimacing and took a swig of his coffee.

'Such a ruddy cock-up, that,' Brian said, finally, the English cut-glass curve to his voice pure Melbourne royalty. 'If only that idiot Bollos had kept quiet.' The accent made the frankness of his words compelling, cool almost, instead of uncouth. 'If she had,' he continued, 'you'd already be a Partner by now. I'm sure of it. Things being as they are though …' He sighed. 'It might be quite a while I'm afraid.' He gave Cressida a sympathetic look, but then his eyes drifted to the floor, and a pensive look crossed his face. Cressida shifted uncomfortably.

'So … what's up?'

Brian glanced up. 'Michael will fill you in.'

There was a sheet of paper on the couch next to him and Michael leaned over to pick it up. He passed it to her. 'Brian's ex-wife emailed him the link this morning.'

She read. It was a copy of the front page of *The Age*. GOTCHA, screamed the headline in capitals, above a half-page image of a smiling young woman in school uniform. In the colour photo her face was ruddy, the cheeks pink as if she'd just come in from the cowshed.

'Holy fuck,' she said, looking closer. 'Sorry, I mean—' She reddened, glancing up, but her gaze was drawn back to the page again. 'Gosh.' She slurped her tea, reading: *A 22-year-old woman was taken into custody last night in relation to the NSW power outage. Charges under Commonwealth terrorism laws are expected.* 'They got someone.' *Outage*, Cressida thought. Bit of an understatement.

Brian remained silent, his face concealed in his coffee cup. Then he looked up at a photograph on the opposite wall. In it rows of smiling young women on bleachers wore red and navy sports uniforms, a set of hockey sticks crossed in front. *Ascham*. It was the Ascham hockey team. She'd played against them at PLC.

'Two hundred thousand dollars in private-school education,' he sighed. 'Down the drain.'

Cressida wasn't sure whether they were talking about the girls in the photograph now, or somehow the girl in the story – or some combination of both. All she knew was that things seemed to be going weird. She grasped for something to say, but Michael stepped in again.

'Cressida,' Michael began. Then the doorbell rang. 'Ah,' he said, with palpable relief, standing up. 'That must be Sandra.'

He crossed to the front door and a moment later there was the clop of heavy heels on parquet, and a large woman in a two-piece suit and rimless glasses entered. 'Sandra,' Michael beamed, standing up. He shook her hand then turned to Cressida.

'Cressida, this is Sandra Crane. You probably know she's a criminal defence barrister. Among other things.'

Criminal defence barrister? Cressida stared at the frizzy-haired woman in front of her. Last Cressida had read, the woman before her had been in The Hague, defending the former Syrian president against charges of torture and genocide. A Senior Counsel renowned for winning impossible cases, she had seen three of Australia's most notorious murderers acquitted on appeal, one following a Commission of Inquiry twenty years after he'd been put in gaol. Cressida didn't know whether to shake her hand or curtsey. She chose the former.

'Cressida,' Sandra said, appraising her with cool grey eyes.

'A ... an honour to meet you,' Cressida said, sweat springing out on her palms and making her want to wipe them on her trousers. She resisted.

'You're a jolly champion for coming, Crane,' Michael said, kissing her cheek. It seemed like a brave move to Cressida but she figured they must be well enough acquainted. 'Coffee?'

'Black thanks,' said Sandra, and sat down on an armchair opposite.

There was the blare of the coffee machine again and over it Michael called out, 'How was the Netherlands?'

'A bloody circus,' the woman answered, putting her bag carefully beside her on the floor. Her tone was soft but emphatic, her voice deep and somehow both authoritative and laconic. It was such a contrast to how Cressida spoke, she thought, she who always found herself speaking quickly and loudly, to get everything out in case people moved on before the end of what she was saying. Sandra, however, sounded as if she knew every word she said would be strained for, and probably written down, so there was no need to make sure people could hear her. How wonderful that would be, Cressida thought. *To know people were going to pay attention. To not have to make an effort to make them.*

'Is that the girl?' Sandra asked, flicking her gaze at the printout. Brian handed it to her. 'Young,' she observed.

'That's what I thought,' Cressida said.

Sandra glanced at her and continued, 'Where is she? Silverwater?'

Brian's eyes strayed back to Cressida. 'I don't know. That's the first thing we need to find out. The article just says she turned up at the temporary cop van at Muswellbrook LAC.'

Michael returned with the coffee and passed it to Sandra. As he sat down Brian started speaking, almost to himself.

'She always was so bloody passionate about things. Used to fly into a rage at the slightest injustice when she was a child. Then of course she had to go to Iraq. *Iraq*. As if she wasn't mad enough already.'

Sandra took a small square container out of her bag and opened it to tip two small white tablets into her coffee, then stirred it. Cressida was wondering how Brian knew so much about a terrorist's biography, and also what all this had to do with her, but mainly she was thinking that what he was saying and Sandra being here, at least it didn't *sound* like it was going in the direction of a dismissal conversation, so she allowed herself to relax a little.

'You seem to know a lot about her,' Cressida said.

Brian looked at her. 'I should do. She's my daughter.'

'What?'

Brian nodded. Cressida thought that maybe she shouldn't sound so appalled. But she didn't know how she should sound. There wasn't anything in her internal Hannes Swartling handbook for this. She felt flustered and embarrassed, as if he had just put a bucket of offal in her lap. It would have been less awkward if he'd said the girl in the paper was his teen lover, for God's sake, or a love-child from his past, who was now a hooker up on drug charges or extortion or, God, anything but terrorism. Then, she would have flicked to 'understanding'. Compassionate. Non-judgemental.

But this information made her feel instead like she might vomit. She looked across at him, trying to keep the judgement out of her eyes. Immediately she found herself thinking about what the hell had gone wrong with his parenting that his daughter had ended up in this mess. Her second thought was the photo. The girl had gone to *Ascham*?

Cressida swallowed and turned her gaze to Sandra, just for somewhere to look. The other woman's pale grey eyes were inscrutable though, and Cressida's discomfiture slid straight off them. No help there. *I guess you'd have to be pretty impassive to defend a war criminal*, Cressida found herself thinking. Above such base notions as judgement.

'But' – she picked up the paper off the table again, speaking just for something to fill the silence, and scanned it – 'it says here explosives offences.' And hang on … *Liddell*? Wasn't that one of the power stations owned by the client they'd met with on Saturday? She looked at Brian.

Wow. He was seriously in the *scato*.

'For now,' Sandra said, sipping her coffee.

'The thing is, Cressida,' Brian continued quietly, regarding her, 'we both know that when scandal gets out in the legal fraternity, it's really hard to live it down.'

Cressida felt herself flush to the roots of her hair. She glanced again at Sandra, unsure whether the woman opposite knew about her father, then in the next moment feeling certain she did. As well as *The Australian* Leo had been front page news in the legal circulars for weeks, and the lead story in *The Sydney Morning Herald* twice. And Brian was right. People remembered. Cressida gave a low whistle. Sandra's eyes flicked to hers and she thought she saw humour there, but the woman remained silent.

'We can't brief an outside lawyer on this,' Brian announced. 'Sandra here of course has the discretion of a Swiss banker, but there is no way I am trusting this to an instructing solicitor outside the firm. You've got experience at the highest levels of criminal law practice, Cressida. You know most of what there is to know about the Criminal Code jurisdiction. Sandra can tell you anything you don't. We need to get her acquitted.'

Cressida was still so stunned at the idea that she was being asked to act on a criminal matter, for an M & A Partner's daughter she had never met, with *Sandra Crane*, that it took a moment to take in the last thing Brian had said.

'Acquitted,' she said. 'But ...' She picked up the article again. 'Didn't she do it? I mean, it says here that she gave herself in. Confessed.' She pointed to the word for emphasis.

'That need not be a problem,' Sandra said. 'We don't know what she's confessed *to*. In fact we don't even know *what* the charges she's up on are. There may be several. Or none at all. Newspapers don't always get these things right. *Or* it could just be a beat-up by that rag,' she said, flicking her hand delicately at the curl of paper. 'Although I will say – with the New South Wales Counter Terrorism unit involved, we have to assume Code charges are likely.'

'Yes. Of course,' Cressida said, wishing she either had more time to think or that her brain worked faster. She couldn't think which would be worse: discovering your daughter could be up on terrorism charges, or finding it out *from the paper*. Except possibly finding it out via your ex-wife. The immediate problem, though, was that they were all looking at her. Come on, she told herself, say something intelligent. Fortunately, Michael spoke.

'I couldn't get anyone on the phone at Muswellbrook copshop,' said Michael. 'God knows what they do with criminals in these conditions. Normally they go to Silverwater first, right, Cressida?'

'What? Oh – yes,' said Cressida, suffused with relief to know at least something.

'She may still be there though,' said Sandra. 'At Muswellbrook LAC. Last night isn't much time to get her down to Sydney.'

Brian stared at Sandra, his blue eyes bright. 'It's unlikely she'll be found guilty of terrorism offences though, right? I mean, yes to explosives, probably even sabotage, or whatever – but *terror*ism?'

Sandra set down her coffee. 'The terror crime list was written for what these people have been up to, Brian,' she said, softly. 'The government is going to be licking its chops. Not to mention ropable about not picking it up beforehand. And there's also the probability of property damage and sabotage offences under State legislation. Maybe some explosives offences. And something under the *Electricity Supply Act*?' she mused. 'Interference with power supply and so on. Oh and of course conspiracy, acting in company,' she said, like rounding off a list of cake ingredients. 'I imagine we can give the double jeopardy prohibition a good swing on some of those. But there's a very specific intent for the terrorism charges,' she said, squinting upwards, remembering. 'Let me get it right. An action done or a threat is made,' she recited, as if of a well learnt poem, 'with the intention of advancing a political, religious or ideological cause, *and*' – she paused – 'with the intention of coercing or influencing the government or the public *by intimidation*. Section 101 of the Commonwealth Criminal Code,' she said, almost with a flourish. 'There are about ten different types of charge of course too. Commit a terrorist act, receive training for terrorism, possession of something in connection with a terrorist act … What else is there, Michael?' she asked him. Colleague to colleague, thoughtful.

Brian's eyes widened and he shook his head. Cress reached for her bag and scrambled to find a pen.

'Let's see …' Sandra continued. 'Direct activities of a terrorist organisation, recruitment for a terrorist organisation … That's assuming they can prove terrorist organisation, of course. We'd be putting – I imagine?' – she glanced at Brian – 'that there wasn't one, I think? Ragtag band of belligerents, et cetera? Anyway, the other potential charges – the State ones: sabotage and these explosives offences – their mental element is just the standard you'd expect for property damage.' She shrugged. 'You know, intent to injure, intent to destroy and so on. Depending on the offence. What do you think?' she said, turning to Brian. 'Did she do this with intention to intimidate the government into doing something? Taking action on climate change, for example?'

Brian's face was slack. 'I have no idea. Like I said – I haven't seen her. Not for four years, now. Though she's always been known as what I think is referred to as a "peacenik".' He enunciated the word as if it were a curious term in a foreign language. 'For as long as I can remember. She has her faults, of course, as we all do, but … well, the Joanne I knew would never have wanted to hurt anybody. Mind you that was before she went to Iraq.' His jaw clenched and abruptly he dropped his face forwards, pressing his eyes with a thumb and forefinger.

'Well, I'm sure you'll agree she certainly failed there,' Sandra said, 'but that's another matter.'

'What do you mean?' asked Cressida, trying to sound less piping. She didn't care though, she decided; if she was going to represent this woman, she had to understand. 'Were workers injured at the plant?'

'I have no idea. I was thinking of *since* then. Harm from lack of power, and so on. Anyway for our purpose it's immaterial,' Sandra said, briskly. 'It will be relevant to sentence but not the choice of charges per se. For that the point is motive – whether to intimidate or not. If the CDPP' – ah, of course; this would be the Commonwealth Director of Public Prosecutions, not State, thought Cressida – 'can't get corroborating evidence to show the terrorist intent, they're left with just the basic criminal stuff. Sabotage, mainly. Which has a maximum twenty-year sentence instead of life.'

Michael straightened, all efficiency while his co-Partner was losing it. 'Let's say they can establish that, Sandra,' he said, clipped. 'The terrorist intent, as you call it. What then?'

'Guess she'd have to investigate plea options.' Sandra shrugged. 'Or mental impairment? Or that she was drug-addled and driven into it by some charismatic leader. Something. Depends on her instructions, of course.'

Wow, Cressida thought. Either way, no babies for her, then. She looked down at the photo on the printout. Had she thought about it, this girl who had turned herself in to Muswellbrook LAC at 9pm last night? Did she know that by blowing up a power station she'd said goodbye to any progeny? Cressida looked at Brian. What did that feel like, she thought, knowing your own child would be locked up away from the sunlight for the next two decades, with humans that were for the most part walking scar tissue, all of your care and investment in raising them come to a screaming halt in a prison cell? She didn't know anything about Brian's family life, but that had to hurt.

But as unfortunate as all this was, Cressida thought, putting down her notebook and biting into the pastry, it had nothing to do with her. Sure, there'd be lawyers who'd think she was insane to turn down a job as Sandra Crane's instructing solicitor – on *anything* – but federal crimes wasn't a career direction she had any interest in. It certainly didn't seem like it would help her get partnership. And even if he *had* stuck up for her at the partnership meeting, she knew she couldn't afford the poo that was about to stick to Brian anywhere near her: it was hard enough getting ahead in the firm as a female even when you *did* do everything right. Anyway, she thought, what about the fact that the power stations were owned by a Hannes Swartling client? If she took this on – and if she did, under the professional conduct rules that meant the firm did – it would be a massive professional conflict. Even so-called 'Chinese walls', where you kept everything to yourself and didn't discuss it with any other lawyer in the firm, wouldn't avoid that. She glanced at them. How could Brian even ask her? And Michael, for that matter. If they thought she'd put her prac-tising certificate at risk over this one he was mistaken.

'I'd love to help, Brian,' she said. 'Really I would. But – I'm surprised Richard didn't already tell you – I'm lead solicitor on InterConnex, so …' *In other words, I wouldn't touch this if I was the last lawyer alive.*

Brian looked at her in surprise, a small furrow creasing the skin between his eyebrows. He glanced across at Michael.

'Yes,' Michael said, turning to her. 'Richard did mention that. A very exciting project, I agree. I don't think there's a way you can manage both, though.' He sighed. 'I know the client asked for you, but I don't think it will be a huge problem to find someone else. At least at first, anyway,' he added. 'This whole thing should be done and dusted well before any ink's ready to be put on any road contracts. I imagine you'll spend, what' – he glanced at Sandra – 'six months on this? And then you can come back in on InterConnex.'

Six months? He had to be kidding. Even if she agreed to risk the con-flict, by that time she might as well get a job as a paralegal on it, Cressida thought. All the main work would be done, the relationships cemented, the chain of influence – and therefore prestige and reputation – estab-lished. Instead of making a name for herself she'd be a worker bee again, slogging it out for no recognition and bugger-all pay. She was supposed to be spending the coming week travelling to the construction sites, for goodness sake. She'd been intending to ask Esma to book the flights as soon as the power was back. No. It wouldn't do.

'It could be over that quickly, yes,' Sandra confirmed, nodding. 'Depends on whether the government wants to string it out or not. Or alternatively be seen to get her behind bars as quickly as possible. Them, I should say.'

Of course. There were other suspects. Why the hell wasn't this person getting the same legal representation as *them*?

'I should warn you though,' Sandra added, 'other cases like these have taken years to run their course. Three at least.'

Cressida swallowed. That was unthinkable.

'Well what *is* happening with the other suspects, by the way?' she said. 'On Eraring and the other plant ...' She scanned the newspaper article. 'Bayswater. Surely they have legal representation?'

'I have no idea. Brian's daughter is possibly the only one that can afford me,' Sandra said, glancing at him. 'The rest will have Legal Aid, I imagine. Depending on their finances. Of course I wouldn't act for any of the others anyway. In my experience this sort of thing turns into a professional conflict pretty quickly. The knives tend to come out between suspects before the first mention. Which reminds me. We need to get back to basics.' She turned to Cressida. 'The first thing to do is to get instructions, obviously. Find out whether she's happy for us to act for her – which I assume she will be – and get as much detail as you can about what charges have been laid. Of course don't ask her too many questions about the incident itself at this point,' Sandra said. 'Then you'll need to get the papers – from the CDPP, if the client doesn't have them. Either way, the first thing is to find out exactly what they're levelling at her so far. And find out how she wants to plead, of course, once we know what *to* – charges *and* full brief of evidence before she decides, of course. Once they've had it transferred up to the District Court, seek orders for one at the first mention. That will take a while – I'm rarely in the Dizzo, but I think it's eight weeks on strictly indictables? Again, depends what the charges are. But I'm sure you're familiar with the Practice Notes.' She added, 'Anyway, once we've got all *that*, we'll know where we are.'

'Here's my secretary's number,' Brian said, scrawling it on the back of the news article with his heavy wood embossed pen and handing it to Cressida. 'Esma. Worth her weight in gold. Consider her yours for this, Cressida. And whatever else you need.'

An unfamiliar feeling began to stir in Cressida, and she tried to pin it down. Ah, she realised with wonder. That was it. *Power.* For the last four years, since Leo's conviction – well, her whole time at Hannes Swartling, actually, but the last four years had been the worst – it had been the other way around. As if, despite all her work and dedication, Hannes Swartling were doing her a favour by keeping her on. Four years of embarrassment, worrying about what they thought of her, proving how different she was from Leo over and over again – how *trustworthy*, because her father had turned out so much the opposite. Even walking up the stairs to this meeting she had been afraid for her job, she reflected with some bitterness.

By doing this, they would owe her.

But she knew that if she did do it, there would have to be cast-iron Chinese walls, and she was going to be asking Sandra a lot of stupid questions. Terrorism and sabotage would be very different from defending on insider trading. And, she thought, looking across at those inscrutable grey eyes, Sandra was not someone she wanted to look stupid in front of.

'Any thoughts on a junior?' Cressida ventured, to give herself time to think. 'And what about bail? Should we appeal?' If there was a junior barrister involved that would make the second issue easier; she could ask them all the stupid questions and still look good to Sandra.

'I'll ask round my chambers,' said Sandra. 'We'll need to see what the charges are first, and that will give me an idea of who would be good. Byron's good on property crimes,' she mused. 'You could try a bail application, of course, always worth a go – but on this? No way.'

Well there was some leeway on the timing then, Cressida thought. She would keep working on InterConnex at the same time, at least during the beginning. Eight weeks for the brief of evidence, that was a start. Once she had found the client, she'd just go out there and introduce herself, get the instructions to act for her, advise her about the charges and then there was nothing to do till the first mention in four weeks. Maybe file a bail appeal, but Cressida thought Sandra was probably right – it would be pissing in the wind. *It's going to be okay*, she reassured herself. *You can keep this on the rails.*

'I'll do this on two conditions,' Cressida said, ignoring Sandra's surprised look and the slight, incredulous smile that sprang to Michael's mouth. Yes that's right, she thought. It's not all up to you now. 'First, I keep the road project, unless and until I tell you it's too much. Second, you reschedule the partnership vote within a fortnight. And,' she said, marshalling courage, 'I get it.' *And don't give me any crap about how it's democratic*, she thought. *I know you two are the numbers guys. Except for those two in Melbourne. I don't know what's up with them.* 'Otherwise, well, I'm …' – she took a deep breath; eleven years – 'I'm looking elsewhere.'

Michael's eyes widened and his jaw twitched, and for a moment something flashed across his face. It was a look she hadn't seen there before. *Respect.* Brian, however, was looking decidedly dark.

'Cressida, come on,' he said.

'I'm sorry, Brian, I mean it. You talk about how hard it is to live things down in the law. Well I'm sick and tired of being judged in my father's shadow. It's time this firm gave me the value I deserve.'

'I'm sorry,' Sandra began, in a voice that said she was anything but, 'I thought we would have the instructing solicitor here. You three work that out, and whoever it is, get them to this woman as soon as the power's back on. We need things while they're fresh.' Cressida flushed in embarrassment at Sandra's tone, but kept her gaze on Michael. They couldn't refuse her, she thought – they'd already told her everything. How could they disagree?

'I'll organise it,' Michael said, quietly.

'I'll call around and see if I can find out where she is,' said Brian. 'Then you can get in to see her tomorrow, either Silverwater or Lithgow, probably.'

Of course he was in a hurry, it was his daughter, Cressida thought. But rushing around and doing things in a panic wouldn't make things happen any quicker. Anyway most of the scheduling would be up to the prosecution.

'Uh-uh,' said Sandra. 'That won't be happening.'

'What? Why?'

'All Corrections is in lockdown until the power's back on. You can imagine the security issues.' She sighed and drained her coffee. 'The prisons have generators, of course, but everything's being run on the absolute minimum. Your daughter is going to be twiddling her thumbs for a little while yet.' She smiled. 'Ironic, really. Well, gentlemen, Cressida,' she said, standing. 'If that's all?'

'But,' Cressida interrupted, a thousand thoughts flying around her brain at once, 'but what about—' *What about the conflict of interest?* 'Oh nothing,' she said, stupidly. 'Ms Crane, I'll let you know when I get in to see her. And you can expect a full brief twenty-four hours later. I'll add the police brief when we get it.'

'Excellent,' Sandra said, standing up.

As Michael showed Sandra out Cressida sat, shaky with adrenaline aftershock. She turned to Brian. 'Brian,' she ventured. 'This is a huge fucking conflict. Don't you need to ask SinoGen? And get the rest of the Partners' okay, for that matter?'

Brian looked at her. 'No, I don't, Cressida. Never been a better application of the phrase *Chinese walls*, I would have thought. SinoGen is not your client. They're not even mine. They're Richard's. There's no problem. Oh and Cressida,' Brian said, as she started for the stairs.

She stopped, her hand on the balustrade. 'Yes?'

'Is Hannes Swartling listed as your contact on the Law Society website? Maybe amend that – your name will be on the court papers ...'

Cressida frowned. He was really serious about this confidentiality thing.

'Sure. Do you want this?' She held out the printout. Brian shook his head.

'It's okay. I'll get another. Her name's Fairbank,' he added. 'Joanne Fairbank. She ... she took her mother's name when we split up.'

'Ok,' said Cressida. 'Thanks.'

Downstairs at the sink as she poured the rest of her cold tea down the drain, Cressida leant against the counter and looked out at the pool, feeling disembodied. Across the room Pip was sitting on one of the bench seats tapping into her laptop. Cress folded up the article and slipped it in her handbag, then approached her.

'Hey,' Pip said when she saw Cressida. 'I've got all the EOI precedents on a zip folder now. So if you email me the tenderer list, I can start filling them … Hang on. You're paler than the lychees in my martini last night,' she observed, eyes narrowed. 'What's up?'

'What? Oh. No. Nothing. That sounds good. Yes. Um. I have to talk to Esma about a couple of things, quickly, and then …'

'Cressida? You're acting really weird,' said Pip, frowning.

'Really?' She brightened her tone, smiling. 'No, I'm just thinking about the road project. Oh, Brian just gave me a new file, but it shouldn't take long.'

'Brian did?' said Pip, eyes homing in on Cressida. 'What, in M & A?'

'No.' She shook her head. 'Criminal, of all things.'

'Criminal? You're kidding,' Pip said. 'But what do you know about that?'

Cressida looked at her. 'My thoughts exactly.'


# 11

The cafeteria at Randwick Private was air-conditioned and crowded with a two to one ratio of health workers to civilians when Cressida pushed through its heavy double doors that night. Among the pale green of the orderlies and purple of the nurses, Felipe stood out as one of the few in surgical dark blue. He was still wearing his cap, and she slid it off his head as she sat down.

'Sweetheart.'

He turned and crushed her in a hug, tipping her face up for a kiss, then turned her bodily to face the overhead menu a few tables down. 'Now look. There's no chilli prawns I'm afraid,' he said, looking chagrined, 'but they do have …' – he paused for effect – 'keftedes.'

'Ohh,' she said, imagining. 'Not today. I'm keeping with the juice diet for the moment.'

He kissed her forehead.

'You're so disciplined. They might have just the ticket. Let's see.'

They queued and Cressida ordered a spinach and kale juice, Felipe the Caesar salad and a bottle of water for each of them.

'How was surgery?' she said as they sat down. 'Better now you have your instruments?'

'A success, thank God,' he said, stabbing a chunk of bacon. 'Thank God I'm done muddling through on the hospital kit. The lights flickered twice and we all held our breath, but everything stayed on. We had to get in and out quick smart though – there's only one theatre on the genny, apparently,' he said, rolling his eyes. 'So I just did the metatarsal – the other two ops will have to wait till the power's back. I'm going to have to talk to the president about better emergency backup for this place.' He shook his head. 'It's just unacceptable.'

Cressida took a long, character-building suck of her smoothie. Yep. Foul. She regarded Felipe. He'd been grumbling about the presidency of the Australian Orthopaedic Association for the entire six months they'd been dating. Since the news about the standing down of the president, all he'd talked about was the election of a new one.

'Any word on candidates? How's the field looking?'

Felipe looked glum. 'Mark was trying again to convince me to run today,' he said, and grimaced. 'He wants to be deputy, of course. I just don't think it's the right year. It's a win that Clarkson's not in the race, but that Queensland contender …' He unscrewed one of the bottles of water and passed it to her. 'Although of course I do have my secret weapon,' he said, and squeezed her hand.

'What Queensland contender?'

He gave a tight smile. 'That new bloke, just back from five years in Germany. Mark says he's running.'

'What, you think he'd be a threat?'

'I don't know.' Felipe shrugged. 'He was acting chair of the equivalent body in Germany, apparently. Got three million in government funding for a new training program they wanted to implement, bringing refugee medicos from Algeria or some such. *Three million.* Complete opposite of what we need, of course.' He sighed, swigging water. 'It seems I'm the only one with any drive to make this organisation entirely self-sufficient. I mean, how else can we maintain our independence? Anyway.' He brightened. 'Not to worry. How are *you* faring, my beautiful girl?'

'Well … I'll get into that in a minute,' said Cressida. There was no way she could tell him about the Liddell matter, of course, but she was still deciding whether to tell him about the travel on the road project. He was always criticising her work for being 'too demanding', as he put it. As for the terrorist case, she thought, it was probably a good thing she was bound by confidentiality. Felipe would have an apoplexy knowing she was acting for someone who had had a part in causing this mess. 'How're your next few weeks looking?'

'Well,' he began, 'of course the absolute highlight is taking my gorgeous fiancée to be the belle of the ball ...'

The ball? *Oh God, that's right. The big one.* Next Friday. The Surgeons Ball. The invitation had been pinned to her noticeboard for months.

'But as well, I'm glad to say, they've rescheduled last Saturday's meet to next weekend,' he continued. He paused and looked at her over his salad. 'You *have* been training, I presume?'

Cressida blinked. 'Well, no, actually,' she said, trying to sound offhand. 'I had to get into work early this morning. God, things have been so chaotic, as you know.' She shook her head and grinned. He was still looking at her though, a familiar stormy look overtaking his face. 'Chillax, Felipe,' she said, keeping her grin intact. 'I'll go tonight. But,' she said, slowly, trying to keep the hope out of her voice, 'surely the ball won't be on? Given the blackout?'

'They've moved it to the hospital fifth-floor balcony especially,' he said. 'Honestly, Cressida. You can't go *tonight*,' he said. 'It's 7.30 already. We've *talked* about this.' He shook his head and stabbed a piece of chicken. 'Three of the committee members are going to be there, for goodness sake.' He put his head in his hands, peering out at her from between meaty surgeon's fingers. 'How many times do we have to go through this?'

She hated it when he got like this. But he was right. When she didn't train, they always argued. She changed the subject.

'Three committee members? Really?'

'Three. *And* they're probably the ones least onside for me as chair. Oh Cressida. You *know* how important this is to me.'

'I do, Felipe. Of course I do. I'll go tomorrow. Twice,' she added. Why the hell her triathlon time had *anything to do* with his chances of becoming chair of the Australian Orthopaedic Association she didn't know, but he was convinced of it, and now it had become a 'thing', so she didn't press it. Something about being able to best represent orthopaedic surgeons to the rest of the surgical profession at multidisciplinary gatherings and internationally. She couldn't believe they'd all be that superficial as to care what someone's *partner* looked like – much less how many triathlons they'd won – but had been through it enough times with Felipe to know there was a lot she didn't understand about the surgical world, and never would. The wife of the current chair had been Miss Universe Burundi, and apparently that had been a crucial deciding factor.

'That's great that it's on this Saturday,' she continued. 'Despite the blackout, I mean.' *And the exercise will mean I can drink an extra glass,* she thought. 'How's *your* training going?'

Felipe grinned. 'Broke forty minutes. This morning in the staff gym.'

'There you go,' Cressida said. 'That's better than the current chair's, isn't it?'

'By nearly a minute.'

'Fabulous.'

Well it was only Monday, she reassured herself. So what if she hadn't trained for three days; there was still time between now and the weekend. Maybe she *could* have that keftedes, she thought, savouring the description on the menu board. Especially if she trained extra in the morning. Four meatballs, she thought, calculating the running time. It could be done.

'Actually you know, I was just reading an article the other day,' Felipe was saying, scooping up the last of the shaved parmesan in his bowl. 'The research is now showing there is a forty per cent correlation between strenuous heart lung exercise in the thirties – like disciplined triathlon training' – he paused and looked at her for emphasis – 'and the prevention of weight gain in the forties. More so than weights, boxing, sprinting or other strength exercise. Good to know, eh?'

Cressida flushed. Even though she tried to pretend it didn't, even the suggestion that her weight mattered to him made her embarrassed.

'*You* don't need to worry of course though, darling,' he said, pulling her face towards his. 'You've got such excellent genes, I know you'll stay reed thin.' He swallowed his mouthful and kissed her. She looked up at the menu board again. It was good he was supportive. It wasn't for him that it mattered though. Being thin just felt good. The keftedes probably *were* fatty. And the tzatziki wouldn't be low-fat yoghurt. She was glad she'd stuck with the juice.

'Hey look,' she said. There was a TV on the wall and on it a drone camera was arcing a bird's eye view across the smouldering remains of a building. The name of one of the power stations flashed up on the screen. *Holy moly*, she thought. It was unrecognisable. Fires scattered the picture and burned with oily black smoke, while in the centre bulldozers were pushing mounds of smoking metal and debris into a gigantic pile. *Liddell*. On the other side of some cyclone wire, passengers in matching red caps and oversized tags on lanyards tumbled out of a bus.

'Oh for God's sake,' Felipe said. 'I mean, of all the *poor taste* …'

A banner of text ran along the screen: *Emergency services to divert power from Victoria … Electricity back in twelve Sydney suburbs …* Then the footage cut to a basketball stadium like the one she had been in yesterday, filled with beds and people, and after that a crowd with placards. Cressida caught the word *renewables* and one saying *Free the Climate Five*. Then came a talking head of a man in a suit with bright red hair, so pale he looked albino. She swallowed and turned back to Felipe.

'I had a meeting with Prendergast this morning,' she said. 'You know, Brian Prendergast. "God".' She saw the cogs turning in his head until he remembered. 'Anyway – he *said*' – she paused for emphasis – 'the partnership vote would be reconvened within a fortnight.' She couldn't conceal the grin.

'Oh lovely,' Felipe chuckled, opening her palm and kissing it. 'I saw the wedding invitations on the bench at Helena's, by the way. Are you happy with them? I'm so glad all that stress will be behind you soon, darling. It's so ageing,' he said, pushing a lock of hair off her forehead.

Cressida looked at him.

'Yes,' she said. 'Life should be a *tad* less stressful when I'm a Partner. Though going by some of them,' she said, shaking her head, 'it gets a lot worse. Oh that reminds me.' She extracted her hand. 'It looks like Pip can help me out on—'

'You know that's not what I mean, Cressida,' Felipe interrupted. She stared down at the table, feeling a familiar flush of anger and hurt. *Why* did he persist in this? In this trying to pretend she would turn into someone she wasn't?

'You know, Felipe,' she began, trying to find a way to say it that wouldn't sound angry. Then her mobile phone trilled on the table and they both stared at it. Whoops. They had an agreement to keep phones off during meal times. But it was Brian's number. She gave Felipe an apologetic glance and picked it up.

'Brian.'

'Cress. It's Esma. I'm so sorry to disturb you. Can you talk?'

'Of course, Esma. Go ahead.'

'Look, I just thought I would call you. It's – the weird thing is – I can't find her.'

'Can't find her? Joanne?'

'I've called every number you gave me from directory assistance, and then a few more. Corrections, Silverwater, Lithgow, even Wellington. It's still ringing out at Legal Aid. And when I got through at one of the prisons, they looked her up for me – and nothing. I even ended up with someone in Victoria and they looked on the central list, but there was no mention of her.'

'Did you mention the article? The one from Brian?'

'Cressida,' Felipe said, through clenched teeth.

She covered the receiver with her hand, cringing and mouthing an apology.

'I'll just be a sec. Sorry. Esma? Go ahead.'

'Sorry, you're at dinner. Yes I did mention that – they didn't even seem to know that anyone had been taken into custody though. It was so weird.'

Cress sighed. How was she supposed to act for this client if she couldn't even find her?

'It's okay – thanks anyway. We'll try again in the morning.'

'Alright, pet. Sorry again. And sorry for interrupting your dinner.'

'Oh Esma, that's totally fine, please always do. See you tomorrow.'

'Bye.'

'Sorry,' said Cress, reddening and putting the phone back in her bag. Jeez, surely the rule against work at the dinner table could be suspended during an *actual* state of emergency. 'Anyway. We should get an early night then. If I'm going to be up for an extra long run tomorrow,' she said.

He sighed and took her hand again, squeezing it. 'That's my girl.'

Felipe stayed at the hospital to finish some paperwork, and when Cressida got home the house was dark. As she passed Leo's study, the shadowy outline of the desk and its oversized iMac monitor was visible. She paused with her hand on the doorknob, inhaling the smell. Books and paper, furniture wax, wood – and there, faintly, the chocolate and camphor trace of her father. How strongly the sensation brought back his image: Leo, throwing himself back from the desk in joy when she appeared at this doorway after school, tossing his glasses and inviting her round to sit on his knee and joking about how glad he was she was here, to let him out of his 'bastille'. Then when she was older, she would sit and they would discuss cases, Leo receiving without the slightest hint of ennui her excitement over *Carbolic Smoke Ball* or some other first year seminal judgment she had learnt that day. The desk had always been spread with papers and the tiny macchiato cups of strong coffee Helena would bring him, but the bookshelves – they were always immaculate, holding a treasure trove of thick, delicious textbooks, on all areas of law. And along the top three, his most prized possession: original, leatherbound *Commonwealth Law Reports*, their ridged red and black spines dating back to 1903. And above them, along the top shelf, in alphabetical order the length of the wall, sat the white spines of every major piece of State and Commonwealth legislation he was ever likely to need, a habit from his days in practice before the internet. He had kept them up to date right up until he went inside. She pulled over the chair to the Cs. There it was. The New South Wales *Crimes Act*. She pulled it down, together with the *Criminal Procedure Act* next to it and – ah, yes – the Regulation. Thinner, next to them, was the Federal *Criminal Code*. No need for that one yet, she thought, feeling involuntary goosebumps. She pulled it out and read its cover, swallowed and pushed it back.

# 12

The dark was pure and soft as Cressida set off for her run the next morning. She loved the fresh, opened-up feeling she had after exercise, and the sense of accomplishment, knowing that for one more day, the guilt of not training would stay in its goddamn box. On her return the house was silent, the pool still as glass as she lowered herself into it. The water was cool on her skin as she watched the first ripples of the day arc outwards and buffet silently against the tiled edge. Tendrils of bright green moss were starting to grow under it, but she decided it would be alright if she didn't put her head under. Inside the shadow of Helena passed, waving sleepily on her way out to get coffees; a takeaway down the road was doing a roaring trade with a cappucino machine on gas bottles.

The whole thing was just so bizarre, Cressida thought as she worked her legs in the water. I mean, how did you *do* that? Go into a bunch of power stations and wipe out a chunk of the entire state's electricity? With a whole lot of conviction about *something*, for a start, she decided. Imagine having that level of certainty about *anything*. The only thing Cressida felt certain about was that she wanted to be a Partner of Hannes Swartling; working to attain it had taken up too much time to think about much else. Towelling off, she put on her cotton robe and dug some sticky notes and the third volume of the road documents Richard had given her out of her bag and sat down by the pool. Then her phone rang. Esma.

'We found her.'

'Oh!' Cress said, the bound document sliding to the floor.

'Well, Brian did. He's been on the phone since 7am. Sorry to call so early. She's at Silverwater.'

'Oh, you gem, thank you! How did you find out?'

'I ended up emailing the journalist who wrote that article you gave me. She replied this morning. I've emailed off an appointment request.'

'Oh wonderful. For when?'

'Well – possibly optimistically, I said Monday! If the power's back by then. I'll keep you posted.'

'You're a genius, Esma, thanks!'

The sliding door opened and Alessa emerged wrapped in a bath sheet. Cressida caught a glimpse of the foam cups and frilly skirt of Helena's bathers underneath as her sister dived in. When she emerged her sister swung onto the shallow pool seat opposite.

'You say a word and I'll kill you.'

'My lips are sealed,' Cressida said, still reading. 'I think you should be flattered though – you look much better than the average octogenarian in those.'

'Zip it,' Alessa said. 'The other pair's in the wash. Anyway, Helena's barely pushing sixty. Well,' she said, tipping her head back so the water smoothed back her hair into a glossy cap, 'you're looking unusually pensive this morning. Pondering the finer points of building law?'

'Mm, something like that,' Cressida said, not looking up. 'How's your corporate float?'

'Hmm?' said Alessa, swimming an arc to the stepladder. 'Oh, fine.' She flipped her hand. 'M & A Singapore is a well oiled machine. I haven't given it a thought. I've been too busy trucking canned food to the stadium with Helena,' she said, rolling her eyes. 'I reckon half the people there just go for the free feed. God I'm so *bored*, Cressida,' she moaned. Then she brightened. 'Maybe I can come into work with you! You must need some help on something?'

Cress laughed. 'You're on holiday.'

'Yeah well. Holidays and I have never really got along. Come on,' she pressed. 'You must have *something* I can turn my fine legal mind to?'

'Sorry,' said Cress. 'All top secret.'

'God, that settles it,' Alessa said, pressing the heel of her hand to her forehead, 'I'm going to die. I can't even go *shopping*.' Her brows knitted in disbelief. 'I mean, that's half the reason I *come* here.' She regarded Cressida, deadpan. '*And* I'm going to have to extend my stay if I ever want to see Dad. I was reduced to reorganising Helena's wardrobe yesterday.'

'You're kidding,' Cress said with a laugh. 'That must have taken all of five minutes.'

'I know – the extent of her array of clothing is pathetic. If only she'd let me talk her into buying something *new*, rather than being everything from Vinnie's. Oh look,' she said, with mock excitement, 'here's another mustard-yellow moth-eaten tweed coat that still stinks of poor person! Every time I come here I try and get her to go shopping with me, and she's not having it.'

'Well. I'm sorry you're finding relaxing so trying. What about a book?'

'I've read them all. Don't worry, I'm going to get started on your wardrobe today. *That* is going to prove more challenging.'

'What? No you're not.'

Alessa smiled sweetly. 'Darling, you're not going to be here – try and stop me. Which is why you should take me into work,' she concluded. 'Anyway,' she said, turning to float on her back, 'you know this is all because I can't get in to see Dad. I'm almost at the point of just going out there, demanding they let me in.'

Cressida looked up. 'What?'

'Don't look at me like that.' Alessa smirked, stretching. 'He might be a criminal, but he's still Dad, and I'm not back for a year. You know he's up for parole in three months. We can't let his whole sentence go by and not visit him.'

'Maybe *you* can't,' Cressida said, anger rising. 'I can. Anyway, I already went once. That was plenty.' She looked back down at the documents. Conversation closed.

'He made a fool of me too, Cressida,' Alessa said, softly. 'Come on. You're being childish. Come with me.'

Childish. She resisted the urge to throw the wad of road papers at her sister's head as it bobbed at the side of the pool. If they all just *forgave* Leo, just acted like nothing had happened, how did anyone know he wouldn't get out of gaol and bloody do it all again? That was her worst fear – that she would finally make Partner and put the whole miserable business behind her, and then he would come out and rip someone else off. Not as a solicitor, of course – the Law Society had red-lined his 1963 name entry in the roll of legal practitioners with stony and well publicised relish – but in some other, horribly creative way that no-one could now predict. How Helena continued to buy the line that he'd done it for the plaintiffs, she didn't know. That's what happened to you when you fell in love: you lost all sense of perspective, any hold on reason; replaced it with blind loyalty to your mate even if the entire world said it wasn't warranted. Thankfully her relationship with Felipe was more mature than that; the two of them were like two sides of a coin, compatible in every way that mattered. And the day she stopped being able to think objectively about his behaviour was the day she'd, well, she didn't know what she'd do, but she was determined never to get there so it didn't matter.

'A *fool* of *you*?' said Cressida. 'Yeah well he nearly landed *me* in gaol, Alessa, so give it a rest.' She shut the document with a snap. 'Anyway I can't. I've got about a month's worth of work to do before next week. Not all of us are on holiday. Enjoy the water.'

Just as she moved to open the sliding door it opened and Felipe stepped out.

'And what work is that, darling?' he asked, stretching and slapping a tune on his naked torso. 'Sounds terrible.' He reached across to kiss her and just as he did so the kitchen lights inside flickered and came on, together with the TV, the oven and the extractor fan over the stove, and moments later her mobile pinged. *Hi!* followed by a carnival of smiley faces and exercise emoticons. Christ, her personal trainer? *Hope you're well! Wow, what a trip that was!!! Training tomorrow?* Cressida's anger at Alessa evaporated, her flounce entirely undermined.

'Oh.' She turned back to her sister. 'The power's back.'

'Oh thank *fuck*,' Alessa exclaimed, and sprang out of the pool. 'That's me in a hot shower.'

'At *last*, I can finally look at my *emails*,' Felipe said emphatically, and squeezed her to him. At the same time they turned to see Helena running for cover to escape the water from the sprinklers that had suddenly come on.

'Ha!' Helena laughed, looking down at her wet clothing in bemusement. 'Well, how about that,' she said, taking a cup from the tray and handing it to him. 'Felipe – short black, dear.'

'Ah – thank you,' he said, taking it, 'but I *think*' – he strained to look past her at the downstairs bathroom – 'this will be even more pleasurable after a *piping hot shower*. Ladies,' he nodded, took the coffee, and was gone.

Helena and Cressida looked at each other and laughed. Then Helena looked into the kitchen and grimaced.

'Here, hold this.' She handed Cressida the tray. She did a quick round of the kitchen turning off the appliances and returned.

'That's better,' she sighed, looking relieved and taking her coffee. 'I had begun to enjoy the silence.'

They stood sipping their drinks and watching the sprinklers scatter drops onto the pool, then two noisy miners swooped down and basked in the artificial rainstorm, weaving their wet heads under the water and flicking drops from their wings. Still watching them Cressida spoke. 'Alessa said she was going to visit Dad today.'

'Oh, of course!' Helena clapped a hand over her mouth. 'Quick, what time is it?' She switched the coffee to the other hand and looked at her watch.

'Um, nearly eight – why?'

'Ai – if we go now we might get to the front of the queue … Cress, come. He misses you so much.' She reached up to touch Cressida's cheek. 'Four years without his youngest daughter's beautiful face.'

'Yeah well,' muttered Cressida, avoiding Helena's gaze. 'He should have thought of that.'

'Oh darling. You know he thought he was doing the right thing. He didn't do it to hurt *you*.' She gave Cressida a pained look. 'He was doing it for them.'

*Them*, Cressida thought. The ubiquitous, conscience-salving, collective pronoun.

'Yeah well,' she said, draining her coffee and checking her watch. 'The road to hell is paved with good intentions. I've got to get organised. See you.' She kissed Helena quickly on the cheek and picked up her phone from the table next to the banana lounge.

'Um Cress,' Helena continued. 'Also …'

Cressida stopped and looked back at her.

'I took the gun back. Thank you.'

Cressida laughed.

'No worries.'

# 13

---

The entrance to Silverwater Women's Correctional Centre was marked by a white sign with large, efficient letters and a row of palm trees that tossed in the wind. At the end of the driveway the prison's high brick walls sat silent, breached by roller doors several storeys high and circled by a cyclone fence. Cressida swung the Fiat into a marked bay near the guard's station and killed the engine.

Across the carpark another, lower building stood, and with her hand on the car door handle Cressida stared at the dashboard, trying not to look. It was useless though, and she gave in. *Fuck.* Four years and still a tiny fissure opened in her chest. *And what are we doing today, Dad? Stuffing cutlery into plastic bags for Qantas? Stop*, she told herself. *He got what he deserved.* Half an hour. *Half an hour and you'll be back in this car and out of here. Get it over with.*

In the end they had secured an appointment for the Tuesday, just over a week after Esma's email. The white file on the seat next to her was thin, containing only a blank Hannes Swartling intake form, the email from the prison yesterday finally accepting the appointment request, and the copy of Joanne's CAN – Court Attendance Notice – Esma had got from Legal Aid, together with some very sketchy Facts. At the back of the file was the newspaper article. Oddly, only one charge was listed on the CAN: *Crimes Act 1900 (NSW) section 93FA – possession of explosives. A person who possesses an explosive in a public place is guilty of an offence. On the evening of Friday 16 March the Accused did possess explosives being forty-five kilograms of C-4 plastic explosive in a public place, being Liddell Power Station.* But it was usual to start soft to secure a defendant, while the police got the evidence they needed for the real case. The papers included an order refusing bail at Muswellbrook Local Court yesterday. Come on, how hard could it be, she asked herself. Regardless of the specifics, her job as Joanne's lawyer was the same in principle as acting for corporates, right? Get instructions, make the prosecution prove everything, and hope for a vaguely humane sentence. That was all anyone could ask of her, wasn't it?

She jammed on a wide-brimmed hat and fell in behind the crowd converging on the footpath; past the security office and up a slight rise to the large concrete building. *Silverwater Women's Correctional Centre*, oversize silver letters on its front wall declared. Correction, Cressida thought as she climbed the hill; good luck with that. Maybe it was different in a women's prison, she decided, looking at the enormous wall. Weren't women likely to be kinder to each other? But then again, she wouldn't know. All her criminal clients so far had been male, and minimum security.

Visiting hours were twelve till three. At the foot of the building people were already waiting, sprawled on the long benches or leaning against the wall, smoking. The men stared at her as she clicked up the footpath; the women gave one glance, sniffed and looked away. She perched on one end of the bench as a rivulet of sweat broke loose from her armpit and ran down her ribs. Dispensing with the jacket wasn't an option, with so many pairs of mirrored sunglasses looking on, but she resolved there and then to get more natural fibres in the wardrobe if she was going to do much more of this outdoor work in a suit thing. At least on road projects, jeans and a hard hat were the norm. Discreetly she found a tissue in her bag and wiped perspiration from under her eyelids, declaring inwardly to the sunglasses – *it's hot, alright, it's **not** because I'm nervous. Even though you are*, she countered. So? There was plenty to be nervous about, wasn't there? What if the client was, well, violent or something? She'd carried forty-five kilos of explosives two kilometres, for God's sake. And you had to be pretty intense to go blowing things up.

Time check: 12.31. How typical of a government institution to be late. Although, hadn't they privatised some of the prisons recently? She'd read that somewhere. Leo had spent his first three weeks here too, she remembered, albeit in the men's section. But then he got sent to minimum, Dawn de Loas, with all the other pansy white-collar criminals. *Ascham.* She still couldn't believe Joanne Fairbank was an Ascham girl. The remand centre at Silverwater would be a long way from the pearls-and-princess-curls life her client had probably had. What a fall from grace. She'd known a couple of Ascham girls who'd gone the 'radical' route in their twenties – horizontally recruited to the Socialist Alliance at Uni, or run off with the ferals, like her brother on *Sea Shepherd* – and they'd all still ended up living on the North Shore and married to some titan of grass seed or the manufacture of pen lids. Joanne was probably feeling like she had bitten off way more than she could chew right now, Cressida reflected. But then, she thought, looking at the hard faces of the women waiting, maybe a private girls' school was just the thing to sort you out for women's maximum security.

The glass doors opened, and with careful nonchalance cigarettes were stubbed out, mobile phones pocketed, and bodies pushed away from walls. Cressida shoved the hat in her bag and dispensed with any pretence of sangfroid; once inside the glacial foyer, she weaved to the front of the queue. A jaded-looking female guard regarded them from behind glass, gesturing to the first person to approach; a woman in a flowered muu-muu with bleached blonde hair and mottled skin lumbered forward and pushed a piece of paper through the slot. The guard said something and the woman began to argue, something about having already been photographed. But she was to be photographed again, and the guard called out for everyone to move back out of the line of sight of the camera so it could be done. Each person gave their papers and was photographed, identity recorded in the biometric iris reader that stood to one side of the counter, and told to reconvene near security. With a sinking feeling Cressida realised that the woman at the counter was the only guard on duty, and everyone's paperwork was to be checked by her first before she would start letting them all through the x-ray machine. And at the pace this guard was going, it would take forever.

When Cressida's turn came she slipped the confirmation email from its plastic sleeve and crossed her fingers inwardly that everything would be in order. The guard regarded her blandly and said she had to be fingerprinted. Cressida complied, deciding it would take longer to argue that they already had her prints on file. Instead she groaned inwardly at the time all this was taking, knowing she'd have to make it up tonight if she was going to get the brief to Sandra prepared and then get anything on the InterConnex T & C draft done at all. At last she was processed and sat down on one of the long red foam couches to wait, while across from her a man in his twenties took up the staring. To distract herself Cressida focused on a sign taped below the window on the guard's office: *Pyjamas MUST be patterned, no lace or plain colours*, next to a picture of short flannelette pyjamas, black covered with white stars. *Buttons must be as shown on this picture. Full length microfibre dressing gowns only.* A fluffy pink garment was demonstrated. *Slippers must have no back or lining. To be provided on receipt of valid prisoner request form only.* Cressida looked around discreetly at what people were carrying. Were there any pyjamas in those bags? What would happen if their characteristics were in breach of the protocol? Would the inmate be required to parade their lacy, plain coloured nightwear with its inappropriate buttons and account for herself? What would the punishment be – pyjama confiscation? But then what would the inmate wear? It was all too complicated to contemplate.

Fortunately at that point the guard came out of her cubicle and stood in front of the entrance to security, a small anteroom one side of the foyer that looked like a clear-glass double-doored lift. In a rattle of plastic and keys she held a card on an elastic band to a sensor and it glowed green.

'Legal first,' the guard said.

In surprise Cressida stood up.

'You're the one here to see Fairbank?'

Cressida nodded. The guard took a lanyard from around her own neck and gave it to her. There was a large plastic circle hanging off it.

'Put this on.' She picked up a walkie-talkie and murmured into it. 'One for special K. Western Entrance.'

Special K? What was that? On the other side of the glass box another guard in pale green descended the stairs, and the first guard nodded towards her.

'She'll take you. Press the button.'

The light glowed blue at Cressida's touch and the doors whooshed open. She stepped inside the box, something invisible considered her, and in a rush of hot air the other side slid open.

'You for Joanne Fairbank?' the next guard said.

'Yes,' said Cressida.

They ascended the stairs and entered an air-conditioned building. Inside people in white jumpsuits sat at tables, looking most of all to Cressida like a company of astronauts waiting for liftoff. Except for their faces, she thought, all of which were watching the door with a naked longing they were trying desperately to conceal. Then she was out on an asphalt open area where groups of women in bottle-green tracksuits sat smoking. Her heels crunching on the stones was way too loud. Feeling their eyes on her she focused on the torch swinging from the guard's belt in front of her. A couple of the women called out. *Hey honey. Give her my love. Nice suit. I'll swap ya.* She nailed a half smile to her face, torn between wanting to ignore them but afraid it would incite aggression, and smiling at the risk of generating ridicule. By the time she had decided which approach to take she had reached the other side of the asphalt and stood, sweat prickling her armpits, as the guard opened another glass door and stood aside to let her through.

They passed along a covered walkway until they reached another building. The guard mounted the steps and opened the door with a pass. They entered a bleak corridor, silent as they walked except for the clip of Cressida's heels and the squeak of the guard's shoes on the linoleum. It was lined with doors with small windows in them, through which Cressida glimpsed the metal frames of hospital beds and, in one, alarmingly, a leather strap on a chain hanging off one side of it. The whole place smelt of bleach and mildew.

'What's this?' said Cressida, her voice echoing off the bare walls.

The guard replied without turning round.

' 'firmary.'

'What, is she sick?'

The guard only glanced back at her, impassive. They emerged into the sunlight again, onto a grassy area that was empty except for a small building on the other side. It was featureless weatherboard except for a letter K on the wall. The guard turned to her.

'You ever visited category five before?'

'No,' said Cressida, trying to sound more confident than she felt. 'But I know the rules.'

The guard turned to face her, taking an at-ease position with her arms crossed.

'Do not touch her, do not give her anything, do not accept anything from her,' she recited. 'Do not discuss anything other than issues pertaining to your legal representation of her.'

'What, not even the weather?'

'Your visit is limited to fifteen minutes. If you feel in danger at any time press that button.' She indicated the item on the lanyard around Cressida's neck. 'I will be within arm's reach outside the door.'

Cressida looked down at the plastic thing.

'Oh for God's sake. It's a panic button?'

'We don't want your family suing us in the event of your death.'

'That is the most absurd thing I've ever heard,' said Cressida, hoping it was. This girl went to *Ascham*, she wanted to say. Spring trips to the south of France and pilates at lunch time, for goodness sake. 'And why do I only get fifteen minutes?'

'The prisoner is on administrative segregation. If you have an issue with that you may take it up with the Governor. Please follow me.'

Cressida stood for a moment, watching after her. How was she supposed to get proper instructions in fifteen minutes? Screw that. She'd talk as long as she needed to; they could drag her out. She squared her shoulders and followed.

The corridor was short, with a closed metal door on the left and then, a short distance away, another. As Cressida followed her heart was racing again. *Oh for God's sake*, she thought, *this is all hype, there is nothing to be afraid of.* The guard stopped outside the second door. With a thud of D-bolts she unlocked it and pulled it ajar, nodded at Cressida and stood back on the other side of the passage. Cressida looked at her, waiting for her to leave.

'That's not necessary you know,' she said, whispering and not sure why. 'You can move further down the corridor.'

The guard just looked at her.

'If I've only got fifteen minutes at least give us some privacy.'

The guard stayed put, and Cressida sighed and turned back to the door. She put her hand on the outer casing. The door itself was five inches thick. *Come on*, she told herself, *you know how to do this.* She took a deep breath and knocked with conscious firmness. The sound it made was barely audible. She tried again and hurt her knuckles. She gave up and spoke through the gap.

'Hello? Ms Fairbank? It's Cressida Mitsok. From Hannes Swartling. We have an appointment?'

No answer. She spoke louder. 'The law firm?'

She peeked in. On the table an arm was visible. It wore a thin string bracelet, and there was a spiral tattoo on the wrist. She slapped on the door, feeling ridiculous, but it still made only a muted clap. She opened it enough to enter and looked in.

The occupant had her head on one forearm, asleep on the desk. She wore an orange jumpsuit that still had the box creases on it, and dangling from the back of the collar was a tiny silver set of keys. The other arm was in a heavy cast supported by a sling. Cressida's gaze strayed to her ankles. Around them were inch-thick chains, the links of another snaking to her wrists on the table, one running up to the white of the cast. Cressida paused, a sluice of fear hitting the back of her throat. Why would they put those on her, if she wasn't dangerous?

But when she pressed in further, feeling ridiculous but not wanting to startle her, the woman's face in repose looked anything but dangerous.

The first noticeable thing was that she looked like Brian. There was that same delicate, aristocratic nose, the fine bow-shaped mouth; cheekbones that looked a little bit Native American. Her face was even more childlike than in the photo on the paper, but as well as the pink, there were dark lines angling down from the inner corners of her eyes, and a dressing plastered the side of her sweat-damp forehead. Under the short messy dreadlocks her blonde hair was dyed pink in some places and hacked close to her scalp in others. Round her neck under the jumpsuit were several woven necklaces. Against the white walls, the hard laminex of the desk and the medieval whiff of the chains, the whole effect was of some sort of soft wild creature chastened by captivity, a piece of mangy almost-roadkill brought into hospital for rehab but tranquilised to stop her biting someone.

Cressida stood wondering what to do. She'd never had a sleeping client before.

Eventually she sat down on the chair on the opposite side of the desk, her zipped compendium containing the file on her lap. The room was stuffy, and so small their knees were nearly touching. She swallowed, concerned even that small noise would be enough to wake the other occupant up, at the same time wondering why she was so worried when that was exactly what needed to happen. There wasn't much point spending fifteen minutes with her asleep, was there? *Come on, get a grip on yourself. Shackles, panic button, guard outside; what more do you want?* She cleared her throat. Nothing happened, and in the silence she listened to Joanne's breathing. But the longer she sat there the more awkward it felt. In, out, in, out. She tried to match her breathing, partly to calm herself and make it more real. Then a door slammed outside and the inmate sat up with a jerk, saw Cressida, and yelled, knocking the chair over. The guard burst in just as Joanne threw herself back from the desk in a crash of the chain on laminex, hands raised.

'It's fine, it's fine,' Cressida yelled at the guard. To Joanne, she said, 'Take it easy. Cressida Mitsok.' She righted the chair and sat down in it. 'From Hannes Swartling.'

'Christ,' Joanne said, slumping and rubbing her eyes. Then her face broke into a grin and Cress nearly kissed her with the relief of it. 'Gave me a heart attack.'

The guard stopped and glared at Cressida.

'Sorry,' she said. The guard sighed and went back out again.

'I must have fell asleep,' said Joanne. 'They were full-on grilling me till four this morning. Oh my God it is *so hot in here*' she yelled, raising the bandaged arm to her forehead. Then she frowned, focusing on Cressida. 'Sorry, who are you again? I've been talking to *so many people.*'

'Cressida Mitsok,' Cressida said, slipping a name card from its silver case and holding it out to her. She was annoyed to notice her hand was shaking. *Surgeons' hands, surgeons' hands*, she recited inwardly. *Pretend they're Felipe's.* 'Your dad sent me. Brian Prendergast.'

The woman stared at her.

'My *dad* sent you?' She exhaled. 'Wow. How did he know I was here?' She reached across and took Cressida's card with her left hand. This was much better, thought Cressida. They were talking.

'You're kidding me,' Cressida said. 'Well you're all over the papers for starters; he'd have to be on Planet Zorg not to hear about it. What happened to your arm?'

'Oh.' The woman glanced down. 'I slipped on the way out the cooling pipe. I bashed it on the side and then the force of the water … Can you get me a drink? I'm fucking parched.'

'Oh. Sure. Um, excuse me?' Cressida called out to the corridor, standing up. 'My client wants a drink of water.'

There was a pause, and then the guard answered, 'She can have one back in the cell.'

'I can't fucking talk to my lawyer with a dry mouth,' Joanne yelled. They both waited for a response, but none came. She sniffed noisily and stared at Cressida. 'Interrogation,' she said, shaking her head. 'Takes it out of a girl.' The smile broke through again. It transformed her whole face, exposing a rack of perfect white teeth; beneath the dreadlocks, for a moment the North Shore girl was still there. That skin like fine suede, Cressida thought, plump with top-class nutrition and an abiding hat rule from birth. She found herself smiling back involuntarily.

Outside there was a sigh and a creak of shoe leather.

'You'll need to come out.'

'Oh for God's sake,' Cressida said, rolling her eyes. She stood up. 'Is this cutting into my fifteen minutes?'

She picked up the file and her bag and waited outside while the guard went to the kitchen. She heard him talking into a walkie-talkie. Five minutes later another guard appeared at the front door to the unit with a bottle of water.

'What was wrong with a cup from the kitchen?' said Cressida, dryly.

'Potential weapon,' the guard said, shouldering open the door again. 'Sharp edges.' She unscrewed the bottle and handed it to Joanne, and Cressida waited while she glugged the water. Then the guard took the bottle back and nodded to Cressida, who rolled her eyes again and pushed herself off the wall. How much damage would Joanne have done with an empty plastic bottle? She sat down again.

'Fuck, that's a whole lot better,' said Joanne, grinning and wiping her mouth with the back of her hand.

'Are you getting care for the arm?' said Cressida, deciding to start with the pastoral angle. 'I mean, did they set it properly and things?' *And what the hell is with those chains?*

'Oh I had that done before I turned myself in,' she said. 'Mate of mine.'

'Oh. Okay.' Some accessory after the fact. Let's not even go there, she thought. Not yet. 'Well anyway, I won't keep you long.' She unzipped her metallic pencil case and found a pen.

'You'll be happy to know your dad has organised Sandra Crane as your SC.' She pulled Sandra's business card from the inside cover of the compendium. Joanne looked at it with only vague interest. 'Sydney's, possibly Australia and the world's, best defence lawyer,' Cressida explained. 'Bizarrely, your father has asked me to be your instructing solicitor. If that's okay with you,' she added.

'Yeah sure.' Joanne shrugged. 'What about bail? They refused it, of course – don't worry, I was expecting that. But the solicitor at the court said something about I could appeal it. And when do I get to get out of this dog box, by the way?' She looked at Cressida, head cocked, and made a sort of musical noise, then shook her head like a dog shaking off water. Her dreadlocks danced. 'If I'm going to be here for a while I want to make some friends,' she said.

'Um …' said Cressida. 'I think they'll keep you in segro for a bit. At least until they classify you. That's … that's not something we can challenge with bail I'm afraid. It's up to them where they put you.'

'Oh. Oh well. I've already been here for a week. What's a few more days? The walls in my cell have padding,' she laughed. 'It's like they think I'm nuts or something. I think I annoyed them though. Kept saying the same thing. Admitting to everything, basically. I think they expected more of a fight,' she said.

Cress stared at her and swallowed. 'You told them everything?'

'Yeah.' Joanne laughed again. 'Why wouldn't I? I had nothing to hide. I *meant* to do it, remember?'

*Jesus Christ*, thought Cressida, trying not to let the alarm show on her face. Well. The only thing for it was to get the record of interview for each one she'd done and hope for minimal hand grenades waiting in them. Unless … unless there'd been no recordings because of the power failure. Oh God. This was getting worse by the minute. *Get ROI*, she wrote on the notepad in her compendium. *Research interview exclusions.*

Cressida took a deep breath and changed topic. 'Okay. On that padded cell you mentioned. Now. Why do you think they would have put you there?'

'What? Am I crazy, you mean?' Joanne snorted. 'Hah. No.'

'So no treating doctor at the moment or anything,' Cressida said, slowly. 'I mean, before you got here.'

'No.'

'Sorry. I just have to ask.'

'Well,' Joanne sighed, 'there *was* a shrink when I left the army. But not anymore.'

'And what was that about?'

Joanne shrugged. 'Nothing.' She paused, and Cressida waited. 'It fucks you up, alright?' Joanne continued, holding Cressida's gaze. 'Seeing dead people. Seeing people kill them. What do you expect?'

'You were in the army?'

'Yeah. Well. Anyway, I'm over it now. I left, and that's why I'm fine. It only screws you up permanently if you don't get out. It's feeling trapped that gives them PTSD, you know. Feeling like they can't escape the horror. I did.'

*And then you blew up a power station. No dramas.*

'I know what you're thinking,' Joanne continued with another laugh. 'The shit from the army's not why I did it. I was one hundred per cent stone-cold rational when I decided we'd blow up Liddell.'

That's by definition debatable, thought Cressida, but said nothing. Aloud, she said, 'Well anyway, there's absolutely zilch chance of getting bailed I'm afraid. Once we get the brief of evidence though, we can start tearing it to shreds.'

'Oh that won't be necessary,' Joanne said with a yawn. 'I'm pleading guilty.'

Cressida looked at her. 'Guilty.'

Joanne frowned slightly, then laughed. 'Of course,' she said. 'Why bother making the police prove it? I did it on purpose. I *wanted* to do it. Sorry, I thought Dad would have told you that.' She sighed and scratched her armpit. 'He doesn't know much about me, but I would have thought he'd work *that* out.'

'But ...don't you want to wait and see what all the charges are before you decide?'

'Not really,' said Joanne. 'I already know what they'll be.' She scratched the inside of one ear with a finger vigorously, then inspected the spoils. 'The gist of them anyway. Blowing shit up. I didn't kill anyone at the plant though' she said, suddenly intense. 'They do know that, don't they?'

'I ... I don't know. Although ...' Cressida thought back to the newspaper article and pulled it out of the back of the file. 'I do remember reading that there had been no deaths at Liddell.'

'Right,' Joanne said, visibly relaxing. 'Good.'

Cressida lay the article on the table. Joanne clocked what it was and grabbed it.

'What the fuck?' she said, staring at the caption under her photo: *Police expect to lay terrorism charges shortly*. 'Terrorism? That's fucking absurd. Oh my God, now I've seen everything.' She laughed, slapping the paper down on the table. 'Don't let a good story get in the way of the truth, right? Bloody hell. You know it's *this* type of reporting that's got us in this fucking shitstorm,' she said. 'If newspapers had bothered to tell the truth about climate change, instead of being bought off by every stinking coal corporate in the country, the world would have taken action long ago. God that's pathetic.' She tossed the page back to Cress. 'Jesus. God it's so *hot*. Can you ask them to get some fucking air conditioning on in here?'

'But Joanne,' Cressida began, 'like it says – it's very likely they *will* charge you with terrorism. If they haven't already. Surely you knew that.'

'Nah,' Joanne said, shaking her head, laughing. 'But that's ridiculous. I blew shit up. How is that terrorism?'

'Joanne,' Cressida began. 'When they were interviewing you – did they go on about intention at all? The police?'

'What, you mean about why I did it?'

'Yes.'

'Sure,' she said, folding her arms awkwardly over the cast. 'And I told them. To stop climate change of course. Contribute to stopping it, anyway. I imagine there'll be copycat acts around the world,' she said, airily. 'If there haven't been already. Have there?'

'I don't mean that. Look I think we can all accept that you did it to "advance a political or ideological cause", right? But what—'

'What?' said Joanne. 'No! That's not true at all. I did it to advance what's right. To call it "political" – that makes it sound like it was a … a choice.'

'No it doesn't,' sighed Cressida. 'Anyway, even if it wasn't political, it *was* ideological—'

'Wrong again,' Joanne retorted. 'You make us sound like some kind of extremists. We were just doing what was *necessary*.'

'Joanne, that's fucking crazy,' Cressida said. 'But look, I don't need to debate that with you—'

'Well I do. Sorry,' she said, irritably. 'How on earth can you be my lawyer if you don't even believe in what we did?'

Cressida sighed. 'It's beside the point what I think of what you did. In fact it's better if I don't "believe in it", as you put it, because *most* people wouldn't agree with it even if you gave them a million bucks. And it's "most people" that's going to be on the jury. But anyway,' she said, kicking herself for starting an argument, 'we can wait to sort all that out once we've got a formal idea of all the charges. The main thing I need to do today is' – she unclipped the Hannes Swartling intake form from her folder – 'have you fill this out, get your instructions to file a bail appeal, appear at the first mention in three weeks or so on no plea, and seek orders for the brief. Oh – and here's the CAN – the Court Attendance Notice. Well, the only one so far.' She slid the paper across to her.

'No,' Joanne said.

'Sorry?'

'I don't want you acting for me if you don't believe in what I did.'

Cressida stared at her. 'Okaaaay …' She waited a moment for her to say more, then asked, 'Who do you propose getting to act for you, then?'

'I don't know' – Joanne shrugged – 'Legal Aid. They were fine at the bail hearing. They do this sort of thing, don't they?'

'Sure.' Cressida shrugged in return. 'You can probably even get the forms from the guards in here.' She couldn't very well do what Brian wanted if the client refused. She stood up. 'Nice meeting you.'

'They'll have some shit-hot barrister too, won't they,' Joanne said, sticking her chin out.

'I have no idea. Not one that's just got a Syrian warlord off crimes against humanity,' she said, 'but an adequate one nonetheless. Probably even a good one. I'm assuming the means test won't apply to you because you're incarcerated, but if it did, would you qualify?'

'What means test?'

Cressida shrugged. 'They have a means test for Legal Aid. But they don't know about your dad, and I assume you're not loaded yourself, so you'll probably be fine.'

Joanne stared at Cressida. Then she looked away, chewing on her lip.

'Actually I … He did give me some money a while ago. When I turned twenty-one. Trying to suck up to me,' she said, top lip curling.

'How much money?'

'Thirty thousand.'

Cressida sat back in the chair.

'Do you still have it?'

'Um, yes … but I'm giving it to someone. At least, I was, before this happened,' she said, her face sad.

'Well it's too late now, isn't it,' said Cressida.

'Can you do it for me? If I give you my details?'

'What, operate your bank account so as to defraud Legal Aid, you mean?'

'It wouldn't be defrauding it, would it? I mean, it's not like I'll still have it.'

'Joanne,' Cressida said firmly, 'No. Anyway, you shouldn't be giving out your bank passwords.' She sighed and dragged out the form again. 'Shall we proceed?'

Joanne slumped into her seat, regarding her. Then she sighed and rolled her eyes. 'Okay.'

*Big of you*, Cress thought.

'Any other names you have been known by?'

'Yeah,' said Joanne. 'Andromeda Numbat Proximus Rigil. Fairbank.'

Cressida took a deep breath and wrote it in the space.

'By deed poll?'

'Yeah. But then I took out the Numbat bit. It made it too much of a mouthful. And folks call me Andy.'

'Andy. Okay. Date of birth?'

'Twelve October 1997.'

*Wow*, Cressida thought, writing it down. Five years ago, the woman in front of her would have been in her school uniform, that awful Ascham checked thing with sleeves she folded up. Loner? Maybe. Wouldn't that fit the profile? Loner until she found a place to belong, with the terrorists? Could be.

'What?' said Joanne. 'Why are you staring?'

'Hmm? Oh, nothing. Sorry.' She looked back at the Hannes Swartling form. The rest was easy. *Address: In custody – MRRC, Silverwater. Email: N/A. Phone: N/A. Mobile phone: N/A. Occupation:* ... Prisoner? That seemed a bit uncharitable. Terrorist? Saboteur?

'Did you have a job at all?' she said. 'Before last week, I mean?'

'Yeah course,' Joanne said with a laugh. 'I was a Level 3 childcare worker.'

'*Child*care worker?'

'Sure,' Joanne said, her eyes soft. 'Frogstomp Early Learning, Clovelly.'

'Right.'

'And before that, as I said before, I was in the army.'

Wow, this woman was *full* of surprises, Cressida thought, trying to get a vibe for trauma. Maybe Sandra might be able to make something of that, for a case on diminished responsibility by abnormality of mind. Or at least sentence mitigation. She pulled out her notebook.

'Which section?'

'Iraq. Task Force Taji 5.'

'What's that?'

'Us and the Kiwis. Training Iraqis how not to blow themselves up.'

Hmm. Possible. She'd draft a consent form for next time, to get the army's files on her.

'Okay great. Thanks.' She wrote in 'childcare worker'. *Type of legal problem: criminal. Income source:* ... Prison wages? That one could be left blank. What about the signature? She wrote in the space 'injured therefore unable to sign'.

'So, right now – let's talk about the charges.' She opened to the CAN. 'It's weird, but the police have only got you up on one charge so far. Possessing explosives. Section 93FA.'

She held the document out to Joanne, but Joanne ignored it and pushed herself away from the desk. The chains scraped on the laminate.

'I can't remember what they said,' she said. 'I thought there were a bunch of them. Or maybe that's just what they *said* they were going to do ...' She petered out, rubbing her eyes. 'Sorry.'

'The police mentioned further charges?'

'Sabotage and shit, I think?'

'Well this one's just possession of explosives at the moment,' said Cress. 'I think we can expect more. I mean, not just terrorism.' When Joanne bristled again she hastened to explain. 'I mean – more under the New South Wales *Crimes Act* as well.'

'What?' Her eyes focused back on Cressida. 'Oh. Sure.'

'Any idea why they've charged you with this in particular?'

Joanne looked at her flatly. 'Er, yes.'

Cressida blushed. 'What I mean is – did they do any tests at the station when you turned yourself in, or since? Why possession in particular? I mean, rather than the whole enchilada. Sabotage.'

'Yeah,' Joanne said, frowning. 'It was weird actually. I was in the middle of being interviewed—'

'Sorry, I have to ask – did you consent to this interview?' Then she told herself not to ask so many questions at once. The girl was finding it hard enough to concentrate as it was.

Joanne shrugged. 'Yeah. I have nothing to hide.'

'Go on.'

'Well. There were heaps of interviews. Waking me up in the middle of the night was their favourite. I started to get pretty cranky about that.'

Cress frowned. 'In the middle of the night?'

'Yeah. That happened heaps.'

Cress wrote herself a note to ask about conditions while she was in custody. Later though. She needed to get on with the legal stuff right now.

'Ok, and then in one of those interviews,' she prompted.

'Oh yeah – well they came in with one of those wandy things. Like you have at airports. Asked me if I minded if they took a sample from my clothing.'

'And did you?'

'No. I'd already told them I blew up Liddell. I didn't care if they knew. It was C-4 though, and I wasn't anywhere near the blast when it happened. Don't know how they got anything.'

'Were you wearing the same clothing? As on Friday night?'

'Um …' Joanne paused. 'Yeah I was, actually.'

Cress sighed. Oh well. On one level it made her job easier: there would be little doubt about the possession aspect.

'Okay. Well. This charge – possession of explosives, without lawful excuse. Presumably you didn't have one?'

'Yeah,' said Joanne, and stuck out her chin in the way Cress was becoming familiar with, 'protection of Mother Earth.'

Cress sighed. 'Yes. But under some, you know, recognised law of Australia?'

'No.'

'Okay. So. If you admitted in your ERISP – in the interview – that you were at Liddell and had explosives, well …' *You're cooked*, she thought. Unless they could challenge it on the public place bit. Wasn't Liddell private property? Maybe that was the angle. For now, anyway; but it did seem likely they'd drop this charge eventually, once they had evidence for others.

'I didn't admit to the explosives,' said Joanne, and smirked. 'I thought it was obvious. But yes – I did admit to being there. At 1900 hours on Friday 16 March blah blah. So I guess with that and their little wandy thing,' she said, 'voilà section 93F' – she leaned forward to check the section number on the CAN – 'A'.

'Mm,' nodded Cressida, concealing annoyance. Could she be any more glib about all this? 'So anyway, section 93FA is what's called a Table offence,' continued Cressida. 'Means you can choose whether to make the Prosecution do it on indictment or not. Assuming their brief establishes the elements, I mean.'

'Whoa whoa whoa,' Joanne interrupted, getting louder with each repetition. 'C'mon sister, speak in plain English. What's a Table offence or whatever and why do I care?' She stuck her chin out again. 'I'm pleading guilty, remember?'

'I know. Look, here's the thing. That section 93FA is a pretty – no, a very – light-on charge to give someone who's just admitted to blowing up a piece of major infrastructure. So, it's pretty much guaranteed there's more coming. And, well, we don't want to go around giving them free guilty pleas when we may … well' – she stopped for emphasis – 'need them.'

'Need them.'

'To negotiate down others.' She sighed. 'When they charge you with seven different terrorism offences, for example.'

Joanne clenched her teeth and spoke through them, biting out the words, 'That's not going to happen.'

Cressida barrelled on. 'Besides which, I'm not advising you on plea until we've seen the police brief. Their evidence,' she clarified. 'And there will probably be some strictly indictable ones as well. I mean – more serious charges they have to do by indictment – which is just, like, a full document from the Crown where they formally establish the elements of their case against you.' *I think.* White-collar crime was never strictly indictable. This was where she really wished she had a phone-a-friend.

'I'm already confused.'

'I know,' Cress conceded. 'I'm sorry. It's just very confusing. There are two separate processes depending on how serious the charge is, basically. Your section 93FA is a minor one, and their brief on that is due in' – she checked the date on her watch again – 'nine weeks if they follow the Practice Note. So – at the mention, which is four weeks from charge' – she checked the CAN – 'Monday three weeks away; that's your first court appearance – I propose we not enter a plea, have a brief on the section 93FA charge ordered, and file a motion to have the refusal of bail overturned. How does that sound?'

'That sounds awesome,' Joanne said. There was that rack of whites again. Instant North Shore princess.

'It's very unlikely we'll succeed on that though,' Cress said gently. A bail appeal? On one view, she was better off not even mentioning it – just because it would then be so much more devastating if an appeal was denied. 'There's generally a benefit in pleading guilty early if you're going to, but no-one's going to hold it against you if you at least wait for the brief. Their evidence against you, I mean.'

Joanne shrugged. 'Yeah fine. Whatever you think.'

Cressida clipped the intake form back into the folder. 'The only other thing I was going to do was ask you whether there's anything you need,' she said. 'In here, I mean.'

'Oh,' Joanne said, and smiled. 'Well, now that you mention it … Can you bring in some chocolate? You have to buy it on some dumb thing called *buyup* in here, and that's not till Friday. And … if it's not too much to ask, some Vicco toothpaste. Have you heard of it?'

'No,' Cressida said.

Joanne rolled her eyes. 'V – i – c – c – o,' she spelled for Cressida, who wrote it down. 'It's Ayurvedic and vegan. They've only got that chemical shit in here. I'd rather gouge out my eyeballs than use that.'

'Um, sure – where do I get that?' Was toothpaste anything other than vegan, she wondered, reading the name.

'Any health food store,' said Joanne. 'You should try it. The supermarket stuff is poisoning your brain.'

'Oh. Right. Okay,' she said, thinking maybe this woman was just crazy. She wrote it down and made a quick note of the instructions to file the bail appeal, then looked at her watch. Perfect. Just shy of twenty minutes. But Joanne slouched back, with the demeanour of someone settling in for a chat.

'So what'd my dad say?' she said.

'Not much,' Cressida said briskly, sliding the notebook into the file folder. 'But he's very concerned about you.'

Joanne grunted. Her eyes strayed to the article still on the table, and disgust curled around her mouth again.

'Have you … has there been any coverage of the others? In the paper, I mean? Flame, Skydark?'

*This is where I should stop listening*, Cressida thought.

'What others?' she asked. Best not to allow any discussion of co-accused at this point. *Don't ask any more of her than you need to.* It kept her mind clean for disputing the police case down the track. 'As far as I knew, there was only you.' And having to cease acting for knowing facts going to conspiracy before the police did might be her own preference, but Brian would go nuts.

Joanne looked at her quizzically, then smiled.

'Oh. Yes of course. Well anyway, if you see anything, can you let me know? I haven't seen any of ... *them* ... since Friday night. We all ...' – she sighed – 'we all went straight into hiding.'

Friday night. The memory of the failed partnership vote sprang back.

'Can I just ask one question?' Cressida said, getting up. 'Why that Friday night?'

'I don't know,' Joanne said. 'It just turned out that way. Why?'

'Oh nothing. The lights just happened to go off in the most important meeting of my career, that's all.'

'Oh,' Joanne said. 'Sorry. Yeah I know there were a lot of people inconvenienced. That was never our intention. Except that it was, because the convenience of coal-fired power is exactly what's killing us.' She looked at Cressida as if willing her to argue.

'I'll call you when they send through the other charges,' she said, and left.

# 14

Meanwhile, a few blocks from Cressida's firm, David Butcher was looking at the drooping peace lily on his office windowsill and, for the seventh time that morning, making a mental note to water it. He had taken seven phone calls that morning, and always, always he reminded himself to water it when he was on the phone, because it was the only time he looked out the window. The lily was at the perfect spot on the windowsill to catch his gaze as he had his ear bent by another defence lawyer, simultaneously watching the outside world and asking himself what the normal people were doing. A gift from his receptionist, Lois, in her continued efforts to help him 'get a life', as she put it, the lily was now down to two remaining leaves, the brightly optimistic white flower that had once thrust up from its depths rendered a weak and flaccid browning envelope on the end of a stem. It had even lasted his week-long absence, valiantly surviving waterless as the entire Commonwealth Department of Public Prosecutions closed and everyone flailed about, the machine of prosecution momentarily stalled by the lack of electricity to power it. It had almost given him vertigo, the sudden halt – from relentless paperwork and court attendances, phones that rang off the hook and an ever-growing pile of files on the end of his desk – and he'd found himself suddenly just wandering about at home, sort of furtively gardening and drinking consecutive cups of tea he'd made for himself and his wife on the camp stove, as if waiting for something to happen. He would be standing in the kitchen admiring the crocuses and then remember an email he hadn't replied to or a phone call he hadn't returned, and put down the tea in a panic to reach for his computer or mobile, only then remembering that the world had temporarily stopped and, in fact, nothing was required of him. The sense of growing acceptance of impotence was delicious. It had been five years since he'd had a holiday, and this one, the email from HR had said, wouldn't even be eating into his leave. On the third day he had even considered just packing his field book and driving, heading to the Watagans or somewhere with Tania to find some of the last specimens for the *Rhizopogan* collection. But the weather was over forty degrees, and instead he spent three glorious days catching up on his fungi photos, cataloguing the last of the *Lenzites* he'd found at Strickland State Forest in the autumn. The power was being largely diverted from Queensland and was still unreliable, but miraculously there had been no outages that day so far. Regarding the peace lily with sympathy, he was flooded with renewed determination to get control of his life; this time – *this* time – when he got off the phone, he would get up, walk to the kitchenette, return with a glass of water and empty it *into the pot plant*. He *would* water it. It was ridiculous. Surely he had time in his day to *water a pot plant*. In fact, he was going to write himself a note. That way he wouldn't forget. *WATER PLANT*, he wrote. There. It was certain to happen now. *Don't worry, plant*, he communicated silently, *it's your lucky day*. He looked at the dog-eared school photo of his teenage son tacked to the corner of his computer screen. It helped, to talk to him throughout the day, and he did so now. *There's life in us yet, Dan*, he telegraphed. With fresh enthusiasm he returned to the caller.

'What did you say your name was again?' he said, interrupting the speaker.

There was a heavy sigh. 'Philips. Andrew Philips.'

'Well, Mr Philips, I'm sorry, but it is the CDPP's policy not to take plea bargains. Not in the interests of justice to the victim and, more often than not, bad for the defendant. If you and your firm have an issue with this I suggest that you do what I tell all the other defence lawyers from big firms to do when I have this conversation, and that's take it up with the Crown Solicitor. Once you've brushed up on the CDPP policy on this, which is, handily,' he said, brightly, 'on our website. Thanks for calling.' Resisting the urge to mimic static into the phone he hung up and stared at the unit. There was something he had to remember to do. Put a court date in his diary? He checked his electronic calendar. No, they were all in there, colour coded the way he liked it. Mention, committal, sentence hearing, trial. It made his calendar look like the gay pride flag on his son's bedroom door, of course, and also gave the impression he was going to be in court until he was seventy, but it helped. He looked down at his desk. He'd written a note ... something he was reminding himself to do. Then the phone rang. Resisting the urge to bang his head on the desk he sighed and picked it up again.

'David Butcher.'

'Good morning, Mr Butcher. My name's Cressida Mitsok. I'm the solicitor acting for Joanne Fairbank.'

Fairbank. That sounded familiar.

'Is that right,' he said. 'Give me a sec ...' He dug under the pile of files on the end of his desk. One had FAI along the spine and he pulled it out. Ah. Well well. The red edge. It had arrived on his desk this morning, together with five others from the phone bail applications during the blackout. He flicked to the back and found the CAN. Explosives. Section 93FA.

'Yes?' he said.

'I was wondering,' she said, 'are you intending to charge her with terrorism?'

David paused, sitting back in his chair.

'I'm sorry?'

'Well, it's just – she's only been charged with possessing explosives at the moment, which seems very, well, you know, *light on* in the circumstances ...'

'And what circumstances might those be, Ms ... Mitsok, was it?' Now, why was *that* name familiar, he wondered. Didn't sound like a defence lawyer though, asking a question like that. Usually they called to ask him to drop charges, not imply he should add them.

'Um ... well, you know, she ...' The speaker coughed and there was a long pause, then she continued, 'We – that is, my client was very surprised to read in the paper that she's being charged with terrorism. Can you confirm that?'

Ah. Hence the red edge.

'I'm sorry, Ms Mitsok, but the decision about all charges to be laid has not been made yet, I'm afraid. Despite what the papers may say they know.'

'So – none proposed at the moment?'

'Look, I'm very sorry but I'm not at liberty to say anything further.'

The woman sighed. 'Why not?'

'Um, because, like I said ... that decision hasn't been made yet.'

'When will it be made?'

'I have no idea.'

'Well anyway,' the woman said, her tone abruptly affecting nonchalance, 'if she *were* to be charged with terrorism – the Commonwealth might like to know that she *does* intend to plead guilty on certain State charges … were that of any interest to your state colleagues, of course. Because if it *was*, I assume we could then discuss' – she took an audible deep breath – 'options.'

David laughed. *Well good for you, anyway*, he thought. That put a new meaning to starting early. 'Guess you'll be the first to know.'

'I'm authorised to accept service of all court documents for Ms Fairbank and accept service by email. I'll send one to you so you have my address. By the way, any idea why she's in a psych ward?'

Psych ward. Interesting. He'd ask Lois to get him updated case law on mental impairment. Of course, it could be just because they had nowhere else to put her in isolation in the gaol, he mused. Had there even been a female terrorist defendant before?

'Nope,' he said. 'Why don't you ask her? Maybe they've just never had a female Category 5 before.'

'But she's not Category 5,' said the defence lawyer. 'She's just criminal damage at the moment.'

David laughed. 'I think that's splitting hairs, Ms Mitsok.'

'Hardly,' she said. 'She's in solitary in a psychiatric ward. Sorry, what was your name?'

'David Butcher,' he said. Suddenly he felt tired again, and looked across at the peace lily. That's right. The reminder note had been to *water it*.

'Well, Mr Butcher, on these charges she should just be on maximum security remand. Category 5 segro is complete overkill and inhumane.'

Ah, these passionate defence lawyers, he thought. As if he had any control over *that*.

'That's as may be, Ms Mitsok,' he said with a sigh, 'but it's nothing to do with me. You'll have to write to the prison governor. Nice talking to you. Bye.'

He hung up and the phone rang again. That plant really wasn't going to get any today, he thought, despondent on its behalf.

'David,' a familiar voice said. One of the senior NSW Police officers at Central. 'How's things. Sent you an email. Did you get that red edge?'

'Popular file this morning,' said David, pulling it back to the blotter in front of him. 'Just a sec.'

He sorted his emails by 'From' and found the one. *[SEC-UNCLASSIFIED] [Joanne FAIRBANK – Charges]* – and then a string of sets of numbers after a letter. Attached was a draft CAN on further charges. He opened it.

'Yep. Got it.'

'Good stuff. No rush, but I'm told the Feds are preparing a brief. Just getting you in the loop on what's happening state side.'

'A lot of charges there,' he said, counting. 'Seven. All of them? Or is this just a bit of a fishing expedition right now?'

'It was a big crime,' the police officer said, a note of dry humour in his voice.

'And you're intending pressing these even if terror charges are brought?'

'I expect so.'

'Fun times. Okay. I'm meeting with counsel next week. When do you think you can get the brief to me?'

The officer gave a dry laugh. 'Not by then I'm afraid. But how about we send you what we've got.'

'Love that.'

'Done. Thanks.'

He turned back to the email to read it properly but the phone rang again, this time his receptionist.

'Hi, David. I've got the Minister on the line.'

David frowned.

'The Minister? The Police Minister? Or the Attorney-General?'

'Um ... neither. Julie Quentin.'

'Federal Minister for Home Affairs Julie Quentin?'

'Seems so.'

'Um, right ...' he said, everything suddenly going very quiet in his head. 'Put her through.'

The line clicked and nothing happened. He began awkwardly into the silence.

'Um – Ms Quentin?'

'David, hi, it's Julie,' came a set of rounded vowels. 'You're well?'

'Um – yes,' he fumbled, reaching for a notepad and pen. It was just a reflex. He had a hunch that whatever she was going to be saying, he would not be writing it down. 'You?'

'Calling about this Fairbank matter. Trust you're prosecuting?'

'Sorry?'

'On terrorism, I mean?'

'Um, Minister – that's – that's fairly complicated. We're still waiting on the brief.'

'And?'

'Well, we haven't decided yet.'

'David?' She chuckled. 'Yes you have. Goodbye.'

He looked at the receiver, beeping at him, and slowly put it down.

# 15

In the Silverwater carpark, Cressida hung up the phone and sat back with her eyes closed, waiting for her heart to slow. She leaned forward and turned the air conditioning up to full bore, picked up the bottle of water in the footwell and downed the lot. *Food*, she thought, *I need food.* There had to be some somewhere. She opened her bag and tipped it up, searching for a cracker or some dried fruit. Nothing. She looked across the carpark. On the other side of the path, a green pennant snapped in the breeze, next to a sandwich board with an icecream ad on it. She jammed on her hat again and got out of the car. Up some steps the glass-walled cafe's interior was dark and empty, but an Open sign hung on the door. She pushed it and made for the fridge. There was one dry-looking fruit salad left, next to a wan-looking ham and salad roll. She bought both.

'Let me guess,' the clerk at the counter said when she approached. 'Legal.'

He wore bottle-green tracksuit pants and a poloshirt. *And what are you in for?* she wanted to ask. They had inmates from Dawn de Loas in here on cafe detail sometimes. Part of integrating them back into the community before release. But she'd been a lawyer long enough to know that wasn't the sort of question you asked.

'Something like that,' she said, handing him the money, and left.

Chewing on the roll in the car again she felt calmer. Well, at least the prosecutor hadn't yelled at her, or worse, laughed. Not much, anyway. Or said the words that were tolling in her own head – why the hell are *you* acting for this woman, you're *not qualified* etc. Anyway, Cressida thought as she started the car, the quicker they could get the charges reduced on a guilty plea the quicker she could get back to her real job. What a relief that would be.

On the drive back to the office Cressida hatched a plan. She could ask Esme to do the initial leg work on Fairbank – track down the Legal Aid solicitor, get the rest of the papers, type up the authority form for her army records, e-file her a Notice of Appearance, and draft the motion on the bail appeal. Then she'd pack it all away to read tonight and spend the afternoon on the road project T & C draft. There was a catchup on the project booked with solicitors from all three offices for early next week, and then she needed to get out west for site visits. Once back at her desk, she wrote up the email to Esma with the list of tasks and, feeling a wave of relief, opened the marked-up T & C precedent Melbourne had emailed that morning. Reviewing the draft worked on her like a mild opiate, so that when Pip slid onto the seat next to her, she was almost back in the zone.

'Easy tiger,' her friend laughed, when Cress jumped. As usual Pip's outfit was burlesque-cum-dominatrix, today a close-fitting crushed-velvet top and pencil skirt, a stack of resin bracelets clattering on one arm. 'What's got you all in a tizz?'

'Hmm?' Cressida began, road technical jargon still filing through her head. 'Oh – nothing, just working on the T & C. How are you going, anyway? Are you getting any work done?'

'Oh God, don't ask me about work,' said Pip, slumping back into her chair and flapping her hands. 'Brian's just moping around being a *total sad sack*. He just wants to drink coffee and stare into his computer. If he doesn't snap out of this soon, I'm going to the Melbourne office.'

'I was thinking of popping down to Melbourne myself next week. Can you be at a meeting on Monday? To go over the T & C draft.'

'Yes. Monday. Sounds great.'

Esma appeared at the door.

'Cressida?' She nodded in greeting to both of them and held out a sheaf of papers. Cress folded them quickly, avoiding Pip's eyes. It was the bail refusal papers from Legal Aid.

'What's that?' her friend asked.

'That? Oh, nothing.' Cress grimaced and shoved the papers into the side pocket of her laptop bag. But Pip was still looking at her. 'Sorry,' she said, blushing. 'Chinese walls. If I told you I'd have to kill you.'

Pip laughed. 'What? Chinese walls my ass,' she said, eyes narrowed. 'C'mon, you know I'll keep it confid—'

'Sorry – look, I've got to go and attend to this,' said Cressida, waving her bag. *Or at least leave immediately in order to avoid blurting the entire situation out to you*, she thought. 'I'll email you about the meeting—'

'Sure,' said Pip, shrugging. 'Any chance of a drink on Friday? There's that hot new floating bar in the harbour – you get to it by water taxis. There's topless waiters I've heard.'

'Really,' Cressida said, laughing distractedly. 'Can't. It's the Surgeons Ball.' She'd do the rest of the T&C from home. Then she'd have to get started on researching the other possible charges on Fairbank.

Pip had lost interest though; her blue eyes were flashing at something over Cressida's shoulder. She sat back against the seat in a feline lean.

'Oh,' she said. 'Brian. Hello.'

'Philippa. Cressida. Cressida—' Brian glanced at Pip, then continued. 'Pop up before you leave will you?'

'Sure,' Cressida said. 'Now's good. I was about to go home anyway.'

'I'll be with you in a minute.' To Pip she said, 'I'll see you later', and leaned across to kiss her on the cheek.

'Ooh,' Pip said as she watched Brian go. 'First a wad of confidential docs and now a private meeting with Prendergast. You're getting more interesting by the minute.'

'Ha ha thanks,' said Cressida. 'Maybe see you on Thursday for a pickleback. I'll let you know.'

On the drive home Cressida's phone rang. She checked her voicemail while stopped at a traffic light. It took a moment to realise the voice recorded was Joanne's. She sounded tearful.

'Cressida. Something terrible's happened,' she said. 'You have to come. I can't … I can't talk about it over the phone. Please. Oh hell, I don't know what the number here is … hang on …' There were muffled voices in the background and then she came back on again and gave the digits.

It was after four. After lockdown. She pulled over and dialled, but got the gaol's voicemail. Damn. Well, it wasn't like her client was going anywhere. She'd try again in the morning.

# 16

She was on the phone by eight am.

'You got a phone appointment?'

'What? No.'

'To talk to her today you need a phone appointment. Twenty-four hours' notice.'

'What? For a *phone call*?'

'Affirmative.'

'Even in an emergency? Even if I'm her *lawyer*?'

There was a pause.

'What kind of emergency?'

'I don't …' She stopped. *Quick, think.* 'My client has urgent information she needs to tell me for her case.'

'Hmph.'

Silence.

'Um, well?' Cressida prompted.

'When's her next appearance?'

'Um, three weeks, but …'

'Can't be that urgent then.'

*Oh for fuck's sake.*

The next words popped out before she knew what she was doing. Lying to a prison guard wasn't such a great thing to do, but things were desperate.

'Um – there's been a death in the family.'

'A death in the family.' Clearly it wasn't the first time this prison guard had been lied to either.

'Yes.'

'We prefer you don't tell her anything distressing over the phone. For that you need to come in person.'

*You're going all pastoral, now?* 'I do?'

'Yep.'

'But I can't wait twenty-four hours – that's the whole point.'

Another silence.

'Just a minute.'

After an interminable pause the voice came back on the line.

'For emergency appointments you can give four hours' notice. Has to be in writing as well. Name?'

'What, hers or mine?'

'Hers,' the voice continued, sounding bored.

'Fairbank. Joanne Fairbank. So I can come today? At 12.30? Will you tell her?'

But there was silence, and it took a moment for Cressida to realise she'd been hung up on. Well. So much for customer service. She rang back, but the phone rang out. She'd just have to send the request when she got to work, and take her chances at 12.30.

This time it took more than twenty minutes to get to the front of the queue at the desk at Silverwater. Cressida resisted the urge to grind her teeth as she waited.

'Fairbank ...' the warden said, looking through a list of names. 'Did you send a request?'

'Yes,' Cressida said, peering through the hole in the glass. '8.22. Today.'

'It's twenty-four hours you know.'

'I know. I rang. Look, I'm legal, and he said if it was urgent four hours would be okay.'

The warden flicked through an ancient card filer, looking unimpressed. Then she hauled herself up and went to a small desktop printer in the corner.

'Mitsok?'

Oh thank God, they'd got it.

'That's me.'

'I'll have to check,' the guard said. 'Inmate might not be here.'

'What?' Cressida frowned. 'But I saw her yesterday.'

The warden perused a stapled list on the desk, then scanned each page again. Her gaze flicked to Cressida and she picked up the phone, dialled, murmured something and put the phone down again.

'Thought so,' she said. 'No longer at this facility.'

'What?'

'I said, she's no longer at this facility.' She nodded towards the queue behind Cressida. 'Now can you move aside please?'

'But ... where's she gone then?' Cressida asked, hating how plaintive she sounded.

The warden shrugged again.

'You don't know?'

The woman shook her head, then called again to the person behind her. 'Next.'

'Wait,' Cressida said, turning to the queue with a pained look, then back to the warden. 'Sorry. I need to know where she's gone. At least give me a number.'

'You can call the Corrections central number. I can't help you I'm afraid. Once they've left here they're out of my jurisdiction. Now please move aside or I'll call Security.'

Security? *Jurisdiction?* Cressida didn't know which word to be more offended by. Judges have jurisdiction, she felt like saying, and maybe sheriffs in bad American westerns, but you're a *Corrections clerk.* But instead she swallowed and walked as calmly as possible out of the line and towards the stained red couch. So. How exactly did one go about finding a client who had disappeared? She didn't want to ring Sandra and look like an idiot. *Er, sorry, I seem to have **lost the client**, any ideas on how to find her?* How could they just move her like that, without any notice or the opportunity for her to call someone? This had never happened to the white-collar criminals she'd helped prosecute. It almost felt faintly *junta,* like the stories Jerome had gone on about when he was in his Amnesty International letters to dictators phase, where 'disappeared' was a fancy word for 'executed'. She looked down at her phone. Corrections central phone line. Whatever that was. She opened a browser in Google on her phone.

'Don't bother with that, love,' a woman next to her said. 'Try this one.' She was holding out her phone.

Cressida read the screen. 'Oh. Really?'

'Unless you want to be sent all 'round the world and get off the phone at

dinnertime without finding your friend, unna,' the woman said. 'Fuckin'
pathetic. Happens all the time. They moved my Richie three times last
year before we found him. Once was on Father's Day.' She shook her head.

'Oh. Okay, thanks,' Cressida said. She wasn't sure whether to follow
the clerk's instructions or these, but decided the voice of experience
would be more reliable. She thanked her and copied the number into her
keypad. After three rings it was answered, and with relief she grinned
at the woman in thanks. After explaining the situation to the clerk she
was transferred to someone else, who put her onto a third person, and
then finally she found someone who said they'd look it up if she'd wait a
moment. After another few minutes they came back on the line.

'Wellington.'

'Wellington?' The woman next to her heard and her mouth dropped
open, then she rolled her eyes in sympathy. 'Where the hell's that? ...
*Dubbo?*' The entire queue as well as the clerk at the desk swivelled to look.
She flushed and continued more quietly. 'Since when?' This morning,
obviously, Cressida thought. 'That's, like, hours away. Don't you have to
give her some notice or something?'

The clerk on the other end laughed. In a strained voice Cressida asked
for the address and hung up. She turned to the other woman and sighed.
'Thanks.'

The woman shook her head in sympathy. 'They're bastards. You're
lucky it's not Broken Hill.' The last person had been processed in the
visitor queue and she stood up. 'You should ring and check the visitors
hours,' she advised. 'They're probably between the hour and five past.'

'Oh. Oh God,' Cressida said. 'Thanks.'

'Sorry for you, love,' the woman said. 'Good luck with it.' She lumbered
off to join the queue at the security scanner.

Cress dialled Brian's number and got Esma.

'Hi, Esma. Is Brian there?'

'Not at the moment, lovey. In a meeting with – with Pip, I think, actually.'

Pip? Must be some M & A business. Cress sighed and said, 'They've
moved her. My client. To Wellington.'

'They've *moved* her? Just like that? Can they do that?'

'Apparently.' She rubbed her temple.

'What a headache.'

'I know. I'm a bit worried – she rang last night and left a message
that something terrible had happened, but I don't know what. Anyway.
Nothing I can do. Even to make a phone call I have to book twenty-four
hours in advance. Can you put in a request for a phone call straight away?
Say tomorrow at one?'

'Okay. I'll tell Brian.'

She gave Esma the number and her visitor reference number to use and rang off before Esma could ask any questions. Keep things professional and separate, she thought. Otherwise ... well, otherwise trying to get the boss's daughter out of gaol would all just seem too overwhelming and she'd give up without even wanting to try.

It could be anything, she reasoned with herself. No vegan toothpaste or something. She wouldn't have to get to Joanne physically until she had the police brief of evidence to go through with her – right now, InterConnex was more important.

Except if it was just that, why had Joanne said she had to see her in person, and couldn't talk about it over the phone? Without knowing her very well it was hard to tell whether it was just some sort of post-incarceration freak-out, or whether it really was important. No matter. She'd find out tomorrow on the phone soon enough.

On the way back to the carpark, her phone rang. Brian.

'Hi.'

'Cress, what's going on? Esme said Jo called – apparently in some distress ...?'

'Um – yes – I missed the call, it was yesterday afternoon, she just said she wanted me to come to see her. So I'm here, at Silverwater, but they've moved her.'

'Where to?'

'Wellington. I've asked Esma to book a call for tomorrow at one.'

'You'll have to go out there.'

'Sorry?'

'If she said it was urgent and she had to see you, Cressida,' said Brian, an edge in his voice, 'you'll have to do that. As soon as possible.'

'But ...'

'The firm will pay. Just get on a flight.'

'There's no plane flights out there,' Cressida said. 'The closest one is Dubbo. If their power is back on.'

'Dubbo it is then,' said Brian.

'Right. Um, yes. Absolutely,' she said, through partly clenched teeth. 'Could you – it's okay, I'll take the road documents with me. Done.'

'Cheers,' said Brian. 'I'll put you back on to Esma.'

'Thanks.'

'Hi, Cress,' came Esma's voice. 'Yes – I'm just looking – um, look, I'm sorry to tell you this – but there are only morning flights to Dubbo. The airport's up and running, but they're all done for the day. The next one's eleven tomorrow. Only takes an hour though ...'

*Fuck.*

'And when are the Wellington visiting hours? Would you mind looking those up?'

'Just a sec ...' There was silence, then Esma came back on. 'Nine till one.'

'Fuck. Sorry. How far's the drive to Wellington from Dubbo?'

'Yep ...' Cress waited again. 'Google Maps says ... damn. Forty-five minutes. Oh dear. Which means you'll miss them.'

'It does.'

'Only five hours from Sydney though, if you drive. You'd get there tonight and could see her tomorrow morning.'

*Drive? To Wellington?*

'Also, Cress. There's another email from the CDPP. It's in your inbox.'

Great. More charges probably. At least if she left tonight ... she'd have a bit of peace and quiet away from Alessa to do the road project work. She'd have to text Inge and cancel training tomorrow again though. Damn. Were there gyms in Wellington? She was beginning to think of the entire topic of this criminal matter with an expletive before it.

Three hours later Cressida was on the M4 west, her zip-up trolley bag neatly packed with a capsule wardrobe, her suit hanging over the back passenger door of the Fiat. Wads of road documents sat in the footwell. If she managed to read them between now and getting back to Sydney that would be an achievement. When she'd cleared the Sydney traffic she asked Siri to call Esma on speakerphone.

'Esma. Did you find me a—'

'Hotel for tonight? Yes I've actually ... Ah, here it is,' Esma said. 'Wellington Motor Inn. That's the best I could do, I'm afraid, dear. There's a caves convention on – so the whole town's filled to the gills. It was either that or a room at the pub with something called a mechanical bull pit.' She pronounced the phrase as if it was an exotic concept. 'Quite the thing on a Wednesday night I'm told.'

'Oh God,' Cressida said, laughing. 'Thank you, I owe you one.'

'Did you find petrol?'

'Had to queue for ten minutes to get it, but this baby's full to the gills now. You sent that request, right?'

'Certainly. 9.50am.'

'You're a star.' Cressida sighed. 'I can't believe we couldn't do this over the phone.'

'Frustrating.'

'Not much privacy in prison, I suppose. Which reminds me – she wanted chocolate. And some weird toothpaste. I'll have to get some at a supermarket ... I guess they have those in Wellington, right?'

Esma laughed. '*Yes* they have supermarkets in Wellington, dear. You're what they call a good sort, I think, Cressida. See you when you get back.'

A good sort, Cressida thought, ringing off. She didn't think anyone had ever called her *that* before. It was nice.

Ahead of her darkness was falling on the road, a band of orange on the horizon. She had to call Felipe. Best to do it while still flushed with good feeling from Esma's words.

'Siri, call Felipe.'

There was a ring tone and he picked up.

'Hello?'

'Darling,' she said. 'How are you?'

'All the better for hearing your voice, my darling. Are you getting beautiful?'

*Not particularly*, Cressida thought, glancing down at the tailored blue jeans and white cotton shirt she'd put on for the drive.

'No, why?'

'Oh you are funny,' Felipe said. 'No matter, I always know you'll be the most beautiful woman in the room wherever I take you. Cressida ...' There was a note of thrill in his voice.

'Mmm?'

'I filed my candidacy.'

'Oh Felipe. That's wonderful news! What convinced you?'

'Oh, you know, Mark was just very persuasive. About how my talents were just what the organisation needed, et cetera. Quite a charming man, actually. Oh darling, I'm so *excited*. Finally there's a chance for me to make my mark on this organisation, end the rot,' he said, barely able to contain the excitement in his voice. 'That German interloper will be there, and it's official – he's *running*. But with you there I know you'll charm the room, which is an enormous relief. So I was thinking – now that this dreadful blackout is over, I thought we could go for a bite to eat beforehand to this *adorable* little French place that's opened up in Potts Point, and then ...'

Oh dear. Felipe was always taking her along to medico cocktail parties and she could barely keep track of them ... What had she forgotten? The Surgeons Ball was on Friday, but tonight?

'Um, Felipe ... oh darling, I'm so sorry. I've obviously totally screwed something up. I'm ... I'm halfway to Bathurst,' she said.

'Ba ... what? What the hell are you doing going to *Bathurst*? Oh Cressida. I told you about this *weeks* ago. The NSW Hand Surgery Association's Annual Scientific Meeting welcoming cocktails. It's *imperative* that we make a strong showing and I mention my new approach to ...'

He used a Latin phrase that Cressida didn't know, but the tone was clear. 'And what about the triathlon? The German is almost *certain* to beat us, darling, unless we have your cycle time on our side!'

Cressida cringed. 'I'm so sorry, darling. I completely forgot. I've got a lot on at work and—'

'Oh piffle,' he said. 'I need you here. How far away are you? Look, I'll have my secretary bring a dress and you can meet me there.'

'What? Oh God, Felipe I can't do that. I've got an appointment with the client tomorrow. In Wellington.'

There was a silence on the other end. Cressida realised she was holding her breath. When Felipe spoke again his voice was soft.

'I see. Well then. I suppose I will just have to make other arrangements.'

Cressida felt a chill at that, but said nothing. What could she do, except apologise again?

It didn't matter the next moment though, because he'd hung up on her. She pulled over on the side of the road to collect herself. *Other arrangements* – she knew what that meant. Even though they were engaged, she knew he had options 'on the side'. For function escort purposes, as it were. Any doe-eyed young registrar at the hospital for a start; one who didn't have to worry about the *slowing of her metabolism* as she neared forty, Cressida thought, because she still had more than a decade to go. *Oh don't be silly,* she admonished herself; *he's your fiancé. He asked you to marry him. Between Sydney Heads on a private cruise by moonlight with lobster and a $50,000 engagement ring, the one that's weighing down your left hand. He's not going to go off with some bit of fluff just because you're unavailable for one night.*

In the silence cicadas called, and then she noticed another sound. Out the window dark shapes moved and she realised they were cows, less than a metre from the car. She could hear their feet on the earth and their slow, satisfied munching.

Ah, Felipe. He could just be so … rigid. And something else she couldn't put her finger on. *Overbearing.* She looked at the clock on the dashboard. Nearly six. Suddenly she was starving. What on earth would there be to eat out here though, she thought, looking out at the cows. It had to be carbohydrate. A big bowl of icecream. With caramel sauce and nuts on top. Then suddenly all she wanted was a hotdog. With the lot – mustard and cheese and fried onion and tomato sauce and a big fat real barbecue sausage. Maybe two of them. The lights of Bathurst were spread out below. She'd never been to Bathurst, but hey, it was country New South Wales. And that meant in the way of food, a jaw-dropping hotdog was a real possibility.

# 17

It was a fact of which David Butcher was now fairly confident, after twenty-two years in the profession, that the more expensive the barrister the less comfortable the chairs in the lobby in which one would be required to wait. Having noted his presence to the large and powdered Italianate woman behind the reception desk, he eyed the sagging Eames rope number that sat a short distance away on the plush wool carpet and let out a sigh. It looked more like a Japanese sex prop than a chair. Wide strips of leather slung between chrome piping were all that came between you and an undignified passage to the floor, and just looking at it was enough to give David welts on the back of his thighs. He sniffed and stood by the window instead.

The view below was hardly more cheering. It reminded him of the view from the budget hotel he and his wife used to stay in when they visited Thailand. A kind of worker ant vertical wind tunnel; through the swivel windows running down its wall could be glimpsed the austere skirts of wooden desks and bookshelves, surfaces scattered with briefs and red binding tape, and three storeys below, a hand sitting flaccidly beside a keyboard. They might earn a million dollars a minute, these surgeons of the legal profession, but he'd take his shabby office and 6pm clock-off at the CDPP any day.

The desk phone burred and the receptionist looked up. 'He's ready to see you now.'

'Oh. Thanks.' David picked up the red-edged folder and headed down the dark wood-panelled corridor. The door was fourth on the left. He knocked and waited.

'Come.'

'Janus,' said David, stepping in. 'Hi.'

Inside, Janus McDuff SC sat behind an oceanliner-sized wooden desk in a room lined with bookshelves, a scruff of peppered red hair and wire-rimmed glasses his dominant features. Behind him double wind-out windows gave onto an identical view as the one from the foyer; on the desk neat stacks of pink-bound briefs looking like so many wads of cash piled up. He grinned broadly and stood, peeling off his glasses and extending a hand.

'David. How *are* you? Have a seat.' He indicated the considerably more comfortable black leather bucket seat that was in front of the enormous desk. 'Scotch?'

*Jesus*, thought David.

'Ah, not before eleven,' he said with a chuckle, sitting down. 'Busy?'

'Murder.' The barrister rolled his eyes and sloshed the drink into a glass. He glanced at David. 'How's Daniel?'

David blinked. It was always there, that little sting, whenever anyone mentioned it. Three years and it still caught him by surprise.

'Um, not sure,' David said, extracting the red edge from his briefcase and busying himself cleaning his glasses with the hankie he always kept in a pants pocket. 'Haven't heard from him in a couple of weeks.'

'No date yet?'

'Um. No – not as far as I know.'

'Ah well. No news is good news, eh?' The barrister sipped his drink and eyed David with sympathy.

'Not sure whether you've had a chance to read it yet,' David said. 'I emailed a brief through yesterday?'

'Ah yes,' said Janus, turning to his laptop. 'Any representation yet?'

'Spoke to her yesterday,' said David. 'Sounded to me like her first criminal matter.'

'Really,' said Janus, glancing back at David. 'What, she wants to make a name for herself?'

David shrugged and flipped open the folder. 'It didn't read like that to me, but you never know, I guess.' He reviewed the Notice of Appearance the lawyer had filed. 'Mitsok. Cressida. Never heard of her.' He shook his head. Green as. This defendant was going to need more than an excitable newbie.

'Mitsok,' said Janus, reinstating his glasses. 'Now why is that name …' He swung back to the laptop and tapped something into the keyboard, peering at the screen. 'Not related to … hah!' he barked gleefully. 'That's his daughter.'

'Whose daughter?'

'Leo Mitsok. You know. Went up for fraud against one of his firm's clients. You must remember – four years ago …?'

'Um …'

'Gee, probably up for parole this year.' Janus tapped out more words. 'Hmmm … yep. Went in four years ago this July. Sentence was six years, parole in four.'

David joined him looking at the screen. *Personal Injury Lawyer Defrauds Client for Millions in False Settlement Case.* He nodded and sat back, saying, 'Right. Never heard of it.'

Janus shrugged. 'He was one of the big ones in personal injury,' he said, leaning back in the chair. 'Before the changes to the *Civil Liability Act* limiting damages came in. When *quantum* was still at large. He won some huge ones – don't you remember? That 1.2 mill for the kid that burnt his hand at school? And the class action against the pharmaceutical company? Massively overreached in the end, of course,' Janus shook his head. 'Which is why he's now in gaol.'

'Is that right.'

'It says here – oh my goodness – "daughter Cressida Mitsok was also investigated but no charges were laid",' he read.

'You're kidding me.'

'Anyway, sorry' – Janus clicked back to the brief on the screen – 'Fairbank. Any antecedents?'

'That's the weird thing,' David said. 'Pure as the driven. Childcare worker, of all things.'

Janus glanced at David over his glasses.

'State Police have issued the CAN.' David flicked to it in his folder. 'Only explosives, but there's a draft for property damage, sabotage, two under the *Electricity Supply Act* … I'm instructed to consider terrorism offences too though. As you'd expect.'

'Should bloody think so.' Janus shook his head, expression serious. 'Where's the AFP brief up to?'

'Still a few weeks away. With five of them, again as you'd expect it will take some time.'

'Any word from lawyers for the others?'

David shook his head.

'They'll include interviews with the workers I assume, CCTV footage, reports from forensics?'

David nodded.

'When you spoke to Mitsok – did she give any indication of plea? On the explosives charge?'

David chuckled, then said, 'No. She was already talking *options* though. As she put it.'

'Cocky.' It was Janus's turn to chuckle. 'What's your thinking on the intent point?'

'What, on the State charges?'

'No,' Janus said, pinning him over his wire-rimmed glasses. 'Prospective terrorism charges. What is it – intent to … let's see …' He tapped into his keyboard again. 'Section 101 – commit terrorist act – "terrorist act" defined as …'

David flicked to the Commonwealth Code excerpts in the folder that Lois had so efficiently printed for him that morning, and skim read: 'Serious damage to property … done with the intention of advancing a cause by coercion or intimidating the government, not being …' He lifted the page. '… intended to cause that damage, and (c) who intended by that conduct to cause: (i) extensive destruction of property, or (ii) major economic loss, is guilty of an offence.' He took a breath. 'That's to paraphrase.

It's two pages long in its entirety.'

'*Intention to create a serious risk to the health or safety of the public or a section of the public,*' Janus read from his screen, savouring the words, '*in order to coerce or intimidate the government.*' He turned to David and gave a brusque grin. 'And what do we have on that?'

'I'll make inquiries.'

'So, nothing as yet.'

'Not so far, no.'

'Well,' Janus said, with a laconic sigh, 'without that, all you have is sabotage.'

'Imputation from circumstance?' David offered. Janus pinned him again over the glasses, and David swallowed. Yeah. Not strong.

'What was it with that Richmond defendant?' Janus mused. 'They found what, a diary, wasn't it?' The leather creaked as he swivelled his chair away from David and looked out the window, chewing on the arm of his glasses. 'Do we have any addresses yet? Boltholes and such?'

'I'll ask.'

'Once you have one, see if anything turns up at the house. Frequently these people have all manner of ideological paraphernalia,' he said. 'There'll be something.'

'And if there's not?'

Janus shrugged. 'No case. Not on terrorism, anyway.' He smiled benignly. 'Probably a good thing,' he said, turning back to the computer. 'Those Feds get altogether too hot under the collar about these things. Now, anything else?'

'Yes, one thing – apparently she's in the psych ward.'

Janus gave him an inquiring look.

'My thoughts were it may just be because they've nowhere else to put her,' David explained. 'Female Category 5. I've subpoenaed the medical records.'

'Good. Get them to me the instant you have them.'

'Will do.'

'Well,' said Janus, minimising the documents on his screen and standing up with a flourish, 'I'm due at the Melbourne. The AG has promised me a bottle of excellent Andalusian wine.' He shouldered on his jacket. 'Two weeks in Spain on a study tour, apparently. Which just happened to be spent at the region's best wine resort,' he said. 'Join me?'

'Hmm? Oh – no. Thanks though,' David said, closing the folder and slipping it into his brief case. The Melbourne Club's muted velvet ambience made David feel suffocated, as did its draconian no-women rule. As a married father of three grown girls as well as his son Daniel, anywhere without the laughter of women just felt, well, *wrong* to him. He had lunch in the park booked with Tania at one, anyway.

As he followed Janus out to the lifts listening to him talk about golf, David thought about the lawyer again. What must that be like, he wondered, having a father in the same profession as yours in gaol for breaching its rules. Almost as bad as being a lawyer with a son in gaol. All told, doing so in a third-world country with gaols like sewers of human misery probably won for awfulness, he decided. But only just.

# 18

Driving west through the Liverpool Plains Cressida felt like she was on the set of *The Sound of Music* rather than farmland half a day's drive from Sydney. But then black loam and canola gave way to red dirt and cattle that matched and by the time she turned into Wellington's wide, coppery main street, its boarded-up buildings and quiet streets felt more *Wolf Creek* than anything with Julie Andrews in it. There was a new-looking Woolies that dwarfed the buildings around it and she found the Vicco and some vegan chocolate inside; half a k down the road, the Wellington Motor Inn was an expanse of yellow pebblecrete with not a blade of grass in sight, the tiny swimming pool visible from the road a puddle of green with a decaying plastic chair in it. Cressida turned into the concrete driveway and parked under the awning, then wound down her window. In the silence the motor ticked and cooled and the air smelt of dust and hay.

A bell jangled over the door as she let herself into the office. In the tiny room was a high counter on one side, a mesh security door on the other, brown and gold shag carpet on the floor and a tear-off calendar from the local smash repairer's behind the desk. Cressida was about to ring the bell on the desk when she heard the clattering of feet on linoleum and the security door slid open.

'Sorry,' a woman said, smiling as she finished a mouthful. 'Help you?'

'Oh, sorry to interrupt dinner,' said Cressida. 'My assistant made a booking earlier today. Cressida Mitsok.'

'Mitsok …' The woman manoeuvred behind the desk and scanned an enormous booking folder. 'Oh yes. You were lucky to get in. Power only just came back on this morning.'

'You lost power?' she said. 'All the way out here?'

'Yep,' the woman confirmed, rolling her eyes. 'And wouldn't I like to wring a few of those necks. Such selfishness. We had no air-con for two weeks. Can you imagine? Well' – her expression brightened as she held out a form – 'here for the conference?'

'Um, no,' Cressida said, taking it.

The woman was still looking at her expectantly.

'Here to see someone in the prison, actually,' she said, with an attempt at noncommittal.

Eyebrows went up. 'Oh yeah. Legal Aid?' Then she frowned. 'Not those terrorist people. I heard they were bringing one of them up here this morning.'

'Did you?' Cressida said, carefully neutral. And maybe her client might even still be here, she thought, dryly, busying herself with the form.

'My sister's mother-in-law works in the laundry there. She says they brought in twenty extra guards the day before she came. Good idea if you ask me. This town doesn't like climate activists. It's a woman, you know.'

'Is that right. What makes you think it's about climate change?' she asked, pushing the form back.

'Are you kidding?' The woman's clear green eyes were incredulous. 'Of course it is. What other reason would there be? Why on earth would you blow up a power station otherwise? She's Muslim apparently. Was wearing one of those headdress thingies and refused to take it off for the strip search. They would have sorted her out though.' The woman handed Cressida a key and said, 'Your room's number 32. I've put the air-con on for you. We're here, and you're round here' – she tore a map off the pad and circled two spots at lightning speed. 'No noise outside the rooms after ten pm thanks. Will you be joining us for dinner?'

'Thanks, I already ate.'

'Oh. Well anyway breakfast's from seven, and if you want room service you'll need to fill in that form by eight pm tonight – which is right about now, so ...'

'No that's okay, I'll get breakfast in town. Thanks anyway.' She put her pen down and asked, 'Just ... what's wrong with climate activists?' It seemed like a funny thing to be passionate about, here in the middle of the country miles from any of the power stations.

'You're kidding me,' the woman said, staring at her. 'You have *heard* of the Liverpool Plains, I take it?'

'Um ...'

The woman rolled her eyes. 'If those pollies've got any sense it'll be the next big open-cut coal district. Ten thousand new jobs in it here in the next ten years. Bring it on, I say,' she said. She rolled her eyes again. 'It's not like much else is happening, right?'

'Oh,' Cressida said. It had looked like farming country to her on the way up. There'd been a sign: *Food Bowl of Australia*. 'I thought it was mostly agriculture.' And some other signs, come to think of it. *Shenhua out.*

'Maybe used to be. Not anymore.'

'Oh.'

'Just the one night is it?' the woman asked.

'Yes thanks. 'night.'

Number 32 was dark and cool when she entered, the air conditioner giving off a low hum from over the bed. A polyester-quilted bed and chest of drawers crowded the room, a small TV hanging from the ceiling in one corner. The tiny bathroom smelt of mildew but looked clean. Cressida swung her suitcase and three volumes of the road project Technical Documents onto the luggage platform and sat down on the bed with a sigh. Hotel rooms always filled her with a sense of giddy freedom. Just her, alone, not expected to answer to anyone. What she most wanted was to sit out on the verandah and have a cup of tea after the long drive, and then bolt off for a run. But the email Esma had mentioned was bothering her. It was sure to be more charges on Joanne. She dug her iPad out of the side pocket of her bag and clicked on the email app. Ah, there it was – standing out in capital letters. *[SEC-UNCLASSIFIED] [Joanne FAIRBANK – Charges]* it said, like the last one – and then a string of sets of numbers after a letter. Only one attachment: another CAN. Still no Facts accompanying.

Steeling herself, she clicked on the CAN: *COURT ATTENDANCE NOTICE. DEFENDANT DETAILS. Joanne Crispin FAIRBANK. DETAILS OF OFFENCES.* This time there were pages of them. She scrolled, annoyed to notice her palms were sweating. Ah, no terrorism charges yet. *Whew.* Well, that was something. Six offences under the New South Wales *Crimes Act* and two under the *Electricity Supply Act*. There was the offence under s 93FA, but then some others. Christ, they all sounded the same, though:

1. 55. Possessing explosives in a public place.

2. 195. Possessing or making explosives with intent to injure.

3. 196(1). Destroying or damaging property with intent to injure.

4. 196(2). Possessing explosives during a public disorder with intention to injure or damage property.

**Destroying or Damaging Property.**

5. 203B. Cause damage to a public facility with the intention that it cause extensive destruction of property.

All with a listing date in four weeks, Muswellbrook Local Court. Ah. And 6: *Intentionally destroy property in the company of others.* She felt a fizz of trepidation. That wasn't good. What evidence did they have about *that*? If they had evidence of others at Liddell, they could potentially give evidence against her client. Unless they meant the other power stations – would there be a separate criminal enterprise argument available on that? She read the details: *At 7.05pm on 16 March did destroy property, being the public facility known as Liddell Power Station, in company, being with four individuals known as ...* and then were listed four female names she didn't recognise. Who the hell were *they*? And they were *women*? She didn't know why that was so surprising, but it was. And she'd had had the impression from Joanne that she'd done Liddell alone. Had these other accuseds appeared for bail on the same day as Joanne? She wrote the names down. And why were they charging her with so many minor offences? And then there were aggravations on the other major ones that were also double-ups: 'in company' or during public disorder; with fire or explosives – why not nail sabotage and leave it at that? So much less paperwork for a start, she thought with frustration.

She filled the kettle from the bathroom tap and put it on to boil, then pulled out the fat wads of legislation from her luggage and cracked open the *Crimes Act*. With a pad of orange sticky notes and a pen she tagged each charge in the thick stapled document. *Wow*, she thought, *no clipped corporate language here.*

**55 Possessing or making explosives or other things with intent to injure**

Whosoever knowingly has in his or her possession, or makes, or manufactures, any gunpowder, explosive substance, or dangerous or noxious thing, or any machine, engine, instrument, or thing ...

The phrases read to her like heavy missives from an earlier age.

**195 Destroying or damaging property**

(1) A person who intentionally or recklessly destroys or damages property belonging to another ...

**196 Destroying or damaging property with intent to injure a person**

(1) A person who destroys or damages property, intending by the destruction or damage to cause bodily injury to another ...

(2) A person who, during a public disorder, destroys or damages property, intending by the destruction or damage to cause bodily injury to another...

And sabotage.

**203B Sabotage**

A person:

(a)   whose conduct causes damage to a public facility, and

(b)   who intended to cause that damage, and

(c)   who intended by that conduct to cause:

(i) extensive destruction of property, or

(ii) major economic loss, is guilty of an offence.

As she read, responses to the elements of each popped up in her brain like mushrooms after rain. How could they know what she intended? Was a power station even a public facility, given it had been sold to the Chinese? What proof was there it had been her client who had possessed the explosives? And the explosives were obliterated, so how could they tell how much there was? Who was she supposed to have intended to injure? The public? Who was that, specifically? It was kind of irritating, the way after years in litigation her brain did this automatically, because many of the responses were irrelevant to a jury that, by its nature, focused on the big picture – this defendant had allegedly done something bad; the only question was, did they do it? But she'd also learnt it paid to note those first reactions when she read a charge, because sometimes they turned out to be the best of the arguments. She dug out her notebook from her file box and started jotting things down.

And then the penalties. They sat below each section like tombstones. *Imprisonment for 5 years. Imprisonment for 3 years or 50 penalty units, or both. Whosoever does ... shall be liable for imprisonment for 10 years. 16 years. Sabotage: 25 years.* Were the sentences consecutive or cumulative? If consecutive, with all of the aggravations included, it would be – Cress did a quick calculation – 77 years. Even if they were cumulative, with the sabotage maximum, her client would be in gaol until she was forty-seven years old. The best part of her life. What the hell did they even need to charge her with terrorism for? She was going to be locked up forever as it was.

How on earth could something like this have been this important to her, Cress thought. To give up the sunshine, the ocean, even just the smell of fresh baked bread or the ability to walk out her front door into the sunshine when she felt like it. The feel of a baby's soft skin on her own, or the touch of a lover. It was almost too much to contemplate. But then, Cressida suddenly thought, how much of that had she herself ever had? She left for work when the world was still dark and came home when everyone else was going out for a drink or a meal with their friends, too exhausted to do anything but shower and fall into bed. And Felipe. How he touched her never felt like anything special. The sex was mechanical, if anything. Sometimes it almost felt like something she had to tolerate. The prostitute, Tiffany Lux or whatever her name had been, booked that night for the Westin, had been an attempt to inject some passion. And that was how it would be for at least the next twenty-five years at home and work as well, going by how things were at the moment. How was her imprisonment in Hannes Swartling any different than Joanne's imminent lifetime imprisonment?

*Oh for God's sake, what's got into you?* she chided herself, sitting up. *You know what it's all for. When you're a Partner you know you'll have freedom. It's nothing like being in prison. It's those two hotdogs. That's what's making you feel shit. It's poisoning your brain. Come on.* She threw the legislation to one side and pulled out her running shoes and shorts – the special saggy unflattering pair – and its holey t-shirt mate, kept especially for diverting male attention. *I'm going, I'm going*, she told the voice in her head. *And don't worry, tomorrow will be cups of tea only.*

Forty minutes of interval training later, she felt clean and renewed, as if the guilt had run out of her body in her sweat, as well as those stupid thoughts about her life, and under the extra-hot shower she felt light-headed from the absence of it. As she towelled off, the Technical Documents beckoned. But then, so did a solitary plastic chair on the verandah. She boiled the kettle again and extracted a licorice tea bag from the pocket of her bag, pouring the hot water over it into one of the cups. It would be okay to sit just for a moment, she thought; those Tech Docs weren't going anywhere.

So she sat down with her cup of tea and blew on it. On the ground next to the chair was a can with cigarette butts in it, remnants of the room's previous inhabitants. The low murmuring of another room's TV sounded down the verandah. As she watched, one tiny star and then another dropped to the horizon in the inky sky. Right about now Felipe would be arriving in some chandeliered ballroom with an unknown woman on his arm, she thought, looking jaw-drop charming in a lounge suit and starched white shirt. There was going to come a point where she would have to let him in on the Joanne thing, she realised with a sigh. She didn't know which she was more apprehensive of – his reaction to the terrorist aspect, or the fact that, with InterConnex as well, it seemed likely she'd be tied up 24/7 for a large chunk of the future.

It wasn't pleasant picturing Felipe at his dinner, so she forced herself to think about something else. What would Joanne be doing now, anyway? It was odd to think of her only a couple of kilometres away. Would the other inmates form some kind of mining wife lynch mob inside? Well she was safe for now, anyway. Locked in her cell at 4pm or whatever they did. Lying there, looking up at some ceiling crawling with cockroaches, wondering what the hell she had done with her life.

# 19

The drive out to the prison the next morning took Cressida through fields dusted green with the first flush of grass from the autumn rains, underneath a sky that was a sear of blue. For miles the only living things were bands of crows that burst up from roadkill as she passed, and once a clutch of galas startled from their grainfall lunch. When the entrance to the prison appeared she almost missed it and had to swerve to make the road to the small cluster of buildings, set in a hollow and invisible until she was almost on top of it.

In the foyer she set her bag down on the counter and pulled out her ID. The guard was a hale woman of fiftyish who turned from her game of computer solitaire and called into an anteroom as Cressida arrived.

'Hey Bec. Can you come and work the reader?' She rolled her eyes in Cressida's direction. 'It's new.'

A second guard emerged from the anteroom and motioned Cressida over to a biometric reader standing on a post, while the first guard regarded them both.

'So. Where you from?' the first guard asked.

'Ah,' said Cressida, putting her ID back in her wallet, 'Sydney.'

The guard raised her eyebrows, impressed. 'And what got you *this* gig?' Her voice held a grain of dry sympathy.

'Legal Aid, wouldn't it be?' the other one, Bec, chimed in. 'Lean in,' she motioned.

Cressida blinked into the machine as the first guard continued. 'Not likely. These terrorists are loaded, aren't they?' She grinned at Cressida. 'Be silks from arsehole to breakfast time.'

'Alright. You're good,' said Bec. 'Come through.'

Cressida followed the guard and threw her keys and bag into the tray on the security conveyor, then stepped through the frame.

'It's a bit of a walk,' said Bec as she scanned Cressida goodnaturedly with a handheld reader. 'You got your comfy shoes on?'

Cressida smiled tightly, thinking her three-inch Louboutins were anything but.

'Why, where is she?' she asked, shouldering her bag again.

'Segro,' the guard said. 'Or as we call it – Si-fucking-beria. And about as far from the entrance, as you're about to discover.' She leaned across to zap open the external door.

'She only just got here, didn't she? Surely she hasn't mucked up already ...' Through the walls of the corridor were bangs and muffled yells and feet on metal staircases, but there were no prisoners to be seen.

Bec was walking in front of her and at first her reply was muffled.

'Sorry, what was that?'

The guard glanced back at her. 'Danger to other prisoners.'

'What?' said Cressida, stopping. 'What do you mean? What danger?'

Bec shrugged, throwing her next words over her shoulder. 'Political views.'

'Political what?'

'There's a policy. Look it up on the internet,' Bec said, scanning her card so another door in front of them opened. She glanced back at Cressida. 'It's up to the governor. Anyway, cheer up,' she said, moving through the door. 'It's only for a coupla weeks. In a little while she's getting her very own facility.'

'What?' Cress hurried to catch up with her. 'What very own facility?'

'The new one. You'll see it in a minute,' she said, turning to let Cressida through another door. 'For permanent segro.'

'*What?*'

'Assuming she's convicted, of course,' the guard said.

'But what do you mean? What do you mean *permanent* segro?'

'We don't have permanent segro so they're building one. We've only got it for, you know, punishment segro – for a month or so. Not as a dedicated living facility. Come on, don't want to keep her waiting,' she said, nodding for Cressida to follow her through the door then stepping through and onto some asphalt. 'Come on. This way.'

Too stunned to speak, Cressida followed her. They passed a long low building next to a broad area of asphalt with razor wire along the wall on the other side, and through another series of doors along a corridor opening onto workshops and training areas.

'Where is everyone?' said Cressida.

The guard looked at her watch. 'Smoko. Nine fifteen.'

By the time they came to a door in a high cement fence topped with more razor wire, Cressida's feet were killing her and the satchel felt like it was digging a trench into her shoulder. On the other side of the fence a bulldozer was clearing some dirt and next to it a site office had been set up. Cressida stopped and stared out at the clearing.

'Come on, don't look so shocked,' the guard said. 'A whole new block all to herself? She should feel right special.'

'But – what – you're telling me that, if she gets convicted, she'll be here, *by herself*, for the rest of her life?'

'I dunno, you tell me. I would have thought that was your department.'

They came to some steps at the front of a long, low building. The guard turned to her.

'Here we are. Standard rules apply,' Bec said. 'You probably know them, but I'll tell you anyway. No touching, no giving her anything, and talk only about those matters necessary for legal instruction.'

'Sure,' said Cressida, thinking of the chocolate and toothpaste in her bag. 'Yes.'

Inside the building was an area the size of a classroom, filled with desks bolted to the floor. Sunlight slanted in through the far windows, and it took Cressida a moment to notice Joanne. She was in a beam of light in the far corner, slumped in a chair, eyes closed. When the door slammed her client jumped, flinching away from the sound. Bec took up a position against one wall nearby. Cressida approached.

'Joanne,' she said, putting her bag carefully on the chair in front of the desk. 'Hi.'

Joanne's eyes took a moment to focus, and then when they did, her mouth dropped open and she launched herself at Cressida.

'Hey,' Bec bellowed, pushing herself off the wall, and Cressida yelled out as ninety kilos of panicked guard hurled itself at Joanne.

'Cool it, it's fine!' Cressida yelled, as in one movement the guard threw her client to the floor and landed on her back, hands on her head. Joanne screamed and struggled, thrashing, and Cressida stood rooted to the spot, hands over her mouth.

'Stop,' Cressida yelled. 'Stop it! She's got a broken *arm*.'

The guard still had her hands on Joanne's head, her knee in her back, face red and breath coming in ragged bellows as she struggled to hold Joanne down. Her client's face was white with pain.

'What the fuck is your story, hey?' she said, leaning into Joanne's face on the floor. 'This is your lawyer, dickhead. Will I send her away again?'

All that came out of Joanne was a muffled sob, but it was clear the answer was no.

'Right then,' said the guard, relaxing and sitting up a little, but still heaving, 'Just so we're *crystal clear*, any more behaviour like that and it's the hole. Got it?'

With her face squashed against the lino Joanne hawked and spat, and the guard pushed down on the knee on her back, hard. Cressida stepped back, sinking into a chair.

'Are you pushing it?' the guard said.

Joanne didn't answer, her breath coming in ragged pants.

'I said, are you pushing it?' the guard yelled again, bouncing on Joanne's shoulders with her knee.

'Jesus, stop,' Cressida said, but her voice was inaudible.

'No,' Joanne muttered, as much as she could get the word out with her face in the lino. 'No.'

The guard gave an inch, watching Joanne's face, and sat back.

'Alright then,' she said.

She climbed up, avoiding Cressida's gaze, and in one motion put her arms around Joanne's chest under the sling and lifted her into the seat. Cressida thought she was going to be sick. The guard ran a hand through her hair and sniffed, then turned and walked across the other side of the room where she leant against the wall and watched them, breathing heavily.

Cressida couldn't move, wanting desperately to say something but unable to. Her client was doubled over, holding her arm, and Cressida watched as she rocked in silence for awful seconds. When she sat back up her face was a mask of pain, but then she gave a furious sniff and shook her head hard, as if to knock it out of herself, and wiped her face on a sleeve. 'Sorry. I just wanted to … I just wanted to hold your hand for a minute, actually.'

Cressida asked, 'Are you alright?'

'What?' Joanne hawked and spat again. 'Yeah,' she said, gaze flicking to the guard. 'Cockhead.' Her green eyes were hollow, but her face was defiant. 'Sorry. You seem to only ever see me when I'm falling apart.'

'Joanne, from what I can see that's the least I would expect.'

'You are a fucking legend,' she said, wiping her nose with the back of her hand. 'I can't believe you found me.'

'What's going on?'

A muscle in Joanne's jaw worked. 'Yeah. Right down to business, I guess.' She glanced back at the guard. 'It's such an irony – I got you out here instead of talking on the phone, and now I can't get away from them to tell you. Fuck,' she moaned, grimacing. 'Can you ask that turd for some Nurofen?'

'Hang on,' Cressida said. She got up and approached the guard, who was still puffing and blowing as she leant against the wall. 'Thanks to you,' she spat, 'my client needs pain relief. Get some. And a private room.'

'She's already had some today. Too bad. And no facilities here of that sort.'

'Hmm. Right. Well … my client has the right to discuss her case confidentially. So. Any chance you could, you know' – *fuck off for a bit*, she wanted to say, but didn't – 'give us a moment?' She gave her most ingratiating smile. 'We'll only be ten minutes,' Cressida pressed. 'Come on. I've come all the way from Sydney.'

The guard looked towards the guard station near the prison entrance.

'You could just sit in that chair on the other side of the window,' Cressida said, gesturing towards what looked like an exercise yard. 'Then you'd still be able to see us, but my client could talk confidentially.'

The guard sighed. 'You know she's dangerous?'

'Of course.'

'Alright. But you're at your own risk. And just ten minutes.'

'Sure. Maybe fifteen. But no more I promise.'

The two of them waited awkwardly until she had left, and then Joanne turned to her.

'Okay,' she began. Joanne started crying again. Cressida got out some tissues and tried to find a topic to calm her, or at least ease the tension.

'I was wondering,' she said, 'what's the tattoo on your wrist?'

Joanne's tears momentarily stayed. 'What?'

'That spiral. It's pretty.'

Joanne looked down at it. On her left wrist was a whirl of three lines radiating from a central point shaped like a coffee bean.

'It's ... thank you.' She looked to be on the verge of crying again, but rallied. 'It's ... it's Sagittarius A and the Arm of Orion. Nothing to do with astrology,' she said, wiping her nose. 'The Galactic Centre, probably a black hole. That's Perseus' – she traced along one of the lines – 'and that's Scutum Centaurus' – she traced another – 'what you commonly refer to as the Milky Way.'

'Ah.' Cressida regarded it. 'And you have it tattooed on your wrist ... why?'

Joanne shrugged, wiping her face. 'It calms me. You know. Gives me perspective. We're all stardust, and all that. So,' she said, letting out a sigh, 'don't suppose you saw the news the other night?'

'No,' said Cressida. 'So you're getting TV privileges, that's something.'

'Hah,' Joanne replied with vehemence. 'No. I saw it for two minutes when they were walking me from the intake room to my cell. Anyway there was a news report on. That revolting woman from *Sunrise* or whatever it's called; the robot one. Looks like a Stepford wife after she short-circuited. Well anyway. We ... we had a safe house of course, didn't we. In the mountains.' She stopped, as though checking Cressida was listening. Cressida motioned for her to continue. 'The full cliché,' Joanne said, charm returning as she regained her composure. 'It wasn't for anyone who was going to be directly involved, of course, because we were all going to turn ourselves in straightaway afterwards. Well, near enough anyway. I had a few things to do first,' she said, 'but I got there eventually. Anyway so this safe house' – she wiped the last of the tears from her cheeks and glanced briefly out at the guard – 'it was miles from anywhere. And the night before last, I saw on the TV ... they found it.' Tears welled and she held them back. 'Fuck knows how, they must have got a tipoff. Anyway they raided it, of course, didn't they. I watched them kick the fucking door down. There must have been twenty of them. All in black, like fucking bikies.' She hawked but continued. 'Anyway. The thing is – there would have been five or six people there, who had *nothing to do with it*. That place was meant to be the *safe* house, where anyone who knew us but didn't want to be, you know, implicated, could go. And they wouldn't have known anyone was coming, you know, so, they would have been just *sitting there*, and then …' The crying started up again. Cressida waited until it had subsided.

'Okay. So you're concerned about what happened to your friends,' she said. *What do you expect?* she felt like saying. *You blew up three power stations. Even your herbalist is probably implicated.*

'Well, no, that's not it – I mean, I would like to find out where they are, of course,' she said, 'but we all knew we probably wouldn't see each other after it was over anyway, especially the ones like those guys, that didn't want to be involved … So we said our goodbyes, but … but they said on the news they'd been *arrested*, and the thing is – they just *can't* be arrested.'

'What?' said Cressida. 'Why not?'

'Well one of them's … one of them's really sick. And she always said that she didn't want me involved, because that way they'd track her down as well, and …' The crying bubbled up again but Joanne stopped herself. 'I always said they wouldn't. I said if she went away, they'd never connect us, and she'd be safe. I even told her to go away. I said go to Queensland. Go lie in the sun and get better. But she wouldn't, would she? I guess she was too sick to travel by then.'

Cressida pulled out her phone. 'What's her name?'

Cressida could see Joanne weighing up again whether to trust her. *Oh for God's sake, I've just dropped everything to drive 200 kilometres, and spent the night in the Wellington **Motor Inn** to help you*, she thought. *I think you can let me in on it.*

'Saturne,' Joanna said. 'Saturne Williams. I mean she goes by Saturne Wild Deer. But her real surname's Williams.'

'I can see if I can find out if she was arrested, where she's being held,' she said, writing the name on the back of the CAN. 'I … I won't be able to act for her though.'

'Why not?' Joanne frowned.

'Because there would be a potential conflict,' Cressida answered gently. 'If she's been charged, there's the possibility she would end up testifying against you. Especially if she's got major reasons for not wanting to be in prison. Like an illness. Although,' she added, 'she would get medical care in prison. They're not so bad about that.'

Joanne snorted. 'Oh yeah. Like *chemo*,' she said, nostrils flaring. 'Slug your body full of poison and hope the cancer dies first? Saturne would rather kill herself.'

'She's got cancer?'

Joanne nodded. 'She's only known for a few months. She did try all that, by the way.' Her eyes flashed at Cressida. 'Said it made her feel so shite she *wanted* to die. So she found this woman in Queensland, they FaceTime once a fortnight, and she has to do exactly what she says. It seemed to be working, but then ... I think the stress of what we were doing got to her ... She wanted it that way though. She said this was more important – ridding the world of the cancer of human overconsumption was more important than getting it out of one human body. She's right of course. It's all part of it,' Joanne said. 'Coal consumption is like a cancer. Killing the planet one kilowatt at a time. She knew we were doing it for future generations. It's just' – she have Cressida a hard stare – 'she can't go to prison. It'll kill her.'

Cressida looked at her sceptically.

'I just want you to find her,' Joanne said. 'Tell me if she's in prison, and then, if you can't do it yourself ... get her a lawyer.' She grimaced and looked at the ceiling as if she couldn't believe what she was saying. 'She's *innocent*, Cressida. Do you get me?'

'Surely that will come out then,' Cressida said. 'They'll just do some investigations and let her out again.'

Joanne snorted and shook her head. 'No. I know they're out to finish us. They'll just cook something up. It's happened before. They find something majorly wrong with your car or trump up some drug charges, from grass they planted on you in the first place, just to get you off the forest blockade. They'll do the same to *rid the world of terrorists*,' Joanne mimicked. 'Saturne never set foot in anything illegal. You wait till you meet her. She's like a little fawn or something,' she said, her eyes going soft.

'Don't you have a family member or something? That can track her down for you?' Cressida asked. She didn't fancy going on a wild goose chase through God knows where to find some mystery woman named after a planet. Felipe would have a fit for a start.

But Joanne shook her head. 'Not anywhere nearby. Mum's been in Melbourne ever since she and Dad split up, and my brother and sister are both in WA. They wouldn't help me even if they were here, though. We, um, don't get along.'

'I see.' Why did she feel as though Joanne's problems were rapidly becoming her own? She was just her lawyer, for God's sake, not her life-coach. 'What about Saturne's family?'

'Doesn't have any,' said Joanne. 'They died in a car crash when she was three.'

'Oh,' said Cressida. 'Extended family, cousins? She must have someone.'

Joanne shrugged. 'Maybe. But I've never met any of them, and I sure wouldn't know how to find them.'

'What if I can't find her?' Cressida said. 'I mean, it was easy enough to find you because I'm your lawyer. But they're not going to tell me which prison some random person is in without my having instructions to act for them.'

Joanne's eyes widened and she put her face in her hands. 'Oh God. I *hate* this. I feel so fucking *useless* in here.' She looked up and momentarily brightened. 'I don't suppose you brought the chocolate?'

'Yes I brought the chocolate. And your toothpaste.' She pulled them out of her bag, and Joanne sighed with almost sexual relish.

'Ohhh,' she said, focusing on the chocolate. 'Alter Eco. You read my mind. God, you're a legend,' she said. 'I mean it. Nobody else'll give me the time of day in here, you know. It's not like I *murdered* anybody,' she said, a little too loudly, in the direction of the guard, but the officer had her back to them in a haze of smoke. 'And you travelled all the way out here to see me.'

'It was in Woolies. I'm really not sure about this stuff though, Joanne. Are you sure it even works? Have you been getting cavities?'

'Sure it does. That other stuff gives you cancer you know.'

Cressida resisted the urge to ask whether Jupiter or whatever her name was had been partial to Colgate (she imagined not), but said instead, 'Alright, alright, no need to get soppy. I'll make some calls and see if I can find your friend. You need to realise though, if she's not in custody, that's the end of the road. Unless you have another contact for her.'

'Well that's the thing, actually. I mean, even if they didn't get her this time, it's only a matter of time. She needs to know she's in danger. I mean – from what you said about some of the charges I'm up on, what are the chances they'll try them on her as well? You need ... you need to find her and warn her.'

'What?'

'Well, I mean, I can't, can I? You've got to tell her what's happened to me, convince her to go away somewhere. She's such a softie, she said she'd wait there until I got out of gaol.'

'Even after it got raided?'

Joanne shrugged. 'I don't know. I have no idea where else to look. I'm just hoping ... maybe she figured that since it was raided, they wouldn't go there again. That's if they haven't got her already, of course.' Her face reddened.

Cressida stared at her for a long moment.

'I'll make some calls and let you know.'

'But – how will you contact me?'

'They have phones here, right?'

'Yes but I can't *tell* you the address over the phone. There's never any fucking privacy.'

'But the police already know where the safe house is.'

'Not if they don't have her, they don't. She might have got out before they got there.'

Cressida sighed. 'How well does this woman know you? Could she … could she for example give evidence about your intent?'

'What do you mean?'

'Well that, for example, you' – she looked down at her notes – 'didn't do this to intimidate for a political, religious or ideological cause?'

A smile dawned on Joanne's face. 'Abso-fuckin'-lutely.'

But would that be unethical? Cressida wondered. Get evidence from a potential suspect who later may want to testify against Joanne, but didn't yet have her own lawyer? All the more reason to get to her quickly, Sandra would say. And it needn't be a conflict. If they were both pleading lack of terrorist intent, there was no problem. She pulled out her pen.

'Alright. What's the address?'

'Uh-uh,' Joanne said. 'You'll need a map.'

'I'll need a *map*?'

'Yeah, don't worry, I'm good at them.'

'You're good at them. Joanne, I'm not worried about your map drawing skills, I'm more concerned the place you're sending me needs you to draw one. In fact I'll have to draw it,' she said, glancing at the guard. 'If you do it they'll want to see it before you give it to me.' She pulled out her notebook and laboriously followed Joanne's instructions for a map. When it was finished Joanne nodded.

'That'll get you there.'

'We hope,' Cressida muttered, feeling distinctly uncertain of that. 'I'm not going to tell her to disappear though, Joanne. Since I've got your permission to – I'll tell her the charges you're up against, and suggest she gets a lawyer. Then I'll give her the number for Legal Aid.' She collected the Vicco and vegan chocolate and folded away the map. 'I'll have to give these to the guard out there to give to you.'

'I reckon our fifteen minutes are almost up,' said Cressida. 'While I'm here, I might as well tell you – extra charges have come through. There's quite a few of them.' She opened last night's fresh CAN on her iPad.

'There's still 93FA, as you saw last time – that's the one they refused bail on the first time, that we're appealing. Plus section 195 – *destroying property in a public place.* 203B – *sabotage: intentionally cause damage with the intention that it cause extensive destruction of property, being Liddell Power Station.*' Reading it all out made it all feel so unreal it was almost comical. How had the tiny blonde opposite accomplished all *that*? 'That's your three indictables – criminal charges that must be tried before a jury,' she explained. 'Then the three Table offences – which just means we can elect whether to have a jury trial or judge alone – first you've got section 55, *possessing or making explosives with intent to injure*; 196, *destroying or damaging property with intent to injure a person—*'

'What? I never intended to fuckin' injure anyone – give me that,' she said, reaching for the iPad, but Cressida kept reading.

'And 200 – *possession of explosives or other article with intent to destroy or damage property belonging to another person*. That sounds more like your Christmas firecracker situation, but anyway.' She handed her the iPad. 'All yours.'

Joanne scanned it, her expression dark.

'This is all bullshit. I didn't intend to harm anyone. Only property. And it wasn't in company.'

'Wasn't it?'

'Nuh,' she said, crossing her arms.

Cressida didn't press it. Time enough for that. 'Did you get a copy of that? They should have served you.'

'Yeah, somewhere,' said Joanne, inspecting her nails with studied disinterest. Then she looked up, eyes hollow.

'Cressida. Before you go – I was wondering …' She swallowed and rubbed her face hard with one hand. 'Is there anything you can do about my cell? It's just … it's pretty rugged in there.'

'It is prison, Joanne. It's not meant to be a holiday park.'

'I know, I know that, it's just …' She avoided Cress's gaze. 'It's just being by myself for you know, well, all the time, really. I'm … Well it's kind of making me think pretty dark.'

'What do you mean?'

'Oh, you know.' She brightened, forcibly. 'Don't worry. It's nothing. Everyone goes a bit crazy with no-one else around, right?' she said. 'I'm sure they'll give me a cell mate once I'm sentenced. Won't they?'

'I don't know, Joanne,' said Cressida softly. Joanne rubbed the side of her face again, hard, and her eyes were hard bright stones. 'Let's worry about that if and when it happens,' she said, trying to give her most hopeful smile.

'Yeah.' Joanne snorted. 'Yeah sure. Good point. Sorry. That's what I mean. Being by myself all the time's making me a bit, you know, *negative*.' She gave a short laugh. 'Hey just one more thing – when you see her?'

'Yes?'

'Just … just tell her I'm thinking of her?' she said.

On the way out Cressida stopped at the guard.

'Hi there. Is Bec short for Rebecca? And can I have your last name please?'

In the car Cressida sat down and dialled the number the visitor at Silverwater had given her. Tracking down this Williams woman through the gaols first seemed worth a try.

'Corrections,' a female voice answered.

'Hi,' Cress began. 'I'm a solicitor acting for one of the terror suspects recently arrested in connection with the power station bombings. I'm trying to find whether a' – she looked down at her note – 'Ms Saturne Williams has been taken into custody. My client believes she may have been arrested at a recent raid of suspect premises.'

There was a pause on the end of the line and then the woman said, 'Well, are you acting for Ms Williams?'

'Um, not at this point, no. It's a bit difficult when I don't know where she is.'

When the woman spoke next there was a smirk in her voice. 'In my day we called that ambulance chasing.'

*Well. Yes*, Cressida thought, *Quite.* Aloud she said, 'So you won't tell me whether she's in custody or not.'

'No, ma'am. Not until you tell me you're acting for her. Or you're a family member.'

It occurred to Cressida again that she could lie to her about it, but if she did that it would be twice in one week, and out of sheer force of habit she resisted.

'Thanks.' Cressida sighed and hung up. The criminal justice system was proving to be a real pain in the proverbial. This never happened on road projects. You bloody knew who your key players were, *and* you had their address. You sat in the same room with them and had perfectly wholesome, healthy, male-dominated pissing competitions over who had the bigger contract and the most of someone else's cash to throw around, then you all went out for beers together and talked about sport. But with this Fairbank matter it felt like nothing was *moving*. She hadn't even got the brief of evidence yet. Six weeks was an aeon away compared to the heartbeat speed things happened on corporate matters. Then a thought occurred to her. What about that prosecutor at the CDPP? He might know where she was, or at least whether she was in custody. But no. Even if Joanne's friend was innocent, any mention of a connection could be used to incriminate her client. Damn. Did this ever get any easier? She looked down at the notes again, wishing she'd kept some of Joanne's chocolate. Hang on – she still had some from the Partnership meeting. She ripped back the wrapper and took a bite. That was better. Her mind was instantly clearer. Now what? She would hoof it out to some place called Cobark on the *off chance* this Jupiter woman was still at large? Where the hell was Cobark anyway? She googled it and swore. The line showing the trip was a gigantic S on its side, to circumvent what looked like a bloody great mountain range in the middle. Six hours' drive from Wellington – or four if you went through that scary dark green bit between. She'd done that before on site visits to distant road projects – trusted the Google maps direct route and ended up on unsealed roads in the middle of nowhere, surrounded by cows. Nope. Sealed roads or nothing. And there was only so much driving she could do in two days. She dialled Esma.

'Esma. I have to get to a place called Cobark. As far as I can see it's' – she checked the map – 'back of Gloucester. Can you look up planes from Dubbo?' She'd have to get the Fiat back home too. 'Is there a train or something I can stick the Fiat on? Otherwise it's a six-hour drive. I have to be back tomorrow night for a thing with Felipe. Sorry, that's my fiancé. And then I'll need a hire car at Gloucester.'

'Sure.' There was a pause. 'Hmm. None to Gloucester direct I'm afraid. Nearest is Taree, and there's only two a day. How keen are you? There's one in three hours.'

Cressida looked at her watch. An hour to Dubbo. She'd get there with time to spare. But what about the car?

'That would be fan*tastic*, if it weren't for the car. I was hoping I could put it on the train or something. God, this is a nightmare.'

'Do you have a spare set of keys with someone in Sydney?' Esma said. 'You could leave the car at Dubbo airport, and I'll send someone on a flight first thing tomorrow to collect it.'

Her little Fiat, in the dark at Dubbo airport. If she was to find this woman tomorrow though, there seemed to be few other options. It was this or drive back to Sydney herself, then catch a flight to Taree on Friday after Felipe's gig tomorrow night, get out to Cobark or whatever it was called within the day, get the statement and fly back to Sydney on the nearest flight. It only gave her a day's leeway, and if anything got blown out, she wouldn't be back in Sydney in time for the road project meeting on Monday. And then she was meant to fly to Melbourne, before hopefully – she felt a little thrill – the Partnership vote happened on Friday … No. Cobark had to be today.

'Yes. My fiancé has a key. It's on his keyring. I don't know where he is right now, but I can call and find out. Leave it with me.'

'You've got enough to do. Give me the number and I'll call him. It can't be that complicated.'

*Oh thank God*, Cressida thought, with a rush of relief.

'That'd be great, actually. I *am* going to be a bit pressed for time getting on this flight. You're an angel, Esma. Thank you so much.'

'Not at all. It's been worth it just to see Brian looking happier. He's incredibly grateful to you, you know.'

Cressida felt a flush of pleasure. Her next thought was that it was probably also a good time to bring up the other part of the bargain.

'Well actually, just *on* that ...' she said, 'how are the confirmations going?'

'For what?'

'The Partnership vote, silly,' she laughed. 'We agreed. It was going to be next Friday.' Gratitude was one thing. But she had better not be doing all this bloody work and he'd forgotten.

'Oh *yes*,' Esma said. 'Brian *has* sent out the email – the issue is finding a room with video – but also you know how it is. Several of the Singapore partners are locked in negotiations with the Chinese government over some defence contracts apparently; it's proving quite difficult to pin them down. He's working on it though. He really wants you to get it.'

'We agreed,' said Cressida. 'It's Friday.'

'I'll chase it up with him.'

'Please. Thanks Esma, you're wonderful. I'll text you Felipe's number. Talk soon.'

She looked out over the buttery fields and fought off the fresh waves of frustration. *When* would she finally get back to her Building & Construction projects? She missed her corner office, her lunches with Pip, even the weekend triathlon training with Felipe. Medical functions and gorgeous frocks. At the same time she felt stupidly guilty at even thinking like that, when there was a woman a few hundred metres away facing the prospect of solitary confinement for the rest of her life. How did criminal lawyers deal with this kind of pressure all the time? Of knowing one screw-up could send their client to prison? The whole thought of it made her want to vomit, or eat a three-course meal with icecream and chocolate. She put the car in gear and started for Dubbo.

# 20

The gravel road to Cobark was narrow and winding, and the wind whistling down off the sharp folds of the mountains made the tiny hire car rattle as it ground its way up the ridge. Rain was coming down in sheets. Ahead of her an expanse of treeless fields stretched to the horizon, not a house or other sign of human habitation save a single wire strung between widely spaced telegraph poles. Her phone was at zero bars. When she couldn't see the road anymore she pulled over, the sound of the rain drumming on the roof in a pattern that numbed the brain. And then when it finally eased and she put the car in gear, the wheels spun and the car didn't move. Resisting the urge to keep trying, she swore, dragged the golf umbrella from behind the front seat, and got out.

The rain hit her in an onslaught, tearing at her hair and wrenching the umbrella inside out in a roar of canvas. Madly she fought it back into position and squatted at the back wheel. A small river had been developing round the car as she'd been waiting, and the wheel was two inches in mud, around it the earth soft in a way that meant it would only go deeper if she tried to drive out. *Fuck.* She would have to wait it out.

But then what? Push the car out by herself?

What did Leo used to do, she wondered. He always knew what to do in this kind of situation. If she could put something firm under the front of the back wheel, it wouldn't sink any more, and there was a chance she could drive out. A plank or a flat rock would do. Just as soon as this rain stopped. There had to be one somewhere. The temperature had dropped ten degrees since Gloucester and the rain on her skin was cold. She pulled a raincoat out of her wheelie bag in the back seat and put it on, then ran along the roadside to look for something to use. But there were only rivers of sodden grass and cow dung. In frustration she threw herself back in the car. In the rear-view mirror she saw her mascara had become a Rorschach blot, her blowdry a complete mess. She looked down at her feet. The expensive mushroom-toned knee boots were ruined, sodden and streaked with mud, and her precious white Petit Bateau t-shirt clung to her and had totally lost its shape. She pulled out a merino zip skivvy she'd shoved in at the last minute and her workout hoodie and put them on, the raincoat back on top. Fine and twenty-five, the forecast had said. The guesthouse manager at Taree had said 'unpredictable microclimate'; she'd ignored him.

A headlight appeared and a dirtbike sped past, its driver bent low against the rain. *That never happens in reality*, she reassured herself as she locked all the doors; only in B-grade horror movies. Oh okay, there was *Wolf Creek*, she thought, for the second time that trip, but what was one true story? When the rain stopped she'd get out and go find a tow. To pass the time she made a mental list of all the things she'd bring next time she went visiting clients in a wilderness. Starting with gumboots and a big fuck-off sou'wester. Okay and maybe an axe.

In a few minutes the drumming quietened, and Cressida wound down the window a crack. The rain had reduced to an amiable patter on the muddy road beside her, but outside looked awfully dark and deserted.

Above the outline of the hillside on the right the clouds parted, and a crescent of moon emerged. Then in the distance came the faint burr of a motor, and ahead on the road a single headlight appeared. She wound down the window and waited. The bike slowed, then pulled up beside her. The rider lifted the visor on his helmet and she relaxed a little. Someone with eyes that blue couldn't be dangerous.

'Oh thank God,' she said. 'I'm a bit stuck. I need a push. I just pulled off the side of the road in the downpour and then the wheel got stuck in the mud.' The words came out in a rush. 'And there's not a bloody rock or anything within cooee, of course, is there. In fact there's bloody nothing out here.'

The fellow looked at her impassively and took off his helmet. Thick black hair stuck up in all directions, a double-ring earring glinting in one ear. He hung the helmet from one handlebar and swung leisurely off the bike, then ambled behind the car, disappearing for a moment as he squatted down to look. She got out of the car and followed him. When he stood up again he spoke.

'Yep. You're bogged alright.'

*Well,* Cressida thought, *you're obviously a genius. Any chance of some* **help?**

'Look,' she said, 'I don't mind if you do the whole knight in shining armour thing, you know. I mean I'm a feminist but I'll make an exception given I'm out of my postcode.' She leant against the car and thought maybe that was funny. There might have been a glimmer of laughter in the blue eyes, but none surfaced.

'Thanks for the tip,' he said, watching her. Slowly he put a hand in one pocket of his jacket and pulled out a packet of something. From the other pocket there came a lighter. He was rolling a cigarette. Here she was, stuck in the middle of nowhere and, going by those clouds, about to get saturated in another downpour, and he was having a smoke.

'Look if you drive the car,' she said in exasperation, *'I'll* push.'

That did get a chuckle. He looked at her, clearly unconvinced the bedraggled, thin-hipped chick in front of him could push much of anything, and continued to light the cigarette with hands cupped against the wind.

'You leave that for your babies,' he said, in a drawl that made Cressida flush from head to foot. Slowly he dragged on the cigarette and, after throwing another long look in her direction, squatted down behind the car again. Cressida sat against it again and waited, deciding that if she wanted his help she should probably be polite. Finally the man ground the cigarette into the gravel and pulled out a Kodak film container, dropping the cigarette butt inside. He stood and ambled slowly back to the bike and started unstrapping something from the other side: a large plank of wood, a bit wider than the wheel. Then from the pannier at the back, a brick.

'What, you've had that the whole time?' she said. 'Where from?'

He nodded towards a barn halfway down the valley.

'How long were you sitting over there for?' she said.

'A while,' he said. She looked at him and felt a fizz of anxiety, thinking maybe he wasn't that safe after all.

'Don't worry, love, not everything's about you,' he said then, and his face broke into a grin. 'I was waiting out the rain, wasn't I?' He knelt down behind the bogged wheel. 'Just like you.' She sighed and relaxed again, watching as he jammed the plank in front of the bogged wheel, the brick behind it.

'Get in and try that,' he said, standing up. 'Nice and easy. Just go slow at first.'

She got in, turned on the ignition and pressed the accelerator gently. After a moment there was traction, and the car eased up the plank and onto the road. Grinning, she guided it back onto the centre and fell back against the seat, blowing out a sigh.

'Thanks,' she said out the window. 'You're a life saver.'

'No problem,' he said, and swung back onto the bike. 'Where you headed?'

'Yeah exactly, I was about to ask you …' She peered at the scribbled directions. 'I don't suppose you know where RMB 2459 Gloucester River is?'

His eyes narrowed. 'Can't say I do,' he said, blinking. 'You want to be careful out here without a parks map. Very easy to get lost.'

'Yeah I'm not surprised. I got directions … I guess I'll just keep looking then. Thanks.'

'It's not that way though,' he said, indicating the way ahead. 'There's nothing up there but the Barringtons.'

'The what?'

'The National Park. And you'll be toast without a four-wheel-drive. I'd head back to town and get a parks map from the forestry office. Come back when it's not raining.'

'Yeah I wish,' Cressida said. 'I've got to get back to Sydney by tonight, unfortunately.'

'Sydney? What you doing up here?'

'Oh, bit of this, bit of that. Thanks again for your help. See you.'

'Bye.' The man wheeled his bike across to the side of the road and waited. Cressida realised he wasn't going to go anywhere until she did. It would be awkward now to go the way he had just suggested she not.

'Gotta find somewhere to turn round,' she explained with a grin.

'Don't want to get bogged again.'

'Up there.' He pointed towards the barn. 'There's a driveway into the shed. That'll do you.'

'Sure. Thanks.' He was either being *really* helpful or he *really* didn't want her to go up that way. Dutifully she drove to the driveway and reversed into it, then drove back past him and waved. In the rear-view mirror she could see he was still watching her when she rounded the bend. When he was out of sight she stopped and waited, listening to the low roar of the wind. The map, and something about his demeanour, told her that 'up that way' was exactly where she wanted to go. There was a wider part of the road up further and she reversed again, careful not to get bogged again.

But when she rounded the corner he was still there, and now it really was awkward. *Alright then*, she thought, *we'll play it your way*. When she was level with the bike again she stopped and rolled down her window.

'My name's Cressida Mitsok.' She stuck out her hand, and after a moment he shook it. 'I'm Joanne Fairbank's lawyer. I'm here to see Saturne Williams. Or I mean ... Saturne Wild Deer.'

On his face surprise registered, then the hint of laughter again, followed by satisfaction.

'Interesting. You didn't look like a cop. Got any ID?'

She pulled out her Law Society card and showed it to him; he squinted at it and then back at her.

'Well I'll be. Let's get the hell out of this rain then.' He grinned and pulled the helmet over his head. 'Follow me.'

*Thank God for that*, Cressida thought, flooded with relief. She started up the car again and followed his red and black jacketed back into the rain. They travelled another few minutes down the road and across a swollen causeway. Then around a corner past a copse of bedraggled gum trees a driveway appeared. Deep grooves that looked freshly made cut the wet grass on either side of the drive. At the top sat a house with squares of light in the windows.

'Wait here,' he said. Cressida watched him accelerate up the hill and waited, looking out at the sodden paddocks as the rain drummed on the grass. Next to the cattle grid a scarecrow in a gas mask regarded her, water dripping from the mop-heads at either end of its arms. It wore a button-up flannelette shirt stuffed with straw, its distended belly hanging over soaking jeans and an old leather belt; around the gas mask someone had draped some yellow daisies. She didn't hear the footsteps beside her until the long wet barrel of the shotgun was inches from her face.

'I suggest you turn your car back on, lovey, and reverse right on out of here. Now.'

She swallowed. Without looking at him she turned on the ignition.

'I suppose a reasonable discussion's out of the question,' she said.

'Does it look like it?'

'Yep.'

'You'd be right.'

'Okay,' she said, still looking ahead. 'I'm going back onto the road. It's public property. Then you can go fuck yourself. I don't think you guys want GBH on your rap as well as association with terrorists.'

The gun barrel dropped a few inches. Without waiting for a reply she roared backwards in a splatter of mud. The man stood with his gun lowered, a skinny grey-eyed character wearing a check shirt like the other fellow, his loose brown jeans cinched with a thin leather belt over feet that stood bare in the mud. She stopped a few metres away, looking at him expressionlessly, and he remained with the gun lowered, watching her back. Then a figure could be seen struggling down the driveway towards them, calling something, with the man in the bike jacket calling out behind.

'For fuck's sake, Mousemoon,' Cressida made out her saying. 'Put the gun *away*. I'm so sorry,' she called out to Cressida. 'Put it down. Now.'

'She's fucking AFP. Look at that car,' the man with the gun yelled. Well, Cressida thought. That's what you do with federal police officers. Pull a shotgun on them.

'Saturne. Come on. Can you go back inside?' the bike rider called as he arrived beside them both, out of breath. Then he turned to the other bloke, and indicated Cressida. 'Actually she's a solicitor,' he said. 'Andy's.'

The gun man's eyes narrowed. He hawked and spat on the ground.

'Why didn't you say so.'

The woman came towards Cressida, barefoot also. There was an enormous growth coming out the left side of her neck and a tube coming out of her nose. She paused for a moment, leaning on a fence post to catch her breath. Finally she spoke.

'You've seen Andy?'

'You mean Joanne Fairbank?'

'Yeah. Goes by the name of Andy round here.' With effort the woman held out her hand for Cressida to shake it. 'I'm Saturne.' The hand was thin and cool in Cressida's, with a couple of threadbare woven bracelets around the wrist similar to the neckwear Joanne/Andy had worn. 'That's Dale,' she continued, nodding at the man in the jacket. 'And you've already met Mousemoon. They're harmless.'

Cressida looked at Mousemoon, pointedly. 'Yeah right. If you tell that dickhead to move, I'll come up and tell you all about it.'

At her words Mousemoon gave her a last contemptuous look, shouldered the rifle and wandered back behind the paling fence.

'Sure,' Saturne said. 'Follow me.'

'Saturne, stay there,' said Dale, concern etched on his face. To Cressida, he said, 'Can you please give her a lift back to the house?'

'Of course.' Cressida leaned across to open the passenger door.

The woman's shoulders slumped slightly and she smiled. 'Thanks. That'd be great.'

With Saturne in the passenger seat Cressida put the car in gear and eased over the cattle grid again, driving carefully around Dale as he walked. The woman leant back against the headrest, her eyes closed; there was a sheen of sweat on her skin. She was thin, even thinner than Joanne, with short, shiny brown hair and high cheekbones, but where Joanne's skin was pink, this woman's was olive, and distinctly yellow. Her collarbones stuck out of a threadbare white cotton shirt, over loose pants pale ochre in colour. In close proximity she smelled of lavender oil and sweat, and something else Cressida couldn't put her finger on. Sitting so close to her in the car, there was something raw and soft about her, like Joanne. Both women so far had been unlike any other women Cressida had ever encountered, even the doe-eyed creatures Jerome had used to bring home every couple of weeks. Cressida felt like she just wanted to keep looking at her, but she had to drive the car so she resisted.

As they neared the house two dogs hurled themselves off the verandah, barking. An old man in a bulky woollen jumper and jeans kneeled at the foot of the front door, hammering a panel of wood onto it. He stood as they reached the top of the driveway and stooped to look into the car, past Cressida to Saturne.

'Who's this?' he asked her.

'Cressida,' Saturne answered, opening her eyes. 'She says she's Andy's lawyer.'

'Joanne had a Legal Aid lawyer.'

'Not anymore she doesn't,' Cressida said, turning off the car. 'That was just the duty solicitor on the day of the bail application. Which we're appealing, by the way.'

'Well,' he said, watching her, 'is that right? Got anything in writing from her?'

Oh for God's sake, Cressida thought. It was like these people didn't *want* any help.

'Just the name of some bizarre Ayurvedic toothpaste,' she said, 'and this address.'

She found Joanne's directions on her notebook and her Law Society ID card again and handed them to him.

'Do you really think I'd come driving up here on my own to a house that was just raided by the federal police, without good reason?'

The man glanced at the map and ID card and handed them back.

'Though going by your man on the gate,' Cressida continued, 'I should have come with an armed guard. That's one way to get the police breathing down your neck, by the way. Is that gun licensed?'

'I guess you'd better come in then,' the old man said. He returned her card and held out a large, callused hand. 'Merv. You're a bit wet.'

'That's my fault,' said Dale, as he reached the top of the hill. 'She was helping me get her unbogged.' Cressida flushed and stepped out of the car.

'Come inside, Cressida,' Saturne said. 'I'll make you a chai.'

'Oh, no, honestly, it's fine,' said Cressida, despite her dry mouth. She wasn't about to let this woman lift a *finger*. She looked like she was only barely managing to stand.

'I'll do it, Saturne,' Dale said, crossing back to pull two large bags out of the panniers of the bike, together with a smaller silver one. It looked like coffee and a pharmacy bag. 'For God's sake get back on the couch.'

'I'm fine,' said Saturne, wiping her forehead.

'You need to rest,' Dale said.

Saturne rolled her eyes and spoke to Cressida. 'Follow me.'

Merv stood aside and Cressida acquiesced. Inside the house a warm hallway full of shoes and gumboots greeted her, together with a smell that reminded her of aromatherapy massages and baking bread. The dogs from outside scurried up, sniffing. Merv turned to her, and then just as he spoke the roar of rain swept the roof again.

'Well, we turned on the weather for you,' he said loudly over it. 'How was the causeway?'

'The causeway,' Cressida repeated, simultaneously trying to wrestle with her mac and fend off the dogs as they scrabbled at her knees with pointy claws.

'Yeah, where you cross the river bout ten k's back. Here.' He held out his hand for her notebook so she could shuck her raincoat. 'Bush, Freebie, Castro.' The dogs peeled away and subsided behind him on hair-covered blankets against the wall. He took the raincoat from her and hung it on a hook.

'God I wouldn't have a clue,' she said, unzipping her boots and trying to yank them off. If she got the wet mud off now there might be some chance they'd survive, she decided. 'I crossed so many of them. What's with this weather?' Saturne appeared with a bath towel and handed it to Cressida, who gratefully squeezed out the water from the ends of her hair with it, and handed it back. 'In Dubbo yesterday it was 38 degrees. Have you got any paper towel?'

'Is that where Andy is?' she said.

'Yes. Wellington, actually. The women's prison there.'

Two heads appeared around the corner of the door to the hallway, listening.

'How is she?' Saturne asked softly. 'Can I visit her?'

'She's fine. I mean, well, you probably knew – her arm's in a cast, but she was in good spirits. She wanted chocolate,' she said, trying to sound cheerful. 'They moved her there yesterday. I had a hell of a time finding her, actually.'

'I can't believe you *did*,' Saturne said, looking at the ceiling. 'No-one would tell *us* where she was. How did you find her? I'm sorry – we should go through to the lounge room. We're all going to have so many questions ...'

Cressida grimaced. 'Um, I don't have much time, actually,' she said, following her with the others and Merv behind. 'She just wanted me to find you and ... warn you.' Without becoming an accessory after the fact, she thought. 'About the charges. And suggest you get lawyers.' She paused as Saturne subsided onto a long velvet sofa and pulled a blanket over herself. 'And then I have to get going. I'm on the 3.30 plane from Taree.' She checked her watch. 10.30. She'd left Taree at eight, so if she left here by 12, adding half an hour for good measure and then allowing a half hour at the airport, she would make it.

One of the others indicated a couch opposite Saturne for Cressida, and the rest sat down on armchairs and cushions on the floor. It was a cosy room, with large plate windows opening onto fields beyond, and hooked throws on the back of two threadbare couches. Small squares of coloured material hung across a fireplace that had glowing coals in it. She sat down, self-consciously smoothing her damp hair out of her eyes. It wasn't the most professional first impression she was making, but what could she do? Saturne quickly introduced them all, though the names went straight out of Cressida's head as soon as she heard them. They were all looking at her with such unabashed curiosity. She put her bag and notebook beside her on the floor, feeling like she was about to read a children's book in a library. How to begin?

'You guys were raided the other day, is that right?' she said.

'Fuck oath,' said a man with sideburns and a buzzcut, and a fat silver ring hanging in his septum. His pale blue eyes were underscored with dark half circles. 'Are they allowed to do that?'

'They bloody wrecked everything,' said the other, a woman with a nose ring and half-shaven dreadlocks. 'We had to chuck two of the couches out because they fucking sliced them open. I mean, what were they *looking* for? They pulled all the books off the shelves, smashed crockery, upended drawers ... It was a bloody mess. They had dogs, for God's sake. *Dogs*.'

'Where were you guys?' asked Cressida. 'Sorry, it's a bit hot in here – I might take this off,' she said, peeling off the hoodie. That was better.

'We all got out, thank God. Mousemoon saw a bunch of cars coming up the mountain in his binoculars, and we all legged it. I hid in the roof of the outdoor loo, and Dizzy went under the house, didn't you, Diz.' She looked at a woman with long frizzy hair and a tattoo on her neck. 'Saturne was at the doctor's, thank God.'

'Oath,' Dizzy said. 'I'm not having my ex get my kids.'

'So then,' Cressida said, 'you guys have probably realised this by now. They're calling you terrorists.'

'Terrorists?' Buzzcut said, 'Yeah right. *Terra*ists. Fighters for Mother Earth. Fuckin' A.' He thumped his fist sideways into his chest.

'But that's what I mean,' Dreadlocks pressed. 'We had nothing to do with it. Well. I mean we were totally behind Andy and the ones that did it' – she looked around for agreement – 'but all of us, none of us can go to gaol. Dizzy's got a child in Dungog, Jason's got form and knew they'd throw the book at him – and I'm opening my own interior design business in Gloucester. Reduce, upcycle, roadkill as artwork, that sort of thing. Dale in there' – she nodded towards the kitchen – 'he wasn't even involved until after it happened. He just stepped in to help with a few of them that got hurt. Until they turned themselves in, because they couldn't go to hospital. And then Andy sent him up here to ... to look after Saturne.' She squeezed Saturne's bony knee under the blanket. 'And Saturne, well ... she's got health issues. So, I mean, we were all *miles* away when it happened – we made sure we were. So what the fuck were we being raided for?'

'Well that's the thing,' Cressida said carefully, picking up her folder. She pulled out her iPad and clicked on the new CAN. 'This is Andy's charge sheet. So far,' she said, pointedly. 'As you can see, it's, well, it's long. And the thing is' – Dreadlocks took the iPad from her and swore under her breath as she read the contents – 'with the terrorism laws – it's an offence just to *associate* with a "terrorist organisation". I mean – she hasn't been charged with terrorism yet, but it's ... well I think it's only matter of time. And then there's also' – she hesitated, not wanting to overwhelm them but having little choice, – 'aiding and abetting sabotage and criminal damage under state law. So ... somehow, I guess, they've found out that you know her, or know whoever else has been arrested and charged, decided there's a terrorist organisation involved, and they're ... well they're after you too.'

Dizzy had gone pale.

'No way,' Dreadlocks said, handing the iPad back to Cressida.

'I'm not up on the finer points of it,' Cressida said, 'but basically if you "intentionally associated" with her, knowing she's a member of or promotes a terrorist organisation's activities and you supported its existence, that's enough. If you gave them money or resources, that's also a crime. That's what Andy wanted me to tell you. Particularly you, Saturne.'

'But we're not terrorists. None of us are,' said Jason.

'I know. But they will try and say you are.'

There was a silence.

Then Dreadlocks spoke. 'What are we going to do?'

They were all looking at Cressida. *Jesus*, she thought, *you're asking* **me**?

'Don't look at me,' Cressida said. 'I'm just legal. Anything else and I risk the same association with terrorism charges myself.'

'Shit,' Jason said again.

'Saturne,' Dreadlocks said. Saturne had closed her eyes and was lying back against the pillow. The dark yellow fabric was nearly the same colour as her face. Dale arrived in the lounge room with a tray laden with rounded earthenware cups, a tall glass of dark purple liquid, and a squeeze tube of honey. He offered one of the cups to Cressida.

'Oh, thanks,' she said, looking into the cup gingerly. It didn't look too bad: tea-coloured with leaves floating in it, emitting a tasty clove and cardamom smell. Dale set the tray on a coffee table and held the squeeze bottle over her cup.

'Honey?'

'Thanks.'

He added it to her drink and held out the purple liquid to Saturne, who sat up with difficulty and took it, then he sat on the end of the couch at her feet.

'What is it today?' Dreadlocks asked.

'Beetroot, ginger and kale,' Dale said.

Saturne drank it then put it back on the coffee table.

'Can I have a look at the charge sheet?' she said softly.

Cressida handed the iPad to her. Saturne did a sharp intake of breath when she had read some way down. That would be the sabotage charge, Cressida thought. Saturne put the iPad down beside her and sat back and closed her eyes again. Then she put her hand over her mouth and stood up, throwing off the blanket, and staggered down the hallway. There was the sound of vomiting. Dale put down his cup and followed her.

'Heavy shit,' Jason said.

Cressida stared into her tea. Then she took a deep breath, and said quietly, 'You need to be aware you're all implicated, and get yourself lawyers.'

'How do we do that?' Dizzy exclaimed. 'We're all skint.'

'You might be lucky and Legal Aid will act for you.'

'But that's so *fucked*,' Jason said, standing up. 'We just told you, we had *nothing to do with it*. I mean, I was just a hanger-on, at first, you know, because it sounded kind of exciting.' He started to pace. 'I'm a fucking engineering student, for fuck's sake. And I'm totally down with what they did, by the way,' he said, pausing to glare at Cressida. 'Those fucking power stations were killing us all. But I never went to any of the planning meetings after, I dunno, a year or so. Dizzy just went because they used to meet in the cafe where she worked, said they sounded like people who were finally *doing* something. And Taina' – he indicated Dreadlocks – 'she was the same as me. Thought it sounded cool at first – but then got out when she realised they were serious.'

'So how did they track you down up here, then?' said Cressida. It seemed unlikely a connection with Joanne that thin would lead to twelve federal agents kicking down the door.

'I have no idea,' said Jason. 'Phone tapping? Secret cameras? Man – maybe they were filming us, Taina! That would have given some of them a thrill …' He finished with a bawdy laugh.

'No, I mean, really. What's the connection between you guys? Did you ever live together? Phone each other frequently?'

'Buy ammonium nitrate together?' Jason said, and Taina glared at him.

'Jason, this is serious,' she said. 'Anyway, they didn't use ammonium nitrate, they used … oh.' She looked at Cressida. 'I guess we shouldn't be telling you this stuff, should we.'

'Well, yes, probably best not.' Cressida sighed. 'Best to tell it to your lawyer. Or not,' she said, remembering Sandra's words. 'Do you guys have internet access here? You can go online on the Legal Aid website and apply for …'

Saturne had appeared in the doorway. When she spoke her teeth were stained red, and for a moment Cressida thought it was blood.

'How long is it?' she said.

'How long's what?'

'The sentence,' said Saturne. 'What's the max?'

'Oh.' Cressida swallowed. 'For sabotage?'

Saturne shook her head. 'The other one.'

'Oh. For … terrorism? Um. It's mandatory life imprisonment. And life means … well. Life.'

Taina gasped, and Cressida continued quickly, 'For Andy, I mean. If she's found guilty. For you guys, for association …' – she clicked quickly to the Criminal Code tab – 'three years.'

'Jesus,' Jason said, sitting down. Dizzy went pale, then ran out of the room. Over the rain the sound of cupboard doors being thrown open emanated, then coat hangers jangling.

'Dizzy,' Taina called out, and ran after her. Jason had leant back against the couch with his eyes closed.

'Fuck,' he said, and jumped up too. 'Taina. Where is it? Where *is it*?'

'No,' said Taina, coming back to stand in the doorway. 'There's none left. The guy couldn't get here in the rain, remember? Besides, it's not going to help. Baby it's going to be okay.' She stepped forward and pulled Jason's head towards hers, pressing forehead to forehead as strange animal groans came out of Jason and he pressed the heels of his hands to his eyes, swearing over and over. Then in a flash of frizzy blonde hair Dizzy swept down the hallway, and the front door slammed.

'Shit,' Taina said. She grabbed Jason's hand. 'Come outside. On the verandah. Fresh air. Now.'

She pushed him towards the front door. Saturne was on the floor in the doorway staring at nothing. Dale emerged from the bathroom wearing rubber gloves and holding the toilet brush. He squatted down in front of Saturne.

'Are you okay?'

Saturne looked across at him, her eyes glassy.

'Yeah,' she said. 'I could do with a glass of water though.'

'Sure,' said Dale, and kissed her forehead.

'Thanks for coming,' Saturne said to Cressida, who was standing.

'Oh. Oh God, no problem.' She thought guiltily of how resentful she had been of the journey. These people were in chaos. They were like sitting bloody ducks. She knelt in front of Saturne.

'But what I keep wanting to say, Saturne,' she began, 'is that the whole point of me acting for her is to get her *off* any terrorism charges. I mean, I think we can. We've got the best federal crimes barrister in Australia – probably the planet – working on it, and, well, I never like to say what I think chances are, but if anyone can get her off, she can.'

'Wow,' Saturne said staring at her. 'Really? You organised all that?'

'Oh no, not really,' Cressida looked away. 'I just got roped into it. Um.' Did Saturne know that Brian was Joanne's father? Did she know he was a Partner at Hannes Swartling? She decided she could take the risk that she already knew. If she didn't what she was about to say would be unremarkable. 'Her dad did the organising, actually.'

'That's … that's fantastic,' said Saturne, eyes shining. 'Did you hear that, Dale?' she called towards the kitchen. 'The best criminal barrister in Australia. So … so she might get off then?'

Cressida smiled. 'Yes. She might. I mean, she'll still go to gaol,' she said quickly, 'but the criminal damage stuff, it's just, you know ten years. Paroled earlier if she's a good girl in gaol. That's partly why I'm here. Would you be willing to give evidence, if it came to it? About her motivations, I mean? It will be hearsay, but an exception will apply.'

'Wow. Yes. Oh God, of *course*. Wow wow wow.' Saturne moved to get up, but fell back and Cressida helped her up. 'Sorry. Oh thank God. You're an angel. You're a *bloody angel*,' she said, holding onto her forearm. Dale emerged into the hall again holding a glass of water.

'Whoa,' Cressida said. 'No I'm not. I'm just doing my job. So if I could just do a quick preliminary interview' – she checked her watch over Saturne's shoulder – 'I'll be able to leave by 11.30.' It would be good to get going early if possible, given the weather, she thought. She would be glad to get off those maze-like muddy roads and onto some tarmac.

'Oh,' said Saturne, leaning back to look at her. 'Won't you at least stay for lunch? I think the bread's just about to come out of the oven – has it, Dale? And all one hundred per cent vegan and organic,' she said, smiling.

'Yes the bread's ready,' he said to Saturne. Then he turned to Cressida. 'So that's it?'

'What do you mean?'

'That's it. You're going, just like that. You come, drop your bomb, and piss off before anyone knows what's hit them?'

'Dale,' Saturne said.

'Much less offering to help.' He looked at Saturne. 'I mean it. What was it, best barrister in Australia, for Andy, she's got – and what about the rest of you?' He turned on Cressida. 'You heard what they said. Saturne's got *cancer*,' he said, as if Cressida couldn't see the tumour. 'If she goes to gaol, she could *die*. Dizzy's got a kid. Jason just started at uni. He's got his whole life ahead of him. You heard them. They *weren't involved*. And look at you, driving up here in your posh rented car, with your private-school education, and your flash Eastern Suburbs home to go back to, and you're just going to *drop them in it*?'

Cressida stared at him, feeling all the blood drain out of her face.

'Dale. That's enough,' said Saturne. 'We don't know anything about Cressida's situation. She's obviously doing what she can.'

'Oh yes I do,' Dale said. 'I know everything worth knowing about her. People like you are everywhere,' he said. 'Using your fancy university education to drop a tiny morsel in the social justice bucket, then fuck off to your three hundred thousand a year job at some evil place that screws the same people ten times over. Let me guess. What's in it for you?' he said, appraising her. 'Going by that rock on your finger, you're engaged to someone rich, so it's not the money ... let me see.' He looked into her eyes and considered whatever he thought he could see in them. 'Ambition. Ah yes. Get a terrorist off and make a name for yourself.'

'Dale, you have to stop,' said Saturne. 'Now.'

'No, I've got it,' he said. 'You're doing someone a favour. Ah yes, I thought so. Someone powerful. Who's going to make this all worth your while when it's over. Who is it? Your boss? I just want to know,' he said to Saturne. 'She comes up here, she tells us the world's ending, or at least your bit of it, anyway, and fucks off to her day spa. Unbelievable.'

Cressida swallowed. Her heart seemed to have a death grip around her vocal cords. With difficulty she cleared her throat and spoke. 'Wow. Okay. I guess that's it then. Saturne, now that I've found you, we can do the statement over the phone.' She smiled awkwardly at the other woman, then bent and collected her things. 'If you just give me the landline and your email address, I'll send it to you once it's done and you can swear it with a JP in town. And I'll let Jo— Andy know you said hi.' *And how on earth is this girl going to get to a JP?* she demanded of herself. *She can hardly get off the couch. And what about that tumour? How do you know she'll survive that long?* It was no use though. She ran a hand over her face, appalled at herself for being near tears. She had to get out. 'Just one thing though.' She turned to Dale. 'You think this is social justice? As far as most of the world is concerned, you guys are slugs on the bottom of humanity's toilet, and from what I could tell, no-one else was fighting me for space to help you. So I hope that whole approach goes well for you. Bye.'

She stood up and tried to remember which way the door was. Left. It was left. Her car – where was it? Outside. She walked as quickly as she could towards the foyer and nearly ran into Merv, who was standing in the hallway. Out of the corner of her eye she saw Taina and Jason looking horrified in the kitchen. Great, humiliation *with* an audience, she thought. On the far side of the verandah the rain was still coming down in sheets. She sat down and yanked on her ruined boots, and was about to make a run for it to the car when Merv called out.

'Cressida. Cressida, wait. You won't make it. The causeways are flooded. Look, don't listen to him. He's angry. So many of them are. Come inside and at least have some lunch before you go.'

'You have got to be kidding,' she said, trying to make her voice work as well as be audible over the rain. 'I'm out of here.' She stared down the valley, wondering what he meant by the causeways. No. She couldn't be trapped. She had to get away. *Unbelievable.* She had come all the way up here to help. Nearly at the expense of her own career, she thought, thinking of the road project, and Pip, circling it like a velveteen vulture. *Don't cry*, she told herself. *Don't.*

Saturne appeared behind Merv, wrapped in a blanket.

'Oh God, Saturne, go back inside,' Cressida said. 'Really. It's fine. It's no problem.'

'No, it's just ...' She leant against the door jamb, catching her breath. Cressida ran to her, supporting her elbow. 'Just – what is it that you have to get back for, so badly?' said Saturne, gently.

'Oh, nothing,' said Cressida, feeling ridiculous.

'Look, you have to excuse Dale – he's, well, he's very passionate about … well about a lot of things. Don't take it personally. He's glad you've come, even if this is all you can do.'

More women making more excuses for more men, Cressida thought bitterly. Why the fuck do we do it?

'I'd love some lunch, actually,' she said, evenly. 'I'm starving. But I'll have it out here, if that's alright. Please, Saturne, go back inside. Andy would be cranky,' she admonished, in an attempt at humour.

'Okay,' Saturne said, managing a laugh. 'But only because you're having lunch.' With a final long look at Cressida she turned and disappeared. Cressida took a deep breath and sat down on a stump of wood against the wall of the house. She focused on the sound of the rain drumming on the roof and looked at her watch. It was twelve already. She had to get going. How bad could the causeway be, really? She looked at her hire car. Flash? It was only a little Golf. But then, hardly any of what Dale had said made any sense. And all this *wasn't* only as a favour to Brian, or anyone – not anymore. For heaven's sake, they just had no idea of the mess they were in. *Someone* had to help them.

The front door opened and Dale emerged with a tray of food, set it down beside her without speaking, and returned inside. Cressida looked at it and her mouth watered in spite of herself. It was like something out of a *Country Style* magazine, she thought with begrudged gratitude. There was a handled bowl of steaming, chunky orange soup, a fat, spiralled roll of seeded brown bread, a small dish of olive oil, and a salad of what looked like beetroot leaves, grated carrot, olives and baby tomatoes, all arranged alongside a folded linen napkin and some antique silver cutlery. To her surprise she ate the entire contents of the tray, including the bread roll, in minutes (though she drew the line at the oil). Then she wiped her mouth with the napkin, repacked the tray, and got up. In the kitchen Taina and Jason sat around the heavy wooden table, looking miserable. Merv was at the sink washing up.

'So what's this causeway then,' she said, putting the tray on the table. No-one answered, or even seemed to hear her. Then Merv turned.

'On the Cobark River,' he said, and nodded out the window. 'Where it crosses the road at Hannah's Spur. About five k's that way. It'll be a metre deep by now.' He put a blue colander on the drainer. 'Cars've been known to get washed away in this weather,' he said, eyeing her. 'Get found a hundred metres downstream. You don't want to be in one when that happens.'

'What about the other direction? Can I go round?' she asked.

'Only via Mudgee,' he said with a short laugh. 'And some godawful four-wheel-drive tracks. What's so urgent, anyway? Why don't you wait till tomorrow and see if it clears?'

'Uh-uh.' Cressida gave her own humourless laugh and shook her head. 'Fuck. I'm going to have to risk it. Thanks for lunch,' she said.

'You're mad, Cressida. It can't be done.'

'You don't understand,' she said. There was no way she was missing a second arrangement with Felipe unannounced – and especially not because of work; he'd probably call off the wedding, for goodness sake. 'A tractor. What about a tractor? This is a farm, isn't it? Don't you have one of those?' She peered out the wide plate-glass window, searching the paddocks.

'It's not that kind of farm,' Merv said with humour, shaking his head. 'What time do you have to be in Sydney?'

'Oh, God, I don't know. Any time before eight o'clock. The flight's at three-thirty.'

'I think you can give up on that idea.'

Dale appeared in the doorway to the hall, holding something that looked like a drained hospital drip bag. He wrapped the rubber gloves he was wearing around it and threw it in the rubbish bin under the bench.

'I'll take you,' he said.

'What?' said Cressida.

'I'll take you to Newcastle,' he said, washing his hands at the sink. 'You can fly from there. There's some forestry roads that get us through. Merv'll get us a map. It's only five hours' drive if we go via Moonan Brook instead of Gloucester. Make it by five, there's a flight at six and it takes forty-five minutes. You can ring and book on the way once we're in reception.' He dried his hands on a tea towel and checked his pockets. 'I just asked Mousemoon. We can take his four-wheel-drive. It's a heap of crap but it's the only one here. Since Dizzy's gone I'm the only one with a driver's licence. Except Merv, and he never goes anywhere.'

'But … I've got the hire car,' said Cressida.

Dale shrugged. 'It's four-wheel-drive only up there.'

'That's in the places it's not falling down the mountainside,' said Merv, draining the sink. 'Half the road is washed away at Murphy's pass. You should be right in the 'Rover though.'

'But …' Cressida was frantically trying to think of an alternative. Even crazy ones. 'Doesn't Mousemoon have a licence?'

'He lost his. Driving while unregistered. Besides, I'm not so scary you'd rather go with a gun-toting maniac, am I?' said Dale, with the hint of a grin.

Cressida thought about it. Close contest. 'Don't count on it.'

'I'm all talk,' he said, grinning widely now.

She looked around the table in a last hope that someone would have a better idea. But all of them looked present in body only, as if a spell had been cast. Come on, people, she felt like yelling – do something. If nothing else, make like Dizzy and get the hell out of *here* before the cops come back.

'What about Saturne?' she said.

'She'll be alright until tonight. I just gave her something. She's resting.'

Dale went into the foyer and pulled an oilskin off a hook, then handed Cressida her mac. Merv followed, loading Dale with instructions on how to find the way safely, and wordlessly they ran out into the rain. Cressida pulled her wheelie bag from the back seat and paused to look at the little white Golf.

'Hang on, if we're taking that' – she indicated the rusted truck Dale was heading for – 'what about the hire car?'

'I can ask Mousemoon to leave it at the crossroads. You can get someone to come and get it,' he called over the rain as he threw a daypack in the back of the vehicle. 'You can afford it, can't you?'

Discarding *another* car, Cressida thought. Lucky that Brian was picking up the bill. She threw the keys on the front seat and ran towards the truck.

# 21

On the climb up the mountainside Cressida clung discreetly to the dash, warding off thoughts of the Land Rover rolling into the river below as Dale negotiated bend after hairpin bend. Dried leaves and bird feathers crowded the top of the console, damp from water seeping through the split-screen windscreen; she inhaled their earthy smell and tried not to look down. After an hour driving in silence a log truck came into view, winding its way up the road on the valley opposite; Dale pulled over to wait for it to pass. Against the rasp and drip of the rain on the roof and the faint grind of the truck in the distance, Cressida watched him pull out a packet of tobacco and roll a cigarette. First he draped a corner of the small square of paper onto his bottom lip, then deposited a thicket of tobacco onto it in his palm, licked the sticky edge, and pressed it into shape. When he had struck a match and transferred its orange flame to the end of the paper, he took a deep breath and blew the smoke out a crack in the window.

'Sorry,' he said. 'Filthy habit.'

'No worries,' Cressida said, more to avoid a conflict than because she didn't mind. He was driving and she was in the middle of nowhere; it wasn't time to stand on principle.

'Sorry about my outburst before,' he said, extracting a piece of loose tobacco from his bottom lip. She kept her gaze on the windscreen, watching three drops of water converge and make a dash for it down the glass. 'I mean, I'm not sorry about its content. But I am about its delivery.'

*Oh that's big of you*, she thought, concentrating on the log truck inching up the first of the bends across the drop. It was carrying a gigantic log, and Cressida found herself wondering if it would make it up the hill. It disappeared from view round the curve but she could still hear its engine.

'I just ... I just have a problem with wealthy people who suck it up,' he said.

Cressida paused, considering whether to be drawn in or not.

'What do you mean, "suck it up"?' she asked, trying to sound neutral.

'You know. Enjoy their lavish lifestyles without giving anything back. I mean – see, there, I've insulted you again – you clearly are. Giving something, I mean. It was good of you to come all the way up here.'

*You don't know the half of it*, she thought.

'What you mean is you've got a chip on your shoulder,' she said. 'About not being "wealthy", as you put it.' She knew her words were harsh, but she didn't feel like being tactful.

To her surprise he laughed.

'You're probably right about that. I guess I do. Which is funny,' he said, 'because I went to a private school too.'

'Really?'

'Oh yeah,' he said, nodding and watching the log truck emerge again. 'Only for a year though. I hated it. I was on scholarship. They weren't my people.'

'You were lucky then. Having all that benefit and not having to pay for it. All my dad *did* was work, getting three kids through private school and uni.' She sighed, then she found herself continuing, 'I guess that's why he decided to pinch other people's money instead.'

'What?'

'Oh. Whoops. Sorry. Out of my postcode. Um. Yes, he's a lawyer, but a crooked one.'

'You're kidding.'

'Nope. You probably would approve though. He defrauded a big coal mining company.'

'Wow.' Dale frowned at her. 'What did he do?'

'Well. Don't suppose I could have one of those, could I?' she said, indicating his cigarette. He looked at her with a surprised expression, and pulled the packet out.

'I'm just kidding,' she said, on a short laugh. 'Talking about my father makes me wish I smoked. Anyway. Where was I. He made up a bunch of plaintiffs. Yep. That's right. Totally fake applicants, for a settlement on lung damage from coal dust. And then alluded to a bunch more. The whole claim for the *real* applicants – there were only about five of those – was probably worth a few hundred thousand. Well. He inflated it to 240 million.'

Dale gave an incredulous laugh. It *was* so extreme it was kind of funny, she supposed.

'That's amazing,' he said.

'Yeah well. It would have been especially amazing if he'd gotten away with it. Which he didn't. Unfortunately for the other side though, they only found out the affidavits were fake *after* they'd paid the money into the rehab fund. The company's still trying to get it back out again. Most of it's gone now' – Cressida shrugged – 'to people that never had to prove their case in court. They just had to get a letter from their specialist attesting that their lung damage was consistent with coal dust deposition. It was mostly gone before anyone found out.'

'What?' Dale paused. 'So, your dad had five real applicants, but he made up a whole lot more, and then the company paid out for all of them, just on his word?' He whistled. 'Brilliant.'

'Yeah, I thought you'd like it. Only problem is, he's now in gaol. He wasn't around that much when he was out either, though. Paying for that expensive education of mine. Plus defrauding people. It took years to pull off.' She gave a tight smile.

'So why do you think he did it?'

'Well. He got a cut, didn't he. Forty per cent of the bills.'

'But only from the real clients. The five of them, or whatever you said.'

'Well yeah. I don't know. I have no idea what curly plan he had for making money out of it. I'm sure there was one. Maybe he was planning to run off with the money. Anyway, that's not the point – he defrauded an opponent, lied to them point blank, and … well, there was a lot of other fallout, let me tell you.'

The logging truck ground past them in a clank of mud and noise.

'Like what?'

'Well, like I said, four years away from us for a start. But it wasn't just that. Can we get going? God knows how many of those trucks we're going to have to wait for.'

Dale took a final suck on his cigarette and stubbed it out in the same Kodak film container he'd had that morning.

'Why do you do that?' she asked. He glanced at her, picking up her irritation, and restarted the car.

'Because throwing it out the window is like ashing on your mother's skin. Sorry, did I ask too many questions?' he said, pulling back onto the road.

'Well I'd rather be asked them than judged without your even bothering,' she said, pointedly.

He looked across at her and laughed. 'Touché.'

She pulled her phone out again.

'When the hell is there going to be reception out here?' she said. 'My phone still says emergency calls only. I keep trying to tell it this is an emergency, but it's not interested.'

'I'd save your energy until at least the other side of the range. The nearest phone tower is Muswellbrook. Plus the mountains get in the way.'

'Great,' she said, throwing the handpiece down on the floor. They slowed at an intersection and he hunched forward to see the road on the right before coaxing the steering wheel left.

'You should just relax,' he said. 'Look at the scenery. The Gondwana Rainforests of Australia are just up there,' he said, pointing out his window up the hill.

'The gona what of what?'

'You know, Gondwana. The continent the whole world was originally part of. There's sassafras up there that's over a thousand years old. Imagine that, some tiny little seed, sprouting in the ground on that there mountain when the Vikings were sacking England. Now it's a massive tree. I don't know ... I just think that's pretty cool.'

*Yeah, I guess it is*, she thought, but wasn't in the mood for saying so. *Your turn*, she thought, and asked, 'So what about you? What brings you into the middle of nowhere giving coffee enemas to a woman you hardly know?'

He glanced at her, giving that same quizzical smile, then paused to concentrate on negotiating a bit of washed-away road. When they were safely on the next plateau he answered with a question.

'How'd you know about that?'

'The enemas? Someone ... someone in my family had cancer. She tried all that stuff but ... Well anyway, nice try. I'm asking the questions now.'

'I'm a doctor,' he said, smiling briefly.

'You're a what?'

'A doctor. Halfway to trauma specialist, actually. I had a bit of detour. Got the degree and even made it to senior registrar, whoopy do.'

'Wow. Really?' It was her turn to sound surprised. The first thought she had was, what was he doing smoking if he was a doctor? But he didn't strike her as the usual kind of doctor. More like a dark noirish Frankenstein one. Except for his smile. When he did that he didn't seem dark.

'Yes, ma'am. Seven years at the grindstone. Loved every minute of it.'

'So … so what happened?'

He looked across at her and held her gaze briefly. 'We're doing truth, aren't we?

'Um, well, yes that seems to be the order of the day. Fire away.'

'Became a ketamine addict.' He shrugged. 'If you're thinking about getting hooked on general anaesthetic – which by the look of you I don't think you are, but just in case – be prepared to watch at least half a decade of your life go by, and miss all of it.'

'Wow.'

'Oh I was okay the first time.' He sighed on a grin. 'They spot that sort of thing pretty quickly in the medical profession; more common than you'd think. It was fine while I was at home – went into rehab, the whole thing, got off it. But then I hit Southeast Asia, didn't I?' He slowed at a fork to another logging road and peered down it before continuing. 'Bright-eyed, bushy-tailed, ready to start afresh, and within six months I was on opium. Much easier to get there than here, and about five times as addictive. Well. Hello,' he said, slowing again, and Cressida followed his gaze out the windscreen. 'What do we have here?'

'Oh fuck,' said Cressida. In front of them across the road was an enormous tree.

'I'll see if there's a chainsaw in the back,' he said, pulling over. Cressida sat and stared at the log. The rain had brought out streaks of brilliant orange and pink in its bark. Up the hill its root ball was stark against the sky, mud caking the enormous tendrils that had kept it in the ground. She looked down at her boots. Calfskin or not, they couldn't keep her under house arrest forever. She opened the door and stepped out.

'Here,' Dale said, holding out a pair of gumboots. 'No chainsaw, and you'll swim in these, but at least you'll be able to walk around.' She grinned sheepishly and threw her shoes in the footwell, slipping white-socked feet into the enormous rubber boots. They felt loose and comfortable. She slipped on her mac; the rain was only a pattering now, rendering audible the rivulets that coursed down the muddy clifftop to their right and underneath the tree, in a miniature waterfall, into the rainforest below. She stretched and contemplated the clearing above them.

'I thought you said this was national park.'

'Not all of it,' he said, squatting down near the log and rolling another cigarette. He seemed to do it any time he needed to think or consider something. 'It's in patches. Or rather, holes.' He pointed at the part above them with the tobacco packet. It was mostly black, sodden stumps. 'That's a hole.'

'But that bit's not,' she said, looking down the slope.

'Not yet. It could be. You'd have to look at a forestry map.'

'What, you mean … you mean they'd log this?'

'Oh yes,' he said, drawing on the cigarette. 'Look at all that beautiful Silvertop. They'd be drooling over that. Miles and miles of inner city floorboards. The slope's a bit steep, but they're getting better and better at that these days.' He looked up at her. 'Selling the idea to the government, I mean.'

'But why isn't it in the national park too?'

'Why are your eyes so blue?' He shrugged. 'Twist of nature. Nobody knows why forestry does anything. The greenies would have asked for this whole valley, but they only got some of it. You'd have to ask Saturne.'

'Saturne?' said Cressida. 'What, was she a forest greenie?'

Dale laughed. 'I'm hoping she still is. She only came off the blockade because she got sick. That's how she met Andy.'

'Really? So Andy's a, what do they call it, forest activist as well as a … as well as a climate … um …person?'

'Andy?' Dale laughed. 'She's an everything activist. Saturne told me once that she fell in love with her for that, within ten seconds of meeting her. At the Granite Mountain blockade, back a few years ago. In Victoria. Oh. You did know they're lovers, didn't you?'

'Hah,' Cressida laughed at her own presumptiveness. 'No. But it makes sense now.' She checked her watch. It was nearly three o'clock. *Fuck.* 'Look, what are we going to do? This is making me crazy.'

'What is it you have to get back for anyway?' he said, stubbing out the cigarette. 'Is it really this life and death? This log's not going anywhere. You know we're going to have to drive back in reverse, don't you? At least until we find somewhere to turn around.'

Cressida slumped against the car and looked out at the rainforest.

'There's … something on tonight with my fiancé. He doesn't like being …' – she pondered which word to use; when the right one came, it was bitter – 'inconvenienced.'

'But surely he'd understand.' He looked at the tree and said with humour, 'It's not like you didn't try, is it?'

'Hah. Yes, well. You're right there. I feel like we should give it one last go, though.' *But what's the point of that?* she thought. It was two hours to Taree from Cobark, which meant five hours from here. There wouldn't be a plane to Sydney that would get her there in time.

'At least if we get back to the house I can use the landline and … oh God, tell him I'm not coming.'

Dale smiled at her and shrugged. 'Sure.'

'Sorry. I'm really giving you a run-around, aren't I?' she said, climbing back in the car.

'Don't worry about it,' he said. 'You're interesting.'

In a grind of gears and roar of engine, the car laboured up the hill backwards, Cressida resisting an overwhelming urge to look up to make sure he was keeping it on the road. Instead she had the surreal experience of watching the valley recede in front of the car, like being slowly winched above it. They reversed into a gravel pit on the side of the road and Cressida breathed a sigh of relief as they started on a forward trajectory again.

Once she'd decided it was hopeless though, she started to relax. Like Dale had said, she'd tried. Gone beyond the call of duty, actually. That was what it felt like, she realised. Duty. Maybe she didn't even *like* going to those balls. Her job was mostly, actually, just to stand around and be interested, charming, conversational *lubricant*, while Felipe stood in a corner with some fellow specialist and talked about nerdy orthopaedic surgeon things, or their most bizarre location for a triathlon meet. And sometimes she found herself wondering if that's all she was to Felipe: an accessory. The essential beautiful female accoutrement required for every successful medico's arm. At first it had been wonderful, hob-nobbing round town to suave, chandeliered places even senior lawyers didn't get to go to, unless they were Managing Partners like Michael or Brian. For a start it had been a great idea to buy too many Alex Perry fairytale frocks, appropriately divine shoes and accessories to match. But the events always left her tired and cranky, with sore feet from standing in a pair of gorgeous but ridiculous heels for four hours.

*You're being silly*, she told herself, *and melodramatic*. It was probably just disorientation from her new environment, and hunger – that was always a factor. But it made her think – maybe she could just avoid Felipe until he forgot she existed, and then at least she would be able to do what she wanted without feeling guilty. That was it, she realised. More and more these days he made her feel *guilty*, just for wanting a little … what? Independence. Self-determination, or something. In retrospect it felt ridiculous that she hadn't felt like she could even *tell* him about why she had had to go to Wellington. And, actually, he hadn't asked.

'Jeez,' Dale interrupted her thoughts. 'It really isn't our day. I don't know that I can get past that.' He slowed to a stop on the side of the road. The part of the road left from the bit washed away before had now disappeared completely, leaving a chasm three metres wide to the other side. For the first time Cressida began to think beyond the immediate issue of getting home tonight, and wonder if they were going to get out at all.

'Oh. Right. Fuck,' she said. 'What now?'

Dale had opened the door and the tobacco was coming out again. Cressida stepped back out into the mud.

'Not too close,' Dale said, catching her forearm as she approached the ravine. 'The edge will be unstable. In fact, I'm going to reverse a bit in case it gets wider.' The engine screamed as he drove a few metres back down the hill. Above them was another bare logging coupe, and another fallen tree. Cressida looked up the hillside to the dark clouds above it, wisps blowing across the heavier front behind. A bird called in the valley, its cry floating up on the cooling air. Dale returned and stood beside her.

Cressida looked across the other side of the gulf. Except for the logging coupe on the left there was thick forest on either side, mist rolling up from the valley. 'I guess we're walking then,' she said.

'It's twenty clicks back to Cobark. In an hour we'll be walking in the dark. I reckon we sit tight until someone comes the other way. Then get a lift back with them. And put something on the other side so they don't run into it themselves.'

Great. Fucking great. What an absurd mess this was turning into.

'Sure,' she said. It was rapidly becoming apparent she had no control over anything, this trip, so she might as well stop trying. 'How long do you think that will be?'

Dale shrugged. 'In this weather, a while. At least the car's mostly water-tight. We can stay overnight if necessary, and hope it's finer in the morning.'

'Jesus,' Cressida said, looking out at the forest. That sounded creepy. There were no bears in Australia, she was pretty certain of that much, or mountain lions or other scary stuff from American movies. But the vegetation looked dark and forbidding, and full of all sorts of unknown predators and crawlers.

'There's no drop bears in this part of the national park either, I'm told,' said Dale. 'Plenty down that way' – he pointed to the valley below – 'but none in this bit.' His face was serious, but Cressida caught the twinkle of humour in his eyes and laughed.

'Drop bears,' she said. Alright then. God, she hadn't even brought any reading. Except for the third appendix to the Technical Documents, tucked away in her wheelie bag. She might as well. She opened the rear door to the Land Rover and pulled her bag towards the back, unzipped it and hauled out the fat volume, plus her tags and yellow highlighter. Dale was squatted in front of the car, watching the water run down the slope, smoking his cigarette. She climbed into the front seat of the car and cracked open the document.

It was really boring. Sometimes the appendices to environmental impact statements were interesting, like heritage reports going into obscure facts about the built value of an area, or its Aboriginal history. But this one only had traffic projections, endless sound roses on maps showing predicted noise impacts, and table after table of current traffic data. In half an hour it was too dark to read it easily anyway. She was still ploughing through when Dale spoke.

'Well I'll be. Hey. Cressida.'

She looked up from the appendix. He was in the logging coupe above them, squatting at the head of the fallen tree, watching something. She put her head out the window and called back.

'What's up?'

He kept his eyes trained on the branches as he spoke. 'Come and see.'

There were ropes of lantana spread on the embankment. She clawed onto a pile of them, pulling herself up, and went to stand beside him.

'What is it?'

He parted the leaves and she looked. Tangled in the branches splayed against the ground under the weight of the top of the tree was a small, furry body. Its two tiny eyes regarded them.

'Ringtail,' he whispered. 'Hang on.' He pressed past Cressida in the narrow space between the tree and the drop and jumped back down onto the road. Mesmerised, she squatted down and reached into the mass of leaves. The little body was pressed under a branch as thick as her calf, and it froze under her touch, looking up at her with shining black eyes.

'Hello, little fella,' she said. 'You're a bit squashed there. What happened to your tree?' She wasn't sure why she was whispering, but it seemed to be the thing.

Dale returned with a rope.

'If I put this around the branch,' he said, bending down, 'we should be able to move it just enough to get her out. Can you do that when I pull?' He grinned at her. 'As soon as she's out, put her in your jumper. She needs to stay warm.'

'Um, sure,' said Cressida, still looking at the possum.

'Just be careful on that slope,' he said. 'We don't want you falling into the valley. Or worse – that mud.'

He looped the rope around and under the trunk of the tree and climbed over it.

'I'm not going to lift it, just bend it back a bit.'

That's good, Cressida thought. Otherwise there would be a definite prospect of the tree falling on her and knocking her into the valley to the drop bears.

'Ready?' he called.

'Yup,' she said, bending down to put her hands on the possum. It was bony and soft, and under its skin she could feel its heart, hammering. 'Ready, little fella?'

'The first thing she's going to try and do is run,' he said, 'so be ready. If she can, that's great, but either way, watch out for the claws. One, two, three.'

With a grind and strain of wood and shudder of leaves the limbs of the tree raised up half a foot, and Cressida whispered loudly, 'A bit more. That's nearly it …'

The moment the branch was off the ground the possum scrambled to get up, using its two scrawny front legs to scrabble at the foliage, but its back half wasn't co-operating. Talking softly to it Cressida scooped the animal up and pressed it up her skivvy, zipping the neck closed with her other hand so it didn't crawl straight out the top.

'Got her,' she breathed, feeling an incomprehensible thrill. Its little claws scraped her skin and she held it away from her through the fabric, yelping. It froze and she looked in at and laughed, awash with relief at having captured and not suffocated it in the process. Dale climbed back over the tree and stood beside her. He parted the gap to look inside.

'Awesome. Wow, she's gorgeous.'

'Stop looking down my top.'

Dale laughed. 'Sorry. Let's get her in out of the cold.'

He jumped down, holding his hand out for hers; her other hand stayed firm on the possum. She climbed into the front seat of the Land Rover.

'You did great,' he said, looking in at the possum again. 'Sorry, I'm not just copping an eyeful, I promise. That's what happens to habitat trees' – he nodded at the fallen tree on the hillside – 'They're supposed to leave three a hectare. But with no vegetation around them until the coupe regrows, a lot just fall over. There would have been a hollow in that one probably, that this little critter called home.'

'She's so small,' Cressida marvelled. Its whole body was no bigger than her outstretched hand, its dark fur smeared with mud and rain. She held the gap in her jumper closed and said to Dale, 'Do you think she'll be alright?'

'If someone comes along soon we can get her to WIRES. I should put something on the other side of that ravine, actually. Before we lose the light completely.'

He leaned across Cressida and opened the glovebox. Inside was a ten-inch Dolphin torch.

'Aha,' he said. 'Good old Mousemoon. Mad as a hatter but thinks of everything.' Then he pulled out a long cigar-shaped object covered in tinfoil. 'Hello. Well, I did say everything.' He put it back in and turned on the torch. 'Back in a sec.'

He walked around to the back of the truck and opened the door. She knew she should get out and help but her curiosity got the better of her. She opened the glove box and peered in. When Dale got back in the car, having tied a yellow rope between two bushes across the ravine, she was still holding the object, and the tinfoil was open.

'What is it?' she asked.

He gave her a disbelieving look. 'You're kidding me,' he said.

'I've smelled it and all I'm getting is parsley.'

'Wow. Right,' he said with a laugh. 'I thought private-school girls were meant to be more worldly than anyone. Don't worry about it. Just put it back.'

'I want to know what it is.'

'Why?'

''Cause I don't like not knowing things, that's why. Is this grass?'

'Got it in one.'

'Wow,' Cressida said, lifting it to her nose and smelling it again. It looked so innocuous. 'I want some.'

'What? No you don't.'

'Yes I do. Come on, show me what to do with it. You don't have to have any.'

He gave a bark of laughter. 'If you think you're smoking it and I'm not having any, you've got another think coming,' he said, and pulled out the packet of tobacco.

'What about Mousemoon?' she said. 'It's his, right?'

'Well yeah, what about Mousemoon. It was your idea,' he said. 'No, trust me, there's plenty more where that came from. I think he grows it up the back of the property.'

'Oh,' she said, looking at it. 'Right.'

'May I?' he said, and took the platter of foil. He did the same thing with the marijuana he had with the tobacco, except stuck two rollie papers together instead of using one. *I can't believe I'm doing this*, Cressida thought as she watched him. But she was sick of being so controlled all the time. Always playing by the rules, doing the right thing, behaving herself, when most of the time it didn't seem to work anyway. Starting with spending eleven years trying to become a Partner at Hannes Swartling. It would be nice to stop the constant strategising for a while.

'What does it do?' she asked. 'I mean, I'm not going to go nuts, am I?'

Dale laughed. 'I don't know. Maybe. I doubt it though. And if you do I'll make sure you don't do anything stupid. Like take on a drop bear,' he said. 'We should probably move Miss Possum here, though. I don't think it would be very good for her.' He put the spliff between them while Cressida carefully extracted the possum; Dale wrapped it in a towel and took it round to the back of the car. She watched as he laid it close to the door and left the door ajar. She looked at the spliff. It was like a fat white cigarette. He got back in and pulled the matches out of his pocket, then struck one.

'You first,' Cressida said, handing the joint to him.

'Okay,' Dale laughed, taking it. He put it between his lips and held the match up. His double earring glinted in the matchlight, and as he inhaled the end of the cigarette became a stark orange ember in the dark. After an eternity, where the only sound was trickling water into the ravine in front of them, he let the smoke out in a straight white arrow, into the sky outside the window. 'Wow,' he said. 'It's been a while.' He shook his head as if to clear it, and held it out to her. 'Your turn.'

*I can't believe I'm doing this*, she thought again, taking the spliff. She put it to her lips and took a tiny breath, blew the smoke out and coughed.

'Just take it slowly,' he said. 'Let your throat get used to it.'

She tried inhaling again, more this time, and noticed her face was starting to feel spongy.

'Whoa,' she said on the exhale, and started coughing in earnest.

'That's probably enough for now,' said Dale, and she nodded wordlessly, handing it to him. 'I'll have one more and then we can put it out for later.'

Suddenly the raincoat and merino felt scratchy and hot, and with a surge of impatience she yanked them off. Ah, that was better. Her t-shirt was still damp from the rainstorm, and the coolness felt good. *Later.* What was that? The sound of the running water outside was so clear, like there were a hundred tiny creatures plucking on rubber-band guitars in the hollow. She looked at the leaves on the dash, wondering whether she would feel anything. She noticed how perfect and sharp each of them was, curled there into tiny, perfect fairy blankets like her jumper had been around the possum. The smell of them, that ancient, mossy odour of forest and fungi, like the Gondwana forests up the hill. What had he said about them? A thousand years old? Hadn't she been sitting here that long? Maybe she too had started life as a tiny seed, sitting in the earth that smelled like that, waiting, waiting for the right time to emerge.

'Wow, strong stuff,' came Dale's voice beside her, and it was as if it came from all directions at once, like she was sitting inside a stereo. 'So, Cressida. Tell me again. What is it that means you can't act for all of them at ... Wow, did you see that star?'

He was looking out the window and had laid his head back against the back of the seat, looking up. Cressida turned to see what he was watching, but then all she could see was his throat, and the fat pirate double earring, glinting. She found herself wondering what it would taste like. Or, more accurately, feel. Would it be cold, like metal, or warm because it was nestled there, in the crook of his earlobe against his neck? She stared at one of the earrings, noticing the fat bulb on each end of it, thinking it would tinkle against the back of her front teeth, and then there would be the warm flesh at the middle of it, that tiny delicate little ...

'Cressida,' said Dale. 'Cressida?'

'Yah?'

'You're eating my earlobe.'

'Urgh,' she said, pulling herself off him and mumbling something.

'What?' he laughed.

'Your earring,' she said, turning to nestle against the door on her side of the car again. 'It was warm. I was wondering whether it was cold because it was metal or warm because it was there next to your earlobe and also those little things on the end looked so interesting and I just wondered what the metal would taste like and then there was your earlobe too and that had an *entirely different* texture and by the way what *is* that you smell of?'

Dale laughed again. 'What do you mean?'

She leaned across to him more carefully this time and sniffed.

'It's like … five spice and vanilla. You smell like one of my stepmother's sponge cakes. Oh, *sponge cake*,' she said, subsiding against the back of the seat again at the thought of it. 'A big fat creamy sponge cake with cinnamon sugar and raspberries and then she'd do it with vanilla-scented double cream and we'd put it all on the stove to heat through and then eat it with these tiny little forks she'd picked up at La Maison. Dale, what are we going to *do*? We're in the middle of *nowhere*. And we've got *no food*. We're going to have to walk.' She launched at the door handle and tore it open and was getting out until Dale reached across and stopped her.

'Hang on.' He grinned and reached back behind them. Two shapes wrapped in foil emerged from his backpack and he handed her one. 'Salami and cheese.'

'Oh my God,' she said, taking it and tearing it open. 'You genius.' She ripped off a chunk with her teeth and in her mouth the taste seemed to go on forever, salt and fat saturating her tongue. The bites hardly fit in her throat and she felt like those snakes on the roadside in Vietnam that had swallowed a pig, but she couldn't stop. In four bites it was gone.

'Hungry?' he laughed, chewing on his.

'Is there more?' she said, but he was already handing her a cup of something from a thermos. She murmured thanks and blew on it, relieved time had taken the edge off its temperature and she could down a full mouthful and then another, savouring the fat chunks of potato and pumpkin sweetness. She waited almost clinically for the guilt, the usual flood of internal berating about how many minutes of running she would have to do to work it off, how much less she would have to eat tomorrow to make up for it, all the bargains she normally struck with herself in exchange for food. But her mind was silent. Then she remembered the chocolate in her bag, and opened the door and was out of the car this time before Dale could stop her.

'I'm just getting chocolate,' she called, squelching the few feet towards the back of the car. *Ah, there it is*, she thought, digging the final two squares of Jelly Popping Candy Beanies out of her handbag. She bit off one square and held the last one out to Dale. 'Want some?'

'What is it?'

'Chocolate. It's awesome. It has all these red chewy lolly bits in it, and tiny invisible pieces that fizz in your mouth. Try some.'

He frowned and took a bite from one corner.

'Oh my God, that's so *rich*,' he said through a mouthful.

'I know,' she said, falling back against the seat in momentary chocolate bliss. 'Isn't it divine? Have some more.'

'No you have it, I think I'd probably explode.'

'I'm so glad you said that.' She vacuumed up the last square and spoke through the sticky mouthful. 'Just so you know, I don't normally eat like this. I mean, I was on this juice diet before the blackout but, well … I mean there was no power so it's a bit hard to juice things … I was settling for raw veggies instead but, God, it was *so boring*.'

'So now you're on the chocolate diet. I approve.'

'I don't know what's going on,' she said, unscrewing her water bottle and taking a long drink. She wiped her mouth and continued. 'I've literally just been eating fruit and veg for the last few weeks. No – more. It's been appalling.'

'God that does sound pretty disgusting. What about protein?'

'You sound like my trainer. I've had the odd bit of brown rice as well. And there were two hotdogs at Bathurst. Oh but right now … steak. That's what I feel like. With mushroom and red wine sauce. What's *with* this? All this fresh forest air. Quick, get me out of here and back to the city, I'll turn into a *hontros*. Porker,' she translated.

He laughed. 'Not likely,' he said, shaking his head and pouring another cup of soup. He wrapped his hands around it and took a mouthful. 'So, Cressida,' he began. 'How did you come to be acting for Andy?'

'Hmm? Oh. Andy. Joanne. Um. I could tell you but I'd have to kill you. She … my firm has a personal connection with her, believe it or not.' The spliff had gone out, and she gestured at it, saying, 'Come on, light it again. We might as well smoke the whole thing, right?'

He looked at her, then down at the roach. 'Really?'

'Yeah, c'mon,' she laughed, picking it up. 'Gimme the lighter.'

'Gimme the lighter,' Dale echoed, shaking his head. He laughed, and handed it to her.

Feeling like an uber-cool girl criminal from a noir film, Cressida wedged the remainder of the joint in her mouth and squinted, tilting her head and cupping a hand round the flame as she lit it. She inhaled again and the world went blurry, and then something was biting her thigh and she yelped.

'Shit,' said Dale, brushing her leg. 'It's okay, it's off now,' he laughed. 'You dropped the roach on your leg. Shit. I think it's left a scorch mark. Ow. Are you okay?'

'Oh thank God, I thought it was a fucking tarantula. Where is it? Sorry.' She peered between her knees at the footwell.

'Don't worry. It was done anyway.' He picked it up and threw it in the glovebox. 'I was just thinking that … oh. Um. Actually.' He was staring at something on her upper arm. 'Don't move.'

'What?' Cressida stiffened and followed his gaze, though she couldn't focus that close to her neck. '*What?*'

There was a blurry dark shape on her upper arm.

'Just … just let me open this window,' he said, still watching, and Cressida swallowed. The shape moved a little, backwards, and she looked down to see the spindly legs of an enormous brown spider, sprawled on her upper arm like a bedraggled Christmas decoration. Its legs were so close she could see the hairs on them.

'Holy fuck,' she said through gritted teeth. 'Mary Mother of God. Is that poisonous?'

Dale reached for a stick from the leaf-strewn dashboard. 'Come here, little fella,' he said. Ever so gently he eased the stick towards the spider, and pushed at one of its feet.

'Wait,' she said, not daring to breathe. She'd seen those things move before. They were like lightning. Fifty-fifty if he bothered it, it would go straight down her top. She stared at it, eye to beady little eye. The eyes glinted, set in their square of velvet black. There was a tiny noise coming from somewhere, and then she realised it was her, whistling; the softest angel of breath slipping from between her lips. This went on for a few moments, and the spider didn't move, watching her. Then it shifted one leg back half an inch, and another foot as if in irritation, before putting it back down again. Its body stayed put.

'You're whistling,' Dale whispered. 'I think she likes it.'

Cressida snorted involuntary laughter out her nose and clenched her jaw to stop the giggles that rose up, but even as her shoulder shook with suppressed mirth, the spider remained immobile.

'Okay,' sighed Dale, 'I think we're going to have to get hard-ass on this little darling.' He glanced at Cressida. 'Hold steady.'

He pushed the stick under the spider's body and then she was out the window in a blob of undignified splayed blackness in the dark, and both Dale and Cressida let out a whoosh of air and collapsed in helpless, relieved laughter. He fell on her and then as he turned his face to her she kissed him.

'Oh,' he said, when she had finished.

'Mmm,' she said, looking into his eyes, and then at his mouth, so close and smelling of tobacco. She kissed him again. He pulled back a moment, breathing heavily, and she smiled. He blinked and fell onto her mouth, both of them falling backwards onto the seat. The gearstick got in the way and he lifted her up and underneath him in one movement, lifting one hand to hold her face as he kissed her. There was already a hardness near her groin and she was about to tear open his belt buckle when his hand came over hers and he murmured to her something which she couldn't understand. He pulled himself off her and, breathing hard, spoke.

'Cressida, wait. Stop. You're stoned. You're gorgeous, and I'd do this in a heartbeat with you, believe me. But you're stoned, and you're engaged. Remember?'

Cressida dropped her hands from his neck. He was looking down at her with such passion and seriousness. She swallowed, and looked past him to the roof above, to avoid his gaze and collect herself.

'Yes,' she said, then couldn't remember what she was answering yes to. 'Are we …' She struggled to sit up, and he laughed, brushing her hair out of her eyes. 'Are you okay?'

'Yes I'm okay,' he said, kissing her neck. 'I'm definitely okay. What about you?'

At that she threw herself into his body again, kissing him, and again her hands travelled downwards and he stopped her hands again.

'Twice is my limit,' he said, shaking his head and smiling.

She grimaced, then threw her head back against the back of the seat. 'Yes. Sorry. You're right.'

The combination of the dope and the circumstance and how he made her body feel right at that minute *was* almost enough to make her want to throw her expensive ring down into the rainforest, but a little voice prevailed – *you're stoned, and that's a fifty-thousand-dollar diamond. And there's a small possibility you've gone troppo and shouldn't make any big decisions right now.* She sat up straighter and fixed her hair, while Dale moved back to his own side of the car.

'You don't need to sit that far away though,' she said. 'It's cold.'

'Yes,' he agreed. He gave her a searching look, then shook his head, leaned back and pulled out a blanket. He smelt good, a combination of tobacco and that sponge cake smell, plus an indefinable male aroma that she decided had probably caused all the trouble in the first place. She had read that somewhere – that sexual attraction was ninety-nine per cent unconscious smell. Well maybe not that much, but a lot. And she'd really like to bury her face in his neck again, she reflected, but stopped herself. They sat in the silence until their breathing slowed. Suddenly she remembered Saturne.

'God – Saturne – what about getting back to her? Who's going to look after her?'

'That's okay,' he said, kissing the top of her head. 'Merv knows what to do. She just needs four-hourly meds and the catheter bottle drained every few days. I left Merv with a few instructions for her dinner and stuff.'

'Is … Do you think she's going to get better?' asked Cress. *That tumour was the size of a grapefruit.*

There was a long silence before he spoke.

'I don't know. The prognosis for non-Hodgkin's lymphoma is good, but only … only with traditional methods of treatment, usually.'

'Is that what she's got?'

'Yup.'

'So you mean chemo.'

'Yup. And she's not doing that anymore.'

Quietly Cressida rode out the upwash of panic and sadness that came. It was okay – it didn't threaten to swallow her any more. She could look at the abyss from its lip, now, and not fall in.

'She's so young,' said Cressida, sadly.

'Twenty-seven.'

'*That* is really hard.' She swallowed. 'So. How do you know Andy?'

He sighed and kissed the back of her hand.

'Well,' he said, 'back in the day when I was a wealthy land owner' – he laughed and winked at her, shifting his position to face her – 'she rented a room in my house.'

'Your house?'

'Yes – believe it or not I have one. Despite appearances. In Sydney.'

'Sorry.' Cressida grimaced. 'I didn't mean to sound incredulous.'

'Hey,' he said with a laugh, 'I'm wearing a flanno and an earring. I get it.'

'Well there is that, yes,' she said, grateful for his good humour. 'Go on.'

'When I arrived back from Asia a shadow of my former self, as they say – which perhaps wasn't that crash hot in the first place, hence the addiction – and having gone through one mother of a cruel, expensive but very effective detox program in Bangkok – designed specifically for junkie doctors in rehab from drugs, I think – the house had been on a month to month lease for a year. So I asked the estate agent to let the tenants know I was coming home, and Andy was one of them. But like a lot of what Andy does,' he said, 'she did exactly what she wanted, and that didn't include leaving my house, so she was still there when I got back. Anyway she took one look at me and told me to sit on the couch and made me a comfrey juice. Most revolting thing I've ever had in my life. It made me feel marginally better, though, and after that we were mates.'

'Comfrey juice,' Cressida said. 'I don't even know what that is.' It was nice, admitting ignorance, having this feeling of not knowing everything, or feeling like she was expected to. It felt good to ask questions.

'It's a garden herb; you've probably got it in your veggie patch at home,' he said, making her think it was sweet that he assumed she had one. 'It's meant to be good for healing. Anyway she stayed on for two years after that, rent free, doing all the activisty things she does. I liked it. I felt like I was helping out in some way, even though I was too busy with my own stuff, trying to stay off the drugs, just by letting her be there. It sure made for an interesting life.' He gave a wry laugh. 'Just what I needed at the time.'

He unscrewed the thermos and poured more soup.

She took the cup, saying, 'I can't believe how hungry I am.' She tasted it. It seemed to have got even more tasty since lunch, from stewing in itself.

'It's the dope.'

'But I only had two, whatever you call thems ...'

'Tokes. Yeah. But you haven't had it before. There's a name for it. It's called the munchies.'

*I've got the munchies*, Cressida thought. *I'm sitting in a Land Rover in the middle of nowhere with a man in a flannelette shirt and a pirate's earring, and I've got the **munchies**.* What would be next? She'd throw in her job and go be a forest whatsit? Feral? The thought was clearly absurd, but from what she had gleaned about Saturne and Joanne's lives, it almost sounded fun. Following your passion, living for something. Except that if it landed you in gaol, that kind of put the brakes on anything exciting.

'What's this chewy stuff?' she said.

'Barley.'

'Yum.'

'So. Cressida,' he said, draining the soup, 'tell me about this engagement ring on your finger.'

She swallowed and looked down at it. Yes. *About* that engagement ring.

'Fair question. His name's Felipe. He's an orthopaedic surgeon. He's twelve years older than me. We've been engaged for three months. The invitations came in the mail last week.'

'Ah. Wow. Okay.' He paused. She could hear the sound of his breathing, so close to her in the silence. 'And do you usually accost strange men in the front seat of cars when you've only just met them?'

She laughed, embarrassed. 'No. Definitely not. And if it's any consolation, I totally didn't see that one coming. I ...' – she looked him squarely in the eyes – 'I enjoyed it though. Immensely.'

'Is that right?' he said, a softness in his eyes. She could feel it rising again, that magnetic pull that wanted to inch her face towards his, inhaling the smell of his warm, soup-and-tobacco laden breath, and she wondered vaguely what the hell she was doing. It was the grass. It had to be.

'Oh God, Dale, this just won't do, will it?' she said, shaking her head. 'You've got me all tied up in knots.'

'I've got *you* all tied up in knots? Try being mad for a million-dollar blonde you just met who's twenty thousand seas out of your league,' he said. 'Wow that was a mixed metaphor. I only had two tokes too, but listen to me.'

*Mad for*, Cressida thought. No. That thrill she was feeling at his words? That was not a good thing.

'Maybe that's what this is, then,' Cressida said softly. 'The spliff talking.'

'Yeah,' he said, twining his fingers through hers. 'That must be it.'

When she woke later with a crick in her neck, lying on Dale's chest, he was still asleep, head thrown back against the top of the back of the bench seat. She spent a few moments enjoying the curve of his jaw in the reflected moonlight off the dashboard, noticing that the thrill of it didn't seem to have abated any. How long did that stuff last in your system? Would she be feeling it seven hours later?

Then in the distance came a sound like a trailbike. Joyriders? Or a forestry chainsaw, getting rid of that log for the trucks in the morning, she thought, listening until it stopped. In the middle of the night? Then another out of place sound rose up from the valley. It sounded like the Westpac rescue helicopter when it did a hello lap past North Bondi.

She craned past Dale out the window and then up from the gully in a bone-shaking roar came the helicopter, its daymakers blasting the car and the road and the rainforest below with light, and like spiders rippling down from a web, black-clothed figures dropped down; Cressida's door was wrenched open and she was dragged out and pushed face down into the mud; someone was screaming at her but it was impossible to hear over the blades above them, and Dale had disappeared. She heard the word 'terrorism' but nothing made sense. Something burned around her wrists and she was yanked to standing and forced forward, stumbling and trying to get the mud out of her mouth and yell something until a fierce whack hit the side of her head. Then there were blinding lights everywhere and she was hurled into a box and the light went out.

# 22

When she woke it was in the back of a moving truck. There was pain in her shoulder from where her arm was chained to the side, and the air around her was thick with the smell of urine and worse things. With effort she wrenched her knees underneath her and tried to find a way that was more comfortable to sit. There wasn't one. She grimaced, and then remembered. *Fuck.* The men in black. The guy in front of her had had large white letters on his back: AFP. Australian Federal Police.

They'd come back. That had to be it, she thought. They'd come back to raid the safe house again, and had somehow connected it with the two of them. Oh God. Saturne. *Dale.* They would have found the remains of the marijuana, and probably the half-smoked spliff as well. They wouldn't care that it didn't belong to either of them. There'd be drug charges for them both.

She tried to think. Jesus Christ, she'd need her *own* lawyer before this was over. No. That was absurd. She'd only had a couple of tokes. And as for being one of the terrorists, that allegation would surely disappear into thin air once she explained she was out there as *their lawyer.*

Except she wasn't. She had nothing in writing from them, no signed documents saying she was instructed to act. *And that's because you refused*, she thought. *Oh fuck. Idiot. Dale was right. Why the hell shouldn't you? It would at least get you out of ...* **association with terrorism**. Five years in prison, Cressida thought with a sudden flash of cold in her stomach. *Holy fuck.*

That's not how this was going to play out though, she told herself firmly. She would explain to them. She'd talk her way out of it. She knew how to do that. She was almost pretty good at it. And then the others. She'd get a criminal barrister for Dale. For all of them. Sandra Crane was wrong. It would be fine as long as they didn't go against each other. She'd get them all off, and then that would mean she'd get off too. Wouldn't she?

Her wheelie bag. It was back there in the Land Rover. And those Technical Documents appendices, that she'd painstakingly bloody read and tagged, for God's sake. The laptop with the T & C draft. *Shit.* They'd keep it in a locker somewhere in a plastic bag for months – *years* even. As 'evidence'. Somehow the thought that she'd have to do *that* all over again was the most maddening thing of all. Jesus Christ, if word of this got out. They might even take the road project off her. No, Brian needed her too much for that. But Pip ... Her mind spun. Pip was a different matter. Pip mustn't find out. Maybe she couldn't trust Pip on the road project at all. Maybe rather than keeping her seat warm while she was away, she was actually in the process of yanking it up out of its foundations and installing it in her own lounge room. If the drug charges stuck ... *They won't though*, she reminded herself again. Personal use only. And you're a *lawyer*.

Then the pain in her shoulder started working on her. What if the constriction did permanent damage to her arms? Between sliding off the side of the seat, jarring her head against the wall and falling asleep, she plotted ludicrously a case against the AFP. For everything, from assault and permanent injury, to ruining her clothing, unlawful imprisonment and psychological damage. There was a bump and the road beneath became smooth, and then the pain turned to numbness. The hum of the tarmac ushered sleep, but every time her head fell forward she would jerk awake, and shifting position made the pain return. She found hot tears were filling her eyes and swore, blinking them away. Whatever it took, these people would pay.

Then through the chinks in the wall she saw the flash of duco under street lights and the car slowed. The smell of the sea wafted through the slats, and young male voices laughed a short distance away against the burn of tyres on asphalt. The truck turned sharply and climbed a hill, then slowed to a corner and descended a short dip in the dark. She heard the squeal of rubber on smooth concrete and the truck came to a stop. By then she was wide awake.

The front doors slammed and booted steps approached. The inside of the truck filled with the strobe of red and blue bouncing off the walls outside; there was a rattle of locks and the truck was flooded with light, before a gloved hand reached in and grabbed her upper arm. Another dis-embodied hand held up a unit that looked like the Fat Max she had used to find studs in her flat when hanging pictures; it was held behind her and with a metallic hiss the pressure on her shoulders released as the lock to the wall let go. It was when she climbed to the ground that her knees gave way.

There were four of them, in black helmets above opaque ski goggles that left no skin exposed. The assertive words that sprang to her throat died there. One look at them and she knew she would do anything they asked. She was lifted to standing and spun, and felt cable ties bite into her wrists. A foot reached between her ankles and kicked her feet apart so she was spreadeagled, only saved from falling by the hand on either arm, and rough hands slapped her down.

'Shoes off.'

Her legs were jelly as she stepped out of the white gum boots and stood in socks, trying not to cry.

'What's happening?' she said, hating the near-hysteria in her voice. 'Am I under arrest? What are you charging me with?'

There was no answer and she was pushed towards the lifts.

Some distance away was her wheelie bag, being dragged behind one of them, bright pink in its large clear plastic evidence condom. Her Oroton handbag was wrapped in another, riding on top of it. Her belongings. Her *lawyer* belongings. A bubble of laughter rose to her throat, and she rode its energy to power ridicule into her voice. As they came to a stop in front of the lift she spoke.

'This is fucking crazy. I'm a lawyer. That's my *Oroton handbag.' They are not going to care about what brand of **handbag** you have*, came a tiny voice, but she ploughed on. 'If you open that wheelie bag you will see there are documents in there for the road project I am working on. Go on. Open it. You'll see this is all one massive mistake.'

They didn't answer her, and all she could hear was the sound of her breathing, embarrassingly ragged over the blood that roared in her ears. She shut her eyes tight then opened them again, and tried again.

'What's your name?' She turned and addressed the agent directly next to her, but his face was turned upwards, apparently trained on the slowly dropping numbers above the lift doors. She said it again. He turned to her, which was almost scarier, and she found herself looking at her own reflection in the opaque goggles. She couldn't tell whether he was looking at her or not, whether his eyes were even open, or even if he had any. But she said it again, articulating every word with forced authority. 'What's your name?'

There was a small but barely perceptible reaction. He turned his head ten degrees to look over his shoulder, as if at someone behind her, gave a short chuckle, and looked back at the lift.

*Fine. I'll say it anyway.* 'I'm a solicitor.' Her voice wavered, and she felt like kicking herself for sounding so terrified. 'I have committed no offence, and neither has the man who was in the car with me. I'll have both of you – all of you – indicted for unlawful imprisonment before you can say Bob's your Auntie if you don't release me and Mr …' She realised she didn't know Dale's surname. 'The fellow that was in the car with me. Immediately.' Even to her own ears her words sounded ridiculous. The piping of a self-righteous mouse. They didn't answer.

When the lift doors opened he shoved her inside, and for two excruciating minutes she stood in the dim silence as it whooshed upwards, not daring to move, and trying not to think about images from movies where people were murdered in lifts, their necks snapped or spine broken with a well-executed manoeuvre by the time the doors opened. Then as they emerged onto the floor above she heard voices, and felt almost faint with relief. Other people. Civilisation. *Witnesses.* But she was led in the opposite direction and quickly the voices faded, as she was taken instead to a door that made a sound like a seal being broken when the same handheld unit was held up to the sensor. Soundproofing?

On the other side was a long corridor of doors with peepholes concealed by flaps, eerily similar to the room in which she had met with Joanne at Wellington.

'Wait,' said Cressida, her throat dry, as the guard in front of her opened the door to one of them. Her voice seemed to have gone up an octave. 'I want to see the head of the station. *Now*,' but she sounded anything but forceful. In answer the door slammed shut and the peephole cover slid into place.

Inside the room was a narrow bunk and she went to sit on it. She missed and landed on the floor, and then she was shaking uncontrollably, her mouth opening in silent terror as tears came. There was a camera in the roof, tiny, no bigger than her thumbnail, and she turned her face into the mattress, trying to cry quietly. *Oh for God's sake*, a dry voice said within. *Get a grip on yourself. They're* **cops**, *not* **assassins**. *Or at least, I think they are …* The rest of it didn't bear thinking about. Eventually she got her breathing under control and sniffed, wiping away the tears on the vinyl as best she could, and looked around. It was a small room that she could cross in under three paces. There was a toilet with no seat in the far corner, above it a coffee-mug sized washbasin. The fluorescent light flickered in a cage overhead. Suddenly brazen, she stared up at the camera and slowly, deliberately, mouthed *fuck you* in its direction and hoiked herself onto the bunk. *Don't panic*, she told herself. *If only because it's not going to help. Don't think about how you have no idea where you are and that nobody else does either. These are police. They're not terrorists. They have procedures, protocols. And anyway, you said you were a lawyer. They'll be back in a minute and it will all be sorted out.*

When the noise in her ears started to lessen, the dominant sensation became instead the pain in her wrists where the cable ties were still cutting in, and her shoulder blades aching from her arms being pulled behind her. There was also a throbbing pain in her right shin, though she had no idea why. She looked at the washbasin, considering the miniscule tap. No cup, but she was so parched she would have happily drunk from the toilet, had her hands been free. There had to be a buzzer somewhere to call someone, at least to ask for a bottle of water. That had to be regulation. But none was visible. She swallowed. Four hours. They couldn't hold her for longer than four hours; that was the rule. Funny how useless bits of lawyer information kept popping into her head. Some kind of weird stress response. Fat use they were with no-one to enforce them. *You had water not that long ago*, she reminded herself, *as well as Dale's soup. Plenty of liquid to keep you going. Don't panic.*

*But then, this isn't some minor drug arrest,* she thought. On terrorism the lawful holding time was twenty-four hours. And it could turn into a week with all the time stops. She lurched up and ran to the door, yelling.

'Can I have a drink of water please?'

Her voice sounded ragged, dry, and hearing it made the thirst feel stronger. She yelled again, and nothing but silence responded. She swallowed, trying not to notice how thick her tongue felt. Focusing on that would just make her panic. *They can't leave you to die of thirst. They can't. They won't. These are crazy thoughts. It's just a dry mouth from the dope.* **The dope.** The whole episode with Dale seemed crazy, ludicrous. He was the one who'd gotten her into this mess. Being so … what? Sexy? Irresistible? *But hang on, weren't* **you** *the one that threw yourself at him, not the other way round?*

Trying to slow her breathing again, she returned to the bunk. In the silence she noticed there was ringing in her ears. The more she concentrated on it the louder it got. She started to hum, just to give herself something to listen to. But when she stopped the silence that returned was louder still. *You're freaking yourself out,* she pointed out. *Stop. Lie down. Think about something cheerful. Try and sleep. Look, Dale's got to be somewhere here. And the others.* The thought gave her consolation. *It just* **seems** *like you're on your own in a gulag. They're probably right there, less than a metre away through that wall,* she thought, turning to face it. If not that one, the next. She tried to visualise it, to imagine each of them on bunks along the corridor, and further down – *somewhere* – were people, going about their usual business. At 4am. Was it some kind of terrorist control centre, staffed around the clock to deal with the terrorist operation? *Oh God,* she thought again, *what have I done?*

She had fallen asleep sideways on the bunk when her door was thrown open and she was pulled to sitting, making her just-recovering shoulders scream in pain.

'Ow!' she yelled. 'Where are we going?'

'Shut up,' said the officer behind her, pushing her out the door. Three other officers were waiting outside the cell and she was taken down the corridor to a tiny room like the other one, but with no bunk. Instead there was a small desk with two chairs facing each other in the middle; she was pushed into one of them, and it was then she wet her pants. Once she started she couldn't stop, and below her a humiliating puddle formed on the floor. The officers fell back behind her and another man entered – from his plain clothes, she figured he was a detective of some sort. He towered over her in a baggy grey suit across the shoulders of a rugby forward, his blue eyes hard. He slammed the door behind him and slapped a file down on the desk in front of her. She instinctively moved to raise her arms to shield herself but they were still locked behind her back and all she could do was duck.

'Ow!' she yelled again as the weight of his body on the table jammed it into her ribs.

'What the fuck were you doing with a terrorist cell?' he yelled, his face inches from hers. The pain of the table in her ribs combined with lack of sleep, pee on her leg and hypoglycaemia to finally tip her into rage.

'For fuck's sake, *calm down!*' she yelled, pushing the table back with her elbows. 'You're all so fucking *aggro.* Jesus.' She was shaking violently, but she held his gaze as long as she could before tearing her own away. Momentary defiance but not so much as to make him lose face, she calculated, amazed that she was thinking anything strategic right then. And in a rush of relief she saw that it worked. He spat out a breath and pushed himself back off the table away from her.

'Cressida Mitsok. Hannes Swartling. Building and Construction. Quite the rising star, I'm told. Except for that shit with your dad. If you weren't a solicitor I'd make you sorry you said that,' he muttered. 'Jesus, what's that smell?' he said, searching under the table. He looked at her with a mix of disgust and the dregs of pity. 'Constable Richards,' he said, to an officer behind her. 'Clean that up. Where's your identity card?'

'In my bag,' spat Cressida. 'That you stole.'

'What?' he shouted.

'*In my bag.*' She clenched her jaw and looked back at him. 'The one you confiscated. Everything's in there. You have a look. And by the way, that other guy that was with me? He's a doctor for someone in the valley.' She took a deep breath and summoned courage. 'Now I'm telling you, you better charge us, or let us the fuck out of here.'

The detective stared at her, and the malevolent look on his face slid off, replaced by something much worse. He laughed.

'Tough talk,' he said with a smirk. 'Well, honey, I've got news for you. Even if you are a *so-li-cit-or*' – he let the syllables roll off his tongue – 'that doesn't mean you can't be in a shitload of trouble.'

'I'm aware of that,' she said. Talking was good. The more she spoke the easier it got to get the words out. 'But as it happens, I'm not. Unlike you, if you don't release me immediately.'

The officer came back with a mop and bucket, and the detective smiled again, snorted, and stood up. 'For a lawyer you don't know much about the terrorism laws.' She was hauled to standing while he cleaned up the puddle, shards of embarrassment firing from her every pore.

'You'd be right about that,' Cressida bit back through it, 'seeing that I'm a *building lawyer.* But unfortunately for you, false imprisonment is Legal Wrongs 101. Don't imagine your boss – is it the Minister? – is going to be too happy about the damages claim I'm planning on bringing. With all that lovely free legal help from my firm, by the way. Plus a couple of silks thrown in as return favours.' Oh words. *Words were good.*

'Nope' – the detective laughed again, shaking his head as she was pushed back into her chair and the table shoved back into place; it was a chilling, mirthless sound – 'wrong again,' he said, and rolled his eyes in the direction of the agent behind her. 'You tell me, darlin', exactly how you're going to make a damages claim about this when you can't tell anyone anything about it.'

'What do you mean?'

The detective gave a look of mock melancholy, giving a tiny, slow shake of his head.

'You didn't know about that? Yeah, I didn't think you looked much like a criminal lawyer. Too thin, for a start. Haven't you noticed, Shaun?' He looked behind her again, and three voices laughed. 'Criminal defence lawyers. They're all fat.' He snorted and pushed himself off the wall. 'Anyway,' he said. There was a chair on the other side of the table and he pulled it out, subsiding in it with lavish nonchalance. He was even bigger close up, the skin of his neck tanned and weathered where it met the stiff white of his collar. He laced his hands together, then looked at her. 'Maybe I'm going about this all the wrong way. Why don't you tell us why *you* say you were in Gloucester Tops State Forest in the middle of the night and we'll go from there.'

'Are you formally interviewing me now?' Cressida said, flatly incredulous.

The detective shrugged. 'Don't know. Depends on what you say.'

Cressida took a deep breath and stared at him. 'Where's the fucking tape then? Come on, officer. At the very least. I'm not saying anything until you record this. And it's difficult to do anything with my arms strapped behind my back. I'm sure the four of you can cope if I decide to turn violent. With that secret mixed martial arts training I've got. Joke. *Joke,*' she said.

The detective glanced up at the officer behind her. She felt her wrists come loose, and the relief that flooded her unbound shoulders nearly made her faint. With a baleful expression in his blue eyes the detective pressed a button on the table and a recorded voice started up. *Recording. Four seventeen am. Saturday 31 March. Please proceed.* The detective stared at her flatly.

'Record of interview. Cressida *Mit*sok,' he said, toying with the syllables. 'For the record I have with me Senior Constable Shaun Winfield and Constable Bob Richards. What were you doing in Cobark State Forest?'

'I'm not saying anything without my lawyer present.'

The detective smirked and pulled a laminated map out of his file, pointing at a red Google marker on it.

'What do you know about this property?'

She looked at it. 'I have no idea where that is.'

'RMB 2459 Gloucester River. About thirty k's from where we picked you up.'

'Uh-uh.'

He looked at her, then at the officer behind her.

'Constable, you already cautioned Miss Mitsok when you arrested her, didn't you? I think she needs to hear it again.'

Constable. So they *were* police. At least this one was, anyway.

'You are not obliged to say or do anything unless you wish to do so, but it may harm your defence if you do not mention when questioned something you later rely on in—'

'I know the caution,' Cress interrupted. 'The problem I have is I couldn't respond to your questions even if I had a defence. *Which I do.*'

The detective sat back, regarding her.

'And why is that?'

'I'm not even able to tell you that.'

The detective narrowed his eyes and looked again at the officer behind her. 'Who was the informant, Constable?'

'Anonymous tipoff.'

The detective blinked. 'That's it?'

'There were some Schedule Four drugs at the premises. Plus MJ and amphetamines.'

'There was also marijuana found in the car you were in,' the detective said.

'That wasn't ours.'

'But you admit it was there? And you didn't mind having a toke,' the detective added.

Cressida reddened.

'We can always charge them on the drug possession later, Shaun,' he said, glancing at the officer behind her. 'Why don't you charge the other three with drug possession, and come back on Miss Lawyer here once there's more evidence.'

The other three. So they were here. Cressida tried not to let the relief show on her face.

'Unless she wants to talk now, that is. What was it we were thinking, Shaun? Accessory after the fact?'

'I'm not saying anything until my lawyer's present.'

'I thought you were one,' the detective said, dryly. 'Alright. We'll reconvene later. Bob.'

She was dragged to standing and pushed out the door. When they reached the door at the other end, he took her to a duty officer, who handed over her handbag and, separately, her wallet, keys and other personal items. But no phone and no iPad.

She gritted her teeth and turned to the first officer.

'Any chance of getting my wheelie bag back too?'

'Less than zero.'

'But I'm not being charged.'

The officer gave a heavy sigh. 'You're not being charged *yet*. The contents of the vehicle are being kept for evidence. You'll get your bag stuff back. If we decide not to press any charges.'

'How long will it take you to do that?'

The detective shrugged.

'Dunno.'

Cress swallowed the panic that welled.

'My laptop's in there with confidential client information. I have to get it back within forty-eight hours.'

'Not possible. The lift's that way,' he said, pointing down the corridor. Then the door slammed shut and she was alone. That was it? Arrested in the middle of the night, dragged here, locked up and now they release her? She wasn't sure then whether the wall leapt towards her or she collapsed onto it, but all sensation went out of her legs and she was leaning on it, the room spinning. The lift – quick, before they changed their mind – where was it?; but the lift to *where*? And where was Dale? She wanted to stand there, wait for him to emerge, but at the same time every instinct told her to flee onto the street, get as far away from here as possible. She looked back at the lift, torn with indecision. Was he in there, she wondered, looking back at the door that had slammed. She ran past the lift to the other end of the landing and peered through the glass in the door, but the room on the other side was empty.

And then with a suck of plastic and a grind of hinges the door opened again and Dale emerged. They saw each other simultaneously, and in an instant were in each other's arms, clinging like the last survivors from a sunken lifeboat, and he was pulling her towards the lift. He slapped the button repeatedly until the doors parted and they both rushed in and slammed 'G' and it whooshed downwards; when the doors opened they ran into the corridor, spinning the other direction when the first way they leapt ended in a dead end. They arrived at double doors and for an instant Cressida thought they were locked, but then in a rush of cool air they parted and Cressida took off at a bolt, running until she got to the corner and only then stopping to gulp great lungfuls of air, leaning down with her hands until her breath slowed and her vision stopped spinning. Dale arrived beside her, his breath similarly laboured, until at last she straightened and looked around, hardly believing she was free.

It was sunrise. They were on a deserted narrow road lined with Victorian terraces, and over the road pale orange and mauve was painting the sky above. There was the tang of salt in the air. She wiped the sweat from her face with both hands, her hands shaking.

'Where are we?' she said. There was a street sign on the corner and Dale headed for it. 'City of Newcastle,' he called back softly. 'Yeah,' he said, running back to her. 'I can smell the sea.'

'*New*castle? Jesus.' She put her head back against the wall behind them and looked upward. Somewhere up there, she thought, were individual soundproofed rooms where people got detained and interrogated without charge. She pushed herself off the wall and inspected the building. It was nondescript, featureless, rendered in standard issue '60s plaster. Down on the corner a sign saying *Newcastle Police Station* hung off the awning. 'So it *was* the copshop. Jesus.' She turned to Dale. 'Did you have a bunch of creeps in black ask you questions?'

'Yeah. Not my idea of fun. Are you okay?'

'Yeah.' His hair and jeans were caked with dried mud, and there was a red welt growing on his cheek. 'Jesus,' she said, reaching across to touch it gently, wanting to move closer but embarrassed by her jeans.

'Oh,' he said, passing his hand down his face in an exhausted gesture, 'I think one of them punched me.' His eyes met hers. 'But you,' he said, 'damn.'

He stepped across to her and they stood holding each other again, and she gave in as he pressed his lips into her hair. It was so good, just to feel the warmth and weight of another human body on her skin.

'Do you think they've got the others?'

'I don't know.'

'Why are we whispering?'

'PTSD, I think,' he said, standing back to give her a wry grin.

'God, I hope Saturne's okay,' she said. It wasn't just their awkward little bush love tryst that had to be transitioned, she realised, feeling sheepish. If Saturne was here, her state after going through what they had didn't bear thinking about. It was one thing to be terrorised when you were otherwise healthy. It had to turn things right up a notch when you were fighting a terminal disease.

Dale swallowed and said nothing. He caught her hands and inspected the welts on her arm, sliding to the ground against the street-sign pole.

'Jesus, look at your wrists. We need to wash this.'

'What about yours,' she said, taking his palm and turning it over. 'They're just as bad. And your face.' She touched his cheek gently again, running a finger along the part where it bled, and Dale winced. He caught her hand.

'You're still shaking.'

'I know,' she said. 'I'm hoping it will stop soon.' His touch was helping though. His hand was like a warm, callused glove. 'What do you want to do?'

'Well if it's okay with you,' he said, looking back at the doors, 'I'm a bit shit-scared they'll come out for us again – but I'd like to just wait.'

'I was thinking the same thing.'

'We don't even know if they're in there. They could have taken them anywhere. Or not even gone back to the house tonight. Just got *us*. It's so crazy.'

'I know,' Dale said, rubbing his eyes. 'Did they say that thing to you about how you can't talk about it? Is that true?'

'I don't know,' Cressida said, massaging her upper arms where they were still aching. 'I mean, yes, they did say that to me. I think it might be.'

'Even if we haven't been charged.'

'Yep.'

'Oh shit,' Dale said suddenly, fishing a phone out of the pocket of his jeans. 'The possum.'

'Oh God. Yes,' said Cressida. 'They didn't take your phone?'

'They gave it back – after accessing the data. I'll call WIRES.'

He kissed her forehead and moved a short distance away to dial. Cressida looked down at her clothing. Her t-shirt was ripped; mud was splattered from ankle to knee, and bits of it crunched in her hair. The adrenaline was subsiding and exhaustion crowding in, and as it did, pain returned: her wrists and shoulders burned, and her ankle felt like it had been twisted, though she couldn't remember when. Maybe when she was pulled out of the truck. In a moment Dale called out to her. He looked relieved.

'I got through,' he said. 'They're going to go and pick her up. Let's hope she's still alive.' He started dialling another number.

'Who are you calling now?'

'Mousemoon,' Dale mouthed, turning away to speak into the phone. Cressida jumped up and put her hand on his arm.

'Hang on,' she said, and he paused. 'Don't. They could be tracing his calls.' Realisation dawned on his face. 'Or yours.'

'Oh,' he said. 'Yeah.' He hung up.

A magpie swooped overhead and landed on a powerline above them, trilling discordantly. They sat down. Dale looked back at the building.

'I just wish I knew what was happening in there.'

'We're doing the best thing we can,' said Cressida. 'Waiting.'

'Maybe I should ring the house,' he said, putting an arm around her and pulling her close. 'See if anyone answers the phone.'

'That's a terrible idea,' she said, resisting the urge to bury her face in his warm, very proximate neck. 'They'd be tracing it.'

'Fuck,' said Dale, looking skyward. 'This is so *crazy*. It's not like they've even *done anything*. Or us. What did *we* do? Jesus. And you work in this industry,' he said, though with a half smile. 'How do you bear it?'

'Hey, baby, I'm a corporate lawyer.' Cressida laughed, glad of the relief. 'I have nothing to do with this end of town. I'm as freaked out as you.'

He smiled and picked up her hand again, kissing the knuckle.

'So anyway. Here we are in civilisation. What happens now?'

Cressida tensed. 'I don't know,' she said, suddenly absorbed in picking the mud out of her hair. 'Depends on whether anyone else is in there.'

'If Saturne's here, she's going to be completely wrecked,' he said, dropping his face into his palms. 'I'll need to get her somewhere she can rest, straight away. Jesus.' He looked up at her. 'She only just had the catheter put in a week ago. They better not have hurt her,' he said, jaw flexing.

Cressida heard the words coming out of her mouth before she realised what she was saying. 'Come back to my place. Surely there must be a bus or a train or something, back to Sydney from here? There's showers, hot food, spare bedrooms there. I mean, it's my stepmum's place, but it's ridiculously huge, and she loves a crowd. Gets to do her Greek mother thing.' She glanced down at the entrance to the building. 'If those guys are just up on drug charges, I can find a lawyer to help them. One that knows about that stuff.'

'But what about orthopaedic surgeon bloke?' asked Dale, frowning.

'Don't worry,' she said. 'He doesn't bite.'

A smile emerged. 'No. But I do,' he said, leaning into her neck.

'Well hello,' came a laughing voice beside them. It was Jason and Taina, arm in arm.

'Oh my God!' Cressida and Dale exclaimed at the same time, lurching to their feet. They all fell on each other, Cressida finding herself swept up in the same relieved affection as the others.

'Boy are we glad to see *you*,' said Dale, ruffling Jason's hair.

'But … what are you doing here?' asked Taina, still holding Dale as if she was afraid to let him go.

'They arrested us too,' he said.

'You're kidding me,' said Taina. 'But you guys left yesterday morning.'

'We got stuck. Then the AFP turned up.'

'No way,' said Jason, wide-eyed.

'And what about Saturne?' said Dale. 'Was she with you?'

'I don't know.' Taina shook her head. 'We were asleep. One moment I was dreaming about snowboarding,' she said, 'and the next thing we know we were being chucked in paddy wagons.' She looked at Jason incredulously. 'They didn't even let us get *dressed*.'

'Just fuckin' threw the clothes in after us,' said Jason. 'I tried to convince Tains to have a go in the truck' – he laughed, throwing an arm around her – 'since we were already nude, but she wasn't having it.'

How could he be so jocular about it, Cressida thought. She still felt slightly sick at the thought of what she had been through. But Jason wasn't making eye contact as he spoke. His pale grey eyes bounced off hers when she tried to catch them, and he was sniffing a lot and wiping his nose. The hand he did it with was shaking.

'I'm so fucking *over* this,' Taina exclaimed, sitting down and holding her forehead with both hands. 'Why are they *doing* this to us?' she demanded, looking up at Cressida. 'You're a lawyer, can't you stop them?'

'Hey, they arrested me too,' Cressida said, 'I don't think they give a shit what I think right now.' She squatted down at Taina's elbow. 'Did they charge you?'

'Yeah,' said Jason, and pulled a scrunched-up piece of paper out of his pocket. 'Cannabis leaf possession. Same with Taina.'

'You're kidding me,' Cressida said, taking the paper. 'But why go to all that bother just for a *drug* charge?' It was like with Joanne – minor charges when they could have thrown the book at them. It felt scary not to understand why.

'I have no idea,' said Jason. 'Anyway, fuck it.' He kicked the street-sign pole and pulled Taina to her feet. 'Come on, I'm *famished, and* I can smell the sea.' He laughed and did a little dance. 'We need a swim,' he told her, then turned back to Cressida and Dale. 'Coming?'

*Hah*, Cressida thought, *adrenaline bonding or not, there is **no way** I'm skinny dipping with you guys.* She shook her head and checked in with Dale to see whether he was up for it. But just as she looked at him, all the colour drained from his face. The three of them turned to see a figure walking slowly up from the corner, and then it doubled over and leaned against the wall. *Saturne.* Dale rushed to her and when he arrived at her feet he squatted down, hand on her arm. The rest of them caught up and as he stood up Saturne doubled over again, her eyes closed. Her skin was sheened with sweat.

'She needs pain medication,' said Dale, searching up and down the street. 'She's meant to have it every twelve hours. I don't have her prescription – we have to get to a hospital.'

'The John,' said Taina, nodding west. 'I used to live here. It's just up the hill.'

'Actually,' said Cressida, swallowing, 'I'd suggest the Mater. There's a specialist oncology unit there.'

'Oh,' Taina said, looking at her curiously. 'Even better.'

'Give me that and I'll call a taxi,' Cressida said, pointing at Dale's phone. He kissed the top of her head and gave it to her, and she quickly moved away, flushing pink as Taina raised her eyebrows in her direction. Dale helped Saturne out onto the kerb and sat down behind her, pressing his fingers into her back. 'It's okay, baby, relax. Help's coming.'

Saturne tipped her head back and leant into his grip, letting out a moan. Taina and Jason picked up each of her hands, massaging the middle fingers. Then suddenly she lurched forward and with a splatter vomited into the gutter. Cressida hung up on the taxi service and called an ambulance instead, running to the corner again to work out the cross street and give the address then handing the phone to Dale to describe her symptoms. Then Cress remembered.

'Hang on,' she said, turning to Jason and Taina. 'What about the others? Merv, Mousemoon? Were they with you?'

'I don't know,' Jason said, still massaging. 'We—' He swallowed. 'I didn't see the others. They weren't in the truck with us.' Tears welled and he fisted them away. Taina hooked a finger around his. Cressida looked back at the doors. *Look*, she reasoned with herself, *they've already let you go; they're not going to just grab you again the moment you go in there.* She took a deep breath.

'I'll go check.'

Inside there was a buzzer on one side of the counter and she pressed it. A moment later a fresh-faced officer came out of a door, wiping her mouth with a napkin. Cressida dug up her most confident smile.

'Sorry,' said the cop, swallowing. 'Breakfast.'

'Half your luck,' Cressida laughed. 'I'm just wondering if I can find out the whereabouts of a ...' She paused, realising if she asked by name, and they *didn't* have them, that by itself would be a lead. But how else would they know what had happened to them? 'Those two that were just released. A ...' Damn, she hadn't thought to get their surnames. 'First names Taina and Jason. Was ... was anyone else brought in with them?'

The officer frowned, then with a laugh, said 'I can't tell you *that*, I'm afraid.'

'What? Why not?'

'Are you the person's lawyer?'

'No ...'

'Well then. Like I said. Not at liberty to disclose.'

Taina appeared at the door. 'Cressida. The ambulance has just taken Saturne. Dale's booked an Uber – do you want to come to the hospital?'

'Yes. Look, actually …' She stopped and turned back to the officer. 'I'm a lawyer. If they *do* turn up, could you give them my number?'

The cop's eyebrows went up. 'Sure,' she said, slapping down a notebook from under the counter. Cressida wrote her name and Helena's landline number on it and handed it back. 'Thanks.'

On the street, there was a black car at the kerb. The driver was looking anxiously through the back door at Jason's mud-smeared jeans.

'Wait, wait,' the driver said, getting out. He got a blanket from the boot and spread it on the back seat. 'Alright,' he said and nodded at them to get in.

As the car wound its way up the sleeping streets Cressida's stomach rumbled, and she *really* wanted a shower. But as they waited at the intersection to the Mater, a greater problem presented itself. Seeing the concrete of the hospital towering over them, her heart dropped to her stomach. It had been where they'd taken her mum, when they'd been staying nearby on holiday, a year before she died. She couldn't go in there. In the undercover car park, even the sight of the inside of the lift made Cressida feel nauseous.

'Um, I might wait for you here, actually,' she said, pressing the open door button before the lift doors closed.

'What? Why?' said Taina.

'I just hate hospitals,' she said, making an attempt at a grin.

'Oh,' said Taina, holding the lift doors open. 'But what are you going to do?'

'Wait here I guess.'

'What, in the car park?' Taina looked pointedly behind her, implying the absence of seats. 'Look, there's probably some nice gardeny place upstairs you can sit. At least come and find a nice tree.'

It was so awkward, she wished she could just say she was going to get going, it had been great and everything but now she was going to head home. She longed to get back to solitude, to order, to a shower and a licorice tea by Helena's pool. But she couldn't, not then, because she'd offered the house to Dale and Saturne.

'Okay.' She stepped in and pressed the button, covering her fear with irritation. 'Sure.'

Behind Jason and Taina she held onto the side of the lift, feeling faint. When they emerged there was no garden, just an aluminium bench seat in the piercing early morning sun. She stepped inside the double doors and waved them off, explaining that she'd wait there. It was all exactly the same, twenty years on. Presumably technology had improved, she thought, but the sight of the linoleum corridors, the signs on the wall, the smell of disinfectant, all were like a glove of panic on her skin. So she sat still and focused on her breathing. Didn't they know that it was hopeless, she thought, putting her head in her hands. Just smoke and mirrors to distract patient and family from the fact that death was coming like a freight train. Already Saturne had the look about her. The sunken eyes, the thinnness. This was almost the most heartbreaking stage, she thought sadly. When the traditional treatments had failed and people cast about in a white-knuckled panic for everything from snake oil to coffee enemas to jolt their body into healing itself. But the slow wasting away of life would come anyway. Or sometimes it was quick.

*You have to eat something*, Cressida thought. *You're thinking yourself into a hole.*

She looked up to see Dale approaching.

'Hey,' he said, squatting down in front of her. 'What are you doing out here?'

'Oh, nothing,' Cressida said. 'I just hate hospitals.'

Dale laughed. 'Great. I'm a trauma doctor and you hate hospitals. Match made in heaven,' he said.

Cressida swallowed, trying to laugh, but instead her eyes filled with tears.

'Hey,' he said, getting up and moving to the seat next to her. 'What's wrong?'

'Nothing,' she said, angry at herself. 'I just need a coffee. How's Saturne?'

'I don't know yet,' he said, his eyes dark. 'But she's getting the best care in there. They've given her something for pain and then we'll see where we are once the registrar has had a chance to see her. Could be a while.'

'Alright. I'll – I'll meet you back here, okay?'

He gave her an appraising look. 'You really don't want to come in.'

She tried to smile but failed. 'Nope. I'll get you a coffee though. White with one?'

'That sounds perfect.' He kissed the top of her head. 'See you soon.'

# 23

By eleven o'clock Cressida, Dale and Saturne were on the train to Sydney. Taina and Jason had decided to stay in Newcastle and swim, promising to ask at the police station about the others later in the day. Saturne dozed behind Cress and Dale in a double seat. The change in her was miraculous; there were still shadows under her eyes, but her face behind the tube was in a deep, childlike opiate repose. Cressida was exhausted. Tiredness gave everything a dreamlike quality, but at the same time she was too wired to fall asleep; the coffee she'd had five hours before had left her jittery. As the train slid past the glass waters of the Hawkesbury she rang the hire car company on Dale's mobile and explained where the Golf was. They made noises about the expense of retrieval that far out of town, but agreed to pick it up. Then she used Dale's phone to ring Helena.

'Oh thank *God*,' Helena said, and started crying into the phone. 'I've been – we've all been worried *sick* about you. Where have you been? Where are you? When are you coming home?'

'It's a long story,' Cressida said, looking at Dale as she spoke into the receiver. 'The short answer is, we're on the train home now. From Newcastle.'

'We?'

'Um, yes … I've got a couple of people with me. Again, it's a long story. Look, Helena, one of them's very sick. Could we give her a bed in the spare room for a while? Just for a few days while they work out what they're going to do?'

'Of course, of *course*. Jerome's here, by the way. But he's in the green room. She can have the alabaster. When will you get here?'

'Um, about five, I think. Jerome? Goodness what's he doing here?'

'Would you believe' – Cress could hear the smile in her voice – 'he heard about those terrorists and their blowing up the power stations and he's here … well, he says he's here to support them! He says they're environmentalists! There's apparently a *protest rally* outside Silverwater, because that's where they are. He's calling them the Climate Five. Strangest thing I've ever heard. Anyway. Oh, and you must call Felipe. He's been worried *sick*, Cressida. Why didn't you call and let us know where you were? We've all been trying to ring you!'

'I was out of phone reception,' she said. This was just the beginning of the explanations, she thought. 'And I don't actually *have* my phone any more. Like I said, it's a long story. I'm using a friend's right now. Look, we'll be there in three hours or so. I'll call Felipe when I get in.'

'Well, alright,' Helena said. 'But you know, Cress … you don't want to. Well. Jeopardise things. Do you? You know how Felipe gets.'

There it was again. That female to male placatory reflex. She should give it an acronym: FMPR.

'Yes. I do know,' she said, 'but I did explain to him I needed to go away for work. I had no intention of missing the Surgeons Ball last night, and in fact I made an enormous effort to get there. But it didn't work out.' Next to her, Dale laughed.

'Who's that?' Helena said.

'Oh. Um, that's the other person I've got with me – basically they're all connected to a client I have. Their names are Saturne and Dale. Yes, as in planet and hillside. I'll explain later. By the way, Saturne's vegan. We're going into a tunnel now … I'd better hang up. See you round two. Mothers,' she said with a grin, handing the phone back to Dale. He laughed and put it back in his pocket.

'She's your stepmother, right?'

'Yes. Since I was fourteen.'

'Do you still see your real mum?' he asked, twisting a piece of her hair in his fingers. 'God, you are more mud than hair up here. What's with this?' He started to pick the dried mud out of the strands and she grimaced, pulling away.

'Ow. Have you looked in a mirror lately yourself?' she said, thumbing a flake off one end.

'Hey,' he said gently. 'I didn't mean anything by it. You still look breathtaking.'

'Yeah right. Whatever,' she said, and looked out the window.

'Hey,' Dale said. 'What's up? You've gone all Mrs Cranky Pants.'

She glanced at him and found herself laughing. 'Yes. I don't know. Something to do with being, you know, thrown in the mud, terrified, chucked in a police van, interrogated, threatened, having really bad hospital coffee.' *And pissing myself.*

'Of course.' He put his arm around her and pulled him to her. 'Have a kip,' he said. 'I'll wake you up when we get there.'

'Before I do – can you tell me,' she ventured, 'what did the oncologist say, about Saturne?'

He sighed, and looked back at Saturne before he spoke. She was still asleep. 'Oh, you know. The usual,' he said, keeping his gaze out the window.

'No?'

He sighed again. 'That she should be starting medical treatment immediately, move nearer to medical facilities, stop this ridiculous alternative treatment regime and get onto some evidence-based cancer management. Stuff like that.'

'Oh,' she said. 'And she doesn't want to.'

'Um, no,' he said, rubbing a hand across his face.

'Is that … is that what you think she should be doing?'

He gave a dry laugh. 'One thing I learnt about Saturne, very quickly after I met her, was that what I think is the least of her concerns.'

'But … but you're a doctor.'

'All the more reason to doubt what I'm saying, I think.'

'God, but how frustrating,' said Cressida. 'I mean, to have all your specialist training specifically *so* you can use it to save people's lives – and then living 24/7 with someone who doesn't want it.'

'I know, crazy isn't it.' He pretended to bang his head against the train window, then stopped and clasped her hand. 'I'm no onco. Trauma is just stitch them up and pass them on. I figure I can help her out in other ways though – managing her pain relief, a bit of palliative care – and of course' – he rolled his eyes – 'make juices from dawn till dusk.'

'Plus administer coffee enemas.'

'Oh God – coffee enemas!' he laughed, putting his head in his hands. 'I tell her it's just daily colonic irrigation and a backdoor way of feeding her closet caffeine addiction. If you'll excuse the pun.'

Cressida laughed and flushed red.

'Plus Andy asked me to,' he said. 'It's the least I can do.'

'So you … you agree with what they did?'

'I don't mean like that. I mean that Andy was – is – a friend of mine, and she wasn't going to be around to care for Saturne herself – for reasons I tried and failed to talk her out of, I might add – and I could help her. Plus it's not like anyone else is needing my medical expertise right now,' he said, with a rueful grin. 'I'm actually hoping I might convince her to go see a specialist while she's down here. If we can get into one.'

'Felipe might be able to help with that,' Cressida said. 'I mean, they all know each other, and I've known people to get into specialists he's known on short notice before. I mean, when I've asked him.' She'd known she'd have to bring up the topic of Felipe eventually, and it was as good a pretext as any. Plus it was true. 'Just on that …' she continued. 'When we get there, Felipe's probably going to show up at some point.'

'I know,' he said. 'I'm planning on challenging him to pistols at dawn. What do you reckon? Over the fair maiden's hand?'

'If you do that I'll shoot you both myself. Ridiculous violent patriarchal enterprise. You'll be wagering me on a card game, next.'

'Hah!' he said. 'I could never afford the bet. Hey. No more talking. You need to sleep.'

She kissed his cheek and put her head on his shoulder.

'Whatever you say, doc.'

Of course, at the exact moment the taxi from Central Station pulled up at the kerb outside Helena's house, Alessa arrived in the Jag and Felipe in his Audi. When Alessa saw Cressida she did a double take and marched towards them, peering over the top of her sunglasses.

'Mary Mother of God,' she said. 'What happened to you?'

'Hi Alessa,' Cressida said. 'The driver's eftpos is broken. I need money for the taxi.'

'But – but look at you,' said Alessa, huffily putting down the plastic grocery bag she was carrying and rootling in her handbag. 'Your Petit Bateau's *ruined*.' She handed Cressida a twenty. Then she turned to Dale and Saturne, and said, 'Hello. Who're you?'

Before he could answer, Cressida said, 'It's thirty. I need another ten. We came from Central.'

Felipe was waddling towards them in black knix, his cycling shoes making a brisk tap on the pavement.

'Oh my darling, look at you,' he said, taking both of her hands and turning her towards him. 'Who's done this to you? Helena rang – we've all been *frantic*.' In horror Cressida thought for a moment that he was going to do the whole Humphrey Bogart dip-kiss thing, but then he noticed the mud on her and stepped back.

'Oh. What's that?' He squinted at her hair, taking a strand of it for inspection. 'Oh hello,' he said, noticing Dale and Saturne. 'And you are …?'

'It's mud,' said Cressida. 'This is Dale and that's Saturne.' Saturne put her arm around Dale's neck and waved vaguely. Dale leaned around her and quickly shook Felipe's and Alessa's hands. 'Saturne has cancer so be nice to her. I'm not answering any questions until after I have a shower. Guys, follow me,' she said to Dale and Saturne, and started up the drive-way.

When Helena saw Cressida from the back patio she let out a yelp and ran to her.

'Helena,' Cressida said, returning her hug with as much energy as she could muster. She turned to introduce the other two but they were still back at the gate, staring up at the house. Felipe was stuck behind them, craning to see.

'Wow,' said Dale.

'A pool,' Saturne said, looking at it dreamily. 'Oh Dalesy, I *need* to have a swim. Right *now*.'

'Fentanyl,' he said to Helena. '*May*be after you have a lie-down, Saturne. If you get in in this state you'll forget to swim and you'll drown. Besides your dressing can't get wet. Helena, is it?' he said. He stepped forward and shook Helena's hand. Felipe squeezed past and came around to muscle an arm around Cressida's waist.

'Yes, hello,' Helena said to Dale, giving him a quick once-over and then glancing at Cressida. Meanwhile Felipe was kissing Cressida's neck. 'How lovely to meet you,' Helena said. 'And this is … Saturne, is it?' She frowned at the thin ochre-clad woman, her gaze catching on the enormous tumour. 'Oh you poor darling. Come inside, quickly – I've run a bath for you. Oh but you probably can't have it because of your dressing – I'll let it out; what about a shallow one? Cress said you were arriving around now, and then there's some soup I made – or would you like the soup first? It's completely vegan …'

'Oh no, a bath sounds simply wonderful,' said Saturne. 'I already ate though, I think. Dale, did I eat?'

'Toast. Well, half a piece, anyway. Cressida got you some at the hospital. Peanut butter on Turkish.'

'Oh. Okay. Cressida, you're lovely. Thank you so much,' she said.

'Helena, I am *dying* for a shower,' Cressida said. And an escape from this appallingly awkward situation. What on earth was she going to do? 'I have to go and wash half the Gloucester Tops down the drain. Darling, I'm so sorry,' she said to Felipe, 'I tried *so hard* to get there.' Before she realised what she was doing she had turned to Dale. 'Didn't I?' *We*, she thought. 'Look, I want to hear all about it but right now I *really* need a shower.' Then she was run-walking into the house.

Her sister was standing beside the kitchen counter, her bag of groceries sitting on it untouched.

'Nice one, Cressida,' her sister said. 'Felipe's just going to love that.'

Cressida went to the esky and pulled out a bottle of water, taking a long drink.

'Hang on,' she said. 'Weren't you supposed to fly home yesterday?'

'I cancelled my flight because no-one knew where you were!'

'Oh. Sorry,' she said, surprising both of them with a brief hug. 'I'm in the shower.' All she wanted was hot water and a litre of her French vanilla bodywash on her skin, *now*.

Twenty minutes was almost enough to push the recurring images of the ski-goggled men from her vision; freshly scrubbed and coated in scented almond oil, she wrapped herself in a fluffy blue towel and padded down the hallway. In her room Jerome was lolling barefoot on the bed, absorbed in his iPhone. Cressida let out a yelp at the sight of him and threw herself on the bed.

'Jerome!'

'Hey sis,' he said, glancing up as she hugged him. He was wearing raggedy-hem jeans like Dale's and a Radiohead t-shirt, and had a new piercing in his eyebrow. 'Looks like you've got a story to tell,' he said.

'Oh it's a nightmare,' she said, extricating herself. 'An absolute bloody nightmare.'

'Two men, eh? Well, you always were the belle of the ball.'

'What?'

'I saw you outside with them.'

'Oh God, is it that obvious?' If Jerome could tell, she thought, Felipe probably could too. 'Well yes that *is* a bit of nightmare, but it's nothing compared to the rest of my life. I just collected three new clients this morning – possibly five – to go with a sixth, all in an area of law I know nothing about. I'm terrified they're going to find out and ask for a real lawyer,' she said. 'What's worse, all the charges have sentences with the word "years" in them. That or a four-letter word starting with L. And I just got arrested for drug possession. Yes really. Possibly terrorism.'

Jerome sat up, iPhone forgotten. '*Terror*ism? What are you talking about?'

'Well, I think you already know. Heard of destruction of any large pieces of infrastructure lately? A certain protest camp you're about to attend?'

'I'm beginning to wonder whether I should have my own lawyer for this conversation,' he said. 'Will I be an accessory?'

'Maybe. I don't think so though. When it came down to it the police didn't press any charges. We all got a free lift from Gloucester Tops though.'

'Cress, what are you *talking* about? It's that bloke, isn't it. He took my glamorous corporate-law sister and turned her into a … well, you don't look exactly feral, but maybe this is the beginning.'

Cressida laughed. 'Maybe. Oh Jerome, I am so-o-o exhausted, and I've got so-o-o much to do,' she said, rubbing her face with both hands. 'I've lost my laptop . The police have got it. It's been *two days* since I checked my email. I'm terrified of what I'm going to find on it. I've probably been sacked. Or will be when my boss finds out about the whole AFP thing. Except of course he hasn't been able to *call* me because I don't have my *phone*. And you know what else? I totally missed the Surgeons Ball. I'm convinced Felipe's going to kill me with some dreadful surgical instrument the moment we're alone.'

'Well,' Jerome said, 'I think actually the most *pressing* thing you have to do right now is go and sort that out.' He indicated down the hallway to the general area of the kitchen and pool. 'Flannel shirt,' he said, nodding approvingly.

'Oh God. I know. Glad you think so. What am I going to do?'

'I dunno.' Jerome shrugged. 'Do what I always do. Be honest. And if that doesn't work, lie your pants off. Come on. I'll hold your hand,' he said, heaving himself off the bed. 'Metaphorically of course. Otherwise that really would confuse things.'

Cressida sighed and pressed her brother out of the room, throwing her filthy clothes in the laundry basket. She was running low on clothes, but there was at least a pair of clean undies and a bra she hadn't been wearing for 24 hours straight. She looked in the mirror. The mud was gone, but there was a graze on her forehead, and nasty welts around her wrists where the bindings had bit in. She hadn't worn makeup for days, and the hollows under her eyes were dark. But there was a light in them she hadn't seen before. And though her hair was criminally in need of a blowdry, she kind of liked the way it fell loose around her face. It was sort of wild and wispy, framing her face like she'd just come from the beach.

Outside, Felipe was reading a broadsheet on the banana lounge by the pool. He folded it up as she approached.

'Darling. Here,' he said, parting his feet and beckoning her to sit between them. 'Oh, let me hold you again.' He leaned forward to catch her in his embrace. 'I was so worried about you.'

'I'm so sorry about the ball, Felipe,' said Cressida into his forearm.

'Oh darling, that should be the least of your worries,' Felipe was murmuring into her neck. 'Well? Tell me all about it.'

There was a pregnant pause as he sat with his chin on her shoulder. *Oh God.* What on earth was she going to say?

'I had to go and visit a client in Gloucester,' she said. 'It was pouring and I got a little muddy. That's all.'

'I saw Jerome is here,' he continued, snapping the broadsheet back to open. 'Back from that boat, then? What's it called, the *Ocean Steward*?'

'*Sea Shepherd*,' she corrected. *That's it then? That's all you're going to ask, about where I've been?* 'It's an anti-whaling boat.'

'Oh that's right. Yes. And who *are* those people who were with you, by the way?'

'Um. They're clients, actually,' she said.

'Really?' he said, watching her over his glasses. 'What sort of matter? They look a bit ... what is that word you use? *Pro bono*.'

Cressida laughed. 'Well yes they are, actually. One of them's a doctor though.'

'Oh really?' he said, becoming still. 'What field?'

'Trauma. Said he's only halfway through the training though. Had a few diversions. Aid work in Southeast Asia. Did seven years and then ...' She petered out, hoping he wouldn't notice.

'And then?' Felipe frowned.

*Quick, think of something.* 'Um, not sure – he said ...'

Then the bifolds slid open and Cressida looked up gratefully at Helena emerging with a tray of fruit and antipasto. 'Oh, Helena, wow,' she said. 'You're amazing. Where are the others? They'll be starving.'

Felipe reached onto the tray for a slice of French stick and slathered it with cream cheese, wolfing it down with some salmon on top.

'Darling, we need to talk about the next triathlon,' he said through a mouthful of bread. 'That German is running. We need to train extra hard this week. When you've rested, of course.'

'Felipe, I … look, I don't think …'

Helena sat behind Cressida on the chair. 'Well, what's-his-name – Dale? – he had some soup and so did Saturne – he's in the shower now. And Saturne is lying down, the poor mite. She's so young to be so sick,' Helena said, absently stroking Cressida's hair. 'What an interesting pair they are,' she said brightly. 'I've never seen a man with *two* earrings in one ear before.'

'It's the latest thing.'

'Anyway,' Felipe continued, taking off his glasses and regarding Cressida. '*I* thought, since you appear to have had such a *harrowing* time, that I'd take you out and spoil you. How about …' He leaned over to whisper something in her ear, but before he could, at that moment the screen door slid open again and Dale appeared, wearing only a towel.

'Hi,' he began, 'I was wondering if I could throw my clothes in your washer. They're—'

'Very muddy,' Cressida finished, dodging Felipe and standing up. She pushed past him into the house, avoiding his gaze.

Jerome was sitting in the Eames, tapping with both thumbs into his iPhone.

'Jerome – do you have a shirt Dale can borrow? And jeans or something?'

Still looking into his phone he stood up. 'No problem,' he said, throwing a grin at Dale. Boy crush already, thought Cress.

Dale stopped in the door to the hall and turned Cressida to face him, picking up her hands. Her heart dropped to her stomach and she quickly glanced out to the patio, but Felipe had returned to his paper. Dale was inspecting her wrists.

'How are they?'

'On the mend,' she said, not looking at him. 'Yours?'

'Come here,' he said. He led her into the bathroom and opened a drawer. 'Ah. Every home has some,' he said, pulling out a tube of aloe vera cream and a box of bandaids. *Really?* she thought as she sat on the edge of the bathtub. *Mine doesn't; that aloe is definitely Helena's.* He ran some hot water over a clean face washer and wrung it out, then gently washed one of her lacerated wrists and then the other. Then he dabbed both of her wrists carefully with the cream and covered it in the thick bandaids, two on each wrist. 'You really need some proper dressings for these,' he said. 'But this will have to do.' He smoothed the last one in place, then sat next to her.

'Cressida,' he said. He hadn't let go of her arm. 'I don't want to make you uncomfortable. If this is all too weird for you, I can go. It's fine.' He swallowed then reached up to stroke her cheek. 'It was fun.'

Cressida's stomach flipped over, and she stared at him. *No*, she thought. *Fun? That's it? But I don't want you to go. I want you to stay.* But the words stuck in her throat. She picked up the aloe vera and unscrewed it.

'I don't … I mean, it's just …' she said, painting it gently onto his wrist in turn. His hands were thick-fingered, with broad, callused palms, and there was a thin silver bracelet she hadn't noticed before around one wrist, under the soft cuff of the flannelette.

'It's okay,' he said, tipping up her chin gently so she faced him. 'I get it. Like I said, it was fun. I don't want to mess up your life.' He gave her a soft smile and was gone, leaving her sitting on the bathtub. She was still sitting there when a minute later he returned, wearing a faded grey *Sea Shepherd* t-shirt and a pair of jeans of Jerome's. To see him in her brother's clothing made her heart twist. He looked … Nah, but that was crazy. He looked like *home*.

'Hey, Jerome and I are going to go to that protest camp. At the prison. Feel free to join us later if you want,' he said. 'Saturne's resting, thank God. I'll see you later, hey?' There was no kiss.

She looked at him, still unable to say anything useful, to articulate the words that were crashing round her head.

'Okay. Sure. I …' she said. 'Bye.'

Her bed beckoned, a dark, cool oasis from Felipe's too-direct gaze and the guilt coursing through her. This was ridiculous. She'd just met this bloke. Things had to stop. Ten minutes – she could just have ten minutes, surely, to herself, to try and make some sense of things. It all felt so impossible. But then Helena was standing in the doorway, holding out the phone.

'For you.'

She sat up and took it. It was someone bawling.

'Cressida? Cressida is that your name?' The words came out in a rush. 'You're that lawyer? Oh thank God,' said the caller, starting to sob. 'It's me. Dez. Dizzy.'

'*Dizzy*,' said Cressida, waving at Helena frantically for a pen, who yanked open the bedside drawer and found one, holding it out. 'Wow. We were wondering where you were. Are you okay?' A notebook quickly followed.

'Oh *yes*. No I'm not, actually.' Dizzy let out a sob. 'I'm – I'm fuckin' distraught. They got me at the causeway. I got bloody stuck, didn't I. I've been in the bloody lockup at Newie since yesterday. And now they've fucking charged me with that …' – there was a silence, and her next words were holding back tears – 'that *association thingie*! And like, funding a *terrorist organisation*. Jesus. I mean I don't *have* any fuckin' money. I don't know why they think I was *giving it away*!'

'Dizzy, stop,' said Cressida, swinging her legs off the bed. 'Are you alone?'

'What?' said Dizzy. 'No. There's a copper just down the hall.'

'Okay. Well don't say anything else. Have you got a pen? Get them to email me the charge sheet. Where are you? I don't suppose they're bailing you?'

'What? No – I don't – Newcastle somewhere. What was that word they used? Lack. Newcastle Lack. Whatever the fuck that means. They said they're keeping me here till *Monday*, Christina – but I can't – I was supposed to—'

'Cressida. Mitsok. I'll … I'll get someone to do a bail argument for you.' How, on the ripe end of a Saturday afternoon for Monday, she didn't know, but she'd work that out later. This woman had a kid, didn't she? What other option was there? 'Did you get onto whoever's looking after your child?'

'No. I just …' There was a silence, and when she continued her voice was barely audible. 'That's why I'm calling. I'm only bloody allowed to call my lawyer – I need you to call my mum and ask her to go get Madeleine. I was supposed to get her at ten, for God's sake.' Her voice caught. 'She's only six.'

'Oh Dizzy, yes. I'll get onto them. What's the number?'

'God, *thank you*. I'm sorry – yes, the number – it's 4325 9555.'

'It's okay. Can I just have their names, and your surname?'

'They're Rodney and Doris Barnes. They're in Gosford. And my name's Desiree Barnes.

'Where is your daughter?'

'With my ex, Michael, in Dungog. Mum knows the address, okay, just—'

'Okay, Dizzy, try and relax, okay? I'll get—'

'Relax?! Are you fucking kidding? I'm … Oh God, I have to go,' she said, sobbing. 'Some other fucker wants the phone.'

'Okay – just take my email address for the charge sheet; do you have a pen? It's—'

The line went dead. Fuck and double fuck. She should have given that to her *first*, not last.

Helena was standing in the doorway, a teabag dangling from her hand. 'Is everything okay?'

'Oh *yes*,' Cressida said, scribbling. *T/c D Barnes 3.32pm. In custody. Financing terrorism – s101.??* 'If you don't mind everything going to shit.'

*Pls call mother & arrange pickup of daughter. 4325 9555. Bail refused – need representation for Monday, Newcastle.*

Felipe came in from the pool and slid onto the bed beside her, hooking his arms under hers.

'Darling, look at you, working so hard – after all you've been through.' He nuzzled her neck. 'For goodness sake, come to the club with me. I've got a nice twilight game of golf planned with Roger. In fact,' he said, straightening her shoulder strap and checking his watch, 'how about I call the spa and ask them to fit you in for a *nice massage*, and *then* we can go out for a lovely dinner at Suki's later on,' he said. He paused for emphasis. 'They've got kef*tedes.*'

'She's got a lot of work to do, Felipe,' Cressida was surprised to hear Helena say from the kitchen, appearing at the doorway again. 'Did you say bail argument? Isn't that a criminal thing?'

'Oh *yes,*' Cressida said. 'Apparently I'm a criminal lawyer now. Felipe, I'd love to,' she said, turning to him, 'but can I meet you there later? I just have to make a phone call. Or two. And look some things up for these clients. Actually can I borrow your iPad? I've … I've lost mine.'

A cord in Felipe's jaw flicked. In the kitchen Cressida heard Helena busy herself with the kettle and teacups. 'Sure,' he sighed. 'Yes. Whatever you like.' He extricated himself with a peck on the cheek, and returned with the iPad. 'I'll see you there.'

When Helena reappeared Cressida was still on the bed, staring at the notepad. 'Well,' she said. 'He was a bit cranky, wasn't he. Tea?'

Cressida sighed.

'Yes. Thanks.'

She'd have to email the police herself and ask them to send her the charge sheet. How long would that take, from some general email address until it found its way to Newcastle Local Area Command? Well. It was better than nothing. And she'd try phoning them back. But first she dialled the number Dizzy had given her. A woman answered.

'Yeah?' There was the sound of a radio, and children yelling in the background.

'Is that – is that Mrs Barnes?'

'Ah, yes?'

'Hello. My name's Cressida Mitsok. I'm … Look, everything's okay, but …' *Just tell her,* she thought, walking down the hallway towards Leo's office. 'Your … your daughter's been arrested. I'm her lawyer.'

'Sorry, what? Rodney, *turn that thing down.* Sorry, the grandkids are here. What did you say? My daughter?'

'Your daughter's been …' There was no way to finesse it. 'She's been arrested on some fairly serious charges. To do with the blackout. And not bailed, so …' Then there was a lot of yelling going on and a man's voice came on the line. 'Hello? This is Rodney Barnes. What's all this?'

Cressida took a deep breath and said it all again. She heard Mrs Barnes in the background, then it was her voice on the phone again.

'Dez? You're talking about Dez? Where is she? Can we see her?'

'I think so – she was in Newcastle just now, and they'll probably keep her there till Monday.' She googled the Newcastle LAC number on Felipe's iPad. 'Got a pen?' She read it out. 'They should tell you where she is. And … look, the reason I'm calling is – she actually wanted to know whether you could pick up, um, Madeleine?'

'Hang on – a pen – Rodney – *get me a pen*. What was it again?' Cressida repeated the number. 'Oh God, yes, Maddie … From Dungog? Jesus. Rodney!' Dizzy's mother called away from the phone. 'Is that car fixed yet? Sorry, love, it's just that the Ford's been up on the blocks for a week. The number of times I told him to get rid of that bloody car … Jesus, *charges*? What charges?'

'I … I don't know.' The truth was, she didn't, until she got the CAN. 'She was just most concerned about Madeleine, so I said I'd call you …'

'Oh Jesus. I *knew* she was getting mixed up with the wrong crowd up there! It's not to do with those bloody Gloucester folk, is it?' There was a pause, and some muffled yelling. 'I'm sorry. Leave it with me, love,' Dizzy's mother said. 'Did she say where Madeleine is? With Michael?'

'Is that her ex? Yes.'

'She'll have watched six hours of TV already then.' She sighed. 'Alright. Thanks for letting us know. He can probably keep her until tomorrow, poor mite. He's a good dad. I'll call him. Bloody hell. Have you got a number we can call you on?'

She gave Helena's landline and hung up, subsiding into Leo's chair. The attacks on the power stations were like the tentacles of some enormous octopus, reaching out further and further beyond the actual perpetrators, into the families and houses of people who'd never even met them. Helena appeared and set a steaming mug at Cressida's elbow.

'What's the matter?'

'Oh *nothing*. Thank you. I'm just worried about this client's daughter.' She looked at the tea. 'She's been arrested and the kid would have expected her hours ago.'

'Who's Madeleine?'

'That woman's granddaughter,' she sighed. 'Her mum was meant to pick her up from her ex this morning, except she's in the lockup. And her mum can't do it because their car's out of action.'

'Ai,' said Helena. 'How old is she?'

'Six.'

'I don't suppose there's any point asking you what this is about,' Helena said, regarding Cressida over the rim of her cup.

'Sorry, Hels,' Cressida said. 'No.'

'You tell me if I can do anything, alright?' she said, her eyes filled with sympathy. 'And you know – you could always ask your big sister for help? She's a lawyer too, you know,'

Cressida smiled, thinking that was the last thing she wanted to do, but that it was kind of Helena to suggest it.

'Thanks, Helena. I'll think about it.'

Helena kissed Cressida on the forehead and took back the phone.

'Okay.'

Cressida sat back in the chair, trying to think fast. What about the Junior Counsel Sandra had mentioned? Surely *they* could do the bail argument? But Dizzy didn't have a Junior yet. Or any barrister at all. Actually, nor did any of them; she hadn't booked anyone yet. Maybe Brian … He had a daughter involved too, after all. If he would agree to pay Sandra to act for Dizzy too, or at least pay a Junior … But Sandra charged ten thousand dollars a day, and a junior at least two and a half. But even if Brian agreed, it seemed unlikely that some Sydney barrister, fancy enough to be picked up by Sandra, would agree to leg it up to Newcastle on 48 hours' notice to apply for bail for some penniless nobody on a terrorism charge. On the other hand, maybe they would. Get their name in the papers. Sometimes even flash Junior Counsel weren't immune to that.

Well, she could only ask.

'What's up?'

It was Saturne, leaning against the doorjamb. She was wearing a pair of Helena's paisley silk pyjamas.

'Dizzy just rang to say she's been …' *There was no conflict, right? Dizzy and Saturne were related parties.* 'That she's been charged with the association provision.' There was no point sugarcoating it. 'Financing terrorism.'

Saturne's eyes widened. 'Fuck. That's absurd. But – but Dizzy doesn't have two dollars to rub together.'

'Yeah. We won't know much more until we get the papers. Incredibly frustrating.'

'Where is she?'

'Newcastle. Remanded to appear on Monday. Said they got her on the causeway.'

'The *causeway*? But that was hours before they got us,' said Saturne, taking the chair opposite. She grimaced as she did so, hand going unconsciously to her side. The tumour sat like a miniature second head on Saturne's shoulder, and Cressida tried not to stare at it.

'They must have been waiting,' said Cressida, feeling cold. Had they been there when she was driving up? Seen her car? 'I'm trying to find an agent to do bail. In *New*castle,' she continued, as if it was the moon. 'How are you?'

'Fine, I'm fine. Dale gives good nursing.'

'Yes,' said Cressida, surprised by the sudden wave of jealousy that rose up. 'It seems like it.' Which would you rather, she asked herself, a massage from Dale or a bloody grapefruit on your neck? 'Are you hungry?' she said, to compensate.

'Hmm, food,' Saturne said, looking thoughtful. 'I probably should. Maybe a sandwich? I could go a cuppa … something herbal if you have it? I'll make it,' she said, when Cressida moved to get up. 'You look exhausted.'

'Don't be silly. You relax.'

In the kitchen she opened Helena's enormous collection of herbal teas and called out the labels to Saturne.

'Rooeybos,' Saturne laughed at Cress's pronunciation of *rooibos*. 'It's pronounced *roy*boss. Thanks. That'd be lovely.'

Roy what? Cressida thought, smelling it. It smelt of grass.

'Never heard of that one,' she said. 'Is that meant to be good … for …'

'For non-Hodgkin's lymphoma? Nothing's good for non-Hodgkin's lymphoma, Cress. Except maybe death. Sorry,' she said, as Cress looked away, pale. 'Black humour. It helps. I just like rooibos though. You have it without milk.'

'Sure. Okay …' She turned on the kettle to reboil and set up the teabag in a cup. 'Um, I just need to make a couple of phone calls. Are you alright for a minute?'

'I'm fine,' Saturne said, smiling and collapsing into the Eames. 'I'm not going to drop dead if you leave me alone for five minutes.'

Cressida laughed. 'Sorry.'

She sent the email asking for Dizzy's charge sheet, then found Brian's number on the firm homepage, dialling as she walked out to the patio. It would only be his secretary's number, she realised, thinking she'd have to leave a message. But unexpectedly, he picked up on the second ring. Diverted.

'Brian? It's Cressida.'

There was a pause, and when Brian spoke his voice was clipped. There was the sound of glasses clinking in the background.

'Cressida. How nice of you to ring. I've left several messages.'

'I'm sorry – I've been completely in the thick of it, I'm afraid. Look – I hope I'm not interrupting anything – I spoke to Andy – I mean Joanne – and—'

'Good.'

'She … well, the first thing she said was thank you. For sending me. And we're still waiting on the brief of evidence, of course, but the good news is, they've only charged her with sabotage so far.' *And stop stalling*, she thought, *and get on with it, Cressida.*

'Good.'

'But the thing is, Brian …' She took a deep breath into the silence, and plunged on. 'It's just – well, she's not the only one.'

'Not the only one what?'

'I mean, aside from the Climate F— I mean the five power station suspects. The ones arrested so far, I mean.'

'I hardly find that surprising, Cressida. There's probably fifty of them counting all the hangers on. What's your point?'

'Well, when I was in Wellington,' Cressida began, 'your daughter told me about some … some friends of hers she was worried about. That's what she was so desperate to tell me. So … well … I went to interview them at a house near Gloucester and just after I left, it was raided, and some arrests made … including me, by the way.' The rest of it came out in a rush, as if talking fast would make it all better. It didn't.

'What the fuck?' said Brian.

'That bit was cleared up, thank goodness,' Cressida said, climbing onto the banana lounge. 'And four of them were let go pending further charges on the terrorism stuff. But … one of them wasn't. A Desiree Barnes. She's been charged with financing terrorism – I don't know the basis of it, Brian, but going by everything else, and having met her, it does seem a little odd.'

'I don't see your point,' said Brian.

'Well – it's just, they've remanded her in custody, and it sounds like the Feds intend to oppose bail on Monday. I'm wondering if we can engage counsel for her on the same basis that we're … that Sandra and whoever the Junior is are acting for Andy.'

'What? No! And who the fuck's Andy? Jesus Cressida, what is going *on*?'

'Sorry, I mean Joanne. Joanne. That's the name Joanne goes by. Andromeda. With these people, I mean.'

'What people? What are you *talking* about? Cressida if any of this is going to jeopardise—'

'It won't. Look,' she said, thinking fast, 'it might even *help* Joanne's case – I mean, they can't really get her on conspiracy without co-conspirators, right? Or at least, not as *much*. And I've spoken to these people, and I think they've got a good chance of getting off the charges with quality representation.'

There was a silence, and then Cressida had to hold the phone away from her ear.

'What the fuck did you do that for?' Brian yelled.

'I'm sorry?'

'You never, *ever* act for co-accused in an indictable matter, Cressida. You know that.'

'What? Well I don't know about never. I mean …'

'What's to say they won't give evidence against my daughter? Jesus, Cressida, what were you *thinking*?'

'Look it's not like that,' Cressida hurried to explain. 'Of course I thought about that before I went. But the woman Andy—'

'Stop calling her that.'

'Sorry. *Joanne*. The woman Joanne wanted me to see is …' There was nothing for it. 'She's her girlfriend. Her name's Saturne. She's … she's here now, actually.'

There was another silence, and Cressida resisted the urge to make sure he was still there. She barrelled on.

'So the thing is, I've thought about this whole conflict issue, and I've looked up the Solicitors' Rules to make sure I'm right, and I know Sandra's the intergalactic expert on all this of course. But I've checked and it's okay for co-accused to have the same solicitor up to the point their interests come into conflict. It's certainly alright for them to have the same barrister.'

'But Cressida. Come on. They could "come into conflict" as you put it – or as I would put it, stab each other in the back – at *any time*. *Or* use information they got from you about the other. I can't *believe* you went up there without consulting me. Don't you realise? You could *already* be conflicted from acting for my daughter against her, depending on what this Barnes person has told you about her own situation. Oh Cressida. I was counting on you. Jesus. Have they signed anything saying you're her solicitor?'

Cressida grimaced. This wasn't going according to plan. 'No.'

'Well at least that's something.' Brian sighed. 'What does Sandra say about all this? Have you spoken to her?'

'No. I was going to leave that till Monday.'

'No time for that. You need to call her and get her advice immediately. Then ring me back and tell me what she says. Now, I want to talk to this Saturne person.'

'Oh. Really? Um, she's not well at the moment …'

'Surely she can chat for five minutes on the phone.'

'I'll ask her.' She got up, feeling dizzy, and trying to think back to her ethics training years ago, to remember how it all worked. Had she really read it wrongly? The Solicitors' Rules had said it was fine as long as both clients consented – she hadn't formally obtained Andy's consent yet to act for the other defendants, but she was sure she would get it. She opened the bifolds and called out.

'It's Andy's dad. He wants to talk to you.'

Saturne frowned and put down her tea. As soon as she took the phone Cressida found Sandra's number on the Bar Association website. What a time to have lost her mobile, she thought. Saturne was on the only landline in the house. Alessa – she had one. She hurried down the hallway to her sister's room. It was just a phone call. She could ask for help with *that*.

Alessa was lying on her bed wearing swimmers and a tank dress, flicking through a *Frankie* magazine. Foam pads demarcated fresh polish on her toenails.

'Alessa,' said Cressida. 'Can I borrow your phone?'

'Where's yours?' said Alessa, without looking up.

Cressida swallowed. She tried to sound as nonchalant as possible. 'The police have it.'

'The police have it,' Alessa repeated, staring at her. She put down the magazine. 'For God's sake, Cressida, what's this all about? You're not having a breakdown are you?'

*God, sometimes it feels like I should*, Cressida thought; *it would probably make things easier. I could go and spend time in some nice, white, clean ward somewhere and wait till all this is over.*

'No,' she said. 'But I really need your phone. Like, right now.'

'What for? Give me the number and I'll dial it.'

'Alessa. Look, I need to talk to Senior Counsel about an issue with a case. It's urgent.'

'But Cressida,' Alessa said, laughing, 'you don't do litigation. You're a building lawyer. You need to tell me what's going on.'

'You know what? I'd actually really love to, because there's fuck-all else in the way of people I can talk to about it. But it's so-o highly confidential you might find yourself going to gaol if I did. The AFP's going completely nuts arresting people from here to kingdom come. And one of them just called me from gaol right now, and I really need to check something out. So. Your phone?'

'Okay, Cressida, okay. God, sit down. There's no need to get all uppity.' She held the phone out and Cressida took it.

'I can't let you hear any of it. Sorry,' she said, heading back down the hallway and dialling the number as she walked. She went into her room and shut the door.

'Sandra. Hi. It's Cressida Mitsok.'

'On a Saturday?' came Sandra's calm, rounded vowels. She was probably in a day spa somewhere herself, Cressida thought.

'Yes I know it's a Saturday. I'm sorry about that. It's just … something's happened.' She felt her voice catch. Here it was, the very thing she'd wanted to avoid. Screwing something up in front of Sandra Crane.

'Well just a minute,' she said. 'I'm in conference. I'll just go into the corridor …'

Of course she was, Cressida thought. She was an international silk. She probably worked seven days a week. Cressida heard a door open then close and then Sandra returned to the phone.

'What is it?'

She repeated to Sandra the part she'd told Brian about finding herself acting for both Dizzy and Andy. Then she waited for the sky to fall in. When Sandra listened without gasping, screaming at her or doing anything else, Cressida thought if she'd been in the same room with her she would have kissed her.

'Yes,' Sandra said slowly. 'Conflict *could* be an issue, but can you ask Ms Barnes whether she objects? Do you think she will?'

'No,' said Cressida. 'No I don't. I mean, not at this point. But … she may do later. She has a child. She's going to be really desperate to keep out of gaol.'

'Well exactly, and that's my concern. Perhaps we *do* need to find her another lawyer, Cressida. Listen, here's what I suggest: make a call to a – do you have a pen? – Byron Kent of Counsel, eleventh floor Wentworth, and run by him the possibility of appearing for her on Monday. He's the Junior on the Fairbank matter I was going to suggest you brief. As you know barristers aren't constrained by the same conflict rules as solicitors in criminal matters. Then you'll need to get on the phone and find another solicitor to instruct him – I assume the defendant is impecunious?'

'Yes,' said Cressida. No two dollars to rub together, quote unquote, she thought.

'Then she should apply for Legal Aid to get a solicitor immediately. Unless you can find someone who is happy to be paid Legal Aid rates, then she can nominate them as her solicitor on the Legal Aid form. And remind Byron – April 30's only weeks away and he's down on his pro bono quota for the year. Plus he could do with getting his tailored butt off Macquarie Street.'

'Oh.' Cressida felt weak with relief, letting loose a strangled giggle at her words. It was so great to have someone to speak so plainly with. 'Okay. Thanks so much.'

'And Cressida?' Sandra said. 'Don't go volunteering to act for any more related parties in this matter without discussing it with me first, okay? And I mean that phrase in the *broadest possible sense*.'

'Absolutely. Thanks again,' she said, but Sandra had already hung up. *I am so embarrassed*, Cressida thought. *Can't be trusted to make any more decisions without reporting in. God, what a nightmare.* She entered the mobile number Sandra had given her into Alessa's phone. Calling counsel she didn't know – on a Saturday – for a court appearance – the day after next – in Newcastle – *for free* – was probably at the edges of anything she would have dared before, but this was urgent, and besides, Sandra had given the okay. But after all that trepidation he didn't answer anyway, so she left a message to call back on the landline or Alessa's number. Then she went to the kitchen and yanked open the refrigerator. Saturne had moved to the banana lounge by the pool, the phone sitting limply in her hands, but Cressida didn't go to her, instead rooting through the fridge for chocolate. Where the hell were the Cadbury Jelly Popping Candy Beanies? There weren't any, of course. Only vegetables, condiments, the leftover soup and a couple of neatly labelled health food meals of Alessa's.

'I'm off to the shop,' she called out, to no-one in particular, telling herself she'd go and ask Saturne about the call with Brian when she got back. She jammed her hat on her head and grabbed her wallet. The air was still thick with heat, cicadas roaring from the dense tree canopy across the road in Centennial Park; she could feel sunlight radiating up from the pavement onto the skin of her calves so that they burned. Round the corner was a service station, and she plunged into its cold air-conditioned embrace, pondering the chocolate display. *Clinkers Raspberry Chips and Marshmallows? Now you're talking.* She took three bars and the instant she'd paid ripped open one and stood munching on it with her head against one of the refrigerator doors. *If only I could just stay here for a minute*, she thought, *in this place that has nothing to do with terrorists or saboteurs or accessories to crimes or incomprehensible Solicitors' Rules or incredible kind sexy doctors from Gloucester Tops.*

'Can I, ah, help you?' called the clerk from the front of the shop.

'Oh,' Cressida turned and gave him her most confident, no-nutter-here smile. 'No, sorry. Just a bit hot,' she said, pushing herself off the fridge. 'See you.'

But she didn't want to go home, she thought as she emerged into the sunlight. It was too bloody complicated there. She didn't want to explain to Alessa or ask Saturne what Brian had said. Instead she slapped the button at the pedestrian crossing on the corner of Darley Street and crossed to the racecourse, a vast jewel of iridescent green fringed by massive Norfolk pines and the white of the railing, and immediately collapsed under one of the palms on its rim, pulling her hat down against the glare. It was hot but the heat felt good – so overwhelming that it turned her into a cold-blooded animal, slow and sluggish. The grass and the little-toothed arcs of the pine needles that lay on it scratched the parts of her bare skin. After a while the world stopped spinning, and she looked across at the track. A distance away some late training horses trotted in the afternoon sun, their wiry riders bouncing on bent knees. It was almost as if the blackout hadn't happened, she thought. Everything was back to normal. What had the point of it been, again, she wondered, munching on the second bar. Surely some reason would come out of all this that would make all of Andy's sacrifice, her friends' and family's sacrifice, worthwhile. She hoped so.

# 24

It was six o'clock by the time she got back to Helena's. In fact, she could probably just make the golf club to meet Felipe in time for dinner. But she just didn't want to. The thought of the pressure of not telling him anything about the case was too much, as was the prospect of suppressing the guilt the chocolate bars were rapidly creating – always worse when he was around. Her ankle was still sore and the welts on her wrists stung. And the night of broken sleep was catching up with her. All she wanted to do was crawl into bed. She sent Felipe a text from Alessa's phone saying she wasn't feeling well, then ran a bath, spraying in a liberal amount of Alessa's gardenia bubble bath. Where was Dale? She should have suggested he not go to the protest camp – especially not since the police were suss on him because of Andy's charges. God it was all too hard, she thought, subsiding into the steaming bathwater. She needed backup. Hopefully this junior barrister would be some chop when he rang back. If he ever did.

Her eyes were just beginning to close in the bathtub when there was a tap at the door.

'Cressida? It's Saturne.'

'Oh. Yes?'

'Hi. Look I'm really sorry, but … I really need to go to the toilet. It's the painkillers. They're a diuretic. Well they always make *me* want to go to the toilet anyway.'

'Oh.' Cressida looked down at the bubbles, which were, fortunately, covering everything. 'Sure. Come in. Though there's another toilet down the hall …'

She knew she should offer to get out, but she couldn't seem to move.

'Alessa's in it I think.'

'Oh. Sure. By all means.' Embarrassed, she averted her gaze as Saturne sat down on the toilet. When water tinkled and Saturne simultaneously let out a sigh of relief though, they both laughed.

'Ah. That's better,' said Saturne. 'Sorry.'

'Hey, no worries,' Cressida said, eyes still closed. She heard the toilet roll spin and the rustle of paper, and then Saturne spoke.

'I've finished. You can open your eyes now.'

'Oh. Thanks,' Cressida said, and did. The other woman didn't show any sign of leaving, though. Instead she flushed the toilet and sat back on the closed toilet seat.

'It's a Chinese curse to live in interesting times,' she said, and Cressida laughed.

'Yes. I've heard that somewhere ... Oh wow,' she said, seeing the tattoo on Saturne's wrist. The three lines radiating from a coffee bean.

'What?'

'Your tattoo. It's the same as Andy's.'

'Oh. Oh yeah.' She blushed. 'It's a special one.'

'The star system.'

'Yeah. Yeah, she was really into that,' she said, looking at it.

'Saturne, I was wondering ...' Cress began. *While I've got you and it's easier to talk about something than remember I'm naked under these bubbles*, she thought. She continued, 'Do you know how she came to do this?' Asking Saturne wasn't the same as asking Andy, she decided. And right now, she was too tired to care. She wanted to know. And she also knew she should be recording this, to capture it fresh for a statement, but she was too exhausted. Enough time for that later.

'You sound like that Brian bloke,' Saturne said with a laugh. 'God, what a steamroller.' She rolled her eyes. 'I can see why Andy doesn't like seeing him. He totally grilled me. Why did Andy do it, what was her motivation, who can prove that, make sure Cressida gets statements from people that can say she didn't intend to, what was that word you used? Intimidate. I felt like *I* was the one who'd blown up a power station by the time I hung up.'

'Yeah. He's pretty intense. Which reminds me. We have to do your statement. I mean, I assume that's consistent ...'

'What is?'

'You know, that she did it for non-terrorist reasons.'

Saturne frowned, then laughed. 'Oh. Isn't that obvious?'

'Well,' Cressida said. 'Maybe to you and me. But I don't think the police are going to be that charitable about it.'

'It was just about coal-fired power. She just got to the point where she wanted it to stop. She wasn't thinking about afterwards, even.' Saturne looked into the bubble-strewn water. 'For her it was like, one sale of heroin to a child in a playground is too much. One more part per million carbon dioxide into the earth's atmosphere on top of what's already there, causing climate change, is unacceptable. She kept a record of it, in her diary. When it passed 400 parts per million … that's when they started planning. They just realised that … Well, she said, that no-one else was going to do anything. And then they gave the last approval to Adani and … well, that was it. It was like it took her over. For weeks she didn't talk about anything else.'

'400 parts per million? CO2?'

'In the atmosphere. 400 parts per million – ppm – was the point at which the science was saying two degrees' rise was certain, and then the feedback loops will start. In other words, things start to get really scary, climate wise. That's the concentration it was in the stone age, when ice melted and made the seas rise ten metres. Then they decided – if Adani was approved, it was on. Almost like it was out of their hands, then, they said.'

'That's that coal mine … the one in Queensland, you mean?'

Saturne nodded. 'Well – it is going to be the biggest coal mine in Australia,' she said, sadly. 'Bigger than anything in the US, even, and a gateway to building ten more. And nearly 80 million tonnes of carbon emissions a year. They were terrified about it.'

'And did you think she was serious? Did you really think she'd do it?'

'Andy? Nah,' Saturne said. 'Even though with this, I almost agreed with her. I thought it'd blow over. She was always getting really hot under the collar about things, then she'd go and do something extreme and it would be like the hole was filled, she was happy, for a few days, anyway, until something else happened.'

'Something extreme, like what?'

'Oh I don't know. It depended on what it was. You know, she'd read about human trafficking or animal cruelty or destruction of some last piece of endangered rainforest, and donate her entire bank balance to an organisation working on that, or pack everything up and the next day be off to a forest blockade or a camp outside a drug lab experimenting on animals.' Her gaze became distant. 'It was actually one of the things I loved about her.'

The bubbles were thinning, and Cressida discreetly piled up more.

'Dale said you met on a forest blockade.'

'We did. I remember the first moment I saw her. She came with this band of, I don't know, forest minstrels.' She laughed. 'They were all dressed up in these outlandish costumes. Andy was wearing a pair of ears and a tail, as I remember it – and they poured out of this bus they were all travelling in, playing instruments and yelping like wolves. It was like something out of the *Where The Wild Things Are*,' she said, in a tone of wonder. 'The thing about Andy was – you know how most people have an "off" button? A button that says "enough?" I've done what I can, I can stop now, other people can take over? Well Andy didn't seem to have that. It was almost like she felt like, because she had the power to do something about something, it was *all* her responsibility. She had the opposite characteristic to most people – she didn't *have* an apathy point. She was always *on*, wanting to change and fix and … *transform* things. No moderation,' she said, with a laugh that held both admiration and sadness.

Cressida looked up at the light on the ceiling. Right now, it was sucking energy from some distant furnace, in some amazing process that turned black rocks into electricity and, according to Andy, pumped out poison. She'd barely even thought about it.

'Thanks. I just wondered,' Cressida said, again resisting the urge to ask more questions. That was enough for now. She was a witness. No coaching her. She certainly didn't want to make any more screw-ups.

'No problem,' said Saturne. 'You know, they asked me to give evidence against Andy when I was in the lockup. Said they'd give me a lesser charge if I did.'

Cressida stared. 'What did you say?'

Saturned snorted. 'No, of course. But can they do that?'

'The police? Sure. They can basically do whatever they want when it comes to the charges. It still makes me nervous that they didn't charge you.'

'Why?'

'I don't know. Just because they could at any time, I guess.'

'But if they were going to charge me, why would they let me go?'

Cressida sighed. 'Good question. Maybe because they're still gathering evidence. Because they didn't have anything on you but they hoped you'd let something slip.'

'But they're not meant to arrest me just for that, are they? They have to charge me.'

'Not if they let you out before 24 hours.'

'What's with that 24-hour thing anyway. That's ages.'

Cressida shrugged. 'I guess they figure that's the time they need to investigate properly, once they've got a suspect. They would have been pretty dark on having to let you go.'

Saturne snorted. 'So sue me, cancer has its good points. Hey, can I ask you something?'

'Sure.'

'What are your intentions with Dale?'

'What?' Cressida said. A hell of a question to ask someone who was already naked.

'It's just … I know you're engaged, that's all, and … well. He's a good man. I just don't want to see him hurt.'

*See **him** hurt*, Cressida thought. *He was the one who just told me it had been 'fun'. What about me?*

'I know he is,' she said.

'Cool.' A smile emerged like sunshine from Saturne's serious expression. 'I thought I'd try and rustle up some dinner. Are you hungry?'

'Opiates worn off, eh?' Cressida said, then wished she hadn't. Talk about tactless. 'Sorry. Wasn't thinking. I hope that doesn't mean you're in pain again.'

'It's wearing off, yeah.' Saturne sighed. 'But I've got some other stuff. Don't worry, nothing *questionably legal*' – she laughed – 'Panadeine forte.'

'Do you know much about NHL?' she said.

'Um, no. I'm afraid not.'

'Oh God, don't be. It's not particularly interesting. Well anyway, I have what's known as stage three mediastinal B-cell lymphoma. It's a blood cancer.'

'And what's ... what's the prognosis?'

'The prognosis?' she said, barking laughter. 'I never listen to that crap. What's the prognosis for you, sitting in the bath like that? You could walk out of here and be hit by a bus tomorrow morning. I mean, I hope you aren't,' she said, a grin softening her words. 'But I've never let anyone tell me any of that "four months to live" bullshit. That's self-fulfilling prophecy poison. Some guy in a white coat tells me I've got four months to live and what's the old subsconcious do? Live what it's been told, right down to the hour. You mark my words. I've seen it happen.'

She got up, turning the tap on full bore and soaping her hands.

'Anyway I'm going to a month-long intensive in the States in June,' she said. 'Run by this amazing bone cancer survivor who cured himself just with juices and meditation. Or something. It costs thirty thousand dollars, though.' She dried her hands, face a picture of optimism. 'Andy was going to lend – no, give – it to me, but then she got arrested.'

There was a knock at the door.

'Yes?'

'It's your barrister,' said Alessa. 'Lord Byron.'

Oh God, thought Cressida. When is this going to stop?

'Okay. Can you—' She looked down at the bubbles. He could wait five minutes. 'Could you tell him I'll call back in five?'

'Okay,' Alessa sang.

'Is that about Dizzy's charges?'

'Yeah,' said Cressida. 'Hey – what about your parents?'

'What? Oh. On the money. Nope. Dead.'

'Oh Jesus,' said Cressida, kicking herself. 'Sorry. I did know that.'

'What was with you the other day, anyway?' Saturne asked. 'You freaked out at the hospital. Dale said you wouldn't come in.'

'My mum died of lung cancer. We went to the Newcastle Mater once, while we were on holiday in Tea Gardens. She had a turn and it was the closest place.' Didn't do any good though, she thought, but didn't say so.

'Oh God, Cressida.' Saturne slumped back onto the toilet cistern and looked at Cressida with her head in her hands. 'I'm so sorry.'

'It was twenty years ago now. But thanks. And thanks for the offer of dinner. I'm going to have a kip for a bit. Then get up and see what headway I can make with the charges. If you …'

'Sure, yep, I'm going. Hey. Nice to chat,' she said.

'Likewise,' said Cressida.

The rawness had arrived in her belly again. Damn. She hated talking about it. And she'd stupidly mentioned the D-word, to someone who … well. She'd breached the 'let's all pretend this might not be terminal' code. *You're being maudlin again*, she told herself. *You need some sleep. Yes*, she answered herself, and hauled herself out of the bath.

Wearing a towel, she opened the door and took the phone from Alessa, weak-kneed with relief when Byron said he would do it. He'd get the fact sheet from the prosecutor at court, he said. It would be enough for a first mention. And something about a relief because he'd been looking for some pro bono hours. After she'd hung up and subsided onto the big double bed in her room, her head spun with all the things she had to do. *When I wake up I'm making a list*, she thought. But right now she was so tired it felt like her skin was looser on her face. *I must look an absolute wreck*. The sheets were white and crisp, freshly changed by Helena, and she crawled in between them gratefully. How Leo had managed to hang onto such an amazing woman through four years in prison was a mystery of nature. So it felt disloyal when she opened the top drawer next to the bed and took out the little leather wallet she always carried with her. She opened it, and looked at the photo. It was faded, an image from a time and a place long ago, her mother smiling under an enormous gum tree in the heat of the Queensland sun, in front of her beloved veggie garden. The grief was quieter these days, a sore that was sensitive to the touch but okay as long as you didn't prod it. She had prodded it by going to the Mater. She wouldn't be doing that again in a hurry. She put the photo under her pillow and fell asleep.

When she woke again the LED lights on the bedside clock said 12.17. She had been dreaming of the opening of Andy's trial. When everybody stood as the judge entered, she had looked down to discover she was wearing pyjamas. Then when the judge asked for opening arguments, Sandra and the Junior and the defendants and all of their families had turned and looked at her instead of Sandra, but when she started to speak no words came out. Then it became a dream about trying to dial a number on her mobile phone and no matter how many times she did it the number wasn't right. She sat up, rubbing her eyes and trying to get her bearings. Craziness. The list. She'd feel better when she wrote a list.

Down the end of the hallway Alessa's light was on, the other bedrooms dark. Dale and Jerome must still be at the protest, she guessed. Suddenly starving, she was about to open the fridge and forage when she heard Felipe's iPad give the email ping. Dizzy's charge sheet? At midnight?

She clicked on it. Nope. *[SEC-UNCLASSIFIED] [Joanne FAIRBANK – Charges]*. Ah, at last. The police facts on Joanne. The cover sheet was signed by the prosecutor she had spoken to on Tuesday and included a note asking her, so politely, to please let them know anything contested. Oh, and something else.

Another CAN.

A chill went through her. They were working on her case *now*, on a Saturday night?

Well, as it happened, so was she. Cressida opened the attachment, and, without taking her eyes off the screen, walked towards the Eames and sank into it.

**Offender**  Joanne Teresa Fairbank

**Address**  244 Marrickville Road, Marrickville NSW

**Nationality** Australian  **DOB** 12 October 1996

**Occupation** Childcare worker  **CNI No.** 73120534

Oh God. There they all were. The charges. Like a shopping list of horror.

**Seq No.**  **Offences**

**Act**  **Criminal Code Act (Cth) 1995**

Section 101:

1. Commit a terrorist act

2. Receive training connected with a terrorist act

4. Possess things in connection with a terrorist act

6. Other acts done in preparation for, or planning of, terrorist acts

Section 102.:

2. Directing activities of a terrorist organisation

3. Membership of a terrorist organisation

4. Recruitment for a terrorist organisation

5. Receive and/or provide training for a terrorist organisation

6. Getting funds from or to a terrorist organisation

7. Providing support or resources for a terrorist organisation

8. Association with a terrorist organisation

Section 103.:

2. Financing a terrorist

She clicked on the light in Leo's study and found the *Criminal Code Act* on the shelf and some sticky notes on the neat blotter, then went and sat back in the Eames. *101.1 Commit a terrorist act*. That had to be defined somewhere. She dug into the beginning of the Act. Nothing in the definitions section; she flicked to the start of the Part itself. Ah. There they were. And it was just as Sandra had recited:

*terrorist act* means an action or threat of action where:

(a)  the action falls within subsection (2) and does not fall within subsection (3); and

(b)  the action is done or the threat is made with the intention of advancing a political, religious or ideological cause; and

(c)  the action is done or the threat is made with the intention of:

    (i)  coercing, or influencing by intimidation, the government of the Commonwealth or a State, Territory or foreign country, or of part of a State, Territory or foreign country; or

    (ii) intimidating the public or a section of the public.

But what were subsections (2) and (3)? Below:

(2) Action ... (a) causes serious harm that is physical harm to a person; or (b) causes serious damage to property; or (c) ... death; or (d) endangers a person's life ...; or ...

Ah.

(f) seriously interferes with, seriously disrupts, or destroys ... an essential public utility.

Well, that was pretty straightforward. She'd done that. But what was (3), she wondered, ignoring the cold hand of overwhelm in her chest.

> (3) … advocacy, protest, dissent or industrial action … not intended (i) to cause serious … physical harm to a person; or (ii) to cause a person's death; or (iii) to endanger the life of a person, other than the person taking the action; or (iv) to create a serious risk to the health or safety of the public or a section of the public.

Well. That was it then.

Andy had been adamant she hadn't intended to harm anyone. She hadn't 'intended' to do any of those things. Done. That was the defence.

It wasn't, though. No-one would accept that blowing up a power station was 'protest' or 'advocacy' or 'dissent'. And anyway, in reality, it wasn't. She hadn't been trying to persuade a government or anyone else to act. She had gone right in and done it herself.

So that left them with refuting the base intention: of 'coercing' or 'influencing by intimidation' the State or Federal Government, or 'intimidating the public', so as to advance a political or ideological cause. Again, there was no 'cause': as far as Cressida had been so far instructed, her client had only done it for the end itself – to stop the power station. No ideology necessary.

But to bring these charges, the prosecution must be convinced they had proof. What was it? She opened the police facts sheet.

**ARRESTING OFFICER**

| | |
|---|---|
| Name: | CON ASHLEY HOGAN |
| Station: | Muswellbrook LAC |
| Date: | 19 March |

**COURT**

| | |
|---|---|
| Court name: | Muswellbrook Local Court |
| Court date: | 21 April |

**WITNESSES**

Police witnesses: 3
Civilian witnesses: 9

**BAIL**

| | |
|---|---|
| Bail type: | Refused |

**To summarise the Record of Interview, the Accused attested to the following facts.**

Childhood and early life.

The Accused was born at the Royal Hospital for Women, Sydney NSW, on 12 October 1996. As a result of a variety of issues in her home life, the Accused ran away from home at 15 and was homeless from the ages of 15—17. At the age of 17 she joined the Army Reserve, and then the Army proper a year later. Her army training included the setting and detonation of plastic explosives.

At age 19 she was deployed as part of the Task Force Tajik 5 in Iraq. However due to an aversion to the extreme physical violence of active combat while on tour, she sought a transfer and was re-deployed to Inventory.

Background to events of 16 March

At age 21 the Accused returned to Australia and became involved in a number of environmental and socialist groups. In mid-2017 at a socialist film night she met an individual (whose name she would not disclose) who had recently returned from active sabotage operations against Russian forces in the Ukraine as a paid mercenary on behalf of ethnic Russians.

A close but platonic relationship between the two ensued, with the Accused spending considerable time with this person discussing politics, philosophy, and "the world at large".

The Ukraine mercenary. That had to be Merv. The old man washing the dishes and fixing the door.

Later in 2017 she met a second person (whose name she would not disclose) who was "passionate about taking direct and immediate action on climate change". It is believed that this second person is a Person of Interest known as DESIREE BARNES.

Desiree Barnes? Dizzy?

The Accused then attended a meeting convened by this person at the private residence of a third person, attended by a number of people (whose names she would also not disclose), where the subject of detonating all of the major NSW coal-fired power stations was first discussed.

Between that first meeting and the night of 16 March, the following events occurred:

Weekly meetings of the above persons and additional unnamed persons at the private residence referred to above and then, in the 3 months prior to the incident, at a variety of premises (described as "a different house each week") to avoid detection;

Obtaining plastic explosives from a "contact" within the Australian army for use in training exercises;

Two explosives training camps at locations outside Sydney, as follows:

Cobark, 18–20 October

Leeton, 29 December — 1 January

where detonation processes, security circumvention, strength and fitness, and ecological philosophy matters were discussed and practised, including a film showing and discussion each night regarding the collapse of the Earth's ecosystems;

Persuading at least two other individuals (identity undisclosed) to attend the private meetings with a view to potentially becoming co-offenders;

Organising child care.


Joanne and Dizzy, Joanne with her soft dreadlocks and star tattoo, Dizzy with her frizzy hair and single motherhood, doing all this? Cressida sat, staring out at the pool, the iPad limp in her hands. It was like opening a door to another world she didn't want to see.

A door clicked at the end of the hallway. Cressida looked up to see Dale.

'I thought you were dead to the world,' he said, stepping towards her. He put the glass of water he was holding on the glass coffee table and picked up her wrists. 'How are these?'

'They're saying Dizzy was the one that got Andy involved,' she said.

'What?' He frowned, pulling the wicker two-seater opposite closer. Even side on, his length took up most of it. 'What's that you're reading?'

'The fact sheet on Andy. On my email just now. Did you know all this about her? Andy? Homeless at age 15. Joined the army at 17, Iraq at 19?'

'No. I knew she was in the army for a bit. She never said anything about Iraq.'

Cressida handed the iPad to him and stared out at the dark. Such a life Andy had had. When Cressida was that age she'd been a bright shiny private-school girl with a paralegal non-job at her father's law firm. There'd been a car and a Tiffany diamond as graduation presents.

Not war and homelessness.

'Are you okay?' said Dale, handing the iPad back to her. She put it aside.

'Oh sure, I'm fine,' she laughed. 'I'm not so sure about Andy though. I just …' She sat back in the chair, running her hands through her hair. 'I feel like I'm so out of my depth.'

'You?' said Dale. 'I don't think so. Anyway you've got this stratospheric silk helping you, haven't you? Surely she'll pull you up if you start going *completely* in the wrong direction.'

'Yeah but Sandra's likely to find out only *after* I've done it,' said Cressida, shaking her head. 'I only bother her lordship with matters of, you know, stratospheric significance. Right now though it feels like *all* of it is.' She put her head in her hands. 'I'm just hoping I can fall back on this Junior a bit,' she added. 'You know I only got put on this brief because it was too sensitive to give to a *real* criminal lawyer. But I'm beginning to think even Brian Prendergast's ego isn't worth Andy not getting the best possible help on this.' That's what it came down to, she thought. His precious firm and its reputation. 'And I think,' she reflected, 'that means someone other than me.'

'Really?' said Dale. 'Are you sure about that?'

Cressida looked at him uncertainly, not sure what he was getting at.

'Um, yes? I'm a *corporate building and construction* lawyer, Dale. With a couple of years in white-collar crime. As a *prosecutor*, not a defence lawyer, I might add. It's not really equipped me to advise someone on life sentence charges for terrorism.'

'Forget about the life sentence bit,' he said. 'If you focus on that you'll bring yourself completely undone. Just look at the charges. It's all the same, isn't it? That basic lawyering thing you guys do – taking words and making them mean whatever you need them to mean? Then convincing someone in a wig on a bench your meaning's better than the other guy's, right?'

Cressida laughed. 'Yeah. I guess.'

'*And,*' he said, leaning across the coffee table and catching her hand, 'you have a crucial aspect that some other private lawyer doesn't. You *care about your client*. Some other guy might be better on the finer points of the law, and tactics with the government lawyers or whatever it's called …'

'Prosecution,' Cressida supplied.

'Prosecution. But that's only going to get her so far. The tactical stuff you can learn as you go along, Cressida. But the heart stuff' – he tapped her chest with his other hand – 'that you can't. And it's in here already. Don't underestimate that. And right now I want to kiss you, but I'm not going to,' he said with a gentle chuckle, and sat back.

Cressida looked down at his hand holding hers and reddened.

'Well that's really nice of you to say. But I'm terrified I'll turn out to have been slogging my guts out down blind alleys when the stakes are this high.'

'But that's the thing, isn't it? When you're doing something that matters.'

'What do you mean?'

'Well, just, you know,' he said, contemplating her hand. 'High stakes mean high rewards and high downsides, don't they. In your case, high stakes for someone you care about.'

'Yeah, I guess so.' Was that true? Wasn't she just doing her job? And maybe that wasn't such a good thing. To care. 'I'm not sure I should be, though.'

'What do you mean?' he said, frowning.

'Well, you know. The risk that emotion might cloud my judgement and all that.'

'But Cressida,' he said with a gentle laugh, 'you can't help that. If you didn't, you wouldn't be you.'

'Jesus,' Cressida said. 'But this is *not* normally me. Usually the clients can look perfectly well after themselves. They just go find someone else if they don't like how I do it.'

Dale looked out at the pool, shimmering faintly in the starlight. 'I guess right now you don't have that luxury.'.

He was right, she thought. In some ways not caring *was* a luxury.

'I guess you're used to it – caring but still having things go wrong. But look at you. You're an expert. You're a *surgeon*, for God's sake. I just feel so *unqualified* for this.'

'Not quite – only really halfway,' he said, giving a dry laugh. 'Anyway, it's still the same. There are still so many limits to what you can do.'

'What do you mean?'

'I don't know. All the time. So much of the time with the aid work I was doing, certainly. I had to set up a field hospital in the middle of a shopping centre once.'

'What?!'

'There'd just been Typhoon Haiyan, and thousands of people were homeless,' he went on. 'It was only day two after the cyclone, and the official surgery and trauma contingent hadn't arrived yet. People were coming in day and night,' he said, shaking his head at the memory. 'With everything from cuts and bruises from being washed downstream in the flood, to getting impaled or dragged by whatever was under the water, or just being crashed straight into a wall or a tree. It was just awful.' For a moment his eyes reddened, and he blinked and looked away. 'There were broken bones from jumping from the roofs of houses, for God's sake, where they'd gone to escape rising flood waters. There was dengue fever, and cholera rumoured in the mountains, the full catastrophe. Unimaginable now. Anyway,' he sighed, 'there *I* was, this young intern with only two years' surgical training, all obtained in the gorgeously well resourced hospitals of the west, going from Royal North Shore to a field hospital in Guiyan.'

'Wow,' said Cressida. 'But was this' – she had to ask – 'was this before or after the ketamine?'

'Oh after, God!' He laughed. 'No, I was trying to get myself *off that* at the time as well. Unbelievable.' He shook his head again and looked into the distance as he spoke. 'Well anyway. The first day I got there I felt like turning 'round and running right back out again. I thought I'd escape myself, throwing myself into that maelstrom, but the truth was' – he looked back at Cressida – 'it wasn't till then that I had to face myself fair and square and see what I was made of. The first two weeks are still a blur.' He paused to take a mouthful of water. 'Anyway. One day a pregnant woman came in. She was nearly full term, and on the way to her family's village, the typhoon hit and couldn't get there. So, there I was,' he said, taking her hands and pressing them to his mouth, 'no training but a distant internship in obstetrics – half of which I'd been high for – having to do a caesarian on this tiny, desperate woman about to birth her first child. Her *eyes*, my God. The longing and fear in them. And the thing was, there was no-one else there to do it. There was one surgeon, but he had been transferred up country to supervise the cholera response. And looking at her, and reading the few signs I knew from the medical book that was in the field library, I knew that if I didn't get that baby out, the likelihood was that both of them wouldn't make it.'

'God,' said Cressida, getting up and moving to sit beside him. 'So what did you do?'

'The only thing there was to do,' he said, kissing her forehead. 'I talked the woman through the options, she gave consent, I gave her a pre-med and got on with it. Way back in medical school we'd been taught the basics of doing a caesarian. I knew where the bits were, so I thought to myself well, I've just got to put the pieces I *do* know together, and hope that with all of that I can pull off something I've never done before. So I put my gown on, scrubbed up, and did it. It was the scariest thing I've ever done.'

'So what happened?'

'Well, miraculously,' he said, subsiding into a smile, 'mum survived, and had a gorgeous six-pound baby girl. She left the hospital two weeks later. I have no idea what happened to them. I sometimes think about them still.'

'Wow, Dale. That's – that's amazing.'

'My point is,' he said, turning to her, 'you're it. You're the one in the hot seat. You've got the gig. You might as well dive in.'

'God you're awesome,' Cressida said, picking up his hand and biting his knuckle. He looked down at her, and Cressida's heart started pounding in her chest. She wanted to move away from him, embarrassed, afraid he might hear it. He was going to kiss her. She was hyperventilating, and trying to hide it all at the same time. But then instead, he got up and went into the kitchen. She followed him, still holding the iPad.

'Thanks. Now what about some dinner? I went shopping before. Those fish markets' – he shook his head – 'out of this world. The rape of the seas, right there in front of me. But *this* on the other hand,' he said, pulling a paper bundle in a plastic bag out of the fridge, 'is sustainably fished Yellowfin. That's what the guy said, anyway. Him and the Marine Conservation Society leaflet on the counter. How does chilli salt tuna, wok fried medium rare with green tea noodles, lime juice and orange chutney on the side sound?'

Tuna, Cressida thought: less fatty than salmon. Maybe she would even have a whole piece. She laughed. 'Are you, like, out of a movie, or what?'

'Yeah, something like that. Recovering drug addict lures gorgeous blonde lawyer with raw fish. Very heroic.'

'Dale,' she said in a serious tone, 'there's a bit more to you than that.'

'Where does Helena keep her rock salt? I'm certain she has some ...' he said, opening cupboards above the stove.

'Yep. Jackpot. Right there. *Definitely* some green tea too somewhere. How's Saturne?'

'Oh, good,' he said, rubbing his eyes. 'Gave her a massage just before, and she fell asleep. She always does. Where will I find ...'

'Frying pan under the stove. In the drawer. Knives on the magnetic strip behind it. Spatulas and stuff next to it.'

She looked back down at the police facts. *You're in the hot seat*, she thought. She picked up the iPad and continued reading.

**The night of 16 March**

1. At 6pm on Friday 16 March the Accused attended a pre-arranged drop off point in bushland on Hebden Road, Hebden, on the opposite side of Lake Liddell from Liddell Power Station. There she collected a backpack containing four kilograms of C4 based plastic explosives and a mobile phone on a lanyard.

Cressida stopped. She nearly didn't want to read it. It all felt too overwhelming. *You're in the hot seat.* She kept going.

The Accused put the phone on the lanyard around her neck then posed as someone fishing on the Beach Road pier until darkness fell. Another person (not identified) attended in a small speed boat to collect her.

2. The Accused and accomplice then crossed Lake Liddell in the boat and entered the inlet to Dora Creek, and the Accused disembarked on the beach. The accomplice left the area. The Accused donned an air tank supplied by the accomplice and the backpack containing the explosives, and proceeded to the perimeter fence of the facility. After waiting for any sign of security and finding none, she cut a small hole in the security mesh and entered the facility. She describes what happened next as having occurred within a period of five minutes.

3. She crossed the distance between the fence and the coal burners at a run and proceeded to remove the C4 from her bag, peel off the plastic backing, and attach it to the wall of one burner. She insists that she attached explosive to one burner only, being South/4.

4. The Accused then proceeded to run to the alarm button in the centre of the facility some 50 metres away and trigger it. She heard a shout from behind her and turned to see a member of the private security firm responsible for the plant (see ROI of prosecution witness Security Officer PAUL PINCER) approaching her. She then ran towards the cooling water pipe of the facility some 200 metres away with the security guard in pursuit, and says that at the same time she heard the alarm go off and saw staff start to evacuate the facility down the stairs from above. With the security guard some 10 metres away, she pressed a button on the mobile phone on the lanyard, which detonated the explosives, threw it at the approaching security guard, and jumped into the pool of the cooling water pipe. She then exited the facility into Dora Creek.

5. The statements of four other accuseds Miss RACHEL FLAME RAFAEL, Miss SKYDARK MOON WILSON, Miss BEARHEART JANE SCARLET and Miss ARIEL DIAMOND are materially similar to this Accused's, though they relate to other facilities, suggesting these are the other persons involved in the explosives training camps. The co-Accused's statements are also consistent with the statement of the security guard PAUL PINCER, with the exception that Mr PINCER opines that he had apprehended the Accused before she exited the

facility, but she punched him and evaded his grip prior to exiting via the cooling pipe. The Accused's statements are also consistent with security footage provided by the security company and forensics evidence obtained by AFP. A bucket, fishing rod and folding chair with the Accused's fingerprints on them were found on the pier on Monday 20 March at 7.15. a.m.

So there was zip – nada – nothing on the intent point at all so far. Surely though, the AFP wasn't silly enough to bring these charges without *something* to differentiate it from bog-standard sabotage – evidence of conversations with some of the other accused, or witnesses; diaries; recordings of conversations …? But maybe none of the co-accused were talking about motive, and if the AFP hadn't picked up any intelligence beforehand, there would be no informants of that nature. But why were they charging them with terrorism then?

And there was another thought, that had an edge of awe to it – could these hippies really have pulled that off?

'Have you heard of any of these people?' she said to Dale, reading out the names as he came in to put down a platter of food.

'No,' Dale said, holding a piece of tuna aloft in chopsticks and biting into it. 'Fuck that's good,' he said, after he had sucked it down. 'I may have met some of them after the fact. Some people came to my house with Andy that weekend. I never asked their names.'

'Why not?'

'Seemed like a good idea not to. They probably wouldn't have told me anyway.'

'So … so you had some idea of what they had done, then.'

Dale took a deep breath and looked at her intently.

'Look, no. I would never have dreamed that that mob of messy, dis-organised hippies could have pulled off something like this. A bunch of lock-ins and a sit-in at the plants, maybe. But blow them up? Never in a million years.'

'And if you had known, would you still have helped them?'

He frowned. 'I'm not sure, Cressida,' he said at last. 'I mean, look, no, probably not. The risk to human life would have been so great. I mean, come on, my whole career is dedicated to healing, not harming. So I guess I wouldn't have, no.'

Cressida felt herself relax. Even though she didn't know what she *really* thought about what Andy had done – in the same way she never really thought about what any of her clients had done; her job had simply been to represent them to the best of her ability – it *was* a relief to think she wouldn't have to have it out with Dale if she decided the other way.

'And I guess that means you don't even know whether they were involved, really, do you?' she said.

'Hmm? Oh. No. I guess not. So Cressida,' he said, taking another piece of tuna and swallowing it before continuing, 'how long have you had an eating disorder?'

'What?' She laughed nervously. 'What eating disorder?'

'Don't come over all naïve. I'm a doctor, remember? Apart from a brief aberration where my soup and a rather tasty salami roll following a bout of marijuana was involved, you have barely eaten a mouthful the whole 48 hours we've known each other. Sorry, correction,' he said, looking at his watch, '60 hours. And here I am, putting before you one of the most delicious dishes humanly imaginable – and your favourite food, in fact, which I know because Helena told me – though keftedes were also mentioned – and haven't touched it.'

'I don't know.' Cressida shrugged, looking back at the iPad. 'I'm just not that hungry very often.'

'What are you at the moment' – he peered down at her frame – 'ten kilos underweight? Twelve? What did you have for breakfast? Oh that's right. Coffee at the hospital. Nothing for lunch. And disinterest in the most delicious tuna on planet earth right now, despite the wonders sitting before you. Are you receiving treatment for this?'

'I'm just naturally skinny,' said Cressida, throwing down the iPad and getting up. It's the way Felipe likes me anyway, she thought; he says it's elegant.

'Cressida,' said Dale, 'why do you need to try and do everything on your own?'

'Look I just don't like eating, okay?' she said, pacing. 'It makes me feel …'

'Makes you feel what?'

Heavy, she wanted to say. Dirty. But then he really would think she was mad – know she was, when it came to food. She had come to take comfort in her hunger. It meant she was … It meant she was in control.

'I just don't like it. Although …' she said, relenting and sitting down again. 'In the mountains was the hungriest I've ever felt. I blame your cooking. Either that or your …' She was about to say animal magnetism, but thought better of it. 'Where'd you learn to cook like this, anyway?'

'I'll tell you if you eat some more sashimi,' he said, holding her gaze. 'Come on, it's beautiful, free-range, wild-caught oily fish. Full of the most amazing antioxidants. Omega 6, magnesium, phosphorus, potassium, thiamin, niacin, B6 and selenium,' he reeled off, 'all wrapped up in a protein hit that tastes like heaven. Plus it's less of a mercury risk because of the selenium derivative.'

Cressida sighed. 'When you put it that way,' she said, and took a piece. It melted in her mouth, the pistachio and chilli a divine contrast to the bland softness of the tuna. 'Mmm.'

'This is about Felipe, isn't it.'

'What's about Felipe?'

'The not eating thing. Is that why? Because he wants you skinny?'

'You,' said Cressida, standing up, 'are asking too many questions. I'm beat. I'm going to bed.' She wanted to flounce out, but the bare minimum of hospitality required some discussion. 'Where ... where are you sleeping?'

Dale smiled. 'Your lovely stepmum put me up in the front room. But I think I'll sleep on the couch in Saturne's room. Unless you want me in your room, of course,' he said.

'See you in the morning.'

# 25

The next morning Cressida woke to find Dale sitting on the edge of her bed.

'Oh God,' she groaned, covering her face with her pillow. 'How long have you been sitting there?'

'Not long.' Dale laughed, pushing a piece of hair behind her ear. He held out his mobile. 'Happy April Fools' Day. It's Jerome. He wants to talk to you.'

'Oh,' she said, taking it and rolling over. 'Hello? Where are you?'

'Sis,' Jerome said. There was a lot of noise in the background. 'I'm at the camp. The police have arrived. They say if we're not gone by ten they'll arrest us.'

'Oh.' Cressida yawned and rubbed her eyes. 'So you're going, right?'

'No we're not *going*,' Jerome said, as if that was the most appalling thing he'd ever heard. 'You need to get here. We need lawyers.'

'Me? Oh God, Jerome, just do what they tell you. I don't even know what you're doing there.' She held the phone way from her ear as Jerome started yelling.

'What the fuck do you mean what am I doing here? Jesus, Cressida, I thought you acting for those people meant you'd *evolved*. The people inside this prison are the ones who've finally *done* something. You should be here, all of you and your lawyer friends should be here, shoulder to shoulder with us in support of them. And besides, right now we need to know if they can arrest us or not.'

'Where are you?' she said, sitting up. 'I mean, where's the camp? Are you on prison property?'

'No. We're across the road. In the park.'

'Who owns the park, do you know?'

'The local council I think.'

'Did the organisers get permission from the council to be there?' She reached for her bathrobe on the end of the bed as she was speaking. *Turn around*, she mouthed at Dale, who laughed and did so.

'I don't know,' said Jerome.

'I'm putting you on speaker,' she said, tossing off the bedclothes and putting the phone on the side table as she manoeuvred into the robe. 'Well. If you didn't get permission from whoever owns the park and there's no "campers welcome" sign—'

'Of course there's no bloody *campers welcome* sign,' said Jerome.

She looked perplexedly at the phone.

'Then the owner has the right to move you on,' she said. 'The owner has to do it first and then the police will say something like "if you don't move on you will be arrested". Have they done that yet?'

'I don't know. All I know is there was a mob of police here at dawn tearing down tents and all hell broke loose until police liaison got out of bed and went and spoke to them.'

'Well they're not allowed to be pulling down any tents,' said Cressida. 'It's not trespass until someone asks you to leave.' *At least I hope that's right*, she thought. Unless they'd declared it a lockdown zone under the *Law Enforcement (Powers and Responsibilities) Act*. Under LEPRA, they could do just about anything ...

'I'll check up on all of what I've told you, and if I'm not right I'll let you know in five. And Jerome,' she said.

'Yes?'

'Don't get arrested. I don't want to be representing my brother.' There was no way he'd be eligible for Legal Aid.

'Why not? Those fuckers. This is why the world's going down the toilet. The state's on the payroll of the Earth fuckers. Why the hell are the police protecting these people? The council should have given us use of this park just on principle.'

'That's a great idea,' she said. 'Why don't you call the council and tell them that. You never know, they might be on your side.'

'It's a Sunday. How am I going to get onto them?'

'I don't know, check their website. Use your iPhone. There should be an emergency number there; why don't you call that. And if someone from the council comes to tell you to move on, maybe try and negotiate with them. Buy time or something.'

'Someone did say they knew a couple of councillors who were supportive. Maybe I'll try them. Where the fuck are the environmental groups, that's what I want to know. Usually there's at least one half-arsed lawyer they've organised to help at something like this.'

'Jerome. This is terrorism we're talking about. I doubt they want to get involved.'

'See what I mean? This is why we're *fucked*. Okay whatever, anyway, are you coming down? I can't remember half of what you just said. Can you come and tell everyone what you told me? Before the police come back?'

'Oh for God's sake. Yes. Alright. What's the time?'

'Seven.'

'Give me an hour.' She rolled her eyes and hung up, subsiding back on the bed.

'Silverwater then?' Dale said.

Cressida sighed and nodded.

'Lemme get dressed,' she said, and pushed him out the door. He laughed and took her wrist, putting his other hand on her cheek. Cressida stopped and stared at him. His face was so close, and she could smell that mixture of the maleness caught up in the cotton of his t-shirt. Bloody five spice and sponge cake.

'I haven't seen you smoke since you got here,' she said.

He gave a half smile. 'It didn't seem right. Everything's so neat here. I wouldn't know where to ash. Besides, I have a feeling you don't like it.'

'Oh God, don't worry about what I think. I have plenty of vices of my own.'

'Yeah speaking of – you're not getting out of here without breakfast,' he said, pushing a strand of hair from her face. 'See you in the kitchen in five.'

She picked up Felipe's iPad and searched 'police powers NSW'. A bunch of results about declaring a large-scale disorder under the *Law Enforcement (Powers and Responsibilities) Act* came up. Possible. She bookmarked the tab. Now, what did one wear to a protest camp? She pulled on jeans and a t-shirt; shoes were the question. Remembering her treatment at the hands of the police, she pulled out her running shoes. They weren't steel-capped boots, but they'd be more protection than her usual Sunday metallic slides. She was lacing them when Alessa appeared in the doorway.

'It's seven am on a Sunday, Cressida. Where on earth are you going?'

'Silverwater,' she said.

'But there's no visiting hours on a Sunday,' she yawned. 'Besides, I thought you didn't want to see Dad.'

'I'm not going to see Dad. Jerome just called. I'm going to try and stop him from joining him in prison. Oh wow, thanks,' she breathed, as Dale returned with a fragrant wrap and held it out to her.

'Organic eggs, rocket and haloumi,' he said. 'Hi, Alessa.'

'Hi. What have you done to my sister? She's turning into a hippie.'

Cressida laughed. 'No I'm not. Look I don't think I'll be a squat of help, but he said they needed lawyers. Since I appear to be one I'm going.'

'Well then,' Alessa said. 'I'd better come too.'

'What?' Cressida said, and Dale's face broke into a grin.

'Don't you dare leave without me,' she said, turning back down the hallway.

Cressida frowned at Dale and shook her head in disbelief. Then she bit into the wrap.

'Wow. This is fantastic. Give me five. Do you know the way?'

'Vaguely,' he said, and followed her into the bathroom. In front of the mirror she started putting on makeup.

'You know, you look just as good without that,' he said softly, leaning against the doorjamb.

'Oh yeah,' Cressida said, amused. 'I don't think so. You're very sweet for saying so though. *But I already feel out of my depth enough*, she wanted to say; going without makeup would be like walking in with a sign on her head saying *I have no idea what I'm doing*. 'I've seen photos of myself without makeup,' she continued; 'I look like a female prisoner on day release. Not good near a women's prison. Now rack off, this is secret women's business.' She pushed him out and shut the sliding door behind him. It opened again and Alessa wedged herself in the space next to her.

'What's wrong with the mirror in your room?' said Cressida as she put on eyeliner.

'The light in here is better. Man, that boy is so-o-o cute,' she said, glancing at Cressida. 'I give it a week.'

'Gee thanks,' she said. 'I wouldn't be surprised if he wasn't around for even that long.'

'I wasn't talking about that,' Alessa said, perfecting her mascara and putting the lid back on the tube. 'I meant the survival of your engagement. See you in the car.'

Cressida stared at her reflection in the mirror. What was she doing, actually? She was *engaged*. She was *getting married*. There were *invitations on the sideboard*. Dale was ... How could she be sure he would even stick around? Was she really going to throw all that away on someone she had only just met? Who was – okay, sure – kind, and altruistic, and passionate, and committed to saving the world, but – also a struck-off doctor? And what would he want with her anyway, she suddenly thought

– a neurotic corporate lawyer who'd never done anything altruistic *in her life*? What on earth made her think Dale would be serious about someone like her? Maybe he was just like all the others. He just … She regarded herself critically. It was the blonde hair. They always fell for the blonde hair, like … like lemmings off a cliff. Except it was always her who lay crumpled at the bottom, when they got tired of it and went onto the next shiny object. Felipe was the only one who had ever put his money where his mouth was. She looked down at her ring. At least you could trust an engagement ring to get you fifty thousand on eBay if the engagement died in the arse.

There was a pair of nail scissors on the shelf above the vanity. She grabbed a piece of the precious blonde hair and started hacking. Just as she was finished, the bathroom door opened. It was Saturne.

'Wow,' Saturne said, her face suffusing from initial shock into a grin. 'I like it.'

'Hi,' Cressida said, snipping at the final tufts on one side. 'You're up.'

'Sure am.' She yawned. 'Who am I to turn down the opportunity for a bit of civil disobedience? Ooh Alessa, don't you look like lawyer-boss lady,' she said, looking past Cressida. Alessa appeared in the doorway. She was wearing her best Ermengildo Zegna.

'Oh my God,' said Alessa, dropping her compendium. She stared at Cressida, white-faced.

Cressida ignored her and said to Saturne, 'Um, I don't think that's such a good idea. Given what they said about charging you. This will just give them more evidence against you.' Then she turned to her sister. 'You cracked out the Zegna, Alessa.'

'Fuck,' Saturne said. Despite her energetic words, she still looked pale. 'I never get to have any fun. I guess I'm staying here then.'

'Sorry. We'll only be an hour or so I think.'

She pushed past Alessa and headed for the kitchen. The keys to the Jag were on a hook by the fridge. Dale looked up from packing sandwiches into a bag and froze when he saw her. Then he grinned.

'Wow,' he said. 'You look like Andy.'

'Cressida, no,' cried Alessa, chasing after her. 'You can't go out like that.'

'Oh for God's sake would you all get *over* it,' she said, hurling open the bifolds and heading for the gate. 'It's a *haircut*. Anyway' – she checked her watch – 'it's April Fools' Day. Play along.'

Just as she passed through the gate she heard the blip of an expensive car being locked, and looked up to see Felipe approaching down the driveway.

'Hi,' she said, wrenching open the front door of the Jag. Behind her she heard the clatter of Alessa's high heels, and clenched her jaw. 'We're going out to Silverwater. Jerome's at the protest there.'

'Darling,' Felipe said, pale. He approached her slowly, one hand held out. 'Oh my darling. It's okay.'

'Felipe,' said Alessa, out of breath. 'I don't know what's going on. She just came out of the bathroom like that.'

Felipe reached inside his jacket pocket and fumbled for his phone, keeping his eyes on her.

'Darling, you need some rest,' he said. 'I can get one of Sydney's best psychiatrists on the phone in a minute, there's a little retreat place just moments away in Rose Bay …'

Cressida glared at him. Then she laughed. 'Oh for God's sake, Felipe. I just needed a change.'

As she turned to get in the car she saw Helena standing behind Alessa in her bathrobe, hand to her mouth.

'Jesus, would you all just relax?' she said. 'I'll be back later. You can send me to the psych ward then.'

'Sorry,' Dale called, appearing with two full cloth grocery bags. 'What's up? Oh. I think it looks great,' he said, throwing the bags in the boot and climbing in. 'Kind of *gulag-chic*.'

Felipe's eyes travelled from Cressida to Dale and then back again. His jaw worked. Quietly he exhaled.

'Right then,' he said brightly. He returned to the Audi and popped the boot. 'Just grabbing this' – he pulled out his medical bag – 'I guess we'd better get going then. It's been a while since I've been in *this* old thing.' He gave a forced laugh as he climbed into the Jag.

'What are you doing?' said Cressida.

'They might need a doctor,' he said, stretching the seatbelt around his girth. 'I'm coming too.'

'What are you talking about? You might get arrested.'

'I doubt it.' He laughed again. 'Come on, chop chop, if you'll excuse the pun; don't want to keep them waiting.'

Cressida slid into the driver's seat, and Alessa got in behind Felipe, as Helena stood on the footpath and stared at them. Her hand had dropped from her face. Cressida swallowed, avoiding her gaze. She turned on the car and was glad for the distraction of the giant engine shuddering to life. Staring straight ahead she waved at Helena and put the car in gear, yelled goodbye and rumbled down the drive.

The four of them sat in an awkward silence for most of the thirty-minute journey, and whenever she glanced into the rear-view mirror, Felipe was watching her. His expression was unreadable.

At the prison the sparsely-grassed park on the far side of the road had been turned into a chaos of temporary living; tents that looked like they'd been uprooted from a family holiday leaned around a makeshift campsite of two sagging couches and a smouldering campfire. Everything was splattered with a patina of mud sent up by the previous night's rain and foot traffic. Two bright red police cars were parked on the verge. Hang on, why were they AFP?

Jerome emerged from a tent and came to meet them.

'Sis,' he said, pulling Cressida and Alessa into a loose embrace, then 'Felipe!', shaking the doctor's gingerly offered hand, before finally turning to Dale with a homecoming grin and sharing a handshake that had the force of someone in a serious bromance. Felipe grinned tightly, and Alessa picked up a discarded placard to stand on.

'What?' she said, in response to Cressida's quizzical look. 'These are eight-hundred-dollar shoes. No-one was using it.'

'There's placard-making materials over there if you want them,' said Jerome, buoyant. 'Channel Seven reckon they're coming any minute. Cressida – can you come and talk to the police?'

'Um,' Cressida said, glancing at three police who were in conversation with two of the protestors, a handful of others milling around the campsite. The officers wore navy caps and overalls with *Australian Federal Police* emblazoned across the chest, above a battery of black holsters of different sizes. Why were the Feds handling this? It only took State police to break up a protest. 'I'm not sure that's such a good idea. Why don't you tell me what they've told you and I can brief everyone on their rights.' She looked around. 'I can't believe there aren't any other lawyers here.'

Jerome shrugged. 'Haven't seen any so far. Oh hang on, I think there was a Wilderness Society guy over there, maybe he knows something … He just turned up this morning. Said he wasn't here officially. I'll grab him, shall I?'

'Sure,' Cressida said, pulling Felipe's iPad from her bag. Here's hoping they don't need to know any bloody esoteric detail, she thought. The information she'd found was very basic. But when she looked at her internet screen it was blank. *Problem loading page.* And the reception was only at one bar. Damn, if only she'd thought to download them before she'd left.

Jerome returned, a tall fellow in a checked shirt following behind.

'Thanks for coming,' the man said, holding out a wrinkled hand. 'Vic.'

'Oh, hi,' she said, switching the iPad to her left hand. 'I was just wondering – can you guys try and find a lawyer? I'm not a criminal lawyer – and I'm about to get totally out of my depth, I think.'

'Yeah, not official I'm afraid.' Vic shook his head. 'My organisation is committed to nonviolence. We can give help off the record in kind but …

there's no way our management would endorse official contacts with legal as a Wilderness Society thing.'

'But what else are they supposed to do?'

Vic shrugged. 'I'm sure you understand,' he continued. 'We didn't endorse this activity. We're not even certain it has an environmental motivation. I mean, it probably does,' he said quickly, as Jerome bristled, 'but it's not like we can go and interview the suspects, is it. Sorry.' He shrugged again, spreading his hands palms up.

'Dale – can I use your hotspot? I can't get reception.'

'I can't either,' he said, pulling out his phone. 'It's been saying half a bar ever since we left Homebush ...'

'The reception here is shit,' sighed Jerome. 'Everyone's been using the prison cafe Wi-Fi for internet.'

'Thank fuck for that,' she said. 'Tell me it's going to be open on a Sunday. Alessa, can you go and talk to the cops?'

'What?' she said, pivoting on her heel to look at them. Her eyes homed in on one with high cheekbones and a five o'clock shadow. 'Oh.' She grinned. 'Sure.'

'Be quick,' Jerome said. 'There's no guarantee they won't start arresting early.'

'But – but they said ten,' Cressida began, assessing the distance to the cafe from where she stood. Jerome shrugged.

'I'll come. I need a coffee,' Dale said

'I'll come too,' said Felipe.

The three of them waited on the side of the road to cross, Cressida's urgency fighting the survival instinct to wait for a break in the traffic. Of all the times they had to have no reception, she thought. There was a gap and Felipe took her hand to pull her across, but instinctively she pulled out of his grip and ran forward, leaving him at the side of the road. She pushed her way through the gates to the cafe and up the steps to the entrance, Dale close behind. A grey-haired man in prison green was making sandwiches behind the bain marie.

'Hi,' she called out, perching on the couch as Dale went to the counter. Ah, good: the Wi-Fi had popped up. 'Excuse me but can I have your Wi-Fi password?'

She clicked on the option, watching the maddening blue circle as the thing scanned for a connection. Out of the corner of her eye she saw Felipe push through the double doors and approach.

'Cressida,' Dale called from the counter. 'How do you have your coffee?'

'Um, oh wow, coffee, yes – just a long black, thanks,' she said. 'No sugar. Shit, this is taking forever. Excuse me, is there a password for the Wi-Fi? I can't get it to work.'

When there was no response, she glanced up at the attendant. The man was staring at her. Cressida's eyes caught his. He looked familiar. As she watched, a look of amazement emerged on his face, followed by joy. Then she realised who she was looking at.

'Oh my God,' she said, and the iPad fell to the floor.

He looked so incredibly different. The last time she had seen him he had been raven-haired and invincible, vibrating with the energy of the prime of life and career success. The man looking back at her now was a grey-haired, hollow-chested shadow, bony in a too-big polo shirt. He looked twenty years older than she knew him to be.

'Dad,' she said, crossing the cafe floor. His whole face crumpled like a child's. His mouth was open but no sound was coming out. She leaned across the counter to take him in her arms.

'It's okay. Dad, it's okay.'

All of the things she had told herself she would say to him when they met again, all the angry, cutting words, the derision, the disgust, all of them melted in a wash of compassion and sadness as she looked at his face, which was now wet with tears. He buried his face in her neck, and one sob and then another cracked out of him, echoing off the stainless-steel counters. Then just as suddenly he swallowed it and stood back, regarding her and wiping his eyes.

'God, don't you look like your mum. Except for …' He looked at her head. 'What did you do to your hair?'

Cressida laughed through her tears. 'I needed a change.'

Leo sniffed and grabbed a handful of paper napkins, wiping his nose with them, first one side and then the other. It was such a familiar gesture, except in the past it would have been with a gigantic white handkerchief. It brought the memories flooding back.

'I am so sorry,' he said to Dale, embarrassed. 'Long black, was it?'

'Dad, the coffee can wait. How are you?'

'Hah!' In the echo of his laugh was the Leo she knew, a fat and mirthful sound that belonged in the cafe by the sea, a trilby perched on his head. 'Much better now,' he said, taking her face with warm, callused hands. Then he looked past her to Dale. 'Who are you?'

'Um, this is Dale,' she said.

Then her father's eyes caught the ring on her finger. He looked at Dale, jerking his chin at it.

'You are marrying my daughter?'

Cressida's mouth dropped open and she felt her face burn. Dale laughed, and she turned even redder. What, it's such a ridiculous idea? She glanced quickly at Felipe, thinking she should introduce him. The look on his face nearly stopped her. He was standing, staring, taking in first Leo and then her.

'Felipe,' she said. 'Come and meet my father.'

He composed himself quickly. 'Hello,' he said, his expensive rounded vowels a stark contrast to Leo's heavy accent. Cressida had heard the voice he was using on the phone to rivals on the committee, or a patient complaining about his work. He didn't move.

'Which one are you marrying?' Leo asked. 'Him,' he said, looking at Dale. 'I hope this one.'

Cressida's eyes widened, and she thought that maybe the best thing to do right then would be to turn around and run back out the door. Then it opened, and Jerome came in, out of breath.

'Oh hi, Dad,' he puffed. 'On cafe detail again hey?'

'Oh my Lord,' cried Leo, putting his hands together as if in prayer; Jerome covered the distance in four strides and they fell on each other in a backslapping embrace. 'Is Alessa here too?' he said, shaking his head in disbelief. 'All my children, here in one place?'

'Not now, Dad.' Jerome shook his head, and turned to Cressida. 'Cressida, you have to come. They've just given us ten minutes' warning on the loudspeaker.'

Cressida looked at her watch. 'But it's not ten yet,' she said. 'Alessa was going to talk to them.'

But Jerome was already halfway to the door. Fuck the fact sheet, she thought, she'd just do it from memory.

'Dad,' she said, taking his hands, 'I'll come and visit you. On the weekend. I love you.' Then she turned to race after Jerome.

'I can't believe that was Dad,' she said when she arrived beside him on the roadside.

'Yeah.' Jerome laughed. 'They must trust him to make the coffee. Is that the first time you've seen him?'

'Yeah,' she said. 'In four years.'

'Oh my God,' he said, and pulled her into a sideways hug. 'No wonder you made him cry. Make sure you go and see him on Saturday, okay?'

'Hah, assuming I'm not in gaol,' she said. 'Did you get the okay from council?'

'They said no. Of course. We knew they would. *Now!*' he yelled, and grabbed her hand and charged across the road between a truck and a sedan.

'If everyone leaves they can't charge them with trespass,' Cressida yelled over the traffic. 'I mean, obviously,' she added, feeling stupid. As they reached the other side more scarlet police cars roared around the corner from the motorway, sirens screaming, and one then another pulled up on the verge, stranding Felipe and Dale on the far side of the road. A voice yelled from a loudspeaker atop one of the police cars. Cressida craned to look for Alessa in the crowd.

'*This is an illegal protest,*' boomed the voice. People were flooding out of tents and sitting down linking arms in front of the sodden campfire, singing 'We, we will not be moved'. '*You have five minutes to leave the area or be arrested. This protest has been declared a large-scale public disorder under the Law Enforcement (Powers and Responsibilities) Act. If you do not leave within five minutes you will be arrested.*'

Someone handed Cressida a loudspeaker and she bawled into it.

'You do not need to answer any questions if you are arrested,' she yelled as Alessa arrived next to her. 'You may be searched and your name required but you do not need to submit to—'

But then the loudspeaker was torn out of her hand and a female police officer was standing a foot from her face and yelling at her to leave.

'Gah,' Cressida screamed back, more angry at being interrupted than anything else. 'I'm their lawyer, for fuck's sake, I'm just trying to tell them their rights.' But the police officer just kept screaming at her – *move, move, move* – while others started hauling on the protestors to get up, yelling *move* in the same roared monotone. Alessa bellowed at the officer about giving her a minute, she was trying to, and with pure force of hauteur somehow managed to create a forcefield around herself as she made her way to the cars on the kerb. Her face was pinched and hands held up like someone trying to avoid paparazzi. Cressida took a deep breath and was about to follow, when the police officer grabbed her by the wrist and spun her, shoving it up behind her back, making her shoulderblade erupt in fire. The iPad was knocked out of her hand and she was pushed towards the roadway.

'Stop for fuck's sake, you'll fucking get me run over,' Cressida yelled towards the ground when they arrived on the edge of the road, balancing on the kerb as the cars rushed past. The officer pushed her towards one of the parked cars and she lurched onto it, slumping against the wheel arch in a fog of relief that the pain had stopped. The world spun, and she watched in horror as other police stomped on the tents and ripped up the pegs, tore down placards and kicked the cold logs in the fire in all directions. Next to her Alessa was quietly talking into her cell phone.

'Where's Jerome?' Cressida yelled, and her sister pointed to one of the police wagons. Then there was a scream and she looked towards the sound; next to one of the tents a woman was standing over someone on the ground. It looked like Vic, the old man from the Wilderness Society. She turned to look for Dale; he was still on the other side of the road. Just as she saw him, he saw the man collapse too, and dropped the coffee and ran towards the park, narrowly dodging a bus. She pulled herself to standing, determined to follow him back into the camp, but the police officer pushed her back again and this time she felt the cable ties on her wrists.

She started to shake, violently, and fought back a wave of nausea.

'What the fuck are you doing!' she yelled, her voice several octaves too high. 'I'm the *lawyer*.'

A tiny voice reminded her that she'd tried that last time and it hadn't worked. She felt like an iron band was squeezing her chest. They were taking her again. She fought to make her vocal chords work.

'Didn't you see that guy collapse?' she screamed. 'Call an ambulance, for God's sake!'

She craned to see what Dale was doing, in time to see an officer crash-tackle him to the ground. He yelled something, the look on his face pure fury, and the officer on top of him twisted to look where he was pointing. He rolled off and Dale clambered up, running to the figure on the ground. He dropped his ear to the old man's mouth and said something, then shook him, but the prone form flopped, unresponsive. A change rippled through Dale's face like an occupying presence and he wiped his hand quickly across his mouth. Then he tipped the man's head back and sealed his mouth with his own. The sounds around Cressida echoed like they were coming through water, the yelling of the officer next to her distant. She watched Dale give a breath and start on the chest presses, arms rod-straight trampolining on the bony chest and making the locks of his hair jerk with the effort. Then he was on the mouth again, breathing, breathing. Felipe arrived and he put down the medical bag and in amazement Cressida saw him pull out a face mask with a balloon attached to it. Seeing it mid-chest press, Dale's shoulders went slack with relief as he pumped and Felipe put it on the man's face, Dale still chest pressing all the while. A moment later the man convulsed, threw his head to one side and vomited, just as two blue-overalled paramedics knelt down next to them. There was a roaring in her ears and Cressida wasn't sure whether it was real or her imagination, until she looked up to see a helicopter overhead, the Channel 7 logo on the side. She shielded her eyes against the sun and watched as a cameraman hung out its open door, a heavily made-up anchorwoman speaking into an enormous black microphone next to him. The cameraman aimed at them. Alessa waved up at the anchorwoman and the anchorwoman waved back. She sat and watched as the police dispatched protestors six at a time into the police vans, their wrists angled behind them in cable ties. Then Cressida's attention was diverted back to the ground as the officer next to her wrenched open the patrol car door. He dragged her to standing.

'Time to go,' he said.

'What?'

'You shouldn't have gone back in. You tried to go back in,' he said, shaking his head. 'You were told to leave the area.'

'No,' she said, starting to cry.

'Shut up,' he said, and pushed her head down and into the car. The driver in the front seat was talking on the radio. He replaced the radio handset into its holder and turned to the officer.

'Hang on,' he said. He twisted to regard her. 'Aren't you Cressida Mitsok?'

'Yes. Why?'

The officer grimaced. 'Constable,' he called out to the other officer again, who squinted into the car. 'Not her. It checks out. She's their lawyer.' He looked at her sternly. 'I'm only letting you go because you'd turn today into a total fucking headache, okay? Get out.'

Cressida stared at him, and then suddenly she wanted to laugh. It welled up and she couldn't stop it, collapsing on the seat beside her in a tsunami of giggles. The officers stared, perplexed. She finally got control of herself.

'You guys are hopeless, you know that?' she said, swinging her legs out the door. 'And by the way, you're right about a total fucking headache, I was already drafting the false imprisonment brief in my head. Can you take these off my wrists please?' She turned her back towards the other officer. He cut them and without looking at her got in the front passenger seat of the car. She jumped out of the way as they drove off.

The last of the paddywagons left, all the protestors having been arrested. Vic had disappeared into an ambulance. In silence she and Alessa and Cressida watched it go. Then she looked across at Dale and Felipe. They both stood motionless in the clearing, pale and wide-eyed. Silently she and Alessa picked their way across the grass to join them. Dale took one look at her and pulled her into a hug, and she didn't try to stop the tears that started flowing, awkwardly reaching for Felipe with one hand so that the three of them were in an awkward embrace. On the ground was Felipe's iPad. Cressida picked it up. It was smeared in mud and the screen was cracked. The four of them stood and watched as the remaining heavy-booted police gathered up the paraphernalia of the protest and shoved it into the back of a police van.

'Where's that stuff going?' Cressida called across to one of them.

'The tip, mostly.'

'But it's not yours,' she said.

'It is now, sweetheart,' the officer said back. The other officer turned to her.

'I thought you were told to leave the area or you'd be arrested.'

Cressida opened her mouth to yell back a retort when Alessa spoke.

'Thanks, officer. Yes, we're just going. Jesus, what a *malakas*,' she said to Cressida under her breath. 'Where to now, sis?'

'We follow them to the lockup and get them out of gaol,' Cressida said.

'That's what we do.'

'Which one?' Alessa said.

'Shit,' said Cressida, and started running towards the Jag. 'We'll have to follow them. I have no fucking idea.'

'I'll drive,' said Alessa, pushing Cressida across to the passenger seat. 'You drive like a nanna.'

Felipe and Dale ran up and got into the back seat.

Cressida was still holding the muddy iPad. She reached into the back seat for her bag and gingerly put it in. Just as Alessa pulled off the kerb her phone rang. Cressida dug through her sister's bag and answered it.

'Hello, Alessa's phone.'

'I need Cressida Mitsok please. Richard Branagan.'

For a moment Cressida didn't recognise the voice. Then it came to her. Richard. Her supervising Partner. Supervisor on InterConnex. It felt like a call from a different planet.

'Richard, hi,' she said, her voice strained. 'It's Cress. What's up?'

'I've been trying to call you. You're not answering the phone. I had to get this number from Brian.'

'Oh. Yes. Um, my phone's been confiscated for evidence.' She probably should have made something up, but everything was happening too fast, and before she knew it she had blurted it out.

'I'm not even going to ask what you mean by that,' said Richard. 'P and C want the T and C draft ready by tomorrow, not next week. How far along is it?'

'Tomorrow?' Cressida tried to keep the shriek out of her voice. 'Nowhere near ready. It's fifty pages long, for God's sake.'

'I know that, Cressida. And so have you, for nearly a week now. I can't believe you haven't got at least a draft ready. Even a working draft?'

'I've been … I've been *busy*,' she said. *And the draft I'd already done got confiscated by the AFP. How has my life come to this?* she thought.

'Can you do it?'

'Oh sure,' Cressida said dully. It wasn't a question you said no to. 'Yes I can do it. It'll be in your inbox by seven tomorrow.'

'If it's too difficult I'll get Pip to do it, Cressida. She's been doing background reading on this for a week. I've been really impressed. She's even organised a meeting in Melbourne with the stakeholders for Thursday.'

*Hang on*, Cressida thought, *I organised that.*

'What do you mean?' Cressida laughed to cover her anger. 'I organised that a week ago.'

'Really? Well they've all been contacting Pip about it. She's virtually on a first name basis with the Victorian Premier's Chief of Staff. You are coming to that meeting, aren't you?'

'Yes,' said Cressida. 'Yes of course. And I'll have the T and C draft ready for Monday's meeting, to review as planned. That meeting *is* still on, isn't it?'

'Yes, Cressida, it's still on. I look forward to seeing the draft. Jesus, Cressida,' his voice dropped. 'What's going on with you? You're my rock-star road lawyer. What's with this getting all frayed round the edges shit?'

'I know, Richard. I'm sorry. I'm working on a major case for Brian, actually. It's getting completely blown out.' She held onto the dashboard as Alessa roared onto the motorway. 'I'm getting it back on track though. I promise.'

'Don't promise, Cressida. Just deliver. Okay?'

She swallowed nervously. 'Yes Richard. Thanks for the call.'

'Bye.'

She hung up. Something very odd was going on. She hadn't asked Pip to organise Thursday's meeting. It had all been done before she left on Wednesday – there were only eight of them, it was just the central few, and they'd all replied and said they could make it. No-one had rung her ... but then she realised she had been out of phone contact since Wednesday, aside from a few moments going in and out of reception between Wellington and Taree. A lot could change in four days. *A lot.*

'Alessa,' she said. 'I need to get to a phone shop.'

'I thought we were going to the lockup,' Alessa said. 'Ah, there's one of them.' She swerved to join a lane behind a paddywagon. 'Here's hoping they're all going to the same place.'

'This is more important,' said Cressida. 'Fucking hell,' she added.

'What's up?'

'Oh, you know, just my life's falling apart,' Cressida wailed, opening the window and throwing her head into the wind. 'That was my supervising Partner. Something I thought was due next week is now due tomorrow. I'll never get it done. And, by the way, I'd already done it, but it got *confiscated by the police.*'

'Go home,' Alessa said. 'I'll deal with these hippies. It can't be that hard, can it? What do I do?'

'What do you mean?' Cressida drew her head back in and looked at Alessa.

'Just tell me what to do. I just, what, tell them not to say anything, right? And give them my card and talk in an American accent? I've seen it on the telly, it can't be that hard, right?'

'That's basically it. Wow, you'd do that?'

'If it's a choice between that and seeing you spontaneously combust right next to me and ruin Dad's heirloom car, yes. So. Phone shop then home, right?'

'Screw the phone shop, just put me out here,' she said, flicking to the Uber app on Alessa's phone. 'You need to get to the police station before those people say anything dumb.' Like Andy did, she thought.

'What do you two want to do?' Alessa called behind her, peering in the rear-view mirror. Cressida turned back to look at Dale and Felipe, who had both been silent throughout Richard's call – she had almost forgotten they were there. She was torn between wanting Dale with her and wanting them both to have somewhere else urgent they needed to be so she could *think*.

'Um,' Dale said, looking at his watch, 'I need to get back to Saturne. She was meant to have a treatment at twelve.'

'Treatment,' Felipe said, glancing at him. 'What is it exactly this *treatment* that you're giving her?'

Alessa said, 'You've got three seconds to decide until I drop you out. I don't want to lose that cop car.' The car skidded to a halt at a bus stop and they piled out.

'I'll call an Uber,' said Dale. 'I guess … I guess I'll meet you back at Helena's house.'

'Okay,' she said, watching him walk away. Felipe was staring at her. She stood there, trying to smile and look nonchalant, when an enormous yellow phone leapt into view.

'Hi,' beamed a face from the face hole. He handed her a leaflet. 'iPhone X only $1550 today only – can I interest you in a test run?' She turned and found that they were standing outside a Telstra outlet. 'Felipe,' she said to him, as winsomely as possible, 'come on, let's go look at phones. Besides – I … I'll need to get your iPad repaired.' She looked down at it resting forlornly in her bag. On the rolled-rosegold bottom edge even its little charging port was filled with mud.

'Cressida,' Felipe said.

'What?'

'Look there's something I have to attend to,' he said, giving her an oddly brisk smile. 'We'll reconvene tomorrow, yes?' He picked up her hand and kissed the top of it. 'You go and buy yourself a phone. Are you alright for cash?' He moved to pull out his wallet but she stopped him with a look.

'I'm sorry about what happened in the cafe, Felipe. I had no idea my father would be there. I'm sorry I didn't introduce you properly. I was just … I was flustered.'

'Hmm? Oh. Oh no, that was fine, though I agree it was … well, it was awkward, wasn't it.' He opened his phone and dialled.

'Felipe. Don't go. Can't we talk about this?'

'Yes,' he said, tapping into his phone. 'Oh, look at that.' He held out his arm. A taxi pulled up to the kerb. He leant down to kiss her cheek.

'There's nothing to talk about. I'll see you later,' he said, and was gone.

She stood on the pavement and watched the taxi go, then sat down on the bench seat, trying not to let the gigantic foam phone see that she was crying. She looked studiously away from him, flicking the tears away. Could things get any more screwed up?

'Are you alright?' the man in the phone suit said.

'What? Oh, yes,' she said, 'I just can't believe that's such a great deal. Where do I sign?'

When she got home Saturne was sitting by the pool with Alessa's *Frankie*. She lowered it when Cressida approached.

'Jerome got arrested,' said Cressida, sitting on the banana lounge opposite. The pool was as still as glass. 'Alessa's gone to get him bailed out. And I got a new phone,' she said, showing her the iPhone X. 'Have … did Dale get back?'

'He's gone to find me some more coffee,' she said, sipping on tea. 'For my nether regions. What happened?'

'You mean this morning?'

Saturne nodded.

Cressida could feel pressure behind her eyelids. *It's okay. It's over*, she told herself. *They're not coming back.* She sighed and filled Saturne in.

'Gosh, is that a record for a corporate lawyer?' Saturne laughed. 'Arrested twice in a week?'

'Oh God, probably,' groaned Cressida. 'Though I don't know if I'm going to even keep that job description for much longer.'

'Why? You're awesome.'

'Hah!' Cressida laughed sarcastically. 'Thanks. Tell that to my supervising Partner. He just rang and told me that something I thought was due next week is due tomorrow. So basically, I've got to get done in the next 24 hours something that normally takes two lawyers three weeks to do,' she said, looking glumly at the pool. 'I'm hoping there might be an old mostly done draft on an email I sent to one of the other lawyers. But without that, it seems so impossible I'm not sure I even want to bother. And I think Felipe just dumped me.'

'What?' said Saturne, grimacing. 'Oh well. If it's any consolation – I didn't think he was right for you anyway.'

'What do you mean?' Cressida said. 'Jesus, tell me what you really think. He was perfect for me.'

'Well maybe in all the *obvious* ways. Orthopaedic surgeon, good-looking, talented, loaded, you mean?'

'Well … yeah. I mean …'

'So what happened then? Why did you let him go?'

'What do you mean? I didn't. I just told you – *he* just dumped *me*.'

*Jesus*, Cressida thought, *you're not being very sympathetic.*

'Come on. You've known for days this was going to happen. And weeks before that, I imagine. He treats you like shit.'

'What are you talking about? You've never even seen us together.'

'I didn't have to. I knew from the look on your face when you had to get home from Gloucester. You were willing to risk your life, Cressida, or at least being washed off a ravine, just to avoid pissing him off. I'm sorry, I hope I'm not overstepping a line here, Cressida. It's just that. Well, you know. You've been really good to me. I just think you deserve to be treated the same. And that brings me to …' She closed the magazine. 'I was going to say, Cressida. You've been really kind, but I don't need to stay here forever. I mean, I know the safe house is gone, but I'm thinking I'll go and stay with my cousins for a bit. They drive me crazy, but they do want to look after me. I've booked a train ticket for tomorrow.'

'They're not in Queensland are they?' said Cressida, slumping back against the seat. 'South America, Russia …?'

'Actually …' Saturne laughed. 'Not South America, but yes to Queensland.'

'Excellent. There's just a slight possibility the AFP might forget about you if they have to extradite you.'

'I'm also going to start radiation.'

'Oh Saturne,' said Cressida.

'Yeah,' she said, throwing the magazine aside. Cressida noticed that her eyes were damp but then she looked away. 'I've decided I'm being a bit of an idiot. Felipe was good on that count, anyway.'

'What do you mean?'

'Oh we had a little chat,' she said, rubbing her eyes. 'He told me about how good the radiotherapy treatments are these days, how it's a lot less invasive than it used to be. And …he called a mate of his up there, an onco. He can see me next week.'

'Wow,' said Cressida, falling silent. What a kind thing to do.

'Yeah. I feel a bit mean saying those things about him – I do still think he's a crap boyfriend – but he's got a pretty good heart. And the gorgeous Helena organised a masseuse for me this morning,' she exclaimed. 'Dale gives great massage, don't get me wrong – as I hope you'll one day find out – but this woman. Oh my God. And Helena's *cooking*!'

'I know,' Cressida said, reflecting that she had barely been there to enjoy it. 'It's so obvious she likes you; I don't think she's cooked anything vegan before in her life, much less for two days running. God, did we only arrive yesterday?' Cressida shook her head. She knew she had to get started on the road contract, and that she was procrastinating because it felt so overwhelming. 'Saturne, that's so awesome about the radiotherapy and the specialist. I was really worried about you,' she said, sitting down to hug her. 'I have to get down to work.' How was she going do it without her laptop? She looked through the house to the door at the end of the hall. She'd have to use Leo's computer. 'Have you seen Helena?'

'She went out. Something about a Farmers' Market. This is all so unbelievable.' She sighed heavily, leaning back against the seat. 'What do you really think about all this? Will any of it stick?'

'I have no idea. To Andy, I mean, there's the sabotage, so …'

'No I know that,' she said. Sadness traversed her face for an instant, before it was swallowed up in that cheerful stoicism she shared with Andy. As if a kind of quiet martyrdom was their accepted destiny. 'I mean the others. Dizzy, Jason, Taina, Merv. Dale.'

'I have no idea. Anyway. Gotta get on with this thingie I have to do. Are you alright for everything?'

'Fabulous,' she said, holding up the magazine. 'Get me a peach daiquiri and I'd be perfect.'

'Um, I could make you a dry martini, but that's about it …'

'Cressida. I'm kidding. Go.'

'Sorry.' Cressida laughed, and headed for Leo's office.

# 26

'How's it going?'

Dale was standing in the doorway. Cressida checked the clock on the corner of the computer screen: 1.58. A smell wafted through the open door. *Lamb*.

'Oh God,' she groaned. 'You're *cooking*?'

He revealed a plate from behind the doorjamb.

'Couldn't sleep.' He shrugged, setting it down on the desk beside her. 'And I figured you'd need feeding.'

'Oh my goodness,' she said, looking longingly at the plump, oiled rounds on the plate. 'You made keftedes?'

'Helena said you liked them,' he said. 'Have you got much to go?'

'Nearly done actually. If you'll excuse my French, it's actually just the *fucking pagination*. I've been doing it for the last half an hour. It's all the appendices.'

'Well I was just going to say,' Dale said, 'when you're ready to pack it in, there's cake.'

'You made *cake*?' She hadn't had cake for years, decades even. Not even at birthday parties.

'I wish,' he laughed. 'Helena made it. Saturne and I told her you were pulling an all-nighter.'

'Can you stop being so nice?' said Cressida, still looking at the keftedes and wondering if she could eat them. 'It's freaking me out.'

Dale chuckled. 'Just think of it as my version of pistols at dawn. See you in a mo.'

'Wait, no! Don't leave me with these! Jesus. And Dale—' He reappeared in the doorway. 'Have you seen Alessa? I've been wondering how she went with the protestors.'

'Yeah. She got in an hour or so. Said they hadn't charged them, though. So she couldn't get them bailed.'

'They hadn't *charged* them? What, after …' – she calculated – 'over *twelve hours*?' Damn. Not good. Twelve hours was more than four. Twelve hours suggested more terrorism offences being considered. *For attending a protest?* Would they be on at the Downing Centre tomorrow then? Or would the police keep them for days without charge like they did Andy? And what about Jerome?

'Oh and she said she spoke to that Byron bloke. He called back for you about something on her phone. He's going to do the rest of the people arrested today – yesterday, I mean,' he said, looking at his watch. 'In Sydney at two. If she can get it stood over, she said. Whatever that means. As a direct brief or something, until they can get solicitors.'

'Oh wow,' she said, falling back into the chair. 'What a legend. Did she talk to my brother?'

'No. But she said he was arm in arm with an attractive brunette, as she put it, when she left the lockup.'

'Ha ha. God, my family,' she said, shaking her head. That old Mitsok charm.

Forty-five minutes later Cressida finally loaded up her father's industrial printer with paper and watched with exhausted satisfaction as it pumped out twenty stapled, hole-punched copies of the document that, a few hours ago, had held her future in its omission. When she listed out to the lounge room, Dale was asleep in the Eames, head cradled by the curved headrest. In front of him on the table was a cake next to a knife and two plates. Pineapple upside-down cake. Damn. Her favourite. Careful not to wake him, she sat in the chair opposite and looked out at the pool. But it was his reflection she saw, reflected in the dark glass of the sliding door. Even at that distortion, she could see the dark circles under his eyes, and in his hands the book he'd been reading had dropped as if he had fallen asleep mid-sentence. How many times had she found her father like that, she thought, turning to look at him properly, when as a teenager she couldn't sleep for worrying about Peggy. He'd be sitting in that very chair with a pile of papers beside him, glasses still perched on his nose as he snored gently under the lamplight. Suddenly she felt an overwhelming sadness. What would he be doing right now, she wondered. Trying to sleep on some hard mattress in a cell that had no door? Alessa was right. She had been way too hard on her father. And anything would be worth not having this hole in her chest where her father's love used to be. Even if she could never forget what he had done, in other ways he had been impossibly wonderful, she reflected, somehow buffering the three of them from most of the trauma of her mother's last days and months, as well as holding down the expectations of partnership at Hannes Swartling. She looked back at Dale. It had to take it out of you, she thought. Caring for someone with a terminal illness, 24/7. Always being on guard, thinking about or caring for their welfare, shopping, preparing, cooking, worrying. All the while never knowing whether it was going to make a squib of difference or not.

And he never talked about it. *How can he*, she chastised herself, *you're always talking about **you***. Watching him asleep it was like seeing his life etched in the lines there, in the shadows of old worry between his eyebrows, the lines of strain beneath his eyelids, tracks of all the joys and struggles of the life he had only a little yet described to her. Except the skin under his chin – that was like a secret patch of youth, smooth and unlined. In the corner where it hit his stubbly chin a pulse flickered, as tiny and constant as a bird's. The most overwhelming emotion she felt looking at him was tenderness.

She picked up the book and put it to one side, and very gently moved his arm aside to sit in beside him, her face close to the crook of his neck. His chest rose and fell rhythmically under the red checked shirt, heat radiating off him through the thin fabric. That was the thing that she most noticed about him. He was always so *warm*. Like his body had some kind of internal furnace, pumping out raw, flame-like heat day and night. She leaned forward and kissed the pulse. He murmured something, and she did it again, burying her nose in his throat. Then he was awake and his mouth found hers, and he picked her up and they were in the bedroom and on the bed, and he kicked the door shut and she was kissing him like she'd never kissed anyone – not Felipe, not her first boyfriend, not the jocks she'd kissed in college who practised on pillows and thought they were pretty good at it. This kissing devoured her, threw a molotov cocktail into her insides and tore it apart, and just as her last scrap of clothing came off she heard Helena yelling her name and banging on the door.

# 27

What was the good in pulling off the impossible, Cressida thought the next morning as she stood waiting for the lift, when in the overall scheme of things, none of it mattered? The doors opened with a muted *ding* and she stepped in, dragging the Louis Vuitton wheelie suitcase she'd borrowed from Alessa. It still had her sister's gold monogrammed tag label on it. When the doors were two inches from closed a voice called to wait; Cressida jammed her finger on the button.

'*Xie xie, xie xie*, fuck, sorry, I mean thank you,' said the voice, and a Chinese man stepped in. He looked at her bag and laughed. 'What, you got a bomb in that bag, or what? It's huge.'

'Oh. That. Yes. Enough luggage for a trip back to Wuhan,' she said, unable to muster humour. 'No. Road documents. Going to a meeting. It's Mr Zhou, isn't it? Cressida Mitsok. We met a couple of weeks ago.' She held out her hand.

'Ha ha, that's right!' he said, taking it. 'Fucking meetings.' He pressed Level 58. Emergent tech and renewables. What was he doing getting out there?

'How's the power stations?' she said, as the lift whooshed upwards.

'Hah, *those*?' he said. 'Cactus. Or as you lawyers say, *confuckulated*. This is where it's at,' he said, and pointed as the doors opened. 'Have a good day,' he said, and was gone.

On Level 61 Cressida parked her bag at the back of the meeting room and made straight for the coffee urn, marvelling at how everything was so clean, and calm, and orderly. The people, freshly showered and rested, beetling about on this floor so many storeys into the sky when below, somewhere, her boyfriend, a lymphoma-ridden 28-year-old woman, and possibly her brother as well were being held and interrogated. Jerome would be alright – he was used to being arrested at protests – but the other two; it was thoughts of them that made her hand shake as she put the teabag into the mug; she swallowed, sure somebody would notice. Then she thought better of the tea and shoved the cup under the coffee spout instead, wishing she'd managed more than just mascara for makeup that morning. Today was *not* a day to look like she was losing it.

She gulped the coffee in one and poured another, ignoring its scalding bitterness, and looked around for Pip. At that moment the door opened and in she swept with Richard, wearing a razor-sharp navy number and with a massive matching cocktail ring and stack of beaded bracelets setting it off. Her hair was pulled into a sideways ponytail and her face looked fresh and predatory. Her eyes snagged on Cressida and she approached.

'*Darling*,' her friend said, air-kissing her. 'Where have you been, New Zealand? I've been trying to call you for days.' She put her leopard-skin leather compendium down beside Cressida's document bag and smoothed her hair. 'You look wrecked. What did you do to your *hair*? Pastry?'

Cressida snapped her game face in place. If Pip wanted war, like fuck she'd get it.

'Oh God, no thanks,' Cressida said, wrinkling her nose. 'I was up till three-thirty.'

'Ohh,' Pip purred, dispensing hot water over a teabag. 'Well done you. Oh, Stanford,' she called, eyeing someone on the other side of the room. 'Sorry, someone I've got to see,' she said to Cressida, who watched her make a beeline for a man in a grey suit and allow him a kiss to her cheek. Oh God. But of *course* Pip was going to already be on kissy terms with the fucking *Victorian Premier's Chief of Staff*, she thought, recognising him. She checked her watch: 9.15. She prayed Saturne and Dale were being given a bail hearing somewhere. Her last sight of them had been being pushed out the front door wearing cable ties at their wrists. The images still swam: Saturne hauled from her bedroom half dressed, Dale bellowing at the police to be gentle, Alessa sitting like a terrified cat beside her on that ridiculous Eames chair, staring with eyes the size of saucers with Helena holding onto her forearm and trying to get some sense out of the police, who had ignored her. It was those last images that were burned into her mind the most: the two people she thought of as being virtually invincible – her sister, so unflappable and aloof, and Dale, with his seemingly endlessly capable calm, both incapacitated in the face of that sudden implacable violence, beautiful Helena wittering on all the while. It had been a blessing that Jerome hadn't been there, she thought. She knew he would have fought them, and he wouldn't have won.

After they had left she, Alessa and Helena had sat holding each other on the cane chair until dawn, none of them able to move from it, each afraid the police would come back, Helena repeatedly offering to make cups tea but then not moving, holding them and flooding with wave after wave of quiet tears.

'Cressida? Hello?' Richard had approached and was looking at her. 'Are you alright?'

'Hmm? Oh, yes, sorry,' she beamed, dabbing at an eye with a serviette. 'Mascara in my eye. Ready to start?'

Richard nodded, and she moved into her seat. Pushing thoughts of Dale and Saturne from her mind she put the coffee on the table and unzipped the wheelie bag, pulling out the top document. Despite her exhaustion, it felt heavy and satisfying in her hands. Once this meeting was out of the way she would have some breathing space, to focus on what

Dale and Saturne needed her to do.

'Alright people, thank you so much for coming at short notice this morning,' Richard began, 'and Pip, thank you again for organising it so efficiently,' he said, throwing her an appreciative grin. 'To those of you who don't know her, this is Pip Michelin, and we also have with us this morning of course Cressida Mitsok, whom I'm sure you all know.' Cressida's new mobile phone pinged and she scrambled to put it on silent, then glanced at the text from Alessa. *I found them. Downing Central 9.15. Dale on drug possession and Saturne on membership of a terrorism organisation. Can you come?* She stared at it. Tiny, sickly Saturne, on terrorism? – and Dale on *drug possession*? Richard was still talking. 'Cressida has been burning the midnight oil getting the T and C draft ready for us this morning, haven't you, Cress, and she's going to take us through it.'

'Thank you, Richard,' said Cressida, jamming down the mild panic that had arisen at the text. 'And yes, thank you, Pip, for organising this meeting. We might do a quick trip round the circle to find out how everyone's contribution on the rest of the pre-approval work is going. Were there any questions before we start?'

There weren't, so Cressida turned to the contents page of her document.

'As you can see, we've covered all the usual material in the application,' she began. 'Under amendments to the infrastructure SEPP passed' – she looked at the date on her watch – 'a fortnight ago, this first stage is listed as critical state infrastructure under the legislation. So most of the usual procedures have been omitted. Question one, capital investment value, is below two hundred million so it's excluded from the need to go to the Independent Planning Commission ...'

Richard looked up, a little frown furrowing his brow, and one of the lawyers down the table raised her hand.

'Yes?' Cressida said.

'I'm sorry, I must be out of date – Melbourne told me the CIV had gone up to two-twenty million as of Thursday. Because of the addition of the Eastern Creek component.'

The Eastern Creek component, Cressida thought, struggling to catch on. Wow, she must be more sleep deprived than she realised; she had no idea what that meant.

'The Eastern Creek component ...' Cressida said, trying to jog her brain into life. 'No I think it must be me who's out of date – Pip, can you assist?'

'Oh,' Pip said, reddening, 'I'm sorry. Jesus. You didn't get my voicemail. Um.' She straightened in her seat and beamed at the assembled party. 'Yes of course there was a major amendment to the proposal made last week, once Queensland got involved. Sorry, Cressida, I thought you would have got my message ...' She flicked to the next page of the document at the same time Cressida did, both of them looking at the figure simultaneously. *But that means ... That means the entire application is wrong*, Cressida thought. If stage one was over two hundred million it put it into an entirely different category. It *would* have to go to the Independent Planning Commission, for a start, she realised in horror. And this was the wrong form for that. She gulped, not daring to look at Richard, who was sitting stiffly, staring down at the offending page.

She hauled out a smile and rallied. 'Oh dear, silly me. No, Pip, I'm afraid I *didn't* get your message, how funny. No matter, I'll just have Esma whip up a fresh form ...' It wasn't going to be as simple as that though, she knew. It would take her a whole day to fix it.

'Oh,' Pip said, chewing on her lip. 'Well, actually ... I'm new at this, as you know, so I actually had a go myself, just as a way to learn, of course.' She gave a little laugh, and pulled out her laptop. 'Just give me one sec and I'll run these off,' she said, waving a USB stick and diving into the hall. Cressida smiled awkwardly and followed.

Outside Pip was talking quietly to one of the secretaries in the typing pool.

'Excuse me,' Cressida said, arriving beside her. 'What are you doing? I didn't get any voicemail message. I've ... I've lost my phone.'

'I know, Cressida. I did try.' Pip rolled her eyes. 'Can you save that and run off twelve copies?' she said to the secretary. 'I'll whack it up on the screen in there in the meantime. Where did you lose your phone, for God's sake, Cressida?' she said, irritably. 'I tried ringing you for days. Thank you so much, Kelly.' She turned and headed back to the boardroom, Cressida almost running after her. She grabbed her arm before she reached the doorway.

'But – why didn't you email me?' she said.

'I'm pretty sure I did, Cressida,' Pip said, rolling her eyes again. 'I've been busy too, you know.' She extracted her arm and sauntered back into the boardroom. 'Copies are coming, people,' she announced. 'Meanwhile if you'll just give me a minute ...' She stuck the USB into her laptop and connected it to the projector wireless with practised ease, the first page of the document flashing up in moments. Cressida sat down next to her and turned to the screen, feeling the prickle of eyes on the back of her neck. She knew she'd gone red. At least facing this way she could avoid Richard's eyes. When they got to page three of Pip's document her eye caught the description in the footer. It was her initials, and the file name still had the word 'WestConnex' in it. The paragraphs of description of the project were virtually the same as the one she'd done for WestConnex – paragraphs that had taken Cressida days of careful work, finessing the phrasing so that it sounded both as exciting and environmentally innocuous as possible – but with the name changed everywhere but the footer. Pip must have inserted her own initials and the correct title in the rest of it. Well, why wouldn't you? she thought. Use an old precedent rather than reinvent the wheel. But you'd think she'd attribute the source of it, at least if the author was in the room. She looked across at Pip, wondering whether she would mention it, but her colleague was breezing on with jokes about having a bash as a rookie, as if it was entirely her own work. The receptionist came in and copies were distributed. When Pip had finished there was a round of applause, and the draft was approved without comment. The meeting broke up and Cressida watched Pip as she packed up.

'Nice work,' she said.

'Thanks,' said Pip. 'I was expecting it to be mammoth, but it turned out not to be that hard after all.'

'I guess not, when you used one of my old documents,' she said. 'Of course, you did neglect to change the footer in section three. The one with my name in it.'

'Oh did I?' Pip laughed. 'I never worry about that. That's for Word Processing to fix up.'

'Pip,' Cressida asked, 'what's going on? You're acting really weird.'

Pip frowned. 'I don't know what you're talking about. Hey Richard, wait up,' she said. 'I'll catch the lift up with you.'

'Richard,' said Cressida, standing up. 'What a complete balls-up, I'm sorry. My phone was … well basically it was stolen,' she said, thinking that essentially that's what the police – who had never charged her – had done. 'I've got a new one now. I'll let your secretary know the number.'

Richard turned to her, his expression unreadable. Pip stood behind him, not bothering to hide her impatience.

'Cressida,' Richard said, 'Brian wants to see you.'

'Oh. Do you know what for?' she said, amiably.

'No idea.' He checked his watch. 'He should be in his office right about now.'

'Okay great. Are you two coming?'

'We'll catch you up.'

'Um. Okay. Sure,' she said. In the hall she checked her watch again: 10.15am. Quickly she dialled Alessa's number, but it went to voicemail. As she pressed the button for the lift she tried to feel optimistic, reminding herself that all Brian cared about was getting his daughter out of gaol. And no-one would argue that she hadn't successfully busted a gut on that front. The appropriate thing would be to personally congratulate her. With that firmly in mind Cressida stepped out into Level 59.

Brian was inside his office with his back to the door, which was standing open. He was staring out the window, and for a moment Cressida had a view of his profile. The strong aristo nose, the high cheekbones and hard line down the side of his mouth. His forearms below the rolled-up sleeves were tanned, muscular, testament to hours spent spinning the wheel of his yacht. The M & A Partner sensed her presence and turned.

'Ah, Cressida. How are you. Come in,' he said, indicating the couch. He picked up two glasses from the silver trolley in the corner. 'Drink?'

'Ah, yes thanks,' she said. 'Shut the door?'

'Oh, that won't be necessary,' he said with a wave of his hand. 'What can I get you?' He opened a bottle of Johnny Walker Blue Label and sloshed it into a glass. It wasn't even noon, she thought, but then he was head Partner of M &A, wasn't he. He could do whatever he liked. She was still standing and without meeting her eyes, he held up an empty glass.

'Have a seat. Drink or not?'

'Oh,' she said, perching on the wide leather couch. 'Um, just a soda water? Thanks.'

He pulled a can from the bar fridge next to the trolley and cracked it open with a fizz that knocked out the silence, and handed it to her with a glass of ice from the bucket. When he sat down it was on the couch perpendicularly opposite and he still hadn't looked at her. Instead he stared out the window over his glass, sipped it and then spoke.

'We were all so proud of you when you came back from ASIC, Cressida,' he said, in that caramel cut-glass voice, moistened by the whiskey. 'The clients were clamouring for you. All that wonderful knowledge you gained, working for the other side.'

'Yes,' she said, nodding with more self-assurance than she felt. 'It was incredibly valuable. Not just for that, but for now, working on' – she glanced back at the open door – 'your daughter's case.'

He almost glanced at her, then down at his glass.

'Quite.' He paused. 'So I hear there was a bit of an adventure yesterday.'

'In what sense?'

He laughed, but it was short and humourless.

'You know Cressida, it's a bit of a worry that you don't know what I'm referring to. How many of those kind of "adventures" have you had, lately?'

'Well rather a lot, actually,' she said, with forced humour. 'Do you mean the protest?'

'Yes I mean the protest. Though I realise now of course there was an adventure on Friday as well, wasn't there,' he said, tightly. 'You're becoming quite the arrestee.'

'Hardly. They let me go without charge both times. And Sunday was completely a function of police stuff-up. I was there providing legal … legal advice,' she faltered, realising how that sounded, when the last time she and Brian had spoken he had told her to refrain from doing exactly that. 'How did you know?'

'You were page five in this morning's *Herald*, Cressida. "Top lawyer arrested at terrorism support rally".'

'Oh. Well that's not right for a start,' she said, forcing confidence to cover the shock. The *paper*? Oh that's right. The news anchor in the helicopter. Fuck. 'They didn't arrest me. And it wasn't a rally. It was a two-bit hippie protest.'

'I don't care what the fuck it was, Cressida,' he bit out the words and finally looked at her directly. 'Do you have any recollection at all, Cressida, of the reason we put you on the Fairbank matter to begin with? Let me remind you.' He pinned her with his blue gaze. '*Discretion.*'

Cressida swallowed and looked down at her glass.

'How exactly did you think being splashed across the front pages of the tabloids was going to serve that agenda, Cressida?'

'Oh for goodness sake,' she laughed, trying to ease the tension. 'I wasn't expecting to be arrested, of course. They made a huge mistake – I just told you, they let us go without charging us. I just happened to be in the wrong place at the wrong time.' Twice, she thought.

He glanced back at the door.

'I had thought this would be a fairly innocuous conversation, Cressida, but since it doesn't appear to be going that way,' he said, smiling tightly, and got up to shut the door, at the same time opening the blinds. He sat down again, staring at her with hostility.

'Cressida. This is not working out,' he said. 'You said you'd tell me when both Fairbank and the road project were too much for you. Well, *I'm* telling *you* that they are. Enough's enough.'

'What? Oh great,' she said, slapping her glass down on the table. 'Brian, have you any idea of what you're dealing with here? This mess would be too much for anyone. You need three solicitors working on this, not just one, and that's just your daughter's matter. Pip seems to be doing a fine enough job of filling my shoes on the road project while I'm distracted with Andy – sorry, Joanne – anyway, I might add.'

He continued staring at her and sighed. Then he put his glass down, strode to his desk and picked up the phone. He punched in a number.

'You can come in now.'

A moment later the door opened and Pip walked in, flushed but smiling.

'You're to give all of your file material and contacts on my daughter's file over to Pip,' said Brian. 'She's going to be acting for Joanne from now on. Richard's delegating the running on the road project to the Melbourne office for the time being. Unfortunately it seems that right now we don't have the firepower. Pip will reconvene on that matter once my daughter is free. You can go.'

Cressida stared at him, then Pip, then back to Brian.

'No offence, Pip,' she said quietly, 'but, Brian, you have got to be kidding. Pip has even less experience on criminal matters than me. I've already established trust with these people, Brian. You're talking crazy.'

'There is only one person I care about in this matter, Cressida,' he said, looking at Pip. For some reason she flushed, and he continued, 'And that's my daughter. As far as I'm concerned the rest of the suspects are on their own. And that's the way it should have been from the start. It's probably half the reason everything got so screwed up in the first place. Your job was to represent my daughter and my daughter only, Cressida. You can go.'

Pip had been avoiding Cressida's eyes the whole time during Brian's speech, and as Cressida looked at her she noticed a peculiar thing. When Pip did look at Brian, which was the only place she was looking aside from the floor, it was out from beneath her inky lashes, and her face was still flushed. Cressida frowned. There was something fishy going on. Then it dawned on her.

'Oh my God,' she said incredulously, and laughed. She noticed Brian's features were also pink under the tan. 'Oh my God,' she repeated, more slowly. 'You have got to be kidding me. How nineteen-eighties are we being here, people?' She turned to Brian. 'You're boning your Senior Associate?'

Brian's jaw clenched, and he looked away. 'Cressida, that is just crass. Please just take your things and go.'

She looked at Pip, wide-eyed. 'Pip. What are you doing? That's crazy.'

'I don't know what you mean, Cressida,' said Pip, airiness back in place. 'I'm just stepping into the breach where you don't seem to be up to it.'

'But … wow,' said Cressida. 'This is priceless. You're going to be totally out of your depth, you know that, don't you. And I'm not talking about the case.'

'What would you know about it?' she said.

Slowly Cressida got up, feeling dizzy.

'Okay. Sure. Whatever. Good luck with it.' She turned to Brian. 'I hope this gets you what you want. Because I don't think it's going to get your daughter out of gaol. Goodbye.'

When Cressida reflected back later, she had no recollection of anything between Brian's office and Hyde Park, only of making for the first empty bench seat and sitting on it trying to stop hyperventilating. *This is not happening*, she told herself as she watched water stream from the terrified open mouth of a stag being wrestled by a centaur in the enormous fountain across the grass. I did not just have my entire life vaporise before my eyes. Pip. *Pip.* How could she do this to her? Pip, who had everything; Pip with parents who were both Federal Court Judges, for whom partnership would have shortly been served up on a plate if she had just been able to wait a couple more years? How long had Pip been positioning herself for this, she thought, currying favour both with her, and with the firm's most powerful partner, with those inky lashes and that velvet smile? Maybe their whole friendship had just been a vast Machiavellian conspiracy towards this end. When she had never shown Pip anything but kindness.

She couldn't go back to work. What would she work on? The road project was so huge it had been the only thing she'd been given. Other than Brian's precious daughter's case, of course. After all that she'd done, she thought. *All that fucking driving.* Putting her life at risk for those fucking activists, getting arrested and thrown around by the police, risking her career with terrorism and drug charges of her own, and, possibly, she thought, bitterly, throwing away her engagement. And all because of … one stupid, innocent spliff in the middle of the forest, and a decision made on sleep deprivation, hunger, hormones, and tetrahydrocannabinol. Out of her postcode, and out of her mind. This wasn't fucking darkest Southeast Asia where people's lives hung by a thread so anything you could do was worthwhile. This was vicious, dog-eat-dog corporate-law Sydney, and her actions over the last week had just seen her thrown to the lions by two of her own.

Her mobile phone pinged in in her bag. Alessa. *I've had everyone stood over to 2.15. Can you come?* Holy mackerel. She checked the time. Alessa *had* been busy. The court was a five-minute walk. There was still time to get there.

## 28

It was hopeless, David Butcher thought, staring at the peace lily. No matter how many Post-it notes, reminders, and emphatic mental promises he made to it while he was on the phone, the plant had finally given up the ghost. All that was left were spindles of dried leaves now, with the remains of the flower thrusting up valiantly in the middle. It probably didn't help that he had taken to pouring his leftover coffees into it as a stopgap to filling up the water jug. Watering it properly would involve actually having had time to get up, go to the kitchen, find a suitable receptacle, fill it up and get back to his desk before anyone could waylay him with casework questions, new files, or a demand for ten dollars for the going away present for some fresh young thing he had never met who had been there on work experience for a week. And the coffees from Legal Bean were *strong*, enough to make him insomniac at midnight if he had any after 3pm. He would forget to finish one before it went cold, forget that it was cold, leave the cup there in case he wanted to drink it later, and then because he had forgotten, go buy another one, all within the space of a few hours. This had resulted more than once in him drinking cold soured coffee without realising – sometimes three days old and already laced with mould. It was a tragedy. The plant didn't deserve him. He should have put it on Lois's desk where it belonged months ago, and stopped drinking so much bloody coffee while he was at it.

And overnight, he had received an email from his son's Peruvian lawyer. Daniel's last appeal, on clemency grounds, had been exhausted, and he was facing three years in prison for trafficking cocaine through Lima airport. Ever since reading that, when he'd logged on this morning, David had done little more than sit and stare at the computer, feeling like his brain had ground to a halt just as the CDPP had a fortnight ago ago because of the terrorists. *Terrorists. Hah.*

His eyes found Daniel's picture again. He had just been young and stupid – how on earth did he deserve ... *this*? The thought of him rotting in some godawful Peruvian prison just didn't bear thinking about. There had to be something he could do.

So lost in thought was he when the phone rang that he jumped. He stared at it. He could just let it go to voicemail. Who said he had to answer it? He wasn't a machine. For God's sake – what did it take to get a minute to your*self* around here? It wasn't going anywhere though. In fact, it was keeping right on ringing. David shook his head quickly to clear his thoughts, suppressed the tears and picked it up.

'Butcher. It's McDuff.'

'Ah, Janus. I was just about to call you.' David sighed, bracing himself. Not ideal, but he had to tell him some time. The memo was half done on his desktop. There just wasn't enough evidence of the intent aspect on the Fairbank file. Sabotage, yes, clear as day. But not terrorism. 'I don't think we've—'

'There's been a raid on a safe house in Woollahra over the Fairbank matter,' Janus interrupted. 'Two arrested, including your accused's lesbian girlfriend and, it turns out, a fellow whose fingerprints match those on the bottles they found in Gloucester Tops. Bail hearing at two. The girl's been charged with membership and support.'

'What? On what grounds?'

'Can you get down there? Lois told me she's got the files.'

David stopped looking. 'What, today?'

'Now, I believe. Just had the Minister for Home Affairs on the phone, by the way. She wants you there personally.'

'What? What's wrong with the duty prosecutor?'

'Julie's instructions. How are the AFP going with that diary? Bye.'

The line went dead, and David stared at the phone. In one motion he was up, jacket on and hollering into the hallway for Lois.

'Lois – Janus just called – apparently there's two matters in the list from a raid in Woollahra – *right now*.'

His receptionist was already standing up and handing him a stack of red edges over the ledge of the desk.

'And a few more,' she said. 'Thirty-five arrests at a protest outside Silverwater yesterday. Williams and Taylor are the Woollahra arrests.'

'What, on *Commonwealth* charges?'

'Apparently. I'll call the clerk and tell them you're on your way.'

# 29

At Museum Station Cressida could hear the roar of the crowd from the far end of the tunnel when she got off the train. On the flagstone verandah outside the courthouse, swarms of people were held back from each other by police, both sides hurling abuse. On one side the placards said *No negotiating with terrorists!*; on the other *Ban the police state! Free the Climate Five!* She found Alessa standing under an awning at the far end next to the not-negotiating crowd, looking irritable. It was all Cressida could do to make it to her sister without collapsing into tears, and when she did, she did so.

'Hey, *hey* – what's going on? Oh God,' said Alessa, grimacing and putting her arms around Cressida. 'You're not in trouble, are you?'

'Oh fuck,' Cressida said, burying her face in her sister's shoulder. 'I wish for once you could manage to stop sounding like a prefect. I don't know. Probably.' There was a tissue in here somewhere, she thought, scrounging in her bag, at the same moment that Alessa held one out to her. Sometimes having a sister who acted like a prefect was good.

'I think I've lost my job. Oh God,' she said, pulling back. 'And I've just left mascara on your jacket.'

'Don't worry. It's dry-cleanable. You. Me. Cuppa. Now,' she said, and steered her in the direction of the cafe on the ground floor.

Cressida sat down while Alessa ordered a pot of Earl Grey for two, then pulled in opposite with a look that said 'talk'. When Cressida had finished, she replaced her teacup on its saucer with an icy precision and said, 'That bitch!' Cressida laughed in spite of herself. After all she'd related, it was Pip who Alessa took aim at first. 'And when you've been so good to her.'

'I don't know,' said Cressida. 'Maybe she's hated me all along. Maybe I did something to offend her ages ago and she's never forgiven me.'

'But I mean, Jesus,' said Alessa, 'aren't you the one that got her the rotation into M & A to begin with? She was just a no-brain judge's daughter before that, wasn't she?'

Cressida shrugged, sipping at her cold tea. 'She's sure showing brains now,' she said.

'Yeah but – someone on terrorism charges? Not her Givenchy bag. You watch. She'll take the easy way out as soon as she can, and get back to giving Brian what's-his-name blowjobs under the desk.'

Cressida gave a tearful laugh at the image and finally found the travel pack of tissues in her bag, wiping her eyes carefully so as not to dislodge the remains of her makeup.

Alessa pulled some paperwork out of her compendium. 'Now. What's our game plan with these people in a minute? Including your druggie boyfriend.'

'He's not a druggie,' said Cressida.

'Notice you don't deny he's your boyfriend,' Alessa said. 'You still haven't told my why the hell he was arrested in a terrorism raid and then put up on a drug charge. It makes no sense.'

'I don't know. Especially when they already arrested him once.'

'And why did they do that?'

Cressida hesitated, still reluctant to explain.

'Come on, Cress,' said Alessa. 'You need to tell me. How can I represent him if I don't know the full story?'

Cressida sighed. She was right.

'Look,' she began. 'I don't really know. But I have a feeling that ... that he might have assisted another suspect after the incident. My client. Medical assistance, I mean.'

'Oh,' said Alessa. 'I see. And what about the drug charges? Are they likely to stick?'

'Well ...' Could she really have been wrong about him, all this time? *All this time*, she thought with some sarcasm. All five days. 'I don't really know that either,' she said, with some sadness. 'He did say that in the past he had been a ... Well, he did say he was a ketamine addict.' She hated breaching Dale's confidence like that but felt like she didn't have any choice. 'Up until two years ago. So ... Look, it's possible.' She looked down, not wanting to meet Alessa's eyes. To her surprise, Alessa put her hand on her arm.

'Cressida,' she said. 'I'm not a total monster, you know. I do love you.'

Cressida raised her eyes and, choking with emotion, said 'I know. I love you too.'

'Well,' Alessa said in a bright tone, 'I looked up the charges against our new friends the hippies from yesterday – their bail applications are in the list today as well, by the way. Court 4B. I guess that's why there's every man and his vegan dog out the front.' She glanced at the crowd and back at Cressida, and this time there was uncharacteristic concern in her eyes. 'They're charging them under the Code, Cressida. Including Jerome.'

'With what?'

'Advocating terrorism.'

'*What?*'

'Section 80.2C of the Criminal Code. That's why I couldn't get them bailed.'

'For going to a protest.'

Alessa drained her tea and squeezed Cressida's arm. 'Yep. Come on. Let's get this over with. I hope Lord Byron or whatever his name is turns up soon. Fucked if I want to do this myself.'

Cressida touched her on the arm.

'Alessa.'

'Ya?'

'You are being such a champion. Thank you so much for this.'

Her sister laughed. 'No worries. It's kind of fun. Maybe I'll take up some crim when I get back to Singapore.'

'Except ...'

'The pay's shit,' they both said in unison, and laughed.

On the other side of security Cressida dialled Byron Kent's number.

'Hello? Cressida?' he said when he answered. 'Look, I'm on my way. The train was delayed. I'll be there in fifteen minutes. Stand it down for later in the list if you need to.'

'Okay. Thanks,' she said, and hung up. The two of them were joining the back of the crowd milling outside court 4B when a tear-stained face surrounded by dreadlocks emerged from the crowd. Taina.

'Cressida! Oh thank God,' the woman said, falling on Cressida in a tight hug. 'I saw it on the news. You were there last night – is Saturne okay?'

Cressida hugged her back, motioning to Alessa to come closer.

'Alessa, this is Taina. I don't know, Taina, I ... I haven't seen her. Alessa has though – Alessa, she was okay, right?'

'Um, yes – look, I only saw her briefly. She looked, well, tired I guess.'

Taina's eyes filled with tears again.

'I can't believe this. Why the fuck don't they just *leave us alone*? What the hell's happened to *freedom of speech in this country*?' She was yelling, and two sheriffs were looking over. Alessa gave them a friendly wave, moving closer.

'Shh, or you'll get arrested yourself,' she said through gritted teeth, touching Taina's arm.

'Wouldn't be the first fuckin' time. It's a *police state*, that's what it is,' she said, still raising her voice. 'They'll let her out though, right?' she said to Cressida. 'Cos she's sick?'

'I don't know, Taina. I'm sorry. But we've got the best counsel,' she said, brightening and looking towards the lifts. 'Byron Kent. He did Dizzy this morning.' *If he turns up.*

Behind them the sheriff emerged from the courtroom and locked the door in the open position.

'Come on,' Cressida said. 'We'd better go in.'

Inside, the bar table was crowded with files and solicitors, a lanky defence counsel slouching on the lectern in a beige suit next to a woman with a pile of files in front of her. On the other side was a young police prosecutor chatting to an officer in uniform. Then a tall grey-haired man arrived at the front of the court looking out of breath, followed by a younger man in a much more expensive suit. They weaved to the front row and sat down, the older one checking his watch and running a hand through his peppered grey hair. He rested a stack of files with red edges on them on his lap.

'What the hell is Quentin's lapdog doing here?' said Taina, looking at the man in the expensive suit.

'What? Who?'

'That guy who just came in, sitting next to the old guy with the files. He's that megabitch Julie Quentin's chief of staff.'

'Julie Quentin ...'

Taina looked at Cressida in disbelief and then laughed. 'The Minister for Home Affairs, silly. Julie Quentin. Don't you watch the news?'

'Oh. Gosh ... I don't know ... How do you know it's him?'

'It's him alright. He's always one of those noddy fuckwits beside her when she's on the TV going on about boat people. I'd recognise him any-where.'

'I guess that's the CDPP's client, technically.' Hang on. No he wasn't. The CDPP's client was the Attorney-General. *Definitely* not the Minister for Home Affairs. They were supposed to be arm's length.

'Fuckwit,' Taina declared, sending a death stare in the man's direction.

The sheriff closed the courtroom entrance doors.

There was a thump on the door at the back of the court and the clerk bent into the microphone. 'All rise.'

Those at the bar sprang to attention and in a cloud of black robes the judge entered. When he sat, the leather chair capsized slightly under his weight; he righted it and peered at those assembled.

'Good morning. If you'll just give me one moment.' He reviewed some papers on the bench. 'I might turn to those Commonwealth matters now, stood over from this m—'

The entrance door to the court thudded open and a tall figure in robes of his own entered.

'Ah,' the judge acknowledged. 'Mr Kent.'

Byron Kent, Eleven Wentworth chambers, swept to the bar table, the defence solicitor in the beige suit scrambling aside to allow room. Alessa winked at Cressida and stood, hovering pointedly behind a seated solicitor until he saw her and quickly offered the chair.

'Good morning, your Honour,' Byron replied with a nod, slapping a fat lever-arch folder on the bar table as he took over the lectern. 'Appearing on the protest matters, your Honour. Which for some reason are turning up in our court as *Commonwealth charges*' – he turned to peer behind him at the greying gentleman with the files – 'together with charges against two defendants – a Ms Williams and a Mr Taylor – the Crown is alleging are related.' Byron scrutinised the list in front of him on the table. 'One to thirty-six in your Commonwealth list.'

*Thirty-six?* Cress thought, wondering how on earth they were going to deal with them all. *And a Ms Williams and a Mr Taylor – oh, so that's Dale's surname. Nice.*

A pile of files were dug from the tower on the bench and given to the judge as he turned to the prosecutor. With a flick of his robes Byron sat down, and in the moment available Cressida stepped forward to the Crown prosecutor.

'Mr Butcher. Cressida Mitsok. Do you have some facts on Taylor and Williams we can have?'

'Ms Mitsok. Nice to meet you,' he said, digging out a document from the top two files. She handed them to Alessa, resisting the urge to sit down and devour the contents herself.

'The AFP facts.' She gestured discreetly at David. 'That's David Butcher. The prosecutor.'

'Ah,' said Alessa, looking impressed. She leaned towards Byron and murmured something, passing him the papers.

'As I was saying, Constable,' the judge was saying in the direction of the police prosecutor, 'the Commonwealth matters were stood down this morning pending Mr Kent's availability – something urgent with the

United Nations, no doubt,' he said, with the smallest of smirks in Byron's direction. 'So if you wouldn't mind, now that Mr Kent is available, I will proceed with that matter now … Hope we didn't drag you away from The Hague, Mr Kent.'

'No, not this week your Honour,' Byron said with a grin. 'Only Newcastle. We do what we can.'

'Oh, my apologies,' said the police prosecutor, glancing behind him and scrambling to collect his files and move out of the way. 'Certainly.' David Butcher stood up and moved into his place, murmuring thanks.

'And Mr Butcher. You're for the Crown?'

'I am, your Honour.'

'Very good. I see there are rather a lot of matters in this list – how would you like to deal with them?'

'Ah, as alluded to by my learned colleague,' David said, glancing at Byron, 'all but two of them relate to a particular set of events yesterday, your Honour, while the remaining two – Williams and Taylor – arose from a raid on premises yesterday evening. Just in the interests of efficiency – perhaps we might deal with those first?'

The judge turned to Byron, who was chuckling at the fact sheets Alessa had given him and striking out great chunks with a red pen.

'Mr Kent?'

'Ah, yes, your Honour.' Byron stood up, flicking his robes out of the way. 'If I might first allude to some preliminary matters …' he began, and then, not waiting for a response, continued. 'For some unknown yet no doubt very interesting reason' – he glanced at David – 'in relation to which my learned friend will illuminate the court in due course, Mr Taylor in particular has been charged under the Commonwealth Criminal Code rather than the State *Drug Trafficking and Misuse Act*. I am hoping that we will not hear shortly that it has something to do with intending to charge my client with Commonwealth terror-related offences at some later date, so that it can retain control of the accused in the interim.'

David peeled off his glasses and peered at the barrister with one metal arm in his mouth. Byron in turn raised his eyebrows at the Minister for Home Affairs' chief of staff, before turning back to the judge.

'I should say at the outset, your Honour, that I wouldn't be surprised if your Honour was the recipient of a quick and perhaps even *apologetic* change of heart on this one from the Prosecution, your Honour. We are objecting to almost the entirety of this fact sheet, by the way,' he said, holding up the red-streaked document and passing it back to David.

'In short, as I will elaborate in a moment,' Byron continued, 'the drugs found at the relevant premises were for a patient being cared for there by the accused. This aspect of the charges, at least, seems to me like a complete misunderstanding and waste of your time on that count, I'm afraid, such that the Crown will struggle to make a *prima facie* case.' He glanced pointedly at David again. 'One that could have been swiftly avoided had the Federal Police bothered to ask even the most rudimentary of questions before arresting my client this morning. At 3.05am,' he added, and with a flick of his robes sat down.

'Goodness,' the judge said. 'We *are* off with a bang after lunch. Mr Butcher, is there anything you feel I should know given Mr Kent's opening?'

David stood. 'I must say I am similarly somewhat shocked by my learned friend's bald words,' he said, glancing at Byron. 'I don't know about you, your Honour, but personally I'm glad I had a second coffee at lunch. If he wasn't such a respected member of the bar I'd call what he just said improper. But if we are entertaining some assertion that the Crown will not make proof on the possession charges, all I can submit is that I'm not sure how he can ask the court to entertain that, given the fingerprints on the bottle were his client's.'

Cressida saw Alessa glance at her out of the corner of her eye, but refused to look. At the same time her mind raced. If it was morphine for Saturne they'd found, why wasn't her name on it?

'It's not an *assertion*,' Byron muttered. 'It happens to be a *fact*.'

The judge sighed and said, 'Well then, perhaps we'd just better get on with it. Mr Butcher, which would you like to deal with first?'

David considered his notes. 'It may be most efficient to deal with Mr Taylor's case first, your Honour. It should be fairly straightforward.'

'Clerk – bring Mr Taylor up from the cells please.'

'While that's happening,' Byron said, rising again, 'I should note we are mystified as to why an arrest on a drug charge relating to items found at the Gloucester Tops required a raid on a family home in Woollahra in the dead of night.'

David murmured something inaudible.

'Excuse me, your Honour,' Byron said, and leaned down towards David. 'I'm sorry?'

David said something again and Byron's expression mushroomed into aghast. He turned to the judge.

'I'm sorry, your Honour, but a very serious allegation has just been made. I will need a moment to make further inquiries.'

He went on to David in a stage whisper, 'What possible basis, could you have for asserting that the quiet family abode of an unrelated party – that whence my client was so rudely extracted in the wee hours of last night and in such a way as to put five innocent occupants in fear of their lives – were premises constituting a locale for terrorist planning? And now we have thirty-five – *thirty-five* – individuals exercising their right of peaceful protest who have been arrested under so-called terrorism charges. For heaven's sake, your Honour,' he said, standing again and turning in exasperation back to the judge, 'will there be no end to the paranoid theorisings of the Crown in this matter? Operation Red?' He turned to look pointedly at the man behind David. 'More like Operation World Domination! More like Operation Spurious Pretext for Theft of Civil Liberties!' He glanced back at the gallery as if looking for support. 'I was going to put this submission later, your Honour, but I may as well put it now: in our submission the Crown should be put on notice immediately to show evidence of any connection between my clients and the incidents of 16 March before this matter proceeds further, because it seems crystal clear at this juncture that their *modus operandi* at present is to accuse just about anyone and everyone of being involved in that terrible matter without a whisker of evidence.' He gave an exasperated sigh. 'Is it not enough for them that they already have five defendants who have comprehensively confessed? Speaking of which, your Honour,' he continued, leaning on the lectern, 'I am defending these exact same proceedings – starting with a request for bail in Newcastle this morning – in relation to a Ms Desiree Barnes, cafe worker and mother of one, who has also been charged with association with terrorism, we understand simply for placing some climate change charity coin boxes in cafes around town.' He shook his head as if in disbelief. 'She is now incarcerated – away from her young daughter – and is mystified as to the case against her. And now, here we have two *more* defendants plucked from obscurity, hundreds of kilometres from any place associated with these terrible acts – one a respected medical trauma consultant with a background in international aid work, and the other a primary teacher suffering through' – he flicked to a page in the yellow notebook in front of him – 'non-Hodgkin's lymphoma.' Now Byron was rocking back and forth with one hand tucked in the pocket of his waistcoat.

*Gosh*, thought Cressida, *he sure knows how to lay it on thick*. She wasn't sure whether to cringe or feel thrilled. Were heavy criminal matters always this theatrical?

'I learnt some very interesting things from Ms Barnes, your Honour. That over the last two weeks alone there have been not one but *two* unsuccessful raids on a so-called safe house in the Gloucester Tops – unsuccessful in the sense of, it is now apparent, not showing up *any* evidence of terrorist involvement whatsoever – not a skerrick of explosives, nor a shred of anything suggesting violent ideological intent. Following which second unsuccessful raid, five innocent people – innocent of terrorism involvement, certainly – were arrested and then let go on minor drug charges because of insufficient evidence on the alleged terrorism charges.' *One of which was nearly me*, thought Cressida, with an odd sense of unreality.

Byron turned to David Butler. 'What next, Mr Prosecutor? Will *I* be implicated in these proceedings?' Byron continued, his gaze taking in both prosecutor and judge. 'Or perhaps you, your Honour? The court clerk? Who,
exactly,' he said, turning to David again in triumph, 'is to be immune?'

David took a long look sideways at Byron, sighed and stood up, in
response to which Byron subsided into his chair.

'Your Honour, I appreciate you wanted to let Mr Byron have his
moment.' David spoke in a laconic drawl. 'But I think he's had it now,
don't you? Would it perhaps be time to continue with the actual matter
at hand?'

At this Byron regarded him with a pained expression and sighed,
resting his eyes on the wall in one corner as if in abject resignation. Finally
he stood again and turned to the judge.

'Well, your Honour, I'm hopeful that with you, at least, I have made my
point,' he said, 'but the somewhat carnivalesque tone *all* the proceedings
relating to the incidents of March 16 have taken to date does tax one. For
the moment, I rest.' He sat down, looking morosely at his notepad.

David rolled his eyes and looked back at the judge, who at this point
had slid so low in his chair it looked like he might slide under the bench,
and now refocused as if only just realising it was over.

'Right,' he said, brightly, 'glad we got that off all our chests.' He turned
to the clerk again. 'Is the accused on his way?'

A side door opened and two police officers led Dale into the dock, his
hands in cuffs. From behind the Perspex his eyes scanned the courtroom
and met Cressida's, ever so briefly, before they pushed him into a seat.
He sat back low and tipped his head back against the wall. Cressida swallowed and braced herself.

'Thank you, officers.' The judge turned to David. 'Mr Butcher?'

'Yes, your Honour.' The prosecutor stood again and passed some
papers to the judge. 'Thank you. Um – there *were* some police facts in
this case, your Honour,' he said. He held up the heavily edited document
Byron had passed him by one page, looking pained. 'But as we can see,
Mr Kent has done some rather serious hieroglyphics on them. Perhaps
we might hand them up on the basis that this is merely a bail hearing and
their contents can be a matter for submissions, insofar as there is anything
left of them.' He glanced at Byron, who was still staring at his notepad as
if in deep preponderance of the injustice earlier discussed.

'Any objection?'

'Hmm?' said Byron. 'Oh, no. No objection.'

'What's he done to them?' Alessa whispered.

Cressida shrugged. 'Just taken out anything that establishes the
charges, I guess. Given it's already after lunch– if he stands them over

to get instructions it will go to another day, meaning everyone stays in the lockup. This way there's nothing incriminating in them. He'll make submissions on probity and the rest of the *Bail Act* considerations and the judge will decide it on that basis.'

The judge scanned the facts as Cressida burned with curiosity. If only it was like in the movies, she thought, where when somebody read something the whole world got to see. But it wasn't, and she had to sit in silence, wanting desperately to know what the Facts about last night stated. The judge finished reading and put the papers down. 'Alright. Submissions?'

'Thank you, your Honour,' Byron said, standing again. All traces of disillusionment were gone, and in their place was a tone of buoyant ridicule. 'Our submission in favour of bail in this matter is short, your Honour, and as with the terrorism charges against Ms Williams,' he said, giving yet another slightly pointed glance at the prosecution, 'it rests simply on the weakness of the police case. Mr Taylor's simple defence to the presence of drugs at premises – and he does not assert that he was not there, that is, he admits he has been in residence at RMB 2459 Gloucester River in the recent past – is that they were there for medical administration to his bona fide medical client, that being said co-accused Ms Saturne Wild Deer, also known as Sally Williams, who as we have heard has non-Hodgkin's lymphoma. You may have noticed from the police facts that there is no reference to the name on the bottle, and the facts also omit to note they were contained in a silver paper packet with the words "Happy Herbal Highs" on the outside.' He looked dryly at David, who had opened a file and was scanning it, and continued. 'My client realises that the amount was somewhat in excess of that usually kept by a medical practitioner for that purpose, but states that this is because of the difficulty in securing access to the substance in such a remote location. They apparently have to be ordered and take two weeks to arrive by courier, depending on weather. Ms Wild Deer's pain – or should I say, Ms Sally William's, because that is her registered identity – pain in relation to her condition is, I'm instructed, at times extreme.'

'But Mr Kent,' interrupted the judge, peering down at the fact sheet, 'it was a de facto supply quantity, was it not? Regardless of purpose?'

'It was.'

'It does on the other hand seem rather a disproportionate response to the quantity involved, Mr Butcher. Your arrest of Mr Taylor at the same time as Ms ... Wild Deer, or William, whatever her name is ... as Mr Kent alluded, pending terrorism charges wouldn't have anything to do with it, would it?'

David sighed, and turned to the man in the expensive suit, murmuring. He stood up and turned back to the bench.

'My apologies, your Honour. I'm instructed that at this stage there are no charges under Division Two of the *Criminal Code Act* in relation to this defendant. If that is what you are referring to.'

Cressida subsided slightly in her seat. Thank God. At least that was something. And surely these drug charges wouldn't stick, she thought, if they were just in relation to Saturne's morphine. Of course his fingerprints would be on them.

'Good old clever trousers over there called their bluff before they'd even set it,' Taina whispered.

'Well that's a relief,' Mr Kent was saying. 'So ultimately, your Honour, to summarise: we say Mr Taylor has a clear and obvious defence to supply, your Honour, such that the Crown's case is nonexistent, and you should find that Mr Taylor should be bailed, that is if the police don't withdraw their ludicrous charge in the next five minutes. That and the fact that Mr Taylor is a trauma specialist who has strong ties in the community – he gives his address as being in Enmore – and that this is his first offence.' Byron sat down.

'Mr Prosecutor?'

'Thank you, your Honour,' said David, standing up and closing the file. 'Our submission in reply is also short. And that is that that submission of Mr Kent's was mostly hogwash. The defendant *used* to be a trauma specialist – registration last current three years ago – and is a known drug user. Well, was, at the very least, and listed as a resident on a rehabilitation program only two years ago.'

The judge regarded David with eyebrows raised.

'Brusque words, Mr Butcher. What do you say to the submission that it was for his patient?'

'Nothing definite, as yet, your Honour, but we expect to have that evidence. It was only last Friday, your Honour.'

'I realise that. Nevertheless, you do have him in custody, and I would have expected that to be on the basis of at least *some* evidence I could hear of in this court against the plausible submissions the defence has just made.' The judge turned back to Byron. 'Look. You say Mr Taylor was the doctor of the co-accused, Mr Kent? Of Ms Williams?'

Byron nodded.

'There is some prospect, isn't there then, that he may be required to administer continued assistance to Ms Williams were I to release her on bail today?'

'Yes, your Honour.'

'Right. Well I might stand Mr Taylor's matter over until I have made a determination on the other matter then, alright? Mr Taylor if you could excuse us for one minute … Can we have Ms Williams on the screen, please?'

After some delay and a telephone call from the tipstaff's bench, Saturne's face came up on the videolink. Her face was grey under the fluorescent lights above her, her brown hair hanging lankly over her face. At the catcalls and whistles from the gallery and calls of 'we love you, Saturne', her face broke into a smile.

'There is obviously a presumption against bail in this matter, your Honour,' David said. 'Our submission is that we have a very strong case against the accused in relation to the membership of a terrorist organisation and providing support or resources for a terrorist organisation – that's Criminal Code 101.4 and 101.8. The police facts—'

'Mr Kent?' the judge interrupted.

'Ah yes, your Honour. I object to those being tabled. I haven't even seen them till just now. You have heard my submissions already on the weakness of the prosecution's case. It is circumstantial at best, relying solely on the evidence of an informant the identity of whom we are not, of course, privy,' he said with a pained smile. A ripple of talk passed through the crowd behind Cressida.

'Who the fuck would that be?' Taina said to Cressida. 'The informant?'

'I have no idea,' Cressida replied. It could have been any of them, she thought. Merv, that psycho at the gate. Even Jason. Or Taina, sitting next to her acting aghast.

Byron continued, 'My client's guilt is presumed merely because she was resident at the same premises as those raided earlier on a tipoff from a neighbour as to a resident with an unlicensed firearm.'

'If I could just correct that, your Honour,' David said, standing up again. 'The informant in question resided with the accused for many days at the premises – described in the facts as a "safe house" – and has personal knowledge of the accused's connection with a major suspect in this investigation who has, in fact, confessed, and by that I mean the accused Joanne Fairbank. The firearm tipoff was unrelated, but obviously convenient. From the prosecution's point of view.'

'Fucking Mousemoon,' said Taina, under her breath.

'I'm sorry, my friend,' Byron interrupted. 'But I've just objected to the facts. Could you desist giving evidence from the bar table?'

'Quite,' agreed the judge. 'Is there anything else you can give me, Mr Kent? Is this her first offence?'

'It is, your Honour.'

'Ties in the community?'

'Family in Brisbane, your Honour.'

'Brisbane. Hmph.' Looking at David, he said, 'Could I order that she reside with them?'

'We would object to that your Honour,' said David. 'For obvious reasons.'

'Oh of course,' said the judge, looking slightly sheepish. He turned to Saturne on the monitor. 'They would have to extradite you to get you back for the trial, Ms Williams, I'm afraid. You understand why they are reluctant.'

Saturne grinned, and Cressida's heart went out to her. Being the good girl even when her life was evaporating.

'But of course the overwhelming factor in favour of bail in my submission, your Honour, is her health,' Byron continued. 'To which I have already alluded.'

'There's an infirmary at Silverwater isn't there, Mr Butcher?' said the judge. 'I'm sure Ms Williams would be well looked after, wouldn't she?'

'Ah, there are certain aspects of ... alternative medicine,' Byron interjected delicately, 'that Ms Williams is committed to. She requires fresh vegetable juices every hour, for example.'

'Does she,' said the judge, clearly unmoved. 'Well. Is that all?'

'Um, it is from me, your Honour,' said Byron, sitting down.

David nodded. 'And me.'

The judge collected his things and stood up, to which everyone scrambled to follow suit.

'Court's adjourned till three-thirty.'

# 30

In the end Dale was released on bail, but Saturne and the protestors – including Jerome – were not. Outside the courtroom, Cressida and Dale left Alessa talking to Byron and found a quiet corner overlooking the street.

'Hey,' Dale said. 'Thank you.'

'It was the least I could do,' Cressida said, her thoughts still on Jerome. She'd call Sandra. Sandra would help him. Surely she would. She'd sell her flat if she had to. She turned to Dale. It was now or never. She was sick of the smoke and mirrors. 'Dale,' she began. 'What's ... what's with the drug charges?' *Please don't have lied to me.* 'The morphine was for Saturne, right?'

'What?' He frowned. 'Of course.'

But when he said it, a sharp expression crossed his face, too quick for Cressida to name. Frustration. Guilt. Once an addict always an addict, Cressida thought. She didn't know where the thought came from, but once it was in her head, it stuck. Could anyone ever really get themselves off that stuff and never do it again? *Come on. Deny it*, she thought. *Please.*

'Look …' he began.

'Actually don't tell me,' said Cressida. 'Don't tell me anything. Not until I'm no longer your lawyer.' Then she thought, oh for fuck's sake, why does everything have to come down to work?

'You're not,' he said softly. 'I haven't asked you to be.'

'Oh.' He was right. But she still didn't want to know the answer.

'Hey, Cress!' Alessa called out. She followed her gaze to see Felipe charging across the foyer.

'Thank God,' said Felipe. 'I'm not too late. I was on lunch when I saw this on the news. My darling' – he took her face between two hands and kissed her – 'there's something you need to know. About this Dale gentleman. Though I think you'll agree after what I'm about to say, he is no gentleman.'

'Oh Felipe,' said Cressida. 'Stop being so dramatic. What are you talking about?'

'Very well.' Felipe turned to Dale, who was looking at him a little as if he was an alien. 'Pull up your sleeves.'

'What?'

'Pull up your sleeves.'

'What? Why?'

'Show this good woman what you showed the police this morning. Right before the part where they charged you with *drug supply*.'

'Oh for God's sake,' Dale said, and started rolling up a sleeve. On the inside corner of his elbow were dark spots surrounded by bruising.

'I knew it!' Felipe said. 'Is it still ketamine? Or are you just on heroin these days?'

'It's not what you think,' he sighed. 'But you don't think that anyway, do you, Cressida?'

'Oh God,' Cressida said. 'I don't know *what* to think.'

Dale's expression changed from annoyance to surprised incredulity. 'You're kidding me.'

'No,' said Felipe, 'she isn't. Cressida, I think you need to cease contact with this fellow immediately. He is obviously not what he seems.'

'Felipe, this isn't fucking *Great Expectations*,' Cressida said. As people glanced over she realised she was shouting but she went on. 'You don't get to tell me what to do. And stop talking like it's the eighteenth century. Sorry everybody,' she said to the people who were looking. 'I've finished. As you were.' More softly she said, 'Dale, you need to tell me what's going on.'

'Cressida, I did. These aren't drug tracks. I told you.'

'But what are they then?'

He stared at her, refusing to answer.

'I can't believe you don't believe me,' he said.

'But why would I?' she yelled. 'I only met you five days ago.'

'Yeah that's funny,' Dale said. 'Because I was reflecting in the cells last night, how I feel like it was my whole life ago.'

'This is poppycock,' Felipe said, grabbing Cressida's elbow and trying to pull her away.

'You need to go,' she said to Dale.

Dale smiled, but there was no joy in it. 'I'm going. But you know something, Cressida?'

She waited, not daring to speak.

'You deserve better than this, Cressida. You really do.'

'Ravings of a drug addict,' Felipe said.

Dale laughed sadly. 'Sure they are,' he said. 'Goodbye, Cressida.'

Cressida stood rooted to the spot and watched Dale go. She wanted to run after him, explain everything, have him tell her his explanation, kiss her, do anything but leave. But instead she thanked Byron and waited for Alessa to finish, but then her sister said she and Byron were going for a drink, and in a manner that indicated there was no invitation. Wordlessly she stood beside Felipe waiting for the lifts, in the chaos of defendants and families and lawyers and wigged barristers going to and from the foyer, wondering what was becoming of their lives. When a lift arrived and emptied she followed Felipe inside. He pressed the close-door button before anyone else could get in and turned to her.

'Don't you ever speak to me like that in public again.'

Cressida felt aware of his size next to her in the confined space. 'I was angry. I apologise.'

Felipe smoothed his hair and gave her a tight smile, then sighed, pushing a lock of hair from her face.

'Right then,' he said brightly. 'Coffee?'

She took a deep breath. 'Sure. I'll catch you up. I have to make a phone call.' She dialled Helena. Just as she was doing so her phone pinged with a message from Alessa. *Don't worry. I'll ask Byron to act for him. It will be ok.*

'Oh darling,' her stepmother answered. 'Hello. How are you?'

Fighting the urge to collapse on the nearest seat in tears again, she took a deep breath. Stay focused. Jerome.

'Helena,' she began. 'They've refused Jerome bail. They've – they've charged him with advocating terrorism, for going to that protest yesterday.' There was a gasp on the other end and she pressed on. 'Look, I haven't seen the fact sheet myself, or the charges – but it's something under the Criminal Code. Alessa is organising him a barrister.'

'Oh *God. No.* What is *wrong* with these people?' Then she started saying something in Greek, too fast for Cressida to follow, before returning to

English. 'Why do they want to make us suffer like this? Is it not enough that *Leo* …'

'Helena,' Cressida said. 'Can you take him some things? He'll need stuff for custody. And he'll want to see you. Can you get out to him? I don't know where he is – I think they said MRRC on the video link – that's Silverwater – but I'm not sure. Can you call and find out? I'll text you the number.'

'Oh God. Yes. *Yes*. What about you?'

'I don't know. I'm – I'm having coffee with Felipe right now. I'll call you in an hour. OK?'

'Ok. Ah, the bloody *malakas*. Bye."

In the sunny cafe opposite the court, Cressida was only going through the motions of listening to Felipe talk, of picking at her salad and making arrangements with him for the weekend, feeling the same sort of disembodied rootlessness she had in the forest when smoking the marijuana, but without the elation. Instead it was just a flat, empty feeling, with beneath it a sort of low dread. And this time instead of Dale she was looking across at a man that, actually, she felt she hardly knew, and for whom she felt things she was sure you weren't meant to be feeling about someone you were about to marry. Apprehension. More than that, actually. Fear. How long had she feared him and his anger, his judgement of her, his ridiculous competitiveness about the triathlons and his obsession with how she looked, his reactions should she do something to displease him – and there were so many things that could do that – more than she'd loved him? She looked down and found that she had slid the engagement ring off her finger and it was sitting in the palm of her hand. Then it was sitting on the table beside her cutlery. Seeing what she had done, a rush of anxiety pulled through her, surprising in its force.

'So the next thing I know,' Felipe was saying.

'Felipe,' she said softly.

'Hmm? Hang on. So the next thing I know, the Chair slams down his gavel and—'

'Felipe,' she said again.

He stopped, irritated. 'What?'

But when she lifted her hand away from the ring, the colour drained from his face. Gently she pushed it across to him.

'It's a beautiful ring, Felipe,' she said, eyes filling with tears. 'It deserves to be worn by someone who can make you happy. You are a wonderful, generous, thoughtful man, but I'm afraid that person isn't me.' Then, somehow, she was gathering her things and standing up.

Multiple expressions slid across Felipe's face, first surprise, then disbelief, and then the colour slowly started to rise as his features settled into rage.

She knew what was coming, and she had to get out of there before it did.

'Cressida, we can talk about this' –he smiled forcedly, glancing around – 'you're embarrassing me.'

'No, Felipe,' Cressida said, passing her hand over her face and suddenly feeling an overwhelming tiredness, but so much relief it was almost nausea. 'We can talk later. Right now I have to go.'

'Sit. Down,' he said, teeth gritted. 'Now.'

What would Alessa do, she wondered desperately. Flounce out without a backwards glance? *Come on, get your flounce on*, she told herself, holding onto the back of the chair. But she couldn't. She'd taken the easy way out all her life. The path of most appropriateness, the one that didn't ruffle anyone else's feathers. The path of the fucking Eastern Suburbs Princess. *God* she was so sick of it she could vomit. With a barely perceptible shake of her head she mouthed an apology again, a tear hitting her cheek. Somehow she found her way between the tables and out into the sunlight, keeping her head down and letting the tears fall, and turned away from the footpath she found her sunglasses in her bag and shoved them on. It was only a few steps to the cool darkness of the train station and with difficulty she made it, overwhelmed with gratitude at the blessed emptiness of the platform. Quietly on a seat in the shadows she let the tears fall.

But where would she go now? Back to work? It would just put the icing on the cake for them to sack her, she thought, wiping away the tears angrily. She had become a liability, given how much she knew about Brian and his sordid private life. Terrorist daughter, alcohol habit, floozy. The list was colourful. God, she should probably be on the phone to the recruitment firms already. But all she wanted to do was go home and curl up under the blankets. *Expression of Interest: Lawyer – 11 years Post Admission Experience Though Currently Unable to Get out from Under Doona.* Oh but *Andy!* Pip didn't care two hoots whether she got out of gaol or not, other than to secure her career aspirations with Brian. If his daughter didn't get acquitted, Pip would just blame it on the exigencies of the court system, and then ask for her partnership endorsement.

The train arrived and Cressida sat on a seat on the lower level, empty but for a man with a baseball cap over his eyes and a woman reading a newspaper. She hadn't been on a train on a weekday for years. *This is what I can look forward to*, she thought. *Endless days filling up my time as an out of work solicitor. Plenty of time to catch up on my hobbies.* Except that she didn't have any. Her hobby was work. Even her friendships, the few of them that there were, centred around work. Pip was the one she would have rung about this in any other context. Such a terrible irony that the one person she felt like she could talk to about things had turned out to be an enemy.

They pulled into Bondi Junction and she rode the deserted escalator up to the bus stop. The 380 bus was crowded with backpackers and mothers with prams. Cogitating on her wounds, she missed the stop at Helena's and found herself still on the bus as it wound its way up the headland at North Bondi. She was the last passenger on when it arrived at the stop nearest her flat. She opened the door and stepped into the alien realms of her home.

It didn't seem possible that it had been sitting here waiting, untouched, when just about everything else had changed so much. But it was neat and quiet as usual, and as Cressida kicked off her shoes and put on the kettle, then opened the French doors to the balcony, she wondered what would become of it now that she had broken up with Felipe. She looked down at the bare space on her finger. *I can't believe I did that*, she thought. Her mobile rang and still she ignored it. She didn't want to have to talk to anyone about what had happened. No-one who wasn't a top-four firm lawyer would understand what it all meant, anyway. The depth of betrayal, the dark portent it held for her future as an employable solicitor in any of the big firms in Sydney. Maybe that was the problem: there was a family curse: *you will never succeed in corporate law in this city*. What a terrible irony. She had worked so hard to try and prevent herself being tarred with the same brush as her father, and had wound up sharing virtually the same fate by different means.

And from that moment all she wanted was to see him.

She pulled out her phone and checked the time. Would visiting hours at Dawn de Loas still be open? She dialled.

'You'd better be quick,' the clerk said. 'We close at six.'

In the late afternoon traffic she made the prison in half an hour. In the large open visiting area families gathered around steel tables bolted to the floor, children doing circuits of the slippery dip on the play equipment in the corner of the compound. She searched for her father from the entrance, but he saw her first and stood up.

'My darling girl,' he said to her, pulling her into an embrace. His chest was thin and hard against hers, his torso again too narrow in her arms. She felt a rush of sadness and longing. He had aged so much since she had seen him properly, and she'd missed all of it. *How could you?* she wanted to rail against him. *How could you get so old?*

'Why, Dad?' she said into his neck.

'My darling, what? Why what?'

'Oh, you know, just …' She couldn't say it. 'Why?'

He gasped and held her tighter, murmuring softly in Greek into her ear until her tears had subsided.

'*Matia mou,*' he said, standing back to hold her face. 'You know she loved you more than her life, yah?' He searched for understanding in her eyes. 'You can *always* know. Ah, the things she said to God as she was dying.' He shook his head, humour in his face. 'That she was going to sort him out, you know.' He dropped his hands to take hers. They were warm and rough. 'For allowing a mother of two teenage girls to …'

Cressida laughed and wiped her now on her sleeve.

'Hang on,' she said, and dug a tissue out of her bag. She had a good blow, not caring who looked. They sat in silence, his hand on hers.

'Well,' she said eventually, regarding him, 'you look terrible. What do they feed you in here, devon?'

He laughed. 'Just about. Peanut butter sandwiches and once in a blue moon, a green apple. But, you know' – he leaned forward, conspiratorially – 'what I miss most? Coffee. A good, fat, nasty macchiato. Oh,' he burst out, slapping his hand on the table and grinning. The guards looked over and he raised a hand. 'Sorry.' He turned back to her. 'International Roast, oh my Lord, how much International Roast have I had in here? It's like drinking dust.'

Cressida laughed. 'Can I bring you some? Coffee, I mean. Not dust.'

'Ach, thank you. But it's not the same. There is no pert little barista to make it for me.' He took her hand again, smiling. 'Ah, all this is drivel. I just want to look at you. You are still the same.' He shook his head, marvelling. 'Beauty that stops men's hearts in their chests.'

'Dad,' she said, embarrassed. Then, to change the subject, 'How long till you get out?'

'Ah.' He threw his gaze heavenward, and said with emphasis, 'Two months, two weeks and four days. Seventy-eight sleeps.' Then his expression softened. 'I am sorry I have missed so much.

'No, Dad, it's me that's sorry,' she said, passing her hand across her face. 'Sorry for not coming sooner. I was so angry with you.'

'I know, *matia mou*, I know. You had a right to be.'

'No I didn't,' said Cressida, wiping her nose. 'I was being entirely childish. None of what you did was about me.'

'Meh.' Leo shrugged. 'It is always about one. In one way or another. I should have—'

'Dad. I wanted to help. I did. I just wish you'd—'

'I know. I should have told you about the others. It was irresponsible of me.'

'Well, that's the funny thing. I think maybe even then I might still have helped you. Once I understood.'

She looked intently at him. 'It was about Mum, wasn't it? You wanted to roast them for what their mines did to Mum.'

His eyes went slick, he clenched his jaw and then, suddenly, to Cress's alarm, began to sob, silently, his thin shoulders rocking back and forth as he covered his face. She ached, watching him, not sure what to do, and finally got up and went behind him and put her arms round him, awkwardly, pressing her face into the top of his head until the crying subsided.

'And you know what, Dad?' she got up from her seat and squatted down beside him, smiling. 'I think you did.'

He stopped mid-sob and stared at her. His tears made rivulets in his wrinkles.

'You know you did. All those people with lung conditions that got care they otherwise wouldn't have. Good hospitals, good specialists, the money to move somewhere miles from the coalfields, even if just for a little while. All of them will remember you for that. And now look at you,' she said, pulling another tissue from her bag and handing it to him.

'You've served your time. You're allowed out now. And no more can ever be said.'

He laughed and took the tissue, dabbing his eyes.

'I don't know about that. I don't think anyone will want me for their lawyer again.'

'Don't be so sure about that,' she said, sitting opposite again. 'I'm sure there are loads of people out there for whom you're exactly what they're after.'

He sniffed, and contemplated that, and looked at her again.

'But *paidi*, how are you? You are – what happened to the ring on your finger?'

She looked down at it. Still sharp as a tack, old dad.

'We broke up,' Cressida said. 'Well. I broke up with him.' She looked at her watch. 'An hour and a half ago.'

'Oh darling,' he said. 'Why? Not the nice one with the blue eyes?'

'No. Not him. The other one.'

'The old man.'

Cressida laughed. 'He's not that old.'

'Maybe not in years. Though he was no spring chicken either.' Leo laughed, a booming sound that brought gazes from across the room. 'He was old in the face. The mouth. He did not suit you.' Leo shook his head.

'I know. I just wish it hadn't taken me so long to figure it out. Dad,' she said, 'I need your advice.' She wasn't about to tell him about Jerome – not in here, when he was so powerless to help. But the other stuff – that, she had to.

'Mine? What advice could I possibly give my beautiful solicitor daughter that she could not work out herself? Look at me. My own advice did not go so well, in case you hadn't noticed.'

Cressida laughed again. She had forgotten how funny he was.

'It's just … I've got this client at work. She did the wrong thing – and I mean *really* – but she is determined to plead not guilty, and so she is going to trial, but I … I totally screwed things up, and they have taken me off the case. I'm so afraid the new person isn't going to try, and she'll go to gaol without ever having a chance.'

'Ai,' Leo said, grimacing and shaking his head. 'This is difficult. What do you mean you screwed things up? I am sure this is not right.'

Cressida sighed and told him as much as she could without breaking confidentiality.

'Ah, *malakas*. After how hard you worked,' he tutted.

'I know,' she said.

'You must persevere,' he said. 'This woman is counting on you. They all are, by the sound of it. You have to find a way to help her.'

'But how?' Cressida asked, spreading her hands. 'I no longer have the file.'

'File schmile,' Leo said. 'You don't need it. Everything you need is in here.' He tapped his head. 'And in here.' He laid his hand on his heart.

*Now you're sounding like Dale*, she thought, feeling heartache at the memory.

'Some other solicitor can only act for her if she consents. Have they even asked them if this new person – what's her name?'

'Pip.'

'Hah,' Leo spat. 'That's a thing you find in an apple, not a court. She's already giving me the pip too, by the way, just from what you have said so far. Sorry, how many jokes can I make about this name Pip, I apologise, this is serious. This Pip can only act for your client if she consents to her doing that. If not, well – you are still her solicitor.'

'But how?' said Cressida. 'I … I may not be insured.' That was all it came down to, she realised. She had obtained her unrestricted practising certificate in the preparations for applying for partnership. But she was listed as employed by Hannes Swartling with the professional liability insurer.

'Ach, but what are the chances this client will sue you? Anyway, you can fix that by going down to the Law Society office, can't you? Change your status to sole practitioner. Cressida, this is easy. Hah, you should come to your old dad with such easy problems more often, I like it.'

Cressida laughed. He did make it sound easy. Of course that wasn't all there was to it.

'But also I will be going against my firm's highest-earning Partner. Who just happens to be the client's dad. Though it's not like I could look any worse to him than I already do,' she said.

'Exactly,' said Leo. 'You should do it.'

Cressida sighed and shook her head. If she was going to buy the apartment from Felipe, she still needed her job.

'Thanks, Dad. I'll think about it. You've been great.'

'No problem. Ai, they are closing up,' he said, watching a guard amble over to the loudspeaker. 'So briefly. Three years two months between visits, and then you come for five minutes. You come tomorrow again?'

'I wish,' Cressida sighed. 'If I'm still on this case, I'm going to have a few things to do. But I will come back soon. I promise. You saw Alessa last week, yes?'

'Ah yes, I did. But I would so love to have all of my children in the same room,' he said. 'Like yesterday. Not that long now though,' he said, partly to himself.

'How have you been going in here?' Cressida said, softly. 'Four years is a long time.'

'Longer than you could ever imagine,' he said, looking down at his hands. 'But now – on Sunday week, you should come for cake. This marks three months until my release.'

'Three months?' Cressida said, feeling ashamed that she didn't know this by heart. 'Dad. This is wonderful. What do you think you will do then?'

Leo smiled. 'Go to the beach a lot, and drink a lot of macchiatos. Make love to my beautiful wife.'

'*Dad*,' she said, getting up and leaning across to kiss him on the cheek. 'I am so sorry I haven't been for so long. I will come again soon.'

He stood and embraced her again, and Cressida stood still until he let her go. 'Yes. See you soon.' She waved goodbye and followed the rest of the families out of the room.

# 31

Walking the halls of Level 56 for the next weeks and months, Cressida felt like the girl who'd contracted herpes in year twelve at PLC. It was clear the stench of career death travelled before her, and no-one wanted to catch it. Invitations to client meetings and new matters in her inbox dried up, Partners passed her in the hall with barely a nod, and all the while, as if to add insult to injury, the email's cheerful *ding* was a constant reminder of how dispensable she actually was because, through accident or design, Pip hadn't taken her off the road project group email yet. The launch of the call for tenders for InterConnex came and went, and the closest she got to it was squeezing into a spot in the lift with gaggles of tipsy and sequined tollway glitterati on their way home when she left work for the night. Meanwhile the new Partner-elect's alabaster-toothed, college-boy grin was on high rotation across the firm's website banner and his name in conversations Cressida overheard in the lift, and Margaret Minters had subsided back into the anonymity of Senior Associateship; Cressida had seen her strained smile in the hallways more than once. *Just fucking resign, Margaret,* Cressida thought. *You're entirely wasted here. Go somewhere your talent and brilliance will be appreciated.* These were the same thoughts she'd had about herself once, but now they seemed the grandiosity of the deluded. *Just keep your head down and work for another five years and no-one will remember the power station/road project saga*, she told herself, holding back the angry tears that were never far away these days.

At least the charges against Jerome and the protestors had been dropped, in the face of a comprehensive and blistering committal defence by Byron Kent. And the other silver lining was the reducing gap on her calendar until the date of Leo's release. That morning Helena had burst into tears over her granola. Alessa was due to arrive back on Sunday morning, and then they would all be waiting for him outside the compound when the leaf in the massive roller door opened on Tuesday. Whenever everything got the better of her, she thought about that.

Otherwise there was nothing for it but to hole up in her corner office and wait for either the scandal to pass or for the email from HR to slip into her inbox, whichever happened first. At least the triathlons were off since she wasn't dating Felipe any more. That was something. She wondered whether the AOA elections had been held yet. Part of her wanted to know the outcome, but the rest of her felt relieved she didn't have to play the charade with him now.

'Hi Ashley,' she said to her new secretary, as breezily as possible on Tuesday morning. 'How's things?' As usual she slid through the narrowest possible crack in her office door and closed it behind her without waiting for an answer. On the desk next to the computer sat a file on a proposed new shopping centre that one of the other SAs had passed on to her out of pity. Ground-floor retail podium and twelve residential buildings, 321 residential apartments. *Please find a way to enable 43 more carparking spaces in Carpark F*, the file note said. It was like going from driving Formula One racing cars to driving the local Soccer Under Fives minibus to Randwick. She found herself constantly looking out the window, Dale's face swimming on the glass. She had found some paperwork on the Fairbank matter a few weeks ago – copies of the notes she'd taken in the interview at Silverwater and Wellington – among the papers eventually returned to her by the police, along with her mud-splattered wheelie bag. They needed to go in the file, and she'd been putting off giving it to Pip. The thought of seeing her former friend face to face had been too appalling to contemplate. It was well and truly time to move on, though. She looked up Esma's number and dialled.

'Esma? It's Cressida. I just wondered if Pip was in her office. I need to drop something down to her on that Fairbank matter.'

'Oh Cressida. I've been thinking of you. How are you?'

'Oh you know,' Cressida said. 'Okay.'

'I'm …' – Esma lowered her voice – 'I'm so sorry about what happened. You worked so *hard* on that file for Brian. And for the record I … Well. I think what's going on between those two is totally inappropriate.'

Cressida sighed. 'Thanks.' She didn't really want to be reminded about what Brian and her former best friend were doing. She just wanted all of that to fade into a bad dream. 'I see that Mike got the Infrastructure partnership.'

'Oh I know, Cressida, I *know*,' Esma sympathised. 'From what I've heard, he didn't work half as hard as you. But did you hear? Maggie Minters is suing.'

'Suing? For what?'

'Discrimination. Sex discrimination, because she has so much more experience than Mike. Word is she'll win too.'

'Oh my. Did she resign?'

'Leave of absence. Apparently the Partners are spitting chips, as you young people like to say.'

'Well that's something,' Cressida said, bitterly. 'Do you know, is the file on her desk?'

'Hmm … I'm actually not sure, I'm afraid, Cressida. She hasn't mentioned that one for a while. Well anyway – you could still drop it in. She's in a meeting with Brian at the moment but she'd get it when she's out.'

'Great. I'll pop over.'

'See you in a minute.'

With the wedge of papers in her hand she walked the gauntlet of the typing pool out to the lifts and pressed the button. In the lift the weather report announced it to be sunny and 26. In July.

Pip's office was next to Brian's, a tiny room with a foot-wide slice of glass as its only view onto the harbour. That if nothing else said how little Pip deserved Cressida's job, Cressida thought; unlike Cressida, Pip hadn't had given the firm the blood, sweat and paper cuts necessary to earn the corner office that Cressida had had. Inside too, the two couldn't be more different. Where Cressida's office was all clean surfaces, new issue textbooks and functional accessories, Pip's room was like her outfits: a feather boa was draped across the computer, a two-foot high bunch of yellow flowers screamed from a vase at the end of the desk, and a mannequin stood in one corner wearing a sequin bolero and a top hat. There were no books. The desk was a mess of paper so Cressida pulled out the chair and put the file notes on it, casting about for a Post-it note. She found one and was just about to write on it when she noticed what she was leaning on. It was a heavy bound document with a thick red border like on the folder David Butcher had had in court. Cress pushed aside the papers on top and had a closer look. There was the AFP insignia. *DPP (Cth) v Fairbank*. The police brief. Without thinking, Cressida picked it up and cracked it open. Pages of diagrams, statements, photographs and, at the back, a CD in a plastic insert. Glancing down the corridor she quickly flicked to the index at the front. It was ordered by charge, and then by element, and listed both the State and Commonwealth crimes. Under Part 2 – Terrorism, *Requisite intent* was a subheading.

'It's good,' said Pip, regarding her from the doorway. Cress jumped.

'Hi. I was just …'

'Yes?' said Pip, pushing past Cressida into her office. 'What's this?' Absently she picked up the Fairbank notes and put them on the desk, then sat down to squint at something on her computer.

'Just some notes from the first interviews with Joanne. They're … they were on your chair.'

'Oh okay, thanks. I'll have a look later. Sorry, I'm just in a meeting with Brian …'

'I see they've got both sabotage and terrorism here,' said Cress, still holding the brief. 'The AFP's running those for New South Wales Police, are they? I assume you're pleading double jeopardy?'

'What? Oh. Nope. God, she's in Wellington, isn't she? Anyway. No need. We've got her pleading not guilty to terrorism on the basis of mental impairment. Section 7.3, look it up. And diminished responsibility for the state crimes. She'll still go inside, but it will be to a psych facility. Ah, *there* it is,' she said, finding and opening something and clicking print. 'We've got an A-class shrink and everything,' she said, grinning.

'What?'

'Dr Philip Parsons. Clinical psychologist. Twelve-page report saying that in his opinion didn't know what she was doing. Brainwashed by that Ukrainian bloke and all that.'

'If you mean Merv, he isn't Ukrainian. He just fought *in* the Ukraine.'

'Whatever. Anyway, she had to be off her head, didn't she? To do something like that? It's not even like she *achieved* anything,' Pip laughed, sitting back to stare pointedly at the fluorescents that flickered overhead. 'Do you notice the lights being out? She's still pleading guilty on the sabotage charge, of course, but Brian's not so worried about that. Or at least I'm not, anyway,' she said, brightly, getting up. 'Sorry Cressida I've really got to run – literally …'

'But … have you discussed this approach with her?'

'With who?' said Pip, marching to the printer. Cressida followed her.

'With the client. With *Joanne*.'

'What? Oh. No. No need though. It's the only way she's going to get off.'

'But …' Cressida looked around at the typing pool, but it was empty. 'But that's not true. You know she can get off the terrorism charges on the intention point. That she never intended to intimidate for political or ideological cause, and all that. Why put her through the humiliation of pleading mental impairment?'

'*Do* I know that?' said Pip. '*You* may, but I don't. Could have fooled me, anyway. Why else would she have done it other than for some mad greenie vengeance thing?' She looked back down at the email she'd printed and kept reading.

'But … but that's not the same thing,' Cressida said. 'You can have a political ideal you believe in, and act on it, but that doesn't mean everything you're doing is to *intimidate* the government or the public to take that up. Have you read the cases, Pip? She's nothing like the others charged with terrorism. Sure, she meant the sabotage, but it was to *stop the power stations*. It wasn't to "intimidate" anyone. It was just direct action to get something done. There's a difference.'

'Cressida, I've got a meeting to get back to. I'm not going to stand here and debate the finer points of terrorism law with you. Besides, you don't need to worry now, do you?' She looked up from the email and smiled. 'You're off the case.'

'You bitch,' Cressida said. 'How could you do this? How could you make her plead diminished responsibility when you *know* there's another out? Does Sandra know about this?'

'It was her idea,' Pip laughed. 'But what does it matter? All we care about is whether she gets off or not. There's five billion in insurance riding on this, and Brian and I aren't about to let his deranged daughter – or you – get in the way of that.'

Cressida froze. 'What are you talking about?'

For a moment Pip's composure slipped, and then there was something like panic in her eyes.

'Oh nothing,' she laughed, smoothing her hair. 'Anyway, her girl-friend's probably going to testify against her.'

'What?'

'Yeah, it seems like at least one of them have got some brains, anyway.

Didn't you know that?'

'You mean Saturne's giving evidence on the intention point?'

'Yup,' Pip said, grinning broadly. 'Now, isn't there a shopping centre file you have to get back to?'

'How could you do this?' Cressida said again. 'What … why are you doing this? I thought …' She knew the next thing coming out of her mouth was unbearably lame, but it was out before she could stop it. 'I thought we were friends.'

Pip stared at her, then laughed.

'Oh Cressida,' she chuckled. 'Not everything's about you, you know. But while we're on the subject – in this place? Friends? You have got to be kidding. You know that in this place there's no friends. There's only other inmates, and all of us are out for what we can get. It has to be like that, you know that. *Your* mistake was in not doing the same. Bye.'

Then she was gone. Cressida stood, feeling her face burn and impossibly relieved that the typing pool was empty and all the doors to the offices closed. Saturne, giving evidence against Andy? And what the hell had that been about five billion in insurance? Without thinking, she hefted the police brief under one arm and hurried to the lift, keeping her head down until she got back to her own office. Once in there, she shut the door and sat down at her computer, holding the brief protectively on her lap. If only she could just *call* Saturne and find out what was going *on*, she thought in frustration, but Saturne was deep in the hell of segro at Dillwynia, and even if she had been able to visit her, asking her about what Pip had said would amount to interfering with a witness.

But the insurance payout. Why hadn't she thought of that? Insurance policies invariably included a terrorism exclusion. *Of course they did.* She shut the door and searched 'SinoGen' in the firm's practice management cloud. No listing. Of course, that's a business name, dummy, she thought. It's going to be a legal name. You can't give legal advice to a business name. She pulled up the ASIC web page and searched. There were dozens. SinoGen Energy Limited, SinoGen Energy (NSW) Pty Limited, SinoGen Energy B2 Pty Limited. With one eye on the crack in the door and the shopping centre client tab laying sweetly open on the desktop, it took her until dusk to find the right company, and the contract she was looking for. It was buried in a subfolder called 'Risk', under 'Assets', in the SinoGen (NSW) Pty Ltd folder. *GE Electricity Generation Plant Insurance Policy – Liddell.* Her heart in her mouth, she opened it and scrolled down till she found it. *3.52 Acts of God and Terrorism.*

Exclusions You are not insured under this policy for:

She skimmed. *Oh God.*

4.17    War, Act of terrorism

4.17.1  **war** or warlike activities, including invasion, act of foreign enemy, hostilities (whether war be declared or not), civil war, rebellion, revolution, insurrection, military or seized power; or

4.17.2  any **act of terrorism** or any action taken in controlling, preventing, suppressing or in any way relating to any act of terrorism.

She already knew what an act of terrorism would be. She found the definitions section of the policy.

3.1     'Act of terrorism' means any act, or preparation in respect of action, or threat of action designed to influence the government de jure or de facto of any nation or any political division thereof, or in pursuit of political, religious, ideological or similar purposes to intimidate the public or a section of the public of any nation by any person or group(s) of persons whether acting alone or on behalf of or in connection with any organisation(s) or government(s) de jure or de facto, and which:

3.1.1   involves violence against one or more persons;

3.1.2   involves damage to property;

3.1.3   endangers life other than that of the person committing the action;

3.1.4   creates a risk to health or safety of the public or a section of the public; or

3.1.5   is designed to interfere with or to disrupt an electronic system.

And then at the end, ringing in her head like a bell:

3.2     Conviction in any Australian or foreign court of appropriate jurisdiction of a person on any terrorism or terror-related charge meeting the definition in 3.1 of this Policy is conclusive evidence of an act of terrorism for the purposes of 5.17.2.

The hair on the back of Cressida's neck prickled. Hardly daring to breathe, she went back to the SinoGen parent folder and kept digging until she found the contracts for Bayswater and Eraring. The clauses were the same.

She had to get out to Wellington.

# 32

At three o'clock the next day the fields around the prison, wheat grass green with winter rains, were even prettier than she remembered. But Cressida barely noticed them as she negotiated security at the prison and headed for Andy. She wasn't sure what she was going to tell her client about being taken off the case by Brian, but as far as she was concerned, unless Andy sacked her, she was still on it. She had to be told.

'Hey love, long time no see,' her grinning client greeted Cressida when she sat down opposite in the dustmote-filled empty mess hall. Already thin when Cressida had first met her, her client's collarbones now pressed painfully out of the collar of the orange jumpsuit she wore, the fabric hanging off her legs, and the hairdo had grown out to a bushy buzzcut under the dreads. But the panicked look was gone from her eyes. She's getting used to it, Cressida thought.

'Hi.'

Andy frowned. 'Why so serious?'

'Because I don't know where to begin.'

'Oh. Gosh. That *does* sound serious,' her client said, chuckling.

Cressida resisted the urge to scream. *Why the fuck am I the only one who seems to be taking this seriously?* Instead of screaming, she gave a hollow laugh.

'You don't sound like you're laughing because you think something's funny,' said Andy, squinting.

Cressida put her briefcase down beside her. 'Andy. Let me ask you something. What did you think you would achieve by doing this? By blowing up the power station?'

'What do you mean?' said Andy, throwing herself back in the chair, a hint of the old glare back.

'Exactly what I said. What outcome did you think you and your friends would get, by destroying the plants?'

Andy snorted. 'I *thought* we'd achieve exactly what we did,' she said. 'We stopped a fucking evil monstrosity from sending one more inch of poison shit into the atmosphere. I don't know why you're even asking me.'

Cressida sighed. 'Okay. Thanks. Got it.' She slapped the police brief down on the table between them. 'So. I think you'll find the material behind tab four most informative,' she said. 'Page 64 onwards. It's tagged.'

Andy rolled her eyes and dragged the document forward, folding the heavy first section back with reluctance. When she found the section indicated – the police Facts on the terrorism charges – she scanned.

'Yeah, and? Why do I have to read this? I *know* what they're going to say – I told them. Hang on ... what the fuck is this about?'

'Do you know who those last two are? The informant and the so-called mastermind?'

'Well I guess for the "mastermind",' she said with melodramatic intonation, 'they mean Merv. You met him.' Andy laughed and folded her arms. 'Not surprised you thought he was harmless. Comes across like a pussycat, doesn't he. Yeah he did train in the Ukraine,' she nodded, reading. 'That stuff about him leading me on is bullshit, though. God, why do they always do that? Can't imagine that a chick would be in charge of things, I suppose.'

'What, you mean Dizzy?'

'No, silly.' She laughed again. 'Me.'

Cressida stared. Andy clocked the look and scowled.

'What did you think? Jeez.' She shook her head, annoyed. 'It was me. All of it. I recruited them. I got the explosives. I worked out how to do it. Merv was my 2IC.'

Cressida took the document back and turned to the terrorism charge sheet.

'The real window here is the intention issue, Andy,' she explained.' There's a crucial "and" here,' she said, pointing. 'As I think I mentioned, to be terrorism, the action has to be done both with the intention of advancing a political, religious or ideological cause; and with the *intention* of "coercing, or influencing by intimidation" a State or the Commonwealth government, or the public or a section of the public. And protest acts count if they are found to have intended to create a serious risk to the public. What do you say to that?'

'Never,' said Andy, arms still folded. 'I told you that. No fucking way. If you knew anything about me, Cressida, you'd know that I'm ... I don't know, what's that word you mainstreamers use? Pacifist. I'm a pacifist. I was in Iraq, right? I fuckin' saw people get their heads shot open right in front of my eyes. I saw ... Well. I'm not going to go into what I saw. Because once it's in your head, it's fuckin' there for life, and I wouldn't do that to you.' Her eyes reddened and she looked away. 'But anyway. I'm totally fuckin' committed to nonviolence. It's just that I happen not to think that includes violence to machines: they do violence, they get violence. That's my rule. And we didn't hurt anyone. Not a single fucker died because of what we did to that plant. Even though maybe they deserved to because they worked there. Did they.'

'Miraculously, no,' Cressida said with a sigh, then immediately realised she'd said the wrong thing, and leapt in before anything further could come out of Andy's dropped jaw. 'Look, sorry, sorry, forget I said that last bit. I've obviously left my diplomacy in Randwick. Forgive me. What you're saying to me is that it wasn't to further a political or ideological cause. It was to end the power stations, plain and simple, am I right?'

'Yep.'

'Well. Strictly speaking – and I say that because this trial of yours is going to be political more than anything else, independence of the judiciary aside – but by the book, if they don't meet their burden on intention, you're up for sabotage only. *However*' – she took a deep breath – 'just to be on the safe side, I'm going to get directions for us to file evidence proving lack of that intention.' Even if I have to file it myself, she thought. 'Statements from people you spoke to about why you were doing this. That aren't suspects themselves. Preferably fine upstanding members of the community the jury is going to be persuaded by. Do you have any of those?'

Immediately she said it, Cressida realised the problem: it was unlikely 'fine upstanding people' were the sort of people to whom you would confess your intention to blow something up. If Andy even knew any to begin with.

Andy looked pensive, and then sceptical.

'Um, well … I'm sorry. Not really. I mean, I didn't really tell *anyone* what I was doing beforehand, other than the other people I did it with.'

'Great. Well, you're fucked then.'

'What? What do you mean?' Andy reddened. 'Come on, you're supposed to be my lawyer. You can't just tell me I'm fucked.'

'Andy, I'm not a miracle worker. You *are* fucked – likely to be found guilty of terrorism – if you don't find evidence against intention. I mean, Sandra can't throw doubt on that just through a rousing speech from the bar table. Given you *confessed* to all this,' she said, pointedly. 'And you can be sure the prosecution will be having a nice hard look into how they can make something out of nothing to prove it. Got any assault charges in the past? They'll use that. Any other crimes of violence? There's your tendency and coincidence argument: you're a natural-born terrorist. It's all bullshit and totally illegal of course, but whether they get away with it comes down to the judge you get. And believe me, you don't want to leave it to that. And Dizzy? Oh she'll be loving this. They'll probably offer her five years in exchange for evidence against you on this.'

'Dizzy? What do you mean? But …'

'My friend Joanne Fairbank? Oh God yes. Violent as they come. Used to tell me about how she wanted to terrorise people one by one, make them admit to their role in climate change—'

'What are you talking about?'

'How if she had her way she'd have an inquisition, line them all up and anyone that didn't have green power gets shot—'

'Stop it. What are you talking about? I would never say that. And what the fuck is Dizzy going to say it for?'

'Seems she's giving evidence against you. Tab twelve. That's how it works.' Cressida shrugged. 'If she has any sense she'll say *any*thing if it means it'll get her out of life in prison. Come on, Andy,' Cressida said, loud enough that the security guard looked over at them. 'This is *not a game*. Do you really want this to be your home for the rest of your life? Stuck here in a two by three metre cell and let out for an hour a day? Is that what you want?'

Andy's eyes glistened. But instead of giving way to tears, her jaw set.

'No,' she said, softly. 'Of course it's not what I want. Are you fucking kidding me?' She stared at Cressida, and then her cherubic face was wet. 'You, sitting there with your blonde highlights and your PLC accent, with your fifty-thousand-dollar engagement ring. Where is it, by the way? Hock it for a breast enlargement? I fucking know I'm going to spend the rest of my life here. You don't need to rub it in.'

'But Andy, that's what I'm trying to prevent,' Cressida said, trying not to let the hurt show on her face, or fire back that breast enlargements only cost ten thousand. 'Sabotage is only maximum 25 years. Less if ... less if you're willing to plea bargain. Or *negotiate charges* as we're meant to say these days. Or ... if you're willing to plead mental impairment,' she said, softly.

Andy stared at her, her blue eyes now holding a mix of hurt and disbelief of their own.

'Mental *impairment*? Is that what you think?'

'Andy, it's not what I *think*, it's what I think might get you *off terrorism*. If it's true, of course. Look, in this country it's only ever been a defence to murder, never terrorism as such. But there was a case last year in the UK ... well, one defendant got up on it. The SC apparently thinks there's an outside chance it could be applied here, either in the trial proper, or on the question of your sentence.'

'No.' Andy shook her head vehemently. 'It's important people know I did it on purpose. That I did it for a reason.'

'People,' Cressida said. 'Andy, fuck "people". This is your *life* you're talking about. You're *young*. Don't you want to have children? Bake a cake every now and then, for fuck's sake? Go to France, Italy, the moon? In here for life you can't do *any* of that. You know they're building a special building for you here, don't you, Andy? For you to live in – in solitary – for the rest of your life?'

'You're not *listening* to me,' said Andy, through gritted teeth. 'Of course I do. But I'm not fucking letting them get me on terrorism. I didn't do it for that reason. I can't say that I did. I can't ... I can't have people thinking

I'm capable of that. That *anyone* is.'

Cressida contemplated the woman opposite. To have that level of passion, she thought. About anything. Extraordinary. Then she sighed and shook her head.

'Andy. You need to have a long hard think about whether you really want to do this. Whether for all these lofty ideals you keep talking about, all these things you're trying to *communicate* to the rest of the world – whether all that is worth giving away the rest of your life for.' She tried to gentle her next words with her expression. 'No-one will care. They will ... they will forget about you the moment you go to gaol. You will be interesting dinner party conversation about every five years – *maybe* – or when the anniversary of the incident comes up in the news. In case you hadn't noticed, the lights are still burning. You need to stop thinking about the greater good and think about saving yourself.'

Cressida tried not to flinch from the horror in Andy's stare. She wondered for a moment whether now was the time Andy would launch herself across the desk and try to strangle her, because it certainly looked like she was considering it. Then her face softened.

'What about a diary?' she said.

'A diary,' said Cressida.

'Yeah. I know, it's pretty dorky,' she said, flushing.

'No I wasn't thinking that. I just mean, what sort of diary?'

'You know, a journal. Where you write down your feelings about things and stuff. I wrote a lot in that in the lead-up to doing it. I mean, it's not like I was ever going to deny that I did it, was it?'

'Apparently not,' Cressida said. 'Where is it now?'

'Back at my house. In Enmore.'

'Fantastic,' Cressida said, thinking this was the first glimmer of light she'd seen in Andy's whole case. 'I'll need that. No-one else who could make a statement for you?'

'No. Sorry.'

'What about people who can vouch for your character? Community leaders you've been involved in things with – not this, of course, but before now. On climate change, or other stuff.'

'Oh. Oh yeah, there's heaps of that, I guess. I tried a whole heap of shit before I decided none of it was enough. I can give you a list an arm long if that's what you want.'

'Great,' Cressida said, relieved. 'Do. Give me a list, I mean. And the diary will be great. How can I get it?'

'Just go round there. I mean I packed up my room before I left, but my flatmate's still there.'

'Is that Dale's old place? Would he know where it is?'

'Yes,' said Andy. 'He would.'

If the police hadn't raided that place too and seized it, she thought. Well, if they had, and it said what Andy said it did, it could only work in her favour.

'I'll get it.'

'On that whole mastermind thing,' Andy continued, 'some guy was in here interviewing me about Merv. It was weird. He looked like a shrink. Not that he said that, of course.'

'Yeah,' said Cressida. 'I heard about that. I'm sorry your instructions weren't sought first; I've … Look, Andy. I need to tell you something. I've kind of been taken off the case.'

'What?'

'Yeah. Um, your dad got angry at me for agreeing to represent the others. Your friends. They … oh of course, you don't know all this. I went up and saw Saturne, like you asked me—'

'Oh. Oh thank God. Thank you. Did she say she was still getting bloods?'

'Bloods?'

'She's type AB negative. When Dale was up there she was having transfusions every three weeks. It really cheered her up, but that type's really hard to come by, apparently. Dale's the same and was giving her his—.

'*Dale* was giving her his *blood*?!' Cressida cut in, incredulous.

'Yeah,' she said, face suffused with admiration. 'He used to go down to the blood bank every three weeks and do a bag just for her. They'd treat it and he'd give her the transfusion. He was amazing.'

The tracks on his arms – could they have been from that? That was just too much to think about now. She barrelled on.

'Look, Andy, I need to tell you something else. Saturne and the others. Well, the house got raided again – you're not to panic, okay? But Saturne got arrested, and so did Taina and Jason and Dizzy, and they all got hauled back to Newcastle, but then they let them go, thank God. But then they arrested Saturne again. We think because she refused to testify against you. She said they asked her the first time, and they let her go to have time to "think about it". She didn't get back to them, and they came and got her again. She's been remanded for her case to be heard at the same time as yours. And no, it doesn't mean you can see her.' Cressida tried to keep her face neutral. 'So … my boss – your dad, I mean – found out that I had acted for all of you at the police station, and got mad at me because he thought it would affect your chances of getting off. There were a few more things that happened, but anyway, Brian decided … he decided someone else would be better to act for you than me. That person sent the shrink up. To … assess for the mental impairment point.'

'Oh,' said Andy. 'Well. They're obviously a fuckin' idiot then, aren't they. I don't want them.'

Cressida laughed in spite of herself.

'You'll find no disagreement from me there.'

'So I don't have to plead that, do I? That … mental impairment thing.'

'Look,' said Cressida, 'to be honest, I don't see how there's any reason you could anyway. Especially not given your statement to the police. But … I'm going to be totally blunt here. If you think you might want to do that, whether because of the Merv thing, or for some other reason, that's fine, and I encourage you to do that – I really do – but I will have to stop acting for you. Because of your instructions to date that you knew exactly what you were doing. But this other woman – Pip Buchanan's her name – she would be more than happy to run that line for you if you wanted to.'

'But I don't want to,' said Andy.

'That's fine.' Cressida shrugged. 'But I think you should at least take a day or two to think about it.'

'Whatever,' Andy said with a shrug of her own. 'I'm not changing my mind.'

'Sure. Just let me know.'

'Okay.'

'Andy, there's one other thing.'

Cressida found the insurance contract in her bag and pulled it out.

'Yes?'

'I …' Her throat suddenly dry, Cressida swallowed. *Just do it*, she told herself; *you have to*. She glanced at the security guard. 'Here's some further legal advice I want you to take away and consider,' she said, handing her the document. 'I think you'll find that … that clause 3.2 is of particular interest.'

Andy looked at it and read the title. As Cressida stood up Andy started to speak.

'What? Hang on. But this is—'

'Please.' Cressida held up her hand. 'Just read it and if you want to, give me a call.'

Outside the prison Cressida sat in her car for a long time. When darkness fell she dialled Dale.

# 33

Shortly past eight-thirty the next day Lois appeared at David Butcher's door.

'David,' she said. He looked up. Her face was white.

'Yes?' he said. 'Lois – whatever's the matter? You're as white as a sheet.' He stood and approached her. 'Sit down.'

'Oh – what? No. It's fine. Um – this just came for you.' She crossed the remaining distance, not taking her eyes off David's face, and handed him a handwritten note.

'What is it?' he said, quizzical. 'Are you alright?'

'Yes,' she said, embarrassed. 'Yes I'm fine – just a bit – surprised, that's all. She ...' She paused, searching David's face as he read.

'She was just on the phone. She ... sounded nice.'

David sighed, and spoke flatly. 'Did she.'

He read the note again. 'Can you call her solicitor and make sure it's true?' he said. 'The number's on the file.'

'What are you going to do?'

'Me?' said David, sitting down and picking up the phone. 'I'm going to get onto the Minister.'

'The Minister?'

'The Minister. Oh – actually – hang on. There's one thing I need to do first.'

He smiled and got up. The kitchen was at the end of the hall. In the kitchen was a glass jug. He filled it at the tap and walked back to his office. He watered the plant. Then he picked up the phone.

'Oh Lois. One more thing. Can you get me the number for a travel agent please? And post this.' He handed her a thick envelope. She glanced at the address and looked at it, eyebrows raised. *Independent Commission Against Corruption, NSW.* 'Thanks.'

He dialled the Minister's number, looking wistfully at the space where the peace lily used to be.

The phone was picked up on the first ring.

'Get me Julie. It's David Butcher.'

'I'm sorry,' the speaker answered. 'Julie's not avail—'

David interrupted. 'Just say it's about Operation Red.'

There was a silence, and then the speaker said,

'Just a moment, David.'

David released the breath he'd been holding, and sat back to wait.

# 34

The call came in the morning. Cressida had been up since before dawn, unable to sleep, and when her mobile phone trilled she was sitting in the plastic chair outside the motel room, sipping her third cup of instant coffee.

'That was quick,' she said.

'I'm changing my plea,' said Andy. 'I've already called the DPP.'

'Andy. Are you … Are you certain about this?'

'Cressida, have you … have you heard of someone called James Lovelock?'

'Um, no.'

'He's an environmental scientist, futurist, academic, you know – general all-round eco-guru. Educated at Harvard Medical School, lives in Dorset. Famous for the Gaia hypothesis – the proposition that the Earth is a self-regulating system. That one of the reasons there's life on Earth, unlike anywhere else in the solar system, is that Earth has an intelligence, and works to balance biosphere and living things to maintain the conditions for life on the planet. It ultimately rids itself of anything that doesn't serve it – especially anything that will kill it. I'm part of Gaia. So are you, by the way. I got rid of something that was killing the Earth. I'm not letting it back.'

'You've … Andy. You … you are the most extraordinary person I have ever known.'

'Do you know what else he says?'

'What?'

'He says that if climate change isn't arrested, by the year 2100, all that will remain of the human race is – quote unquote – "a few breeding pairs wandering the arctic circle". I figured it was kind of important. And thanks, Cressida. You're pretty damn fine yourself. Oh, one other thing. Can you get a copy of that contract to the others, tell them what I'm doing? Skydark, Bearheart, Flame and Ariel? They need to know about this too. Bye.'

Before she could let herself think Cressida opened her laptop and typed the letter, emailed it to Esma asking that it be sent off to the CDPP, and checked the time. 8.55. She dialled Sandra's number, hoping to catch her before court.

'Sandra. It's Cressida Mitsok. About Fairbank.'

'Cressida. I wasn't expecting to hear from you on that matter. I've been under the impression another solicitor had taken it.'

'Um, yes they have …' she said, 'it's just that, well, Joanne just rang me.' Best not to mention her maverick visit to her, she thought. 'She's changing

DIRECT ACTION  285

her plea. She doesn't want to plead mental impairment on anything. She never did.'

'Fuck. Why did we think we had instructions for mental impairment?'

'Um ... I don't know. I'm ... I'm not sure those instructions were ever sought.'

'Does Brian know?'

'Not yet.'

'And this was having been fully advised on the implications.'

'Yes.'

Sandra paused and gave a heavy sigh.

'Alrighty,' she said, brightly. 'Does the CDPP know? Onto submissions on sentence, in any event. I'm in a matter all day for the next two days – can you send me a draft by 5pm tomorrow?'

'Yep.'

Sandra hung up, and Cressida sat staring at the phone. What now? Call Pip and confess to having gone out there, or do the submissions on sentence herself? She was saved the trouble of deciding when the phone rang again.

'You bitch,' said Pip. 'What the fuck did you do?'

'You didn't get instructions to plead mental impairment, did you?'

'What the fuck would I do that for? I don't need them if she's nuts.'

'Nuts? What are you talking about? Look, PTSD is one thing, but Joanne is more than capable of giving instructions *now* for what she wants to have happen in her matter, Pip. Did you even assess her current mental capacity before you made this decision? Have you even been out to *see* her?'

'Oh whatever, Cressida. I said before, I don't need to see her – it's obvious that anyone who does what she does is a complete fucking loony. How could you manipulate her like this?'

'What are you talking about?'

'You know full well. You're using her to get back at Brian for not giving you your precious bloody partnership.'

'No,' Cressida said, her voice shaking. 'No I'm not. She's – was – my client. My responsibility is to represent her to the best of my ability. And that means telling her everything I think she would want to know. She's not crazy, Pip. She knew exactly what she was doing.'

'Your head's going to roll over this, you know that, don't you?' answered Pip. 'Brian's ropeable.'

'Yeah well, this isn't about Brian any more. Or my head, for that matter. Anyway how did you find out so quickly that she's changing her plea? I barely spoke to Sandra two minutes ago.'

'The CDPP just rang. Our loony client rang them directly. Here – Brian wants to talk to you.'

Brian came on the line.

'A lady saying she was David Butcher's secretary just rang me,' he said, his voice cold with rage, 'and told Ms Buchanan they just received a phone call from my daughter saying she's pleading guilty to the terrorism charges. Do you know anything about this?'

'Yes, Brian, I do.' She sighed. She was screwed anyway. Might as well go down in flames. 'I gave her the insurance contract. SinoGen's.'

For a long moment Cressida thought Brian had hung up on her. Then he went on.

'I suppose you know this is the end of your practising certificate.'

'How? Unlike you and Pip, I acted on my client's instructions.'

'My daughter is mad. You don't need instructions. And by the way how does imprisonment for breach of corporate in-confidence material sound?'

'I doubt it. I wasn't a party to the contract. I stopped having any obligation of confidentiality to SinoGen once I became Andy's solicitor. Chinese walls, remember? As instructed by a senior partner of a major law firm.'

'Theft then.'

'When I had lawful access to it? I think not. Don't worry, Brian, I'm sure you'll find something. You should never have continued to act for that company. The moment you asked me to act for Andy you were in professional conflict. Does Sino know? Mr Zhou? I bet he'd like to. And to think you lectured *me* about that. It was my professional obligation to Joanne to tell her everything she needed to know in her best interests. It would have been remiss of me *not* to give it to her.'

'Yes and now she's going to gaol.'

'She was always going to gaol, Brian. Even that crazy idea about mental impairment was only ever an outside chance. Sandra knows that, I know that, you know that. She blew up a power station. What's more, she walked into a police station and admitted it, because she believed in it. Give her the honour at least of that.'

There was a silence again, and this time neither of them filled it. Then Pip came on the phone.

'Brian has to go now. I hope you rot in hell, Cressida.'

'Thanks,' Cressida said, but Pip had already hung up.

# 35

Three hundred kilometres away in Canberra, with icy rain teeming down the plate-glass windows of her Manuka flat, the Minister for Home Affairs was working on her downward dog and trying not to think about the Treasurer. By now she had left so many messages, at all three of his offices *and* on the two mobiles, that it was beginning to feel like stalker behaviour even for her. In the Federal Cabinet there weren't many members that ranked higher than the Minister for Home Affairs, but the Treasurer was one of them, and she had clocked up many hours of yoga in the last three weeks keeping her natural tendency towards slight obsessiveness in check. There was a Zoom videoconference booked with the NSW Premier in five minutes and she was loathe to go ahead without speaking to him – confirmation of the funding under the *Terrorism Insurance Act* would no doubt focus the Premier's apparently erratic mind – but she decided, feeling her hamstrings burn, that it would be a good opportunity to remind her New South Wales colleague on whose side all their bread was buttered energy-wise. It had been months since the arrest of the Climate Five, and he'd had plenty of time to get on with making a clear statement of support for the rebuilds.

'Julie,' he said. 'Your 9.15.' Her personal assistant was standing in the doorway, holding out coffee.

'Is Robert on?' she answered with difficulty.

He nodded.

'Excellent.' She gave him her most warm and confident smile and stood up. 'In the conservatory?'

'Ready to go.'

'Thankyou,' she said, and picked up the suit jacket she had slung over the couch in preparation. Her PA always set up the laptop camera facing away from the doorway in the room she held internet meetings, so she could turn it round and they'd see her only once she'd sat down; the other person always had a nice view of the staghorns while they were waiting, anyway. She checked her teeth in the gilded mirror and collected her notes from the sideboard. There was only one line, though, on the notepad, and it was the one both she and her donors wanted to know. *How long?* Well, two, actually. That, and *Why not already?*

'Robert,' she said, spinning the laptop to face her once her lycra-ed legs were safely stowed under the white wrought iron of the table. 'You're well?' Hang on. It looked like he was sitting up in bed. There was a pillow behind him, and a lamp to one side. Well, each to their own, she thought. At least he was dressed.

'Excellent thank you, Julie,' he said. 'Couldn't be better.' She did notice the omission of the title, but figured it was informality to go with the whole in-bed thing.

'How's things?'

'Also excellent, Julie.' *Well*, she thought, *'Julie' again. We **are** being cosy this morning.*

'Hmm yes? And the facility, Robert?' she said, sipping her coffee. 'How's that going? I'm expecting to hear back from Josh on the finance any day now, of course – he's been a tad busy on other things, as you can imagine – but before we can fund anything, Robert, we need your approval of the builds, Robert, don't we? Don't we?' She grinned.

Robert was smiling and looking past something the camera at something, taking a moment to focus back on her.

'But Julie,' he said. 'I can't approve anything until I get a development application, can I? And no-one's going to put one in unless they know whether they've got funding, are they?' It was bizarre. It was like he was barely interested. 'Besides, the thing is, Julie,' he went on. 'I don't know that we need it.'

Mid-sip Julie bit into the rim of the coffee cup, narrowly avoiding her tongue.

'You don't know that you need it,' she said back. 'What, the money?' she laughed. 'But Robert—'

'No, not the money,' Robert chuckled, and gave Julie a look that was almost pitying. 'It's always about the money with you Liberals, isn't it.'

'What do you mean?' – she inserted a chuckled of her own – '*You're* a Liberal. Preselected April 13, 1998, I think, and four years a member before that? So, I'm not sure about that "*you* Liberals", Robert. So. Where were we? The plants. Three of them. Ah yes. You've given Sino the indication you'll approve their rebuild development applications, right? Confidential Minute or some such?'

'Um, actually no – not so far. That would be improper, wouldn't it, Julie? Without a full application and environmental impact assessment? Anyway – word has it the owners are more into renewables these days, actually. Can't imagine why. So they might be applying for consent for *that*. Something about imminent climate catastrophe? Anyway, yes, where were we – the other thing is – oh yes – we still had power. Didn't we?' He spoke to someone off-camera as if to check. 'Yes, we did! Three days, I think, it was out for, so …'

'That's hardly …'

'Um – Julie?' said Robert, helpfully. 'Someone behind you I think?'

She turned around and saw that her PA was standing in the door again. This time he was holding the cordless phone.

'James, *what*?' she snapped. The young man went white, and stammered a reply.

'It's just – it's Josh,' he said in a rush. 'I thought you'd want to know.'

Oh of *course*, thought Julie, he decides to call back *now*. Well. Sudden money snob or not, confirmation of a few gargantuan dollar signs might be just the thing this New South Wales idiot needed to hear. Turning away from the screen also gave her the moment she needed to collect her composure. 'Robert,' she said, smiling as she turned back, 'it's Josh. Can we take five?' Without waiting for an answer she spun him towards the staghorns and wrenched open the door to the patio. Hang on. One more downward dog, she thought, thanking her PA and taking the phone. She placed it carefully beside her on the pebblecrete and breathed in, assuming the position until her mind stopped spinning. Through her ankles she mouthed at James: *My notes. On the sideboard. Purple folder.* He rushed off and she picked up the phone, slipping on her best warm chocolate. 'Josh. You must be so busy. Thank you.'

'Unimaginable,' sighed the Treasurer, in the private-school voice that also always sounded to Julie slightly hit-man. 'Now,' he said, a smile in his tone, 'I imagine you want to talk about the *TIA*.'

'Hmm?' said Julie, annoyed that he had jumped to the topic so quickly, and seemed to be happy about it. She had been thinking for months how to work him round to it and had several minutes of charm booked in first, and he'd ruined it. 'Why yes,' she purred, 'how did you guess?'

'Well,' the Treasurer said, with a note of purr of his own but that didn't sound friendly, 'there's not really much hope of rebuilding the plants without it, is there? And that's what you want, isn't it?'

'Well of course it is,' Julie said, laughing a little too loudly. Her PA came running back and with a one-handed whipcrack motion she opened the folder, bending onto the wet patio and frantically flicking the pages. Damn. Points one to ten had been skimmed over and they were at twelve, without any of the groundwork. 'That's what we all want. Best for the populace, best for the party,' she said. 'Of course.'

'Quite,' he said. 'And your donors, of course.'

'*My* donors?' she said, annoyed that her voice had gone up an octave. 'Last time I checked they were your donors too, Josh,' she said, adding a light laugh.

'Not my donors, Julie,' he said. 'I'd never be so foolish. There's only one thing I need from you,' he said. 'And that's the business case.'

Julie sat down on the edge of a concrete planter. This wasn't going according to plan.

'The what?'

'Treasury doesn't fund anything without economic modelling, Julie, you know that.' There was a musical humour to his voice. 'So. I anticipate you've got some?'

'Economic *modelling*? For rebuilding *power plants* that provide 60 per cent of Sydney's power supply? I'll give you some modelling,' she said, throwing away the folder and getting up. 'Model this. The first terrorist attack on Australian soil. Seven billion dollars' worth of damage. Four hundred thousand people left without power for three days. Businesses, factories, airports all unable to function.' She was jabbing her finger in the air but she didn't care – there were no neighbours anyway; the flat building was only occupied during parliamentary terms and now wasn't one of them. 'How about *that*?'

'Exactly. Right now, there's no case for it.'

'What?'

'It's already over, Julie. Why would we fund a rebuild when the power is back? We don't mind where it comes from, Julie. The system has actually coped quite well. I'm sorry, but we in Treasury have been saying for many years now that coal-fired power needs to be wound back. Do you know how much renewable technology we bought from China this year? Come on – I challenge you. Guess.'

'What? I don't know – ten million? Twelve?'

'None. And do you know how much renewable energy technology the US bought from China in 2017 alone? Two hundred billion. And you know what effect that has on our trade links with the world's newest superpower, don't you? Not to mention that three Chinese-owned pieces of infrastructure got blown up on Australian soil and we did nothing to stop it? Negative. Very negative. So, Julie, I am not going to be funding a rebuild of old technology in the face of renewable energy we can buy from our most important trading partner without a strong business case, okay? Am I clear?'

'Josh.'

'Julie. You can do whatever you like with getting your precious terrorism convictions, and I wish you luck with that. But the Commonwealth is not going to be shelling out ten million dollars of taxpayers' money to undermine our most important trade relationship. Okay? Enjoy your day.'

Then the phone was beeping at her and she pressed the end call button, staring at the receiver. Bloody hell. With an arm that had once been a key component of the Canberra State Softball League championship team she threw the phone receiver hard at the pebblecrete, momentarily satisfied but then aghast that it would shatter into shards of plastic, relieved when it missed and bounced into a potplant instead. Plastering on a smile she plopped onto the garden seat and spun the laptop around again, wondering what on earth she was going to say to Robert. But he was gone, the square on the top toolbar dark. Gone? *Gone?* You didn't just pike out on a meeting with the *Federal Minister for Home Affairs*. What was this ridiculous Premier playing at? Then her PA was at her elbow again, pale. He was holding out a letter.

'By the way. Mail just came.' He was avoiding looking at it, and her. 'I'm ... I'm sure it's nothing. But I thought you'd want it.' The stock was heavy and the letterhead embossed and gold. Julie read the heading and shoved it into her pocket, grinning.

'Oh, thanks,' she murmured to her PA. 'That's all, James?'

'Uh, yes,' he said, and was gone. She pulled the letter out of her pocket and glanced at it, then with fingers that were suddenly nerveless, dropped it to the floor.

Back in Potts Point, Robert rolled over to put his arm back around Colin's waist. He hadn't slept in with his lover in years. Through the French doors to the balcony the breeze carried the tinkle of yacht moorings on masts and the cry of seagulls through the shimmer curtains, and reminded Robert about how appallingly glad he was about yesterday's turn of events. Later he would make Colin a short black on the tiny cappuccino machine in their new kitchen, and they'd sit on the balcony over the water and pore disbelievingly again over yesterday's phone call. The Ram, Colin was calling the caller – the Redhaired Albino Messiah; Aemon Husk, the obscure – to Robert, anyway, though Colin had heard of him – renewable energy mogul who had called the Premier out of the blue and offered him twenty million dollars to refuse consent to any power stations replacing the destroyed plants, which amount just happened to be four times what he would lose in pension if they sacked him from the Premiership before his twentieth anniversary in the Parliament. The quirky billionaire was spearheading 7000 megaWatt hours of new solar, battery and hydro power systems in four sites in the Australian desert with the help of SinoGen, the company that had owned all three power stations, he said, and any new 'dirty old coal' power stations would just ruin the party. And to add to the perfection, the news last night had said Julie was up on a corruption investigation for seeking to influence the CDPP's prosecution of the greenies, as he now affectionately called them. That night, after Robert had told Colin, they'd had the best sex in years. It felt good, this thinking of humanity thing. And now, with the end of – even he was happy to admit – his fairly hopeless political career in sight, he could look forward to more of it. The plan was they would travel around the world doing aid work for the next few years – only in the most delicious tropical locations, of course. He stroked Colin's hair and reflected again on the incredible turn of luck. Sometimes things just turned out much better than you could ever hope.

# 36

The rapidity with which the CDPP got Andy a court date on receipt of Cressida's email about Joanne changing her plea was quick by anyone's standards. Four days after Andy's phone call, Cressida and Alessa, who had arrived back ready for Leo's release the following week, found themselves donning dark glasses and flashing their solicitor cards at police to get through the protestors and waiting media pack and into the court building again.

By the time they had negotiated the slap and jangle of security and squeezed into an available lift, Court 4B was standing room only. There were no seats outside it either. They had resigned themselves to watching the proceedings on the video link in the foyer when Taina stepped through the doors.

'Cressida,' she said, clutching her into a lavender hug. 'What are you doing here? And more to the point, why aren't you in there?' She pointed to the courtroom behind them.

'Taina. Hi,' said Cressida, stepping back. 'You remember Alessa?' Alessa and Taina gave each other a nod. 'Um, I got taken off the case, actually.'

'Wow,' said Taina. 'Really?'

'Yeah. I … Anyway,' she said, switching her compendium from one hip to the other, 'Long story. How are you going? Did you get off those drug charges?'

'Still *pending*,' said Taina with an eye-roll. 'Hearing's on Friday. That barrister friend of yours is awesome. Scary as hell,' she laughed, 'but awesome. Hey. Come on. We can't have you watching this on the telly. Come inside and I'll get you a seat.'

Cressida paused. 'Did you, um, hear about what's happened?'

Taina stopped, hand on the heavy door-handle. 'With Andy? No – we all just saw on the news they were coming back to court – but no-one knows why. We heard the DPP was dropping all charges. The terrorism ones, anyway.'

'What?' *Oh God.* 'No, I don't think so.' They wouldn't need a court date for that. They'd do it by email, and as quietly as possible. 'Anyway I ... I think we should just wait and see though. I'm not her solicitor anymore. Things might have changed.'

'Really? Well anyway,' said Taina, 'I'm just popping to the loo, but give me a sec and I'll be back.'

'Sure.'

A man sitting at the far end of the public seating got up and approached, smiling uncertainly.

'Are you with this lot?' he asked, gesturing towards the courtroom. 'The defendants on the power station matter, I mean?'

'Are you from the press?'

'Me? No,' he laughed. 'I'm looking for Cressida Mitsok. We heard she was acting for one of the accused in this matter.'

'Oh. That's me. Sorry, and you are?'

'Oh,' he said, his face breaking into a grin. He held out a business card. 'So wonderful to meet you. Damien Bollit, Bollit and Associates. I'm not sure whether you've heard of us – plaintiff law. We were very impressed with your father a few years ago.'

Cressida and Alessa shared a look of incredulity. Cressida took the card.

'My *father*?'

'But of course,' he said. 'One of the best in the business.'

'He's in gaol,' Cressida said, flatly. 'Getting out next week, actually. Why don't you look him up?'

'Oh yes I know. That happens. But as you would appreciate, that doesn't always mean one's done the wrong thing.'

'Er ... He swindled two hundred and fifty million dollars from a client.'

'For some very deserving plaintiffs,' said Damien. 'Cressida, I'm surprised to hear you sounding so sceptical. Didn't your mother pass away from lung cancer?'

Cressida gave him a frosty look. 'I'm sorry, what was your purpose in wanting to talk to me?'

'Oh dear. No, *I'm* sorry. I've offended you. I'm getting ahead of myself. Here, look, I can see you're busy; perhaps the best thing is for you to call me when you have a moment. I'd like to discuss your coming to work for us.'

'*Work* for you?'

'Certainly. In plaintiff law. Even you would have to agree, you're a superstar. Anyway. Give me a call,' Damien said, as Taina reappeared at her elbow. Alessa turned and stared at Cress, half mocking, half impressed. 'Will you?'

'What? Look, I'm not sure. I'll have to—'

'Think about it. Good luck in there, by the way.'

'Thanks,' Cressida said, feeling like she had disappeared down the rabbit hole and ended up at the Mad Hatter's after-party.

'What was that about?' Taina said, watching Damien's receding back.

'I have no idea,' said Cressida, doing the same.

'Come on,' Taina prodded, yanking the heavy door open and holding it for Cressida and Alessa. Inside people were crowded along the pews and others were crammed standing against the back wall or on either side of the gallery seats. The first thing Cress noticed, though, was that there were a *lot* of lawyers. Sandra was visible among them, swapping amiable barbs with the prosecution QC – not David Butcher, Cressida realised with surprise, though maybe he was yet to arrive – and expensive-suit man was there, crammed on the end. Closest to Sandra a woman Cressida didn't recognise sat at the bar table fingering her iPhone. With Sandra here at least they would get on first, she thought. With a crush of sadness she remembered what that meant though. No. Make it take forever, she thought, looking at the dock. To take her mind off it she scanned the crowd for Pip, but there was no sign of her.

'Not … not up the front,' Cressida said, grabbing Taina's elbow. She had no desire to be spotted by Sandra.

'Don't be silly,' said Taina, dragging her forward. In the front row was Jason, who grinned and stood up, insisting she take his seat. Next to him was Dale. The two of them shifted sideways to give Cress and Alessa room.

'Hi,' said Dale. He was smiling but his eyes searched hers.

A silly grin tried to make a run for it across Cressida's face but she collared it back.

She looked across at the iPhone lawyer beside Sandra, torn by a torrent of mixed feelings: relief that someone else was looking after Andy now, but also desperate hope that this lawyer would care enough to do an adequate job. It mattered. Most of all she was trying not to think about the fact that today might be the last time there was any hope she would ever see Andy outside prison.

'Hey, sis.' Someone was murmuring into her ear. She turned. Jerome. He was in the row behind, holding the hand of a woman next to him. 'This is Alice,' he said. 'We got arrested together.' He was trying to look nonchalant about it, but Cressida could see through his expression to the delight beneath. Alice reddened and smiled.

'Hi,' said Cressida, resisting the urge to shake her head at Jerome. Some people could make good of any sort of disaster, she thought. Lucky Jerome to be one of them.

'You probably don't want to answer this question,' he said, looking across at iPhone lawyer, 'but why isn't that you?'

'I got sacked,' said Cressida, shrugging. Just don't turn round, she thought towards Sandra's ample back. Its court robes were so close she could see the weave.

'Sacked.'

'Yep. From the case, anyway. The rest of it's a long story.'

She turned back and opened her compendium, fingering again the purple fluffy hardcover book within. How childlike it looked, with its glittery pink and gold stars scattered across the front, and handmade drawings of a circle with a tree in it. The Gaia symbol. The diary was replete with it, scattered throughout the handwritten pages with their looping ps and circles on the I's. The letters 'PPM' were written on the top right-hand corner of each entry, with a date and a number next to them that steadily rose. *12/10. 403.64. The reef is dying!!! Can't stand the waiting!!! 30/11. 405.14. The fuckers just gave in – the Carmichael mine has had FIRB approval. I can't believe it!* All the way to the last few pages, when it stopped on the last entry for 16 March that year and the numbers 407.62. An article from the World Wildlife Fund was glued onto one page: '*24 coal power stations are the largest source of greenhouse gas emissions in Australia, pumping out 170 tonnes of CO2 every year.*' *DIE!!!!* had been written across it, in thick red marker pen. If only any of it mattered, Cressida thought sadly, closing the book gently and holding it to her chest. Knowing her client could have been exonerated of terrorist intent by its contents, and that it wouldn't even help on sentence, made it all the more unbearable.

At that moment the atmosphere was seared by three knocks at the door at the back of the courtroom. To Cressida they sounded like the steps of Godzilla coming for Bambi.

'All rise.'

Cressida steeled herself and stood up. When she sat down again she found that she was holding Dale's forearm, clinging.

'Good morning, your Honour,' the prosecutor began.

'Mr McDuff,' said the judge, taking a sip of water. 'No Mr Butcher this morning?'

'I'm afraid not, your Honour. He's ...'

'Yes?'

'Currently on his way to Peru, your Honour.'

The judge raised his eyebrows then chuckled.

'Half his luck. Holiday?'

'Ah, permanently, your Honour,' the prosecutor said, sliding a glance sideways at expensive-suit man, who avoided eye contact.

'Well, Mr McDuff,' the judge continued, 'Welcome.' His gaze shifted to Sandra. 'Ms Crane,' he said. 'I almost feel like saying it's an honour.'

'Nonsense, your Honour,' said Sandra, leaning on two steepled hands at the bar table. 'May it please the court, I appear for all the accused this morning.'

'Thankyou,' the judge said, finding the files in the pile on his desk. 'No junior?'

'Called away on other matters, your Honour. This matter will be quick though, so I thought I could struggle on without one. I think you'll agree things have changed rapidly in the last few days, in ways even I hadn't anticipated.'

'Well. We'd better get on then,' said the judge. 'Mr McDuff?'

'If I might have the defendants brought up from the cells?'

People started to chant. 'Andy. Andy. Andy.' Then there were other things as well. *Justice. Save Mother Earth*, and other names. *Flame. Bear-heart. Skydark.* The other names from the fact sheet. The other accused. *The other women.* In the noise the judge picked up a *Commonwealth Law Report* and banged it hard on the bench, once and then again, and when that didn't work to quiet the court he grabbed the microphone and bellowed into it.

'Silence *now* or I will have this courtroom vacated.'

There was a wolf-whistle to round off a final yell, and then the gallery fell silent. With studied nonchalance, those at the bar table turned to watch the dock, their faces appropriately grave. Cress forgot to worry about Sandra spotting her and watched the dock too. Muffled through the wraparound Perspex, there was a thud of bolts and a creak of large hinges, and for a moment nothing happened. Then above the ornately carven rail, Andy's head appeared. The patches of short pruned hair among the dreadlocks had grown out, and she wore a sort of rainbow-coloured shift instead of prison greens. Her wrists were cuffed, the sling and cast gone. As she turned to face the crowd a renewed roar went up, and she raised her hands in fists in the universal symbol of defiance. Cressida closed her eyes. She could barely watch.

'Are you okay?' Dale said, close to her ear so he could be heard.

She nodded and squeezed his thumb, on the hand which was suddenly over hers. 'Yep.'

At that moment a *Commonwealth Law Report* came sailing across the room and hit the back wall, dropping into the gap behind the last pew.

'If you are not quiet now,' the judge shouted, his microphone shooting feedback, 'I will have you *all* for contempt.'

The sound grumbled into silence, which stretched until Sandra's earthy drawl broke it. 'Quite a shoulder there, your honour.'

Then something else was happening. Andy was looking down the stairs up which she'd come, and smiling. One by one quiet, rainbow-clad women joined her at the top of the stairs and embraced her, burying their faces in her neck in a way that brought tears to Cress's eyes. The first was small, and dark, and wiry, with hair that fell over her face; the second was a foot taller than Andy and built like a mountain, her grey hair short and purple streaked; the other two could have been school teachers – small, mousy, with short bobbed hair, one blonde, one dark. As they arrived in the dock they joined hands. Cressida's mouth dropped open. They looked such pedestrian women, so quiet and earnest in the dock, but with them was a palpable sense of profound dignity. Seeing the five of them all at once made the enormity of what they had done hit her, as if for the first time. Then Cressida's eyes were filled with tears, and she had to cover her mouth to contain the threat of crying. Around her, it was having the same effect on others. There was no need for a flying CLR now – the court was so quiet she could hear the creak of the floorboards as one accused moved down to make room for the next, the silence underwritten by the sounds of crying behind her. It was as if for one rare, overwhelmed moment the entire criminal justice machine was quelled, its papers stilled, its word clouds silenced, as a hundred people sat in something close to awe as this, the quiet, female, oddly unassuming Climate Five unhurriedly filled the dock. When Cress looked down she could see that Andy's cuffed left hand gripping the next accused's was white.

Another moment passed, and the judge cleared his throat.

'Ms Fairbank,' he continued, his voice gruff, 'do you understand the charges against you?'

Through the wooden slats of the railing, Cressida watched all five women begin to take their shoes off. The court clerk nearest frowned and murmured something through the intercom, but they continued.

'Yes, your Honour,' said Andy, when she had finished.

'And have you had the benefit of legal advice in relation to them?'

'I have.' For the first time Andy looked at the bar table, and for a moment confusion crossed her face. She leaned forward into the intercom again, speaking to the clerk, who stepped forward and listened. He glanced at the bar table and approached the judge. The two bent heads together before the judge spoke.

'Um, Ms Crane,' he said, 'Slightly irregular, but Ms Fairbank says that her solicitor is not here. A ...' He checked with the clerk again. 'A Cressida Mitsok?'

iPhone solicitor looked up at sudden attention and straightened in her chair. Sandra bent to speak to her.

'Your Honour,' said Sandra, somewhat diffidently, 'this is Ms Fairbank's instructing solicitor. Felicia Smith.'

In the dock Andy was shaking her head. She stared at the judge, and the clerk spoke to him again.

'She says she won't enter a plea until her solicitor is here,' said the judge.

Sandra paused, and looked back behind her at the gallery. When her eyes found Cressida she gestured frantically with her eyebrows, jerking her head *come here*. Andy followed Sandra's gaze and her face broke into a smile, eyes filling with tears that looked like relief.

'Go,' Dale said, elbowing her. '*Go.*'

Awkwardly Cressida stood up and approached the bar table, and the other solicitor got up and gave her the seat. The judge continued.

'Thankyou, Ms Mitsok. Ms Fairbank. Are you ready to enter a plea to all charges?' he said.

'I am.'

'Ms Rafael.'

The mountain-woman, Flame, looked up.

'Do you understand the charges against you?'

Flame leant forward, her voice barely audible through the wall, said something and nodded.

'And have you had the benefit of legal advice in relation to them?'

'I have.'

'Are you ready to enter a plea to all charges?'

'I am, your Honour.'

'Ms Wilson.'

The small dark one next to Andy turned, and the same questions were asked.

'I am your honour,' she said, her voice rich with an accent. 'Thank you.'

The same questions were asked of the one called Bearhart and of Ariel, and they answered likewise. The judge donned a pair of wire-rimmed glasses.

'Alright. Well, as you would appreciate, there are quite a few of them. Charges, that is. I'm going to read them out one by one and you each will be asked to enter a plea. It's probably easiest if you each answer after each charge, rather than me reading them all out to all of you. Alright?'

The five nodded.

'To committing a terrorist act – how do you each plead?'

Andy stood forward to the intercom again, and through the Perspex Cressida saw a bead of sweat run down her temple. Then her client turned very deliberately and looked at Cressida, and smiled for a long moment before mouthing the words *thank you*. Cressida felt paralysed, wanting to answer, to yell something, *anything* to make it all okay, set her free, make her reconsider her words, but instead she just sat and felt her cheeks flush. Then Andy turned to look out at the gallery, an expression of beatific joy settling on her face, blew a kiss to them, and spoke into the intercom.

'Guilty, your Honour.'

There was a collective gasp from behind Cressida, and as each woman leant forward and said the same it rose to a crescendo, until the last one's plea could not be heard. The court clerks shouted for silence and the judge banged uselessly on his gavel.

'What the fuck is going on?' Taina said into Cressida's ear. Cress looked down and Dale was squatted behind her, eyes hollow with questions.

'If you do not pipe down,' the judge boomed, 'you will all be arrested. *All* of you.'

'They're innocent!' yelled someone. 'He's the terrorist!' shouted someone else, and the man behind Dale stood up and stabbed his finger at the Crown Solicitor, who turned and regarded them all with a look of appalled fascination. At the same time two court officers arrived at the door and started to march the loudest, protesting, out of the courtroom.

'If you do not be silent,' the judge said, 'I will not only have you arrested for contempt of court *but*, because that seems insufficient deterrent, I will have the clerks clear this courtroom immediately, even quicker than they can arrest you. There will be no further warning. Is that clear?'

He waited until the last voice was silent and then a moment more, and at last continued.

'Receive training for a terrorist act, how do you plead?'

'Guilty,' they said.

'Jesus fucking *Christ*,' Taina said into Cressida's ear, softly.

Cressida closed her eyes and put her head back against the seat, letting it all assault her. *It's not your fault,* she told herself. *She wanted to do this. You did the right thing.*

'Directing activities of a terrorist act, how do you plead? Sorry, Mr Prosecutor, did you …'

'Yes, your Honour, my apologies.' The SC stood up. 'That one has been dropped. As well as' – he consulted his papers – 'all those relating to a terrorist organisation. Directing activities of a terrorist organisation, recruitment, training, membership, support, association.'

The accused in the dock frowned and turned to each other, confused.

'Someone finally realised *dis*organsation was the more applicable term,' Taina said quietly. Cressida glanced at her, amazed at her ability to joke.

'I see,' said the judge, regarding the prosecutor over his glasses. 'Am I to assume that will be the case for all the accused, then? I mean, if there is no terrorist "organisation" here, there can be none for the others.'

'Um …' The prosecutor shuffled his paperwork and turned to the lawyer behind him, then after a short conversation stood again. 'Yes, your Honour.'

'And the State charges? They don't seem to be listed here – have they been dropped too?'

'Yes your Honour. We, er, accepted the defence's double jeopardy submissions on those.'

Bearheart banged on the glass and a solicitor from the bar table went over and said something through it. The woman's mouth dropped open and she said something to the others, and then they were all crying and hugging each other in the box. Skydark squatted with her head in her hands, dissolving in tears.

'Well,' said the judge. 'Given the sentences I am required to give on these, that seems—'

'Only reasonable, yes, your Honour.'

The judge pressed on.

'Right. Is that everything then?'

'Ah ...' He consulted his papers again. 'Yes, your Honour.'

'Right then,' said the judge. 'Submissions on sentence in four weeks. You can see the registry for a date. Court's adjourned.'

The bolts to the trapdoor opened and the courtroom erupted in fresh cacophony. The Five stayed for a moment with their heads bowed, still not looking at the gallery. Then, slowly, first Andy and then the others, raised their right hands in a fist and yelled, muffled through the glass, 'We are Gaia, protecting herself. Long live Mother Earth.' The crowd roared in support and the court clerks started yelling at people to leave, pushing those standing bodily towards the door. The chant rose up – *We are Gaia, protecting itself! Long live Mother Earth!* At the tipstaff's desk in front of the judge's bench someone got on the phone to security. Then the prisoners and the crowd were gone and the dock was empty, but still Cressida couldn't move. She sat staring at the empty box and wondered what on earth she had done. A flustered court clerk stepped towards them.

'Come on, Cressida,' Alessa said softly from behind her. 'It's time to go.'

'You. Move,' the clerk said to those left in the gallery. 'We do have other matters today.'

'Yeah, alright mate, we're going,' Dale muttered, standing up. He held out his hand, and Cressida took it. Mechanically she turned towards the door. Outside Jerome and Alice sat waiting for her. Next to them was Helena.

'You darling, darling girls,' her stepmother said, standing and gathering them in a fierce embrace.

'Sis,' said Jerome, waiting until Helena had released them and then collaring them in a hug of his own. 'You okay?'

'Yeah,' said Cressida. 'I just want to get out of here.'

The five of them walked across to the lifts and Dale pressed the button. He turned and looked at Cressida, and then took one step across to her and pulled her into his arms. Cressida subsided into him, feeling him kiss her hair. When the lift came their small group stepped wordlessly into it, quiet until they reached the ground.

Out on the street clutches of protestors stood in a daze, tear-streaked faces speaking laments to each other that Cressida did not need to hear to understand. Placards lay squashed on the steps beside a bedraggled *Free the Climate Five* banner, which was starting to blur from the rain. Cressida stood and watched the crowd below, suddenly cold, and pressed into Dale for warmth. She hadn't brought an umbrella. At least waiting out the rain would let her succumb to the numbness that had sunk into her bones.

Across the parqueted entryway was an elderly man Cressida vaguely recognised. He was standing in conversation with a woman dressed in the trim suit and overloaded makeup of a news anchor.

'Hey isn't that the guy whose life you saved?' said Jerome to Dale.

'Oh,' Dale said, his arm still around Cressida's neck. 'Vic. Yeah.'

As they watched, the man's eyes widened at something the news anchor said, and then after a few more words of excited discussion, he pulled out his mobile phone. A phone conversation ensued, and as it did he turned back with the same dazed expression. His expression turned to amazement, then delight. He ended the call and hurried over to one of the groups.

'A loudspeaker,' she heard him saying. 'Has anyone got a loudspeaker?'

'Yeah mate, just a second,' someone said, going to another group and pulling an old-fashioned loudhailer out of a backpack. 'Here you go. You know the rally's over, mate,' he said. The man looked at the loudhailer and turned it on, then held it to his mouth.

'Everyone,' he began, 'I would like to make ...' He paused as the loudhailer screamed feedback and settled. 'I would like to make an announcement.' The scattered throng quieted and heads turned to him.

'Um, I don't know if you know me,' he yelled, clearing his throat and sounding nervous. 'Vic – um, Vic from the Wilderness Society. Our colleagues in the media,' he yelled, taking a breath, 'just told me something she heard from – am I right?' He turned to the anchorwoman. 'The Chief of Staff of the Premier's office?' She nodded, and he grinned, hardly able to get the words out, continuing, 'The Premier has just announced, as an election promise ... seven billion dollars in funding ... renewable energy projects' – most of what he said next was lost as the crowd started screaming and he screamed to be heard over the top of them – 'and that no new coal-fired power to replace the plants destroyed will be approved by his government!'

Jerome let out a yell as the crowd screamed some more, waving placards and embracing. Cress grabbed Jerome and yelled, 'What? *What?* I couldn't hear him! What did he say?'

Jerome was laughing and pulling Alice into an embrace, leaning her down Sinatra style across the marble tiles, and someone broke into a loud version of *All we are saying, is give green a chance*, making people in passing cars honk their horns. Cress grabbed Jerome's sleeve.

'Jerome,' she yelled again, four inches from his ear. 'What – just – happened?'

Jerome laughed and took a breath, still holding onto Alice. 'The insurers won't fund a rebuild, and the Premier just announced he won't approve a rebuild even if they do! In other words,' he said, dancing in a circle, 'we won!'

Security guards were coming out of the building to find out what the noise was about, yelling and threatening to call the police, and the people laughed and apologised and converged on the footpath, their joy unassailable. Then Dale saw something over her shoulder that made his jaw drop, and Cressida turned to follow his gaze. Saturne. Both the tube and the tumour were gone, and her skin was awash with warm olive. Then the three of them were lost in a lavender-soaked hug, Saturne's face buried in Cress's neck, and she cried and laughed at the same time.

'Saturne – you,' she began. 'But I thought you were in *gaol*.'

Saturne laughed through her own tears, nodding. 'I was. But then this morning, my Legal Aid lawyer came and said that the DPP had dropped everything. Some senior guy in the DPP had decided to withdraw the charges. Not enough evidence or something. And I got a train straight here! So – we're all out – even Dizzy!'

'Dizzy?' Cress looked about. 'Where is she?'

'I don't know,' Saturne said, wiping her face with her sleeve. 'I bet she's in Dungog with her daughter already.' She fell into a hug with them both again.

'But – are you alright?' asked Dale, standing back.

Saturne stepped back too and looked at him, eyes wide. 'That's the other thing,' she said. 'I had the chemo. Lots of it. And the radio. And I'm ...' – she swallowed, suddenly shaking – 'I'm in remission.'

Cress squealed. 'You're *what*?'

Saturne nodded.

'They did an antigen count again. It's ...' She looked at Dale. 'My 19-9s are probably better than yours.'

Dale's mouth dropped open again. 'Oh my God,' he said, hugging her and looping his arm around Cress to pull her into it. 'That is ...' His gaze caught Cress's and she saw his eyes were damp with tears too. He kissed the top of Saturne's head and stayed there. Then he searched her face. 'You did – you do know about Andy, though? And the others?'

Saturne's face softened, and she nodded. 'I do. It's okay.' She took Cress's hand. 'It's …' Saturne's eyes filled with tears again. 'It's what she wanted. After someone slipped her that contract. That saved us. Saved *her*. Everything…everything she'd worked for,' she breathed.

'What contract?' said Dale, looking confused.

'The insurance contract for the plants,' said Saturne, face beautific. 'Because of the terrorism convictions, the rebuild insurance doesn't cover them. And with this announcement the government won't step in – they'll …' She clapped her hand to her mouth and withheld a disbelieving sob. 'They'll never be able to build them again. Andy, Bearheart, Flame, Ariel, Skydark – *they won.*'

'To the park,' the man who had given Vic the loudhailer was shouting. 'To the park!' He pointed across the road and people ran onto it, those on either end of the group waving at the traffic to stop it so that the rest of the group could rush through. Jerome laughed, picked up Alice and ran down the steps.

'Come on, gorgeous,' he yelled. 'This is the fun bit.'

Cressida stood next to Dale and watched, astonished. She looked down at Dale's hand in hers, and kissed it.

'Come on,' she said. 'Let's go join in the fun bit.'

# Acknowledgements

Thanks to …

My editor at Lacuna Dr Linda Nix AE, for her tireless continuity and grammar vigilance; the much better cover and title ideas; sticking with me all the way through; and wanting me in the first place.

The generous readers of early versions: the forever cherished FicChicks Kerry Rogerson and Judith Flanagan, in accepting voluminous first and multitude drafts, and teaching me with their own; Paula Morrow and Ed Wright, in dissuading me from tangents and dead ends; Penelope Taylor and Patrick Filmer-Sankey, for reading the final draft the whole way through; Greg Bastian, mentor through Writing NSW, for making me start again; Laurel Cohn, for putting me to proof that this one was different; Alan Mills and his Novelist Bootcamp 2012, for getting me to the end; the writing teacher that told me "girls" (sic) couldn't write thrillers (I did); and lastly, the women of my early UTS creative writing class in 2008, giving me those crucial first words of encouragement that made me think perhaps there was something to say after all.

Nigel Milsom and Damien Linnane, for their generosity with endless answers about being inside, and Daniel Matas and Maria Walz about acting for those that are; Kath Teagle, Dr Kim Ostinga and Dr Anousha Victoire for the answers to my medical questions; Patrick Filmer-Sankey for the thoughts on the finer points of power station destruction (which I ignored); and Kerry Rogerson, for calling my bluff on police procedure and pressing me to accuracy. All errors are my own.

Ingrid and Sarah for their adamant views on cover design.

Penny, Patrick, Sean and my brother Tim for always rowdily believing in me, especially when I didn't.

The forests of East Gippsland, the plains of the Gloucester Tops, and the post-industrial grace of Newcastle, for inspiring me to write and write about them, and Badde Manors café, the Carrington Hotel, and the Sydney to Newcastle for the space to do so.

Ben Elton, Marge Piercy and Writing NSW for showing me how it's done (better); and Anne Lamotte, Stephen King in On Writing, and Julia Cameron for showing us all pathways to get there.

My parents, Anne and Ian Svenson, for first bringing me to nature, for always having books in the house, and for the solitude to write; and Grandma Dorothy Michell, for doing it first.

And lastly, my children, Hugo and Max, for whom it is all of course, always, for.

# About the author

JD Svenson is a crack litigation solicitor at the University of Newcastle Legal Centre specialising in environmental law. She has written stories from the time she could hold a pen. She is also a clinical teacher, candidate for the Doctor of Philosophy in Creative Writing at the University of Newcastle, and the single mother of two boys. *Direct Action*, her first novel, is the culmination of a youth spent in environmental campaigning, a passion for the natural world, and fear for the loss of civil liberties for legitimate protest.

www.ingramcontent.com/pod-product-compliance
Lightning Source LLC
Chambersburg PA
CBHW051101030726
47504CB00006B/1729